I0548303

Rise of the Queens

Richard R Hall

Shadow Angels Trilogy
Book Two

Rise of the Queens
By
Richard R Hall

Copyright by Richard Hall February, 2016

TXu 1-993-968

Cover by Elina Dudina 2016

True Look Publications

658 Central Ave.
Albany, NY
12206

ISBN-13: 978-0998780016
ISBN-10: 0998780014

Richard R Hall

For Debbie and Shawn wherever you are.

Books by Richard Hall

Shadow Angels Trilogy:
Shadow Angels
Rise of the Queens
Brendel

Chapter One

S tarting to feel the chill of space, Drake reached out and wiped the condensation from the forward control window. The freighter he was piloting was an hour away from the one planet he had never visited in his life. His routes had always been the outer planets and the moons of the gas giants. He could see Earth on the other side of the thick poly window, the blue world with its wispy white streaks and more water than any spacer could imagine. This was the place of origin for his species, pristine Earth that long ago had survived a terrible apocalypse.

His parents were spacers, and he was born on a freighter carrying precious supplies to Europa. Drake spent the first twelve years of life on the ship. Eventually, his parents worried about his lack of education, bought an apartment in a large habitat on Mars. When he grew older, he became a spacer himself, traveling the solar system, delivering iron ore on an ion powered space freighter. The freighter on this trip was three miles long. The crew consisted of himself, Ray the copilot, and Robert 286, the A.I. robot that fixed most anything on the ship.

They rode in the rear, in the pusher, a spacecraft connected to the freighter that consisted of the control room, a large living area, and massive ion engines. On arrival to a planet or moon, the spacecraft would separate from the freighter and leave it in orbit. He would visit the habitats, spend a few nights in the bars with the women, eat some decent food, catch a few movies at the cinema and then travel on to pick up another freighter. This was how

Drake lived his life. He wiped more condensation from the window and pressed the com button. "Robert, what is going on with the climate control in here?"

The sound of Robert's monotone voice came through the com. "Experiencing a flux in the fusion core."

"What do you mean?" Drake asked, a little exasperated. He always had to pry information out of Robert. "We are going to need the auxiliary engines in less than an hour."

Robert answered in his precise way. "The temperature has dropped five hundred degrees in the fusion core, making the power delivery uncertain, and I cannot find out why. I shut down the ion engines two hours ago to slow our approach to Earth, and the fusion core has been touchy since. Auxiliary engines should work when you are ready to fire them, Drake, baby."

"Funny," Drake replied. Robert had learned humor over his ten-year life with humans.

Drake wiped his forehead with the back of his hand and then wiped it onto his coveralls. Ray, a tall, lanky fellow who constantly banged his head on the overheads, slid into the seat next to him and began start-up procedures for the auxiliary engines. Ten minutes later, Drake fired the forward engines to slow their approach to Earth and to steer them into position for orbit.

"I'm not getting steady power to the aux engines," Drake told Robert in a mildly tense voice.

"I'm aware of that. We should be okay to enter orbit. We'll have a repair shuttle sent up to make repairs when we disconnect from the freighter," Robert replied over the com.

"The power level is dropping. We don't have the power from the aux engines to land," Ray quickly informed Drake.

"We will have to be careful. We certainly don't want to fall below earth's orbit," Drake answered as he tapped the power indicator.

They saw the earth from their location at the end of the freighter, quickly grow, and soon covered the front window. Drake fired the port engines to place them in a position to enter Earth's orbit. He soon felt the intense vibrations of the ship.

"What the hell is that?" Drake yelled into the com.

"The thrusters aren't firing with the same power,"
Robert replied in a calm voice. "There is a pressure build-up. I believe it's in the ion line that goes to the port and starboard thrusters. That's why the fusion core is trying to shut down."

"The ship is committed now. We have to fire the starboards to trim out our orbit," Ray said in a tense voice. "For the love of space, fire them. We are getting too close to Earth's gravity."

"Robert, I have to fire the starboard engines," Drake told the A.I. through gritted teeth. "If I don't, the freighter is going to tumble, and Earth's gravity will take hold of us."

"That will be risky," Robert answered.

"You said they would work," a frustrated Ray yelled as he wiped more moisture from the window and then muttered, "Robots."

"I don't think we have a choice. Firing starboard engines!" Drake commanded.

Drake touched the activator. The engines fired, and the ship again shook violently. He heard Robert start a word and then listened to a loud *bang*. He felt the shock-wave; the force ripped them from the freighter and propelled them toward Earth. Their spaceship was tumbling. Pieces of the spacecraft flew off and sparkled in the sunlight amid the darkness of space. Alarms were screaming throughout the control room. Drake switched to battery power, and the control room went dim.

Drake heard Susie, the computer, come awake. "Catastrophic failure. Main auxiliary line. Catastrophic failure. Main auxiliary line. Gentlemen, we have a breached hull in the auxiliary engine room. Closing all doors to the auxiliary engine room."

"What about Robert?" Drake yelled.

"Robert is no longer responding," Susie replied.

"You're kidding!" Drake muttered.

"No, I don't kid," Susie answered in a calm, soothing voice.

"Are the maneuvering thrusters working?" Drake yelled as he went for the controls.

"Yes, they are working," Susie replied calmly.

"Oh, Susie, baby, they work!" Ray screamed.

Drake worked the maneuvering thrusters like a maestro and eventually straightened the spacecraft to an acceptable position to enter Earth's atmosphere. Handling a spaceship was second nature to a spacer that had spent his life traveling the solar system.

They no longer had the thrust to escape Earth's gravity, and their spacecraft was now committed to landing on the planet. The question now was whether they would have the power to land.

"I want a twenty-degree trim," Drake called out to Ray.

"Twenty-degree trim coming up," Ray shouted back.

Drake wanted the best angle to slow the spaceship over a long reentry path. They soon felt the buffeting of the spacecraft as it plowed into the earth's atmosphere. Warning alarms were screaming that their speed was too fast, and heat was building on the outside hull.

"Gentlemen, we are traveling too fast for Earth entry," Susie warned. "There's nothing I can do about that," Drake yelled back.

"You might want to use the drag chute once we enter earth's atmosphere," Susie said in her relaxed voice.

The chute was a piece of old technology that Drake had forgotten about. The builders had placed it in the aging spacecraft long ago, and he had never used it; there was no need for it. The alarms continued to scream, and Drake thought the buffeting was going to tear him apart.

"Earth Control, this is the spacecraft *Stuben*. I repeat, the spacecraft *Stuben*, sending an SOS. We have lost power and need an emergency landing zone. This is an emergency. Priority alpha. I repeat, priority alpha. We need a glide path to a landing area."

"Spacecraft *Stuben*, this is Earth Control. You are leaking radioactive material into our atmosphere. You must try to control the radioactive release."

"I'm doing my best, but I need those coordinates."

"Spacecraft *Stuben*, keep your twenty-degree trim and follow flight path 330 by 448, and that will put you in the Mohave Desert for your landing."

"Copy, Earth Control. We'll need help once we land." Drake

answered.

"If we're alive," Ray muttered.

"Spacecraft *Stuben*, Space Command will provide aid, but you must try to control your radioactive materials. Radioactive emissions are illegal on Earth. Good luck, spacers."

"We will do the best we can, but that's not our major concern right now," Drake said as he shook his head over the earth's paranoia of radioactive materials.

"Susie, do you think the drag chute will work?"

"The circuits are working, but there is only one way to find out. I would suggest you deploy the chute now."

Drake found the cover to the drag chute initiator, pried it open, and activated the chute. The chute caught the atmosphere, and the drag pushed them forward in their seats. The ship shuddered and moaned as it sliced through the cloud cover. Drake could see the billowy white clouds shoot by his window. Earth's terrain had come into view, and just as quickly, they were over the ocean. Their speed was now starting to slow. The old technology was doing its work.

Another loud *bang* and a section of hull flew off the ship and through the drag chute.

"It's that damned breached hull, the atmosphere is tearing us apart," Ray yelled.

"We won't make the desert," Drake yelled back. "Jettison the drag chute. We are going to have to put her down in the water."

"We're spacers! We can't swim!" Ray shouted as he touched the activator.

"Can't be helped. We're going to put this radioactive, crumbling spaceship in the earthiers' ocean."

"They're going to love us," Ray shouted over the roar of their descent.

Drake dropped the nose of the ship and approached the water. He now saw the white caps on the breaking blue waves. They exchanged looks of dread; the water went on forever. He positioned the maneuvering thrusters forward and fired them at full power to slow the ship as much as possible. The spacecraft loudly protested and shook violently as it slowed.

Smoking and sputtering, they hit the ocean and became a flat stone skipping across the water. As they slowed and made full contact with the water, it threw them forward in their seats. Drake felt his breath leave him against the pressure of the seat straps.

They lost more speed from the friction as they skimmed the ocean's surface. The slower they went, the deeper the hull sank into the water, and this eventually caused them to turn. The spacecraft then flipped more times than Drake could count. He thought his body was going to tear apart from the force and strain from the violent jerking of the craft. Finally, the centrifugal force caused him to lose consciousness.

When Drake came to, he saw pieces of the spacecraft floating in the clear, blue water. A bright yellow sun hung high in the sky, surrounded by white, puffy clouds; the only colors were blue, white, and green. Wires and electronics hung from the ceiling, swaying in time with the rocking from the waves.

"Ray, wake up," Drake yelled.

"Did we live?" Ray mumbled in a hoarse voice.

"We sure did!" Drake replied, not quite believing what he said.

They had been lucky this time. Drake knew someday his luck would run out, but not today. He loved space and the sights he had seen—the rings of Saturn, light creatures below the ice of Europa.

Again, the sound of Susie's voice: "Gentlemen, we are taking on water. I believe the seafaring Earth phrase would be, 'it is time to abandon ship.' I suggest you prepare for your escape."

"Escape where? Into the water? For the love of space!" Ray yelled.

Drake reached over and touched the emergency hatch activator, and, with a small explosion, the top hatch blew out into the water.

"Let's get the raft, and I hope we can find those life preservers," Drake said as he stood and felt the full weight of Earth's gravity.

"I feel like I weigh a good hundred kilos," he said. "Susie, I will send the earthiers for you. You should seal your positron cells now."

"Thank you, Drake."

Fifteen minutes later, they were in their life raft, bobbing in the middle of the Pacific Ocean. This was unnerving for them; they had never seen or been in this much water. Drake also felt the vastness of the planet---it went on forever. He had lived his life in a spaceship or in a habitat on Mars, or on the moon Europa. This was overwhelming for him. He could taste the salty air, and it smelled funny. Earth's atmosphere came with an odor. How strange it felt blowing against his face and wet hair. He felt dizzy and looked at Ray, who wasn't doing any better.

"We'll get used to it," Drake muttered, half believing what he was saying.

"I hope so." Ray gulped and then leaned over and added his breakfast to the seawater.

Soon the spacecraft *Stuben* slipped below the surface of the water. All Drake could see was debris floating in the blue, frosty water, the immenseness of the ocean, the blue sky dotted with white, puffy clouds, and the hot sun.

"Goodbye, Susie," Drake said. "How are you feeling?"

"Better," Ray replied.

"It's like space, it goes on forever," Drake replied.

"Yes, it is, but we were always inside something," Ray said.

Drake scooped some seawater and placed it in his mouth.

"They're right, the water is salty," he said as he spits it back. He held the crook of his arm against his forehead to shield his eyes and glanced at the burning yellow ball in the cobalt-blue sky. He had never been to a world like this---it was so bright.

Soon, Drake heard the low whine of the hovercraft coming toward them and saw the bright, intense sunlight reflecting off its silver hull. He saw two men wearing some type of water gear fall out into the water. They approached the raft, their equipment quickly propelling them through the water. When they arrived, one man lifted his water mask and said, "Do you spacers need a lift?"

"We sure do!" Drake said quickly, with much relief in his voice. "This is a lot of water!"

The man laughed and said, "I guess for a spacer, it must be.

Come on, we will get you out of this life raft and to dry land."

"Thanks, I'm starting to get sick again," Ray, gulped.

Soon after, they were sitting in two comfortable seats and flying thirty feet above the ocean, watching the blue water and white caps skim by.

Drake inquired, "Where are you taking us?"

One man turned and said, "We're taking you to the Seattle Space Port. They will take care of you. Space Command has informed your corporation of the crash. From what I saw, you guys lucked out."

"We sure did," Drake muttered.

Two hours later, the shuttle landed at the spaceport. Medical personnel met them and immediately took them to a hospital. Drake spent two days lying in a bed and answering an endless list of questions about the crash. The earthier wanted to know what kind of radioactive material was on the ship, and how much. Drake wished he had Robert with him, but the robot was gone, floating somewhere in space. The earthiers kept him confined until he signed the salvage rights for the ship over to them. He tried to explain that it was not his place. That didn't matter to them; they wanted to salvage the radioactive iridium out of the ocean as fast as possible, a point that they were not friendly about. He finally relented when they agreed to recover Susie's positron brain before the saltwater finished her for good and to track and find Robert. Drake spent two weeks in the earthiers' custody before they took him to a hostel somewhere in the lower section of the city. The Mars Solar Mining Company also debriefed him, and they were not happy about him signing the salvage rights to the earthiers. They quickly left without him, in a huff, and soon after, Drake's corporation informed him, it would be six months before they would send a spaceship for him. Drake wondered if he might have to find his own ride home.

Chapter Two

D rake was sitting in a lounge on Jackson Street by the Port of Seattle, Ray had traveled on to visit long-lost relatives in Europe. Seattle was now a large, modern city located in the District of Vancouver. He was in a good mood; Space Command had informed him they had retrieved Susie. He liked the bar, it felt familiar to him, it was secluded, and of course, the many pretty girls that would frequent it. The women gave him company while he waited for his ride home. The hostel had been his home for the past three months, and he spent his days at the university studying the latest in space propulsion. It became clear to him that the *Stuben* was a little behind the times in that area.

Finishing his last drink of the evening, he noticed a strange, beautiful woman watching him. Usually, he would go over and start a conversation with a woman as attractive as she, but this woman made him feel uneasy. He had seen her before she'd looked at him, but there was something not right about her. He swore her eyes once flashed red at him. Drake had spent many nights in bars throughout the solar system, and he learned to tell the woman he could approach from the ones to avoid. This woman was definitely one to pass up.

Finishing his drink, he took the remainder of his allotted credit chips for the evening, placed them on the bar, and slid off his stool. It was late, and he had to get up early this morning for a lecture at the university. He glanced at the woman as he was leaving, and she returned a seductive smile. Her eyes were strange—there was something alien about them—and he had experienced alien before. They penetrated him and made his head feel funny. He quickly went by her, out the door and onto the walkway.

Tonight, he would walk back to the hostel to experience the wide, open feel of this world. There was no confining dome or processed air; the city air came rich in order. Looking high above, he saw the lights of the aircars and the faint glow of the high towers and their many different living, shopping, and working platforms. This city had many different levels, and the wealthy lived high above the poor. There was so much space here, with few people to get in his way. The habitats on Mars were crowded, and he always had to move around people to walk the streets. Tonight, he was the only one who walked this avenue.

Even now, he was still becoming used to this world. He loved to take trips into the forest to see all the kinds of vegetation and the strange creatures, or he would go to the flatlands where the horizon went on forever. And there were times the color green would overwhelm him.

There was so much life here--except that of the earthiers--their numbers were low. Human life flourished everywhere in the solar system except here, where it should have, and no one really knew why. Folklore told that long ago, mortals angered the angels, the angels spoken of in their old religion, and now they would not allow it. Drake had heard eathiers talk of guardians and other strange creatures, from different realms on this world.

Footsteps echoed behind him, and when he looked back, he saw the strange, beautiful woman following him. He cursed, quickened his pace, and thought, *why would a woman like her follow me?* What a world it was, where a beautiful woman followed him home! He wondered if she was going to rob him, quickened his pace again, and the woman matched him.

The woman was gaining on him, so he stopped and turned. "Is there something I can help you with?"

The lady approached him; she moved effortlessly over the pavement, feet barely moving, and he knew immediately she was different. He looked closer and saw that her eyes did not blink naturally. They drew him in, deep as a Martian well, and they did flash red. The woman smelled him briefly and then backed away. She reeked of strangeness, and now he realized---unfortunately, for him---one of the strange creatures the earthiers spoke of had found him.

"Why, yes, there is some way you can be of help. I'm lonely, and I want to take you home," The woman said teasingly.

"That's not possible tonight," he quickly replied, looking her up and down. "I have an early appointment this morning, and I cannot be late. Maybe we can meet at the bar some other night."

"No, Drake," she said sternly. "I have decided tonight is the night you come home with me."

"How do you know my name, woman?"

"I know a little about you already. You aren't from this world. And it has been a long time since I've seen a man as handsome as you.

Space must agree with you—a pity for you."

This woman made his head spin like the anti-gravity chambers at flight training school. Reaching out, she tried to touch his cheek, but he backed away.

"That's not friendly of you," the woman purred. "Don't you want me? Don't you find me attractive, human? Would you make love to me?"

"Who are you?" Drake said with a shaky voice. This person was a mystery to him, but he was sure she was trouble.

"My name is Selene, beautiful man," the woman said seductively.

"What are you!" She was making him afraid, something that he rarely felt from a woman. His spacer's instincts were telling him to get away from her as fast as possible.

"You will know that soon enough. I am going to take you for a lover. These days my kind wants nothing to do with me. They say I'm a liar, a deceiver, and they can't trust me. They say I have gone mad."

"They are right about that. Stay away from me, woman, I warn you!" Drake turned and accelerated his walk to put as much distance between him and the lady as possible. Suddenly, she was in front of him. Her eyes burned a crimson red, and she took hold of him with an unbreakable grip. He found himself flying through the air. At first, he flung his arms and legs, trying to regain his equilibrium, and then he clung to her, afraid he was going to fall. Within a minute, he was on a terrace high above the streets of the city. He tried to break free, but he couldn't; she was too strong.

"My brave spacer is afraid. I can hear your heart pounding and smell your fear. There is no escape for you now," the vampire said as she flung him to the ground.

Drake saw the woman change. Her eyes narrowed and glowed red with transparent slits in the middle. The woman had tremendous strength, and she was quickly upon him.

"Look around, Drake. One more time, with your mortal eyes," Selene whispered in his ear. "Look, spacer, and see the world for the last time as a human. You will always be bound to this world now. Never can you leave or go back to your precious space, for if you do, you will die."

Her laugh rang in his head. Her lips became flushed with blood, and two long, white teeth appeared and then went to his neck. A sickeningly sweet smell of perfume emanated from her. He felt the sharpness of the bite, and the life fade from him as his blood left him. His consciousness fell away, and he found himself floating in a light, with a peaceful feeling, and then he was falling.

Drake woke in a room with no furniture, only the grey blanket he lay on. A terrible pain wracked his stomach. Quickly, he sat up, leaned over, and retched out a red liquid. At first, he thought the woman must have poisoned him. Then he saw the steel door that guarded against his escape. The room had no lights, yet he had no trouble seeing. He stood, went to the door, and tried to open it, but was unable.

The woman's laughing voice came from the other side of the door. "You aren't strong enough to open the door. I will keep you weak, my dearest, so you can never escape."

Again the pain in his stomach bent him over, projecting a stream of dark, foaming blood from his mouth. This made the woman laugh harder as he staggered back to the blanket, fell to the floor, and went back to sleep.

He woke again and felt better, but he had wet himself with pink piss. He didn't feel hungry for food, but he did feel a strange hunger that was almost more like a thirst. He smelled blood, its odor coming from the bottle, and strangely, he wanted to take a drink, but as quickly, the thought sickened him. Again, he looked around the room and saw nothing. His senses were far more alive; his sight, hearing, and smell were far stronger. Something else was awake in him now, and he could sense energies that he never knew existed.

Somehow, he knew the woman was on the other side of the door. Drake heard her unlock the door, and he quickly crept to the door. Fear built up inside him as he realized something terrible had happened to him. When the woman came through, he grabbed her to throw her, but the woman had unbelievable strength and threw him against the far wall. He fell to the floor, stunned, and the woman's high-pitched laughter resonated in his head.

"You cannot escape me." To prove her point, she again picked him up and threw him against the other wall. "You have no strength against me. I will decide whether you live or die. You will please me. Do as I say, or I will take your heart from your body and hold it in front of your eyes so you can watch the last beats before you die."

"What have you done to me, woman?" Drake yelled at her.

"I have made you a vampire, so you can be with me, travel with me, and please me. Your look intrigued me, and that sealed your fate. Vampires are vain creatures, my dear Drake."

Vampire, he thought. Drake remembered stories he heard of creatures like her, but they saved humankind, they were good, and this woman was pure evil.

The horrible woman hissed at him as she set a bottle of red liquid on the floor. "Hear me! I will be back in a couple of days. While I'm gone, you will drink the blood from the bottle. When I come back, if you haven't, I will pour it down your throat."

The woman turned, started for the door, and said as an

afterthought, "My name is Selene, not woman. Make sure you remember that." She shut the door behind her, and Drake heard the lock turn.

He lay in the room with his heightened senses, felt the energy around him, heard whispers of people talking in different apartments on the terrace. Sensing them, he realized he was having quick glimpses of their thoughts, and he easily could tell the hour of the day. His new abilities helped him to keep track of the details of his existence.

Selene had left two days ago and hadn't returned. He tried to pull the steel door from the wall but couldn't, and the exertion made him dizzy, so much for vampire strength.

On the third day, he decided to drink the blood. He would sit and stare at the blood, drawing it close with his new eyes to see the shape of the cells floating in the plasma. Strangely, he craved the dark, red blood.

Sleeping was different now, too. Drake heard voices as plain as when he was awake. They came from beings floating with him in his sleep. Last night they told him they were angels and had made his kind. They told him to drink the blood, as it would allow him to live, and he must survive this ordeal and that someday help would come. Eventually, a powerful vampire would come to teach him about what he was.

Drake picked up the bottle, smelled the blood, and it drew him to the opening. Then he put the bottle to his lips, tasted its thick texture, and drank. At first, it made him gag, dribbled out of his mouth and down his chin, but then the taste became sweet like the Poi Syrup on Titan, and it was intoxicating. He felt an energy release in him; his spirit quickened, and he came alive in ways he had never imagined. The bottle rolled from his hand as he fell to the floor. Drake lost consciousness and found himself floating in a bright light. The angels' voices came again, singing sorrowful songs for him and his despair.

The following eve, Selene returned in a bad mood. Something was wrong; Drake could sense it as she walked through the door. Her face wore the mask of absolute disdain.

"I see you have drunk the blood," Selene hissed at him. The dark beauty that was Selene came to him, held his chin in her mighty hand, and said, "Now you are my vampire. I will do what I want with you. How did the blood make you feel when you drank it? It came from a young man that had rude words for me as I passed him. They are still looking for his body."

"The blood made my body come alive, but now I think I will be sick," Drake said as he leaned over and retched. "Will it always do this?"

"Yes, it does, minus the retching. Human blood is for nourishment. You can stop looking at me with disgust. You will have to kill humans to survive as I do. What will make you strong is my blood, and I will never give it to you. I will keep you weak so you cannot escape me. Poor spacer who came to earth and found such troubles." Selene let out a loud, mocking laugh.

"Why did you do this to me?" Drake demanded.

"I wanted you, and angels gave me the power to have you."

"I don't sleep well," Drake said. "I hear voices in my sleep. They say they are angels."

Selene became upset over this piece of information. "The angels have come to you already? Did they try to soothe poor, weak Drake? They cannot help you. Only I will decide what happens to you. My angels abandoned me long ago. They say I'm sick from the radiation I was exposed to when I was human. They say I must become a spirit to fix my soul."

"What radiation?" Drake said. "There hasn't been radiation on earth for centuries."

"Radiation from the Great War," Selene said as she slapped him on the side of the head. "We are vampires, Drake, and I have lived for centuries."

"You're mad, woman!"

This brought a backhand from Selene that sent him plummeting to the floor. "You will not speak to me like that, and I told you my name is Selene, not woman." She wavered and then was in front of him again, holding his jaw in her firm grip. "Get up and follow me. You stink!"

Drake followed her through the door and into the apartment and quickly realized this woman lived well, with the most elegant furniture and trappings, and rare artifacts from times long past. He went through her sleeping area, seeing a strange box in the floor, and then into her bathroom, where many different perfumes invaded his sensitive nose.

"Take those filthy clothes off and wash. You smell like a pig."

Drake stripped his clothes off while Selene watched and dropped the clothes to the floor. The vampire quickly picked them up and threw them into a bin in the wall. Selene approached him and ran her fingers over his chest. "How handsome you are. Wash yourself, and we will lie in my couch."

Drake washed and allowed the soothing, hot water to flow over his body. In this world, there were no restrictions on water; there was plenty for all, and he needed the relaxing waters. Selene watched him intensely, and when he had finished, she took him to the box in the floor. Her scent came from the box, and, strangely, it aroused him.

She kissed him passionately, everywhere, bit him, and suckled his blood. She used her mouth to make him hard and then straddled him. Where she was cruel and caused him pain, in love, she brought him pleasure. Selene was a beautiful and sensuous woman. When she finished with him, she allowed him to stay in the box and lay next to him, so close it made him uncomfortable.

"Why are you so full of hate?" Drake asked her.

This made her angry, and she viciously sunk her teeth deep in his neck. Drake thought she would tear his throat from him, and then just as quickly, she released him, licked the blood from her lips, and gave a smile.

"Careful, Drake, what you say to me. Fortunately for you, I love the taste of your sweet blood and the feel of your cock. I will tell you this one time why I hate. After the Great War, my maker made me a vampire. I was sick from the radiation, and he tried to save me from the burning death. Vampires had forbidden him to do this, as they weren't sure what the effects would be. He had broken other laws, and vampires looked down on him and me. I

16

loved him so much, but he wasn't like most vampires, so the pigs in the Vampire Council sent an eliminator. When I was a century old, they found him, so he buried me, to hide me. They killed him, and I have hated vampires since. Remember this, Drake. Vampires are killers, and they are cruel. Most vampires are worse than me."

"Didn't vampires save mankind once?" Drake said.

"They saved the humans so they could serve them. So they could feed on them. That was their reason. Why do you think there are so few humans in this world? When they find us, they will kill us. That I promise you. Go to sleep, and when the night comes, we will feed. We will hunt humans and take their blood."

Drake woke to the new night, and Selene gave him hot tea to drink to soothe his blood sac. When he finished, she made him climb onto her back and flew him out through the balcony and into the night sky. Clutching her body, he felt waves of panic travel through him. Selene flew around a nearby tower and then slowly descended to the street. There were few people out walking the streets, and they walked for a long time. Maniacal Selene walked hurriedly, and every so often, she would prompt Drake to walk faster to keep up. Finally, they came on a couple and followed them. They were young lovers, and, by their dress, unfortunate for this world, but they were in love, talked, kissed, and laughed as lovers do, held hands, and made their plans for their life together.

Drake became sick at the thought of killing these lovers.

"You can't be serious. We cannot kill these people."

"How are we to survive? We must kill! Do as I tell you, Drake."

"I will not kill. I can't!"

Selene grabbed him and held him in the air by his neck, his feet dangling. You will kill these people, or I will kill you. I know the brave spacer wants to live. The will to survive is strong in you. Vampire law tells us we can only kill evil people, but I have never followed their rules."

Selene tightened her grip, shook him, and set him down. "Follow me!"

Drake followed her and tried to keep the horrible thoughts from his head. She was a coldhearted woman that now ruled his life, but he would wait for the day to make his escape. That he promised himself.

They rounded a corner, and Selene flew at the couple. Their screams came quick and ended at the same time as their lives. Selene broke both their necks and threw the woman to Drake's feet. Out of character, she had taken pity on him and made the killing for him. Drake picked the girl up and looked at her now dead face. Moments before, the couple was planning their life together, the girl's eyes were alive and happy. Now, frozen on her face forever, was the mask of death. Selene again laughed at him as she raised her head from the boy's neck. Her face was covered with his blood.

"Sense where her veins are and use your teeth to pierce them. Drink, and it will make you feel better."

Drake stared at her lifeless neck, his vampire instincts telling him where to find her vein. He lowered his head, bit, and the blood flowed into his mouth. The blood was delicious and sweet. His brain screamed at him to stop that this was wrong, but he could not stop himself. Selene told him to spit the last of the blood onto the girl's neck, and he watched in fascination as it transformed the two ugly holes back to smooth, pale skin. The blood energized him, and his sickness went away. Drake dropped the body and all he heard was the strange sound it made hitting the pavement, like a *thud* from a sack of flour.

Selene grabbed his arm and shot straight up. It jerked him, and then she let go of him, and he desperately grabbed her leg, so he didn't fall.

He heard her piercing laughter. "What's the matter? Is the spacer afraid of falling? Is he afraid of gravity?"

Holding on, he watched the lights from the high towers fly by. They arced over the top of a tall tower and flew down to land on her balcony, high above the street. She dragged and threw him back into the room that kept him prisoner, locked the door, and left.

He spent eight months living in the room, and sometimes Selene allowed him to live in the apartment. It depended on her level of madness. There were times she would have periods of clarity and times of absolute madness. She would take him to feed—some were innocents, some were not—and she would tell him innocent blood was the sweetest.

Sometimes she would take him to places vampires gathered and drank. He would meet other vampires at these places, but most ignored him or acted superior to him, and some would push him out of their way as they passed. They called him a "worthless changeling" and scolded crazy Selene for bringing him to their tavern.

On the way home, Selene would slap and curse him. When they got back, she would make love to him and leave bite marks over his entire body. When she was done making love to him, briefly, her madness would lift, and she would tell him, "I won't hit you again, Drake. I love you so much."

"Then let me go," he would plead to her. "If you love me, you wouldn't keep me prisoner."

A burst of loud, shrill laughter would follow, her insanity returning. "You can't be on your own. You are too young, and other vampires would kill you. Even now, eliminators hunt me. Every year they come closer to finding me. They say I'm a diseased vampire. They do not know my greatness, my power."

"Then let me go before they find you, so I can live. Give me a chance."

"Why would I do that? When I feel love from you, maybe I will think about it. You have no love for me that I know." She would then grab him, dragging him to the room, screaming at him. "When you love me, I will let you out."

"Don't put me in the there!" Drake would beg. "I can't stand that room anymore!

"You are a sorry creature," Selene taunted. "I let you feed on humans to survive, but I will never give you my blood. Not until you love me. Love me, spacer, and I will give you my blood. I will make you strong. So nobody can keep you in a room."

She would slam the steel door, cursing and screaming, "You will never have the strength to open this door!"

He would call her "woman," and this would send her into a rage. This was his blow against her, his resistance, a small defiance to her, and it quickly brought a hard slap from her every time. Eight months passed, and the ghosts still came to him in his sleep. They tried to soothe him to give him hope. They would tell him that soon he would be free. Many times, Selene would leave, and he would spend days in his prison expanding his senses, allowing them to roam outward, feeling the life of the city and the people. This is how he kept his sanity. Finally, he heard her leave for the last time.

A week had passed, and Selene came home crazier than usual. He heard her screaming, "They think they can kill me! They don't know my power! My maker told me I am the most powerful of all vampires!" Drake heard breaking glass—she was throwing her figurines against the walls. The following evening, he sensed a different vampire coming. Power came from this vampire like none he had ever felt before. This was an ancient vampire.

He heard a deafening crash as the vampire came through the apartment door, and a loud, commanding voice. "I have come for you, Selene. You have broken too many of our laws, and now you teach a changeling to feed on innocents. The Vampire Council has sentenced you to death."

"You do not have the strength to kill a vampire like me!" Selene raged with her maddened voice, "I am the most powerful vampire in this world!"

"You are mad. I will send you to the angels, and maybe they can help you."

Drake heard the two vampires battling and the destruction to the apartment. The walls shook, terrible noises echoed through his door, and finally, he heard Selene pleading for her life and her death scream.

Terror overcame him as he sensed the eliminator moving to his prison door. Drake had been a brave man before Selene had found him. The steadiness of nerve was always his allies through danger, quick thinking to remove him and his crew from harm. Now, he crawled to the far corner and cowered in it, consumed by fear as the steel door exploded across the room. Drake thought about how these horrible creatures had turned him into a coward, always afraid for his life.

The vampire was tall, with a dark complexion and curly, black hair. A handsome fellow, but with penetrating eyes that turned sorrowful, as he stood staring at Drake huddling in the far corner of the room.

"What has the vampire done to you, young one?" the vampire asked.

"She made me a prisoner and she tormented me," Drake replied.

"The council gave me no orders to kill you. They left your death up to me. I think now I will let you live. Beware, young vampire. I'm sure someday the council will send me to you."

The vampire turned, and, as quickly as he came, he left. Drake sat in the corner and realized he was finally free. He went to Selene, found a pile of fine grey dirt, kicked it with his foot, and watched it explode and fill the room. He tore her couch from the floor and gathered all of her money. He cleaned himself and wore the fine clothes she had bought for him, went to the balcony, and started his long climb to the streets below, and to freedom.

Selene had once told Drake how to be with humans. She told him what to expect and how to behave with them. Drake spent the next two years living with humans. He never wanted to be with vampires---he despised his kind.

Chapter Three

Tonight, Katherine walked a lonely street in Seattle. A light fog hung close to the ground, and she heard the distant sounds of laughter—party-goers headed to their next bar. Roads in this age were for walking and were the lowest level of these modern majestic cities. Ground-level was where she would find the type of human she was hunting. Seattle had been her feeding ground these last fifty years. Often, she would come to hunt the undesirables, the evil of the world, and sometimes she would move on for a brief visit with her maker in the Great Iberian Bayou.

Fifty years had passed since her maker had returned to her. Katherine was over five hundred years old and a powerful vampire for her age. Few vampires were as powerful as she was. Her maker made her this way, and he was the most powerful vampire in this world. Many times she would think of Shawn: how he had become a recluse over the last fifty years, and she knew he still felt deeply for the loss of Anne and Marilyn. Later this eve, she would go to him like always and try to prod him out into the world.

Stopping her stroll, she whispered to herself, "There you are. I feel your evil."

Rounding the corner, she saw the man across the street, leaning against a building. The soft yellow light of the hovering streetlight lit the mist hanging in the air. She heard the hum of two low-flying air cars as they passed overhead. Katherine hung back by the corner of the street and watched her prey.

He was an endorphin thieve, a tall, lanky man, and she sensed his dark nature. The man held a small machine in his hand, and she saw the titanium needle meant to be plunged into the heads of his victims. He would siphon that precious neurotransmitter of joy into the machine—killing his victim. When he had enough, he would sell the juice for large amounts of money. Later, humans would make it into a drug.

Katherine walked across the street, past the man, and, as expected, he moved quickly toward her and tried to plunge the needle into her head. She caught his arm, twisted it, and listened to the sharp snaps of his bones. Then she took his blood and life, leaving him in a pile on the street, his hand still clenching the machine.

She licked the sweet nectar from her lips and wiped the rest from her chin with a handkerchief. Ascending slowly into the night sky, she felt the warm wind blowing against her face, pulling at her clothes. Higher she went until finally, she reached the top of a high tower to perch. The towers of this time stretched high into the sky and held many platforms, placed around and extending outward, from the towers. Humans built their buildings and living areas on these platforms. At night, these cities would light the night sky. This was how humans lived now in cities of towers, and few lived in the countryside, only the wealthy and people who raised and grew the food.

Katherine sat and watched the millions of lights in the city. Seattle sparkled like a jewel this night. *How beautiful,* she thought. Focusing her powerful eyes, she would bring random areas close and then watch the humans through their windows, smiling or grimacing at the many different scenes she would see. Humans lived their lives, talking, laughing, or screaming at each other. Lonely humans that had no one would sometimes pace their floors at night, unable to sleep.

A fleeting distortion formed in the air, and then a whisper came to her mind—*remember him*—followed by a memory, a story that Renee had told her. The Vampire Council was aware of a young changeling roaming Seattle, living with humans. He was from space, and a crazed vampire had changed him. Renee asked her to be on the lookout for this vampire because the council had voted to send an eliminator for him. Renee told her she voted "no", but the majority voted "yes", and she was afraid for this vampire.

Again, a whisper in her mind—*look for him*. Feeling the night, she projected her senses outward, and finally, she found him, a young vampire by himself to the north. She flew a mile to another tower, and there she could sense the vampire somewhere on the street below. Another message filled her mind—*go to him*. Dropping a half-mile to the way, she began her walk and sensed him a block up.

Katherine made her way to a human bar pulsing with the music of the times and sensed the young vampire strongly inside. She readied her mental abilities as she entered the speakeasy. When passing the humans, she would place thoughts of normalcy in their heads and make them think she was human.

Katherine worked her way through the mortals. It was warm because of the large crowd, and the smell of human blood was strong. The vampire was in the back and stood where the band was playing.

Slowly, she approached; there he was, in the corner, working the band's sound equipment. Effortlessly, she could see what got him into trouble with crazy Selene. He was a strikingly handsome man with a strong, masculine face, brown, shiny hair, and a close cut, reddish-brown, beard. A well-built man. As humans say, "tall, dark, and handsome."

She cloaked herself from him, watched him, and sensed him, took in his smell. He was an uneasy vampire, always looking over his shoulder, and was friends with this band, worked for them, and the leader knew he was a vampire. His name was Drake, and he had gotten himself into some serious trouble with the Vampire Council. However, she felt the angels had taken an interest in him.

Katherine moved closer through the crowd, was now ten feet from him, and smiled as her gaze traveled his body. Slowly, she lifted her shroud, and his eyes immediately went to her. His edgy smile quickly turned fearful when he recognized her for what she was. She nodded at him and promptly sensed his loathing for her and sent him a message: *Greetings, young vampire. I must speak with you.*

Again, she could feel intense hatred and knew he had no desire to speak to her. The vampire was now looking around for an escape route, and she knew he was going to run from her. Worse, the bandleader had noticed his fear, and the vampire nodded toward her. Drake had given her away.

No, young one, you cannot do this, she sent back. Katherine would have to remove him from this city to protect him from himself and the council. He obviously knew nothing about vampire law.

More of his thoughts came to her. Drake knew what she was. Realized she was in his mind, and Drake would glare back at her with hate on his face. Katherine knew his situation wasn't his fault. His maker had never taught him how to be a vampire. Now, the Vampire Council would kill him for what Selene had done and for what he was. That was not fair to Katherine, but the Vampire Council never was appropriate to her. They did what was expedient and then took the easy way and accepted high accolades for it. Her maker would always warn her about the council.

The band played on, and Katherine swayed to the rhythms of the music, following the beat as Marilyn taught her, and watched Drake until the music stopped. The vampire didn't look at her, but instead turned and went out the back door. Katherine followed, and the bandleader stepped in front of her.

"Sorry. Patrons can't use that door."

"Are you sure?" Katherine pressed as she caught his eyes with hers, waving her hand in front of his face and placing the thought to step aside in his mind and to let her use the door.

"Go ahead and use the door," the bandleader said as he stepped aside.

Katherine went through the door and immediately sensed Drake's location. She followed him down the alley and out into a crowded walkway. Bumping into and walking around the humans, she quickly caught up to him. Drake was walking with the humans so she could do nothing but follow him and try to talk to him.

"What is the matter with you, vampire?" Katherine said in a low voice.

"Stay away from me, you filthy whore!" the vampire hissed back. "What you are after is to own me and take control of me!"

Well, he's right about that. I am going to take control of him, she thought.

"Filthy whore, that's not very nice of you," Katherine said back. "Is that how spacers talk?"

"That's exactly what you are. A filthy whore vampire."

"You know nothing about vampires," Katherine said as she hurried to keep pace with him. "I can see that in you. You hate your own kind."

"I hate vampires. I have never met a decent vampire. They all bring pain with them. They want to take control of me."

"How many vampires have you met? Not many, I suspect. I am going to take control of you, Drake. I have to. You have broken vampire laws, and you have not been taught how to be a vampire, you know nothing about being a vampire."

Drake suddenly dipped his body forward, bringing his foot up, arcing, and striking her in the face, sending her flying into a wall. He then disappeared down a side walkway. Drake did this to her with vampire strength and speed. It surprised Katherine; it had caught her off-guard. Blood came from her nose as she sat against the wall, and humans gathered around her. She had not expected him to show himself this way in front of all the humans.

"I'm fine," she said to the gaping humans as she got to her feet and hurried down the walkway. Katherine heard behind her the humans say, "You couldn't see that man's foot move and did you see how far the woman flew in the air." The mortals whispered, "Guardians."

She could sense Drake, and quickly went to the railing he had used to make his escape, watching him climbing the column that led to the next platform that held apartment buildings. She flew to the next platform and caught him crossing the lawn toward one of the buildings. Sensing her, he turned and charged at her; she grabbed him by his arm and neck and threw him quickly back to the ground. Katherine pinned him down as he struggled desperately.

"Calm yourself, Drake!" she commanded as she sat on him. He tried to hit her in the head again, but she caught his fist and held it to the ground.

"Stop hitting me, vampire! You don't want to make me mad."

"Get off me! Let me go! Go torment some other poor soul!" Drake yelled, angrily. "I have done nothing to you!"

"That is what you think," Katherine said as she stared into his red vampire eyes. "You know nothing of what you are. You can deal with me, or you can face the eliminator that the Vampire Council has sent for you. You tell the humans what we are. Vampire law forbids this. Selene has done you a grave injustice. Let me help you. Let me try to save you."

"Let me up, and we can talk," Drake conceded.

"I can tell you are not going to give up, but I will let you up to show you I mean you no harm. You cannot escape me, Drake. You are a weak vampire. Have you ever taken vampire blood?"

"I would never drink filthy vampire blood. Let me up, woman."

Katherine slowly let Drake stand, and as soon he did, he twirled, using his leg, knocking hers out from under her. He shot toward the edge of the platform, and Katherine tackled him from behind. Again, she was on top of him.

"The spacer is not going to give up, is he? And seems to be good with his legs. What is this in your mind? You are from space…Water. Let us go for a swim spacer." Katherine laughed at the irony as she gathered him from behind, wrapping her arms around his chest. He was helpless in her grasp. Flying him out and over Seattle Bay, she dropped him into the water, watching him flounder in the water and hearing his screams.

"Help me! I can't swim, you whore!" Drake screamed.

"Calling me a whore is not going to make me help you. What a fool you are! You can't drown. The Mother would spit you back to the shore."

"Vampire bitch! Help me," Drake pleaded.

"You have a terrible mouth on you, Drake. I will if you promise to stop trying to get away and mean what you say. Remember, I can tell what you are thinking. You must mean it this time."

"Please! I won't try to escape! Get me out of this water!"

Katherine knew he meant it. He was the first vampire she had met who didn't like water. She drifted down and watched him flail in the water, shaking her head in disbelief.

She scolded him and laughed. "Relax!" Katherine entered the water, wrapped herself around Drake, and held him so he couldn't move. She let him float on top of her.

"Calm yourself," she whispered in his ear. "Feel the water. Let The Mother soothe you. You can't drown."

She was trying to reassure him, keeping him in the water until he could feel it was strength to him. It could be soothing for him. Slowly, she felt him settle. Drake stopped his thrashing, and then he went limp. The fight had finally left him.

"I can feel it. What is it?"

"It's The Mother," Katherine whispered. "Let her soothe you."

Katherine let the vampire calm himself and then took him by his collar, flying him to the shore and dumping him in the sand. Sitting next to him, she took her shoes off and spilled the water from them. She watched him lying on the beach, staring at the night sky. Drake pointed, "That is where I'm from."

Katherine felt how tired he was, his disillusionment, and the fear he had for his new life. His mistrust of her had lessened, and now he was finally looking at her—judging her. Drake was thinking about how beautiful she was, and that maybe she might be different.

Katherine smiled and told him, "Selene was a rarity amongst our kind. Not all vampires will abuse you, guardians mistreat you because you are so young and undisciplined, and they can feel your hatred. You need someone to teach you what you are and to give you strength. Give you blood. You must grow and learn."

"I have not experienced this in your world," Drake said. "To me, vampires are cruel creatures. Killers without mercy."

"We are killers, but we kill evil."

"Really? That's not what I saw."

"Selene was crazy. That's why the council killed her," Katherine said. "They sent her to the angels so they could heal her soul."

"Who are you, vampire?" Drake asked. "And why do you care what happens to me?"

"My name is Katherine Bryce, and I don't feel that you should die… not yet. I can see what you are. You are far more than you can imagine. Also, the angels want you to live. That I know."

Drake sighed. "That also annoys me about vampires. They are always looking into my mind. Reading my thoughts."

"Then you should learn how to keep vampires out of your mind. Again, you know nothing of what you are. We have to talk about the danger you are in. You have broken vampire laws, and the council has decided to send you back to the angels. They think you are defective because of your maker, but I see a young, undisciplined vampire who deserves a second chance. There is no rogue in you."

"Let me go, vampire. I don't need help. What I need is for you and your kind to leave me alone."

"The eliminator will not leave you alone. He will take your heart and send you to the angels. He is coming for you, and you will need a safe place. My family is a powerful and respected vampire family, and we can go to them. Maybe my family's name can save you, but now we will find a place to rest and clean up."

Katherine took Drake to a hotel located a half-mile above the streets of Seattle, on top of a high platform. The Crimmian Society owned the hotel, and Katherine exclusively stayed there when she was in Seattle. She always took the room, which gave her a view of the mountains to the east.

Katherine had taken a shower, and when she came back from the bathroom, her brown hair was wet and brushed back, hanging straight as she buttoned the top of her pink silk pajamas. Drake had a towel wrapped around his waist and was staring at the night sky. She could sense homesickness coming from him, and she noticed his wet skin, his broad, muscular shoulders, and his flat stomach. Drake was a man she could spend time with in her couch. A thought she quickly hid from him.

Drake was a young, weak vampire, but she knew he would sense her desire for him if she wasn't careful. Earlier, she had tried to contact her maker, but he had disappeared. A situation that had happened many times over the last ten years. The evil forces of this world were gathering, evil was rising again; Lucifer's witches were coming to this world now, and knowing her maker, he was deeply involved.

"What has attracted so much of your attention?" Katherine asked Drake.

Drake pointed to the bright light in the sky. "My home, Mars. I long to go home and forget this nightmare world and what happened to me. That vampire, Selene, said I could never leave this planet. I'm stranded here for eternity."

"I'm sorry, Drake, but she was right. Your life force can only survive here. You have great powers and eternal life, but only in this world. You can never leave. If you do, you will crumble into dust."

Drake hung his head, and blood tears came to his eyes. Katherine felt his pain, went to him, placed a hand on his shoulder, and tried to soothe him.

"The angels said they would take me," Drake whispered.

"Come to bed and sleep. You will feel better when you wake. When we are rested, we will figure this mess out."

Drake looked at the large bed in the center of the room. "Where can I sleep?"

"In the bed, silly. Vampires sleep together, but it doesn't mean we have sex. Don't you feel lonely when you sleep?"

"Yes, you're right. I do!"

"There is so much you need to learn, but first you must survive the Vampire Council."

The next eve, Katherine took Drake north to travel with him, so she could learn about him, took him to feed, to teach him what vampires fed on, and how they fed. She entered his head, saw he was a decent man that liked people before Selene, and now it seemed, she started to want him. Why she wasn't sure. She tried to reason with herself to answer that question in her mind.

The angels whispered to her about Drake when she slept and told her to take care of him. They told her to accept him without question. After that, she showed herself to him, so he knew she wouldn't harm him or abuse him. Slowly, he started to relax with her, talk with her, and often spoke of the hatred he had for Selene. Still, she hid her attraction toward him.

Three nights later, they arrived at Bryce's family home and stood on the front lawn. She watched Drake kick at the grass, a look of dread having spread over his face. "This is your family home. It's an earth mansion, like in the pictures, and I sense three vampires in there. Do we have to?" Drake asked with loathing in his voice.

"Yes, we have to, and leave the hate out outside. They are vampires like me. Most vampires are like me. I was hoping you were starting to learn that."

"All right, I promised to let you help me. Who are these vampires?" Drake questioned.

"They are Caitlyn, Juliette, and Peter. Caitlyn and Juliette are part of my family. Most likely, Peter Kenmare is here to be with Juliette."

"Vampires have families who would have thought," Drake said.

Katherine looked at Drake. He had finally said something good about vampires. Drake followed her inside, and she introduced him. Caitlyn and Peter were not that friendly, but Juliet was cordial. When Renee wasn't there, Caitlyn was head of the house, and she called a Crimmian immediately to take him to his room. Katherine then went to the sitting room with Caitlyn, Juliette, and Peter.

Renee is coming from Amsterdam," Caitlyn told her. "Last night, the Vampire Council dispatched an eliminator to kill the vampire you brought to our house. Now, the eliminator is coming here. Do you care to explain yourself?"

"He is a decent man. That mad vampire did him a terrible wrong. Renee told me to look for him. He needs help. The council is being unfair!"

"Katherine. Really. Renee didn't tell you to bring him home. Now an eliminator is coming," Caitlyn said. "Have you contacted Shawn?"

"I tried, but he has disappeared again."

"We will help you until Renee comes, and then it's her decision," Caitlyn instructed.

"There is a way you can save him," Juliette added sheepishly.

"What is it?" Katherine urged.

"Give him your blood! Stand by him and take him as your protégé."

"That's the way," Katherine said.

"That's the only way," Juliette replied. "It should work. You can always threaten the eliminator with Shawn's name."

"We'd better hope Renee gets here before the eliminator," Peter added.

Katherine went to Drake's room, slid onto the bed, and lay looking at the ceiling, waiting for him to leave the shower. She was deep in thought when he came from the bath, naked. He quickly pulled a towel around his middle. "I guess vampires don't knock."

"Not with you, I don't."

Katherine watched him dress. She decided she liked to look at his naked body and wondered what he would taste like, what sex would be like with him.

"I'm going for a swim in the lake. Follow me, we have to talk."

"To the lake?" Drake whined.

"Yes, to the lake." Katherine took Drake by the hand and led him to the lake in silence. She went to the water's edge and took her clothes off slowly. Drake sat in a lawn chair with his usual look of horror—the look he had when he couldn't see the bottom of the water, or when the water looked black to him. Katherine watched Drake look at her as she undressed, watched his eyes, sensed his arousal, his hate for her leaving him. She even started to feel a little trust coming from him. Standing at the edge of the lake, she splashed water on her face and breast. "The eliminator will be here in a couple of days. There is only one way to save you."

"Let's leave and run. We can escape him. Let me go, Katherine. Give me a chance," Drake pleaded.

"No, I am not going to let you go. I have decided on that! You wouldn't survive. I could bury you, but you couldn't stay buried forever."

"Bury me? In the dirt?" Drake said.

"Yes, in the dirt! You amaze me how little you know. Mother Earth will hide you from your enemies. Like this water that scares you."

"Who is this, Mother?" Drake asked.

"She is a lesser god, and her name is Eos. An old and powerful angel that inhabits this planet. Do you even know about angels?"

"In my sleep, the angels talk to me sometimes. They give me encouragement."

"They are your angels and have been working on your behalf. What else have they said to you?"

"They said I'm from space, and I will be a shooting star in this world."

Katherine went to Drake and took his hand. "Come. Take your clothes off and let me show you how to relax in the water. Remember how you felt in the ocean when you relaxed."

"If you want, Katherine, we can go into the water." Drake sighed.

Katherine helped Drake take his clothes off, led him to the lake, and pulled him in the water. She let him float on her.

"Relax, Drake, and feel the water. You can feel it soothing you.

"Yes, it is! I feel it, and I can feel you."

Katherine held Drake and pulled him through the water, her hand brushing his erect penis.

"What is this? Do you desire me, vampire?" She turned and faced him, wrapping her legs around him.

"It must be the water," Drake mumbled.

"You want me, I can tell. I can smell it on you," Katherine whispered in his ear. "Can you stay with me for a hundred years? Do as I tell you, follow my teachings?"

"Why should I do that?" Drake asked as he pushed her away.

"That is the only way to save you," Katherine told Drake as she drew near and looked into his eyes. She always saw a sorrow in his eyes, a lost man in this world. "I can take you as my fledgling and give you my blood."

"I don't know if that is what I want. I'm not good at taking orders. I have always given them. Who is to say you wouldn't abuse me? No, I think I will fight this eliminator."

"So you think you should fight the eliminator," Katherine said angrily. Quickly, her caring for this vampire turned to anger. Katherine took hold of Drake and threw him out into the lake. Again, she was on him, picking him up and flying him to the lawn.

She changed to her full vampire form, sunk her teeth into his shoulder, and then bit his neck. She spits the bitter blood out. "Your blood tasted of hate and stupidity. You have never taken vampire blood. I can taste it. You have only the original blood Selene gave you. That's why you're so weak."

Katherine held Drake down by his neck—sat on him—and bit him again in the neck and chest. Blood was running down her chin.

"You are helpless, weak vampire. Try to fight me, Drake! You can't even move! The eliminator is as powerful as I am, maybe more. He will take your heart before you can raise a fist to him."

Katherine released her grip on Drake. She kissed him passionately, guided him inside her, and moved against him, caressing him. She put her thoughts of love in his head, and whispered in his ear. "Let me save you. Let me teach you. You will have to do what I say, but I will never abuse you."

"Then save me!" Drake said with respite in his voice. She felt his surrender to her, felt his release, and sensed he finally knew he had found someone to help him.

"I'm a spacer, and I know when I'm beat and when I need help."

"No, Drake, you are a vampire now, and I will help you live

like one."

She guided his head to her neck. She saw his face changed to a vampire; his eyes were weak in color as if they were not sure what covenant they belonged too. She felt his teeth enter her neck, the touch of his wet tongue, and he drank. She sensed the fear leave him. She saw him fall back onto the grass, shutter, and heard him give a loud, pleasing moan. His eyes opened and were the blue of the Herit Covenant.

Chapter Four

S hawn had taken cover in the tall swamp grass on the shore of a shallow bayou lake to hide himself from the dark witch who was building a fire on the other side of the lake. The brackish waters reflected the soft light of the large moon that hung low in the night sky. The protruding eyes of the gator moving just below the surface also indicated the light. Squatting next to him was Jessamine, the witch—his daughter. They had been shrouding themselves for a week, as they played cat-and-mouse with the evil witch that Lucifer had sent to kill him and bring his soul to Hell. This was the third witch Lucifer had sent, and each time they grew stronger.

Forty years ago, at considerable expense to Shawn, he built a red brick mansion with a white, wooden, pillared Southern plantation porch in the Iberian Bayou. Wood was abundant in this world, but humans no longer used it as a building material and rarely used brick. Shawn shared the house with Jessamine—he lived upstairs; she, downstairs.

The house was on high land, and scattered throughout his three-hundred-acre estate were majestic cypress trees, with Spanish moss draping from their branches. Jessamine had planted beautiful flowers and herb gardens around their home. A lone road traveled the bayou over bridges and through the thick trees to their house, circled the estate, and headed back the way it came.

These days, Shawn rarely left the bayou. The sadness of Anne and Marilyn's deaths was only now starting to fade. Katherine and

Victoria would come for visits but would tire of the swamp and leave. Now, Jessamine was his one constant companion.

She has built a fire, Father," Jessamine told him. "The witch will mix the plants and herbs found in the swamp. I'm sure it will be an evil poison. Made especially for you."

"The witch is most determined. You stay here," Shawn whispered.

"Let me go with you, Father?"

"No, if I get into trouble, then come."

"The witches keep coming," Jessamine whispered.

"I know, it's only a matter of time."

"That's what I'm afraid of, Father."

Shawn took his clothes off, laid himself on the ground, floated through the grass, and into the dark water. He no longer had a slayer and never replaced the one he lost fighting the demons. The lake was shallow, and he moved just above the muddy bottom, around the floating grass swaying in the slight current he made as he traveled by. He startled a gator, and mud exploded from the bottom as the creature made its escape. When he came to the other side, he transformed into a mist and drifted up the bank, through the vegetation and toward the witch.

Arriving at a large cypress tree, he hid and changed back to his vampire form. He peered around the tree, and in the clearing saw the witch stirring her little pot of poison, and heard her chanting her evil words. She was a hag of a woman, an evil entity sent by Lucifer.

Her hair was scraggly, dark red, streaked with purple. The fire danced off her pale face, and dark veins stood out on her flour-white skin. Her eyes and lips were black, and her teeth stained with berry juice. She was a stocky woman who wore little clothing; mud caked her bare feet and streaked her legs. Her breasts were bare, each held a symbolic marking made with mud, and she had drawn a mask of berry juice around her eyes. Evil and a horrible stench came from the witch, and it was hard for Shawn to bear.

The witch sensed him, turned, and yelled, "Vampire filth! Beelzebub, send me fire!" The dark energy of the universe gathered, a blue fireball appearing in her hand, and the witch reached back and threw it at Shawn. He quickly ducked to the ground. The fireball hit the tree and, with a loud *boom* that echoed into the night, exploded into red, fiery trails that went into the dark sky and out over the lake, like evening fireworks at the summer fair.

He watched the witch crouch, getting on all fours and changing into a large black panther with piercing red eyes. The witch turned, took to the forest, and began to circle the lake, heading back toward Jessamine. Shawn changed to his vampire form, ran after the witch, and soon caught the panther, wrestling it to the ground. The beast changed back to the witch, and Shawn held her by her throat.

The witch gasped to him, "Lucifer will have you. There is no escape for you. I'm just the beginning."

The witch's hands held the slimy goo she had concocted, and then it burst into flames; she rose up, wrapping her hands around his neck, burning his face. "Have some fire, vampire?" The witch raged.

Shawn pulled the burning hands from his neck, threw the witch back onto the ground, smashed her in the face, and slammed her head against the dirt. "You are the one that will be leaving."

Her eyes burned red and he heard a penetrating shrill rise in his head—a maddening shriek. He fell back off the witch, holding his head. The witch was on him again, but before he could give the witch a deathblow, a white beam of plasma hit the witch, lifting her off him and throwing her into the brush. Gentle Jessamine had circled around and caught the witch unprepared with her rod.

Shawn followed and again threw her to the ground. The witch spits her blood at him. "Have some blood, vampire. Lucifer will never tire and never forget. He seeks his revenge on you, vampire!"

Wrapping his hands around her neck, he squeezed with all his strength. Her head came off, and she turned as black as night. Dark blue flames consumed the witch and a panther's head with long, white teeth and burning, red eyes came out of the fire, flew at

Shawn, roared, and disappeared.

"Well, Father, that was spectacular," Jessamine said. "Looks like Lucifer is starting to put on quite a show."

"He is. He is a tormentor and likes to have his fun."

The following night Shawn sat on his white, pillared front porch and saw for miles through the swamp with his vampire's eyes. He would sit for hours, drinking his bourbon, watching the night, the stirring of the critters, and thinking of the past. Some nights, as he sat in his rocker, parts of his life would haunt him. Jessamine had gone early to her living area in the mansion, and he had not seen her since. She was probably asleep; after all, she wasn't a vampire.

Earlier, he had sensed Katherine; she had sent him a message only he could detect. She needed him, and he would leave the next eve. It didn't seem serious, more like she had gotten herself into trouble—probably a trick to get him out of the swamp. These days he often thought about leaving the swamp but decided he wasn't ready. He still wanted the solitude. He still grieved for Anne and Marilyn, but again time had gone by, and now he strained to remember their voices. Herit was always after him, telling him to go home to Washington and live life again.

He would ask her: *What about Jessamine?*

She is a witch and part of The Mother. She will be all right.

And then he would ask her question, one he had asked many times before, *will you still come for me? Will you still fight for me?*

Yes, Shawn, I will.

Tomorrow night he would make the trip to Washington. It would do him good to be with his family. He sipped at his bourbon and then saw the white points of light swirl out in the front lawn. More and more, the points of light gathered until they formed a single bright light, floating just above the ground. "Herit," he said to himself as he left the rocker and floated out onto the lawn. Shawn had traveled halfway to the light, stopped, and fell to the ground, sobbing uncontrollably. That terrible pain came again to his heart, that feeling of a terrible loss that would make him choke. Blood tears flowed from his eyes; he looked, and the angel wasn't

Herit—it was Anne.

My love, we have not seen each other for such a long time. Do not cry.

Shawn stared at the light. It hurt his eyes, but he didn't care.

"It is you! I can see you again." Shawn cried blood tears, staining his shirt. "I hear you, a voice in my head…it's so hard to live in this world without you."

You must go on and live, Marilyn and I are happy and content.

"Can I see Marilyn, too?"

She will come to you in the light when you sleep. We have been resting these years, rejuvenating ourselves, healing our spirits. Now, we have begun our existence as warrior angels, and we can come to you. Not a lot, we are still gathering our power, and there will be other vampires we must attend to.

"Why didn't Michael take me?"

You lost faith in him, and The Mother claimed you. She healed you and protected you. The Mother has a task for you now. I have come to urge you to leave the bayou. It is time for you to go on and live a fuller life. Evil is rising, and you must prepare yourself. You cannot spend eternity with Jessamine in this swamp. Stop your grieving for Marilyn and me. It serves you no purpose now. We have gone on to our place in Heaven. Live again, Shawn!"

"When you and Marilyn died, it left such emptiness in me. It was unbearable at times. I have tried to fill the void, but it has been so hard. I have made Victoria sad because she can't make me happy. Katherine comes, but I hurt her, too. She denies it, but I know."

Then fill the emptiness with the knowledge that Marilyn and I live in Heaven, and that someday we will be together again, my love. Now listen to what I have to say. You have made an enemy with Lucifer. You will be his revenge on the warrior angels. He wants to take you to Hell and punish you for what happened to his demons.

"Michael left me behind! Of course, Lucifer will have me…eventually."

The Mother wanted you. She wants you here. Michael had no

choice; he needs The Mother's to help fight the great dark angel. Be careful with Lucifer's witches; he will keep sending them for you, and they will grow stronger and more cunning. Malin will come soon, in the flesh—The Tempter—and vampires will fight a great battle. I do not have the strength yet to stay long. I must go. I love you, and always will.

The light broke up into smaller points of light; it swirled and then disappeared.

"No, don't leave me!" Shawn whispered. Despair flooded him. He could not keep Anne in this world, and he knew Michael would not allow him in Heaven anytime soon.

Chapter Five

K atherine woke in her couch, sat-up, and rubbed her eyes; Drake still slept in the next room. He slowly was becoming more comfortable with her. It had been two eves since their arrival home, and now she felt her maker was close and sensed the arrival of Renee and the eliminator. Floating out of the couch, she went to the bathroom, washed, and then went to Drake's room, crawled in bed with him, brushed his hair from his face, and whispered in his ear, "Wake up, sleepy." She knew he was starting to wake, and he had sensed the arrival of the vampires.

"They're here, aren't they?" Drake sighed.

"They are! I will be with you, and my family will stand with me. And my maker is coming!"

"I hope that will be enough," Drake said. "Maybe the angels are right. I should go to them."

"You will be a vampire, my fledgling, and you need to start realizing that. I usually get what I want, and stop saying the angels want you to go to them."

Katherine sensed Renee coming down the hall and stopping at the door.

"I have to talk to Renee, so don't leave the apartment."

"Will the eliminator come?" Drake asked.

"Not yet. He will formally judge you first. I will be back soon."

Katherine went out into the hall, and Renee stood with her arms crossed, held tight, and a perturbed look on her face.

"We have to talk. Follow me," Renee scolded.

Katherine followed her down the hall and up the stairs to her living area.

"Why did you bring him here?" Renee demanded. "You didn't ask my permission. I am head of this family, and you should have told me before you brought him here."

"I'm sorry, Renee, I didn't think. You were the one who told me about him, and Drake certainly does not deserve to die. This mess is not his fault."

"Whose fault…is not the question," Renee said sternly. "The council believes he is not of this world, and Selene should never have made him a vampire. I do not agree with this, but the eliminator is here, and he will judge young Drake."

"He's here to kill Drake. I am going to stand by him. I am taking him as a fledgling, and I have given him my blood. He has the eyes of a Herit now," Katherine blurted out.

"Katherine, you go too far!" an exasperated Renee informed. "You are just like your maker!"

"What do you mean?"

"You get your family into bad situations!"

"That's not fair, Renee!" An anxious Katherine replied. "Shawn never wanted to fight the demons! He did what the angels wanted!"

"You're in love with this vampire!"

Katherine shrugged, looked away, and said, "I'm not going to let anything happen to Drake!"

"You have put me in a difficult situation, just like your maker used to do with Anne. Have you heard from Shawn?"

"Yes, he lifted his shroud two eves ago," Katherine answered.

"Your maker made a terrible enemy with the likes of the dark angel Lucifer. He shrouds himself when he fights Lucifer's witches."

"Yes, I know. It's becoming a problem," Katherine answered.

"Is he coming?"

"He is on his way."

"We will all stand with you, present the eliminator with the facts, and hopefully, he will see it the Bryces' way. Bring this Drake to the library at midnight. The eliminator will pass judgment then."

"I will not let anything happen to Drake, and I will ask Shawn to help me. I wanted you to know that, and I hope the eliminator is aware of that."

"It looks like you will be saved, Katherine," Renee said. "I'm sure the eliminator knows it. Now I know how Anne must have felt. I am going to take a nap. I will see you at midnight."

Deep in thought, Katherine made her way back to her apartment. She wasn't going to let the eliminator kill Drake. They couldn't kill the eliminator, as that would break the laws of vampires, and would bring the council after them. Maybe the angels that had taken an interest in Drake would intervene with the council. She then sent another telepathic message to her maker: *Hurry, I need you!*

Entering Drake's room, she could sense his fear, and knew once he had been a brave man, a proud man, but she also realized her kind had stolen this from him. Drake lived in constant fear and had lost his bravery over these past two years. Now, he was always scheming, looking for the next danger, the next horror in his life, always searching for a way to escape vampires. She would change that for him, she would make him a brave man again.

"Don't be afraid, all is not lost," Katherine told him. She took his hand and led him to the sofa. "My maker will be here soon, and he is a powerful vampire."

"Maybe this will be for the best," Drake said. "I'm tired of this world, living as a vampire…maybe I should die."

"You are not going to die. I will take you as a fledgling and show you the life you can have as a vampire. We will go to the study at midnight and face this eliminator. I must leave you for now, my maker has arrived, and he calls me."

"I sense the love you have for him," Drake said. "To love a vampire like that…amazing."

"Stay here, and do not leave the apartment."

Katherine made her way to Shawn's room. She now occupied

most of Shawn's old living area, but he still had his messy room. The door was open, and she immediately went to him and embraced him, kissing him. Two Crimmians were changing the bedding in his couch.

"It's good to see you standing in your old room again," Katherine said excitedly.

"How have you been, my love? I missed you!" Shawn replied as he kissed her again. "Jessamine sends her love. So, you have brought home this stray, young vampire?"

"I did, I couldn't help myself."

"I see you love him and can't understand why."

"I do love him, and it came so quickly...my feelings for him. It has confused me."

"Then look to the angels, as I'm sure they know why. Does he love you?"

"No, but he is starting to trust me. He hates vampires because of what Selene did to him."

"I'm sure he does. What do you plan on doing about the council?"

"Bluff them," Katherine said.

"That will be hard. They are old vampires. We will have to reason with them, but usually, that doesn't go well. I will visit this vampire alone."

"Why do you want to do that?" Katherine questioned.

"I want to see what's in his heart, and I can tell better without you there."

****

Shawn went to Drake's door and knocked. He could sense the vampire on the other side of the door and knew Drake sensed him, too. The vampire was now deciding whether to open the door or jump through the window and make his escape. Shawn said softly through the door, "Courage, young vampire. Open the door. That is your best chance."

The door slowly opened, and Shawn looked through "Drake, I presume? Can I come in?"

"Sure, come in."

Shawn entered the room, and Drake quickly backed away. He read the young vampire quite easily, a calculating man, and this came from years of leadership as well as the predicament he found himself in. Drake had been a proud and a brave man, but now he was not so sure of himself, hate was his primary emotion these days, but throughout his life, he had been a good man.

Drake was a handsome man, a powerful man, Shawn recognized, looking at his body. A spacer never had fat on his bones.

"I'm Shawn, and we need to talk."

"I know who you are. I have heard of the vampire Shawn Bryce."

"It looks like I have to figure a way to save you, so no harm comes to my Katherine," Shawn confessed as he took a seat. "You have yourself in quite a unique situation."

"A situation I curse every day," Drake replied.

"I'm sure you do, but that carries little weight with the Vampire Council. They will do what is expedient."

"Let me go. Help me to escape!" Drake pleaded.

"You are a schemer that is for sure. You wouldn't make it to the end of the driveway. We will let the eliminator make the first move. He knows I'm here and is now in contact with the council. He might be looking for a way out, too."

"You can sense this?"

"Yes, I can, and someday you will, too, but now you have to get that sick Selene blood out of you. I will stand with you, young vampire, but you must do what Katherine says for the next hundred years. You will stay with her and become her fledgling. And you will try to get the hate out of your heart. Vampires deal with too much darkness in their lives to have that type of hate in them."

"I don't have a choice that I can see," Drake answered.

"No, you don't. Take this opportunity. A much better existence can be ahead of you. You should realize, Drake, that it was a lucky day when Katherine found you. Take this chance to survive. The angels have been kind to you."

"I'm starting to realize that. I thought that all vampires were cruel, but Katherine has shown me I was wrong. I will do as she says. I will put my fate in her hands. I was born an explorer, a spacer, and sometimes I feel lost on this world."

"I'm sorry you can't go back to your beloved space," Shawn told him as he stood to leave. "It was cruel what Selene did to you. I often wanted to experience space, but the angels won't allow it. Our kind can only exist in this world."

"It's hard to know you can never go home," Drake said as he walked to the window and looked out at the sky.

"Courage," Shawn advised as he went toward the door. "Katherine is coming. I will see you at midnight."

Shawn went back to his room, looked out the window, and pondered, then took off his clothes. Dissipating into a white vapor, he drifted across the floor, up the wall, and out the window. Up the outside wall, he went, onto the roof, and traveled just above the roof's surface. It was a cold, crisp winter's night, snow covering the roof and a burst of wind occasionally spraying the icy, white crystals out into the night. A bright moon hung high in the dark sky, wisps of clouds moving quickly by. He came to the peak, went over, and flowed down to the icicled edge, down the other side, and came to a stop at the eliminator's frosted window.

Drifting above the eliminator's window, he cloaked himself using all the power he had. The eliminator would never imagine any creature could get this close to him without his knowledge. This judge was talking to the Vampire Council with his communicator, discussing the situation he now found himself in.

Shawn wanted to smile but knew he couldn't. The council had changed their mind and were going to spare young Drake for now, if only to wait for a better time. The vampire council couldn't risk a confrontation with him, a fight that would be disastrous for them. Shawn was a powerful vampire and a hero to the vampire world. Vampires held the Bryce family in very high regard, and most vampires disliked the council now. Only the ancients, the heads of the covenants, kept the Vampire Council in power. Shawn knew the Vampire Council would not give up easily, and would wait for the right time.

*****

Katherine led Drake to the library, where the eliminator had set up court. It was almost midnight, and she could sense the apprehension in Drake, and she, too, felt fear. They now stood outside the large double oak doors. Katherine met Drake's stare and gave him a weak smile. She had timed their arrival so they would be the last to enter the library.

Years ago, she had lost trust for the council, when Anne and Marilyn had died, and now was unsure of the outcome.

"Shawn is here. Everything will be all right. Courage," she said, trying to reassure Drake and herself.

"I hope you are right," Drake mumbled.

Katherine opened the door, and they entered, passing Renee, who was leaving. To her right sat, Shawn. Her own chair was set to the left. The eliminator sat behind a large wooden library table and had placed Drake's chair in the front of the table. Katherine immediately took her chair and set it next to Drake's.

"Well, young vampire, I told you we would meet again," the eliminator reminded with a forced smile. He was a big man, a dark man with jet-black hair, and wore many rings on his fingers. He wore the red robe of an eliminator when judging condemned vampires.

"Yes, you did say you would come to kill me someday. You see, sir, I know a vampire will kill me. It is only a matter of time."

"Sit, young vampire. I take no pleasure in this," the eliminator commanded as he waved his hand at the chair.

Katherine and Drake took their seats in front of the eliminator.

"The council has decided you are not of this world, and Selene should not have changed you. Your maker was a sick vampire and passed her blood to you."

"Drake was a human," Katherine quickly added. "Where he was born doesn't matter. Selene turned him, and, like any human, he became a vampire. He was a good man, visiting our world, and vampires did him a grave disservice."

"Please, do not interrupt me, Katherine Bryce. Young vampire, you have broken other laws, including telling humans about our existence. You have fed on innocent humans. For these reasons, the Council has decided to send you to the angels."

"I am ready," Drake declared as his shoulders and head slightly hung forward. "My angels showed me where I would go. They showed me Heaven. They told me I would come there soon."

"This is ridiculous," an angry Katherine shouted as she bolted up. "Why would the council make such a decision?" She then turned and faced Drake. "You are going nowhere! You will be with me!"

"They are old and stuck in the past," Shawn said. "Sit and calm yourself, Katherine. They hold on to the old ways, and the angels told one of them that Drake would become a Bryce. We all know, eliminator, that some on the council want no more Bryces'."

"I have given Drake my blood," Katherine growled. "I have taken him as my fledgling. I claim him as my own."

"That doesn't matter now," the eliminator responded. "Drake has been condemned before you took him as a fledgling, yet the …"

"I will not let you harm him," Katherine interrupted. "He has the blue eyes of the Herit Covenant, and I will protect him."

"Eliminator, this serves no purpose," Shawn said. "Katherine will not let you harm Drake, and I will not let you harm Katherine.

You lift a finger toward this young vampire, and you will not leave this house. You know that. I hope for your sake that the council has given you new orders."

Renee came back through the door, wearing the look of relief. "The council has contacted me, and they have decided to defer this matter. The council members Shawn speaks of have decided to bide their time."

Relief also came to the eliminator's face. "Drake, this doesn't mean your death sentence has gone away. I hope the council forgets about this matter, but I don't think they will. I told you once that I hoped you would live. This matter is closed for now, and, I hope, forever."

"I see no reason to bring this matter up again," Shawn said. "Renee, please inform the council that Drake is under my protection, and I will not look kindly on anything happening to him."

Chapter Six

Fifty years had passed since Katherine took Drake for her fledgling. She had loved him and given him back his self-respect, made him a brave, decisive, self-assured man again. The blood of Herit flowed strongly in his veins, and now his eyes were the vibrant blue of the Herit covenant, and she loved him as she loved her maker.

Waking from her day's sleep, she lay on top of him, guided him into her, and moved with passion and desire as she kissed him. She loved the way he felt, his smell, and the way he tasted. His head went to her neck; she felt his teeth pierce her, smiled, and listened to his moans of pleasure.

Katherine had bought a large amount of land where the town of Dalton had once stood. By the river, she had built a house on a tower fifty feet into the air. Now, she went to her balcony, looked out, and saw the forested hills, the rise of the half-moon surrounded by the flickering stars.

Few people lived in this area now, and the smell of the crisp, clean air found its way into her sensitive nose. The forest, rivers, and lakes were pristine again, and trout swam in the clear river water, making their way south to the vast Delaware Reservoir.

A slight foreboding hung with her this eve, as Anne had come to her in the light. These last fifty years, Anne had visited her many times. Anne was her guiding angel now. Sometimes, she spoke of Shawn, told her how worried she was for him, and told her she would go to him, comfort him, but Herit was his guiding angel.

Anne told her Shawn was finally coming out of his long melancholy, but he was not taking Lucifer's witches seriously. He seemed resigned to this fate.

Last eve, Anne had come to warn her of a witch Lucifer was preparing to send for Shawn. The Mother knew of this witch and the great powers she possessed. Anne told Katherine to go to the mountains of Peru, near the ruins of Picchu, to meet Jessamine. She would take Katherine to The Mother's shrine. The center of Eos power on earth. There, The Mother would teach her about this witch.

Drake came up behind her and wrapped his arms around her, kissing her neck.

"Good eve, beautiful," Drake said sleepily.

"You tell all the girls that. You're such a charmer," Katherine whispered as she raised her head to allow him better access to her neck.

"Why the long face?" Drake asked.

"We must travel to South America, to the mountains of Peru. You will need to pack a travel bag for us, and I will pack my slayer."

"What's in Peru that is so important?"

Katherine turned, stroked Drake's cheek, kissed his lips lightly, and spoke in a low voice as if she was trying to keep a secret.

"The time has come, and now you will learn what it means to be a Bryce. Evil is rising again in this world. Lucifer is unleashing his witches, and we go to meet a witch.

"Well, I love a good witch fight." Drake winked and chuckled.

"She is a good witch. Her name is Jessamine, and she is my maker's daughter. We may encounter The Mother. I shouldn't take you with me, but I have no one to leave you with, and I don't trust the Vampire Council."

"I can handle what I will see. I was a spacer once, and have handled bad things before. I have met my share of witches in the bars of our solar system."

"Aren't you rude," Katherine said, as she gave him a stern look. "You have not experienced the evil I'm talking about. There once were demons on this world, and their evil was so strong it would quickly overpower you if you came too close to them. These demons brought the apocalypse and the Great Dark Age to this world, and they almost destroyed it."

"The battles between the Esmanaa and the Bryces is well known in the vampire world. I have been a vampire for more than fifty years, and I know vampires think of your maker as a hero," Drake said as he became serious. "I have always felt the terrible loss my family feels from those battles. I have sensed your sorrow for Anne and Marilyn. I'm part of this family now, and I'm ready to go with you. I will also be a fighter of evil, and I will not bring shame to the Bryce name. You will see what a spacer is made of."

"I know what you're made of," Katherine said as she kissed him, tasted his lips with her tongue, brushed his hair back, and felt the desire for him once more. "I know how courageous you are and how cunning. We will be together, and I won't let anything happen to you."

Katherine was sitting in a hovercraft listening to the slight hum of the engine rise in pitch and then fall off as the craft rose and descended. She adjusted a display that floated in front of her and showed the map of the Picchu area, following a path she laid out to The Mother's shrine carefully with her finger. She knew Jessamine would catch up to them eventually…at her own good time. Drake was piloting the flier up the Amazon to the River Solimoes. Then it was on to Pucallpa, where they would follow the river Apurimac by foot to The Mother's shrine.

These days, a good deal of her flying was in a flier. Drake loved to fly machines, and she had a hard time saying no. His own natural flying abilities had developed, but he could fly only short distances—he was still a young vampire.

They would travel at night and dock along the riverbank during the day. The sun was intense in this part of the world, and Katherine used the day to sleep, sometimes to make love to Drake. Few humans lived in this part of the world, and still, in the year twenty-nine hundred, the population of the earth was low.

Drake was taking his time with the flier, exploring areas of the riverbank, veering down small tributaries to explore before he would make his way back to the main river. He watched the creatures scurry back into the rain forest, birds taking flight as he came near, and gators bursting from the riverbank and into the murky green water. "Did you see that, Katherine?" He would screech, raising his arms excitedly. Still, after fifty years, Drake explored this planet with the same fascination as during his spacer beginnings. She didn't mind, vampires have plenty of time, and she enjoyed the lazy days and nights she spent with Drake.

Drake was never in a hurry; he had accepted eternity much easier than she had at his age. She would talk to Shawn about Drake, but he would say that Drake still behaved like a spacer and that he was a dreamer. "What a fine vampire": that was all Anne would say about Drake. This bothered Katherine; she knew that when angels stopped talking about a vampire, it usually meant trouble.

It was midday—the sun high in the sky. The heat lay like a blanket on the river, distorting the air rising from the warm water. Drake had beached the flier on the bank of the river Ucayali for the day. Katherine lay next to Drake, feeling sleepy, caressing his naked body, twirling his soft hair with her fingers, and whispering softly to him. "Have you talked to Herit lately?"

"Sometimes I talk with her, but a new angel came to me last month. I meant to tell you. The angel said she would be my angel."

Katherine raised her head and asked, "Who is this angel? Why didn't you tell me?"

"She said when she was a vampire, she was known as 'Marilyn Bryce'. The angel talked about being with me when the time comes for me to go to Heaven."

Katherine sat up and quickly became upset. "She said that to you?"

"Yes, she said she would watch over me. She talked about space to me, talked about you and Shawn, and said she would help me come to Heaven when the time comes. She wanted me to know that."

"You misunderstood. You will live a long life as a vampire, and I will protect you. I will never allow anything to happen to you. The angel is talking about the future."

"Calm down. You are right. You won't let anything happen to me," Drake said as he pulled her back down on him. "You wouldn't have anybody to boss around."

A feeling of foreboding swept through her, the same desperate feeling she had for Shawn.

"I will be bossing you around for a long time," Katherine told him as she pulled him tighter to her and lay on top of him, kissed him, made love to him. Then she drifted into an uneasy sleep.

They left the flier in Pucallpa and proceeded on foot, following a trail that traveled alongside the River Apurimac. They carried their bedrolls, and Katherine brought her slayer. The vegetation was dense but thinned as they went. Katherine took pleasure in watching Drake as he became fascinated with the animals, and always had to move him along when he came upon a tree sloth and their slow movement. She watched him use his vampire eyes to stare at the brightly colored birds, cataloging them in his mind.

"Come on, Drake, we can't stop every time we see the sloths and birds."

"Look how slow they move, and how they hang upside down," Drake told her in amazement.

He laughed with such pleasure as they came upon the big, colorful lizards rising and scurrying into the underbrush. Everything was green here—the trees, the grass, and the moss that clung to the rocks.

The higher they went, the more the vegetation would thin, soon it turned to tall mountain grass, brush, and boulders as the trail climbed higher into the mountains. The sound of the river grew louder as the land became steeper and soon turned into a roar as the clear mountain water rushed down the rocky terrain.

As they went, Katherine realized she was sensing an evil, a different kind of darkness, and it grew stronger as they followed the trail. She then realized it was one of Lucifer's witches, stalking from afar.

Trying to stay calm, she yelled to Drake up ahead: "Remember how I taught you to shroud yourself? Do it now."

Katherine's powerful senses were at their highest now, as she scanned for the witch's location. The devil witch was powerful, and thirty miles to the west obviously sent to stop her from meeting with The Mother. This evil was like the demons' evil; it was dark, deep, and consuming. Katherine's knees went weak. The witch was moving toward them.

How could she avoid contact with this witch, take to the air? No, Drake was with her. He was a young vampire and had limited flying skills, and this was a witch of Lucifer's. She had seen few witches, yet she was close to Jessamine, a powerful witch. Some of The Mother's witches were ill-tempered; she could only imagine a witch sent by Lucifer.

"Are you all right, Katherine?" Drake said as he came to her.

"I'm fine. We are going to have to run fast. I want you to follow me, and do your best to keep up."

"Something terrible is coming this way. I can feel it," Drake said as he pointed west.

"It's a devil witch."

"Why run? We can stay here, make a stand, and fight this witch," Drake said forcibly. "That is what we should do. We are Bryces, but you are afraid for me."

"No, let's try to escape. I don't want to fight the witch here. We need better ground." She knew she had to get Drake away from this witch, but she did not want to tell him that.

Katherine started to run and told Drake, "Follow me, and run as fast as you can." Accelerating to the point that Drake could barely keep up, she ran higher into the mountains. The brook turned to rapids as it spilled its way down the mountain's narrow valley. The water echoed off the sheer rock formations that shaped the narrow valleys and rose high into the starry sky. Katherine knew the witch was gaining on them, and that she would have to bury Drake to protect him.

She yelled to Drake, "Follow me!" as she jumped the brook and started into another valley. Dodging boulders and brush, they ran until she found a patch of ground that held nothing but rich, dark dirt. Katherine stopped, pulled the dank, green moss, and the mountain grass from the field, and laid it aside to use when she buried Drake.

"Start digging!" she ordered.

"Not the ground, Katherine! Let me help you! I have faced danger before!"

"You can't help me this time, love. She would destroy your mind in a blink of those beautiful eyes."

"Hurry, help me!" She told him as she quickly dug at the ground. Fear for him rose in her as she formed the grave. "Get in, you are to stay here. Do not leave here, no matter what happens. Do you understand me? This is one of these times you will do as I say."

"Yes, I understand," Drake mumbled disappointingly as he reluctantly lay in the grave.

"I will come to you if I'm successful. If not, stay in the ground for two eves, then come out and sense the area for a witch. Use your senses like I taught you. If you sense a witch, go back to the ground."

Katherine buried Drake and changed for the fight. Becoming a warrior vampire, she shrouded her mind from the witch's evil. The witch had trapped a powerful vampire protecting her fledgling. She drew her slayer and whispered, "Michael, guide me," and flew back down the valley. There, she saw the witch enter the valley as a panther, eyes burning red, and a cloak of evil surrounding the beast.

Katherine soared over the rocks, the brush, and the brook, straight and true toward the witch. Like a bullet, she flew over the panther, slicing its shoulder with her slayer. She turned and landed as the animal changed, and a witch screamed her indignation.

The witch was a large woman, stout but not fat, pancake-white, and muscular, with black streaks through her face—veins to move her putrid blood. She was dressed in black, with a strange, black cape made of black scales. Her hair was close-cropped, black, and oily. Her eyes were dark; her tongue, a deep red, and she flicked it out past her black lips repeatedly like a deadly snake.

"Beelzebub, I have her," the witch hissed. "Send me your power."

Dark energy appeared in her hand, and the witch threw it at Katherine. The fireball hit a boulder beside her, exploding in the night and throwing her back onto the ground.

"Katherine, my dear," the witch hissed, "Lucifer sends his greetings. He knows about you. He knows what that fucker Michael is up to."

Quickly, Katherine sprang up, crouched, and hissed, then flew toward the witch, driving her slayer into the hag's belly, forcing the witch to the ground. The witch's brown, putrid blood covered her hands and slayer.

"You filthy creature," Katherine yelled at the witch.

"Do you think your pathetic slayer will stop me? Lucifer will have Shawn. He wants you to know that. That is the reason I follow you. Eos will not save him."

A burst of dark energy threw Katherine off the witch, sending searing pain, and a dark melancholy through her body. She erupted from the ground, bringing her slayer down on the witch's back, only to have it bounce off her scaled cape. The darkness became more potent and drove her back from the witch.

Moving around the witch, she mustered her strength, prepared to attack again. Suddenly, a white beam of plasma hit the witch, throwing her back into the brush. It was Jessamine. The dark sickness in Katherine's head stopped, and she quickly attacked as the witch came to her feet. Katherine swung her slayer, and this time it found the witch's neck, taking her head cleanly from her body. The head fell to the ground with a thud, and the witch's body collapsed after it, bursting into dark blue flames.

"I thought you could use a little help, sister," Jessamine said.

It always caught Katherine off-guard when Jessamine called her sister, but she was a good sister. "I thank you for the help. It's good to see you, especially now."

"I sensed two of you earlier," Jessamine questioned.

"I buried my fledgling up the valley."

"Well, let's go fetch him."

As they walked, Katherine asked, "How is Shawn? He tells me he is traveling again."

"He spends a lot of time with Victoria now. The Bryces will be glad to know he doesn't spend all his time in the bayou anymore."

"You are a Bryce, too. Who cares what that silly Vampire Council says."

"I am a Bryce, and you are my sister."

"I know Shawn loves the bayou, and he loves you," Katherine said. "He will return to the swamp. He always does."

"I'm sure you're right. If Lucifer doesn't have him first. And I see my dear sister has found love again. How love suits you."

"I do love him. Probably too much!"

"You always fell in love quickly and intensely. I will take you to The Mother. She has much to tell you, but you will not be allowed to take your fledgling into the shrine."

They came to the spot where Katherine had buried Drake and quickly unearthed him. As Drake stood and brushed the dirt off, Katherine introduced him to Jessamine.

"I'm glad to finally meet you, Drake," Jessamine said. "Shawn told me about you, and the angels speak of you. I'm sorry for your misfortune. But now you have Katherine and a new life."

Drake stood, indignantly brushing the dirt off himself. Katherine could tell that burying him had hurt his feelings. She tried to explain it to him. "I had to bury you. I had no choice. I know you have a need to help, and that you wanted to help, but with a witch, I would have to protect you and fight the witch at the same time."

"You are too young to face a witch like that one," Jessamine told Drake. "You would not keep her out of your head. She would take your mind and leave you a fool. Remember this, young vampire, the devil will take your soul if you let him."

"I'm sure he would," Drake confessed as he wiped dirt from his eyes while giving her a pained look. "You're so white. You look like you have been in space for years."

"I have little pigment," Jessamine laughed. "And I guess this was the way The Mother wanted me."

"I thought you were a witch, but I feel a vampire in you."

"My life force came from The Mother, and Shawn is my father."

"The story of Shawn and Pandora!" Drake said. "So it is real. I thought Juliette was fooling with me. She loves to trick me."

"Come on. I will take you both to The Mother," Jessamine laughed.

Katherine and Drake followed Jessamine up the mountain trail. Jessamine would walk for miles on one path, turn, and then follow another for miles. Eventually, there was only green moss, small scrub brush, and stone. The large granite stones would rise from the earth travel high into the sky to form jagged peaks.

They walked for two days and finally came to the shrine. Supernatural beings long ago made the shrine from perfectly formed, rectangular, polished grey stones laid to make an exact round cylinder that rose four stories into the air. It narrowed as it climbed, and at the top, it opened to the cascading water from the rock face behind, which rose another hundred feet into the sky. Water fell through the rock openings and cascaded over the shrine.

A mist filled the air. There was a large, bright moon surrounded by stars sparkling in the clear mountain sky, and the only sound was of the falling water. Katherine immediately sensed the energy of this place and felt the electrically charged air.

"Can you feel the electricity, Katherine?" Drake said with amazement.

"Yes, there is great power here," she said. Katherine felt the power, felt it building, and turned to Drake to ask, "Are you ok?"

"I'm fine, I can take it," Drake reassured as he turned to the shrine and stood straight.

"Drake, you must wait here," Jessamine commanded. "The Mother will only allow Katherine to enter."

"You're kidding…I have to wait here?" Drake complained.

"Stay here," Katherine told Drake. "You are too young to go in there. What you feel here is a hundred times stronger in there."

60

"Always too young!" Drake complained. "Let me help you."

"Do as I say. Stay here!"

Katherine followed Jessamine through the entrance of the shrine and found the inside was much larger than it appeared on the outside. The floor held polished, brown marble pebbles, and in the center, the water poured down and over a large, clear crystal that stood six feet high. A wet mist streaked with different colored lights filled the air. A soft siren's song and the sharp tinkling of glass penetrated the quiet.

Then came a quick rise of energy, a power so strong it pressed in on her as if there was no room for her. Her life force vibrated with the strength of the shrine. A light filled the crystal and radiated outward. The water broke the light like a prism, and the room filled with many colors, so bright that Katherine shielded her eyes with her hand. She felt a soothing warmth, entered her mind.

I have brought the queen, Jessamine projected.

So you have...well done, Jessamine. Greetings to you, Katherine. I have brought you here to look into your soul and to give you a command. To tell you a little of what the future holds, and to warn you of the horrible witch that is coming. Soon you will lead the fight against evil. The days of the Vampire Council are ending. The catalyst for that change has come. Lucifer sends his most powerful witch for my Trojan Horse. Lucifer sends the witch Malin to bring Shawn to the Gates of Hell, where she can torment him before she sends him to Lucifer. Even now, she has started her change to your world. She is beautiful and powerful and has lived for eons of time on other worlds. She is The Tempter, The Succubus, and she comes for Shawn."

She will never have him, Katherine projected. *I will never allow an evil creature of Lucifer to have Shawn.*

You will have great powers and great losses! Michael will make you queen, and when he does, you must prepare an army. You will follow after Shawn, take this army to the Gates of Hell, and you must kill The Tempter there!"

You are after Malin!

Yes, I told Malin long ago I would see her dead to this world.

Remember what I tell you, Katherine. Build an army and kill The Tempter at her black castle by the Gates of Hell. That is the only way you can save Shawn. Kill Malin at her castle, and she will never be able to enter the physical planes again.

The Mother's energy started to dissipate, and they heard her one more time. *Jessamine, you must prepare yourself. We, too, will have to sacrifice.*

They left the shrine and started down the long trail to the river. When they reached Pucallpa, Jessamine left them and went back to her home in the bayou. Before she left, she told Katherine that Drake was an old soul, sent to Earth by the angels one more time to complete one more task.

Drake needed to feed, as he was young and in need of blood, so Katherine made a detour, found a hover park in Mexico City, and directed Drake where to land the hovercraft. They dimmed the windows, slept for a day in their comfortable flier, and then went into the city.

Mexico City was populated mostly by descendants of stranded Chinese soldiers from the Great War who had mixed with the surviving Latinos. The brightly lit city was alive with people. The Chinese loved colorful neon lights. They flashed and lit the night, bright holograms were everywhere, shouting out their advertisements. A hologram of a giant green dragon wound its way down the street above their heads. The road was alive with humans and plenty of food vendors that stirred long gone memories in Katherine.

Katherine walked the street with Drake, avoiding the people in the crowd. She carried her slayer under her coat—she always brought it when she was away from home and with Drake. Shawn had it made for her; the blade was made of a titanium alloy, fashioned after Deceida, and it was and sharp as a razor. She'd had the honor of holding Deceida a few times, had felt its power, and remembered how it glowed in her hands. Renee now led the Herit Covenant and had possession of the slayer.

Mexico City did not have towers, but still, their buildings were high. Their streets were strictly for walking, and the aircars traveled above. Katherine and Drake were following an evil human, supper for Drake, and to Katherine's surprise, dark energy was with this man and he was going to meet a warlock.

"Can you sense the bad man, love?"

"Yes, I sense him."

"What do you sense about him? Follow the energy, go deeper in his mind."

"He is a heartless fellow and likes to kill. He sells endorphins to make his money and is a hired killer. He is the leader of a large gang and is afraid of something. Someone he is going to meet. It's another man, but he is not sure of him."

"That's right. You do this so well now. The bad man is going to meet a warlock. Enter my mind, love, and feel the dark energy. Remember how it feels."

"I feel it, it's terrible!"

"We are going to follow him," Katherine whispered. "But you must shroud your mind as I taught you. Do not lift it."

She worried for Drake, he was young, and she probably should not be exposing him to this danger, but wanted him near her so she could protect him. Because of the Vampire Council, she had to keep Drake with her. He was always in danger from them, and now the angels kept a secret about Drake, which they would not tell her.

This evil warlock was weak, and he was not aware of them, and they were close to him. The warlock was new to this world and had not gathered his energy.

Katherine would see what this creature was up to and then take Drake home to Washington. The family would be there, and he would be safe. They followed a reasonable distance back, and the man took a few more turns, eventually coming to a nightclub with a large, flashing hologram of a scantily dressed woman with bright, blue hair and light blue skin above the people on the street, inviting them in. The man they followed wore apprehension, he was a bad man, but the evil he was traveling toward even scared him.

"Stay next to me, Drake."

"The evil warlock is in there. I can feel it," Drake whispered.

"Yes, he is there. He cannot be that powerful, to let us get this close to him. He is a netherene witch. A witch from a lower caste and he is not here to fight only to spread satanic misery to the humans. We have accidently stumbled on him. Keep yourself shrouded, and we can see what the warlock's business is."

The man stopped before he went in, received a message from someone, and then communicated to the doorman. Pictures and symbols, projected from the nano positron chips implanted behind his right ear, formed in front of him in vivid colors, and then disappeared. All humans of this age received information and communicated this way. Humans now could project the world's knowledge in front of their eyes. They quickly project symbols and pictures developed and defined. When formed in front of their faces, these pictures would communicate a complete thought or emotion. Humans complemented their speech now with these symbols. They could speak words, project pictures, and symbols from their nanochips, making human communication quicker and more varied and precise.

They entered the establishment, a Chinese man flashed them with red laser light, and a bank instantly deducted the cover charge from Katherine's account. Physical currency had disappeared long ago. Katherine made her way through the crowd. The pulsating techno music blasted her ears, and the flashing lights filled her eyes. Holograms of dancing panda bears or advertisements played out above her head.

"Stay behind me. The warlock is in that far corner," Katherine whispered to Drake. "We will use the crowd for cover."

"I'll be right behind you," Drake said. "I hope the man-witch doesn't notice us."

Katherine made her way to a vantage point directly across the large room from the warlock. She saw him through the crowd, talking to the bad man. The witch was a thin man with waxy, pale skin, and black, greasy hair that he had combed flat on his head. He had small, puckered lips, adorned with a black, narrow mustache, piercing, dark eyes, and black, thin eyebrows. The warlock was supplying the man with a large quantity of the endorphin drug. This drug turned humans into helpless creatures only capable of looking for their next fix of endorphins.

Since its discovery, it had become a scourge for the humans, and it was far deadlier than the old drug, heroin, that ravaged humans long ago. The warlock had an unusually large shipment of the drug, and he was almost giving it away to this drug dealer. This could pose a big problem for the people and the authorities of Mexico City.

The warlock and the man walked to the front of the disco and left to go see the large shipment of drugs. Katherine and Drake followed and made their way out of the disco.

"Did you detect any of that?" Katherine asked Drake.

"Some, but I was concentrating on shrouding my mind," Drake said. "He certainly is a nasty fellow. That I sensed."

"We will fly to that balcony on the side of that building. I know you can fly a little."

They flew to the balcony and took cover behind a solid railing. Drake had taken on a most serious look.

"Listen to me," Katherine whispered to Drake. "I am going to kill the warlock, and you are going to feed on the human. First, we are going to follow them to see where the drugs are. That way, we can alert the authorities." Katherine looked over the railing and then crouched back down. "When the time comes, fly straight and true toward the man. We must strike before the warlock can cast a spell. I don't want to do this with you, but those drugs would do great harm to this city."

"I'll keep up, you don't have to worry about me," Drake assured.

They would fly from one balcony to another, sometimes using a low roof, and eventually, they arrived at a warehouse. Katherine held her slayer, watching the man and the warlock enter the warehouse through the back door.

"Follow me," Katherine whispered.

Katherine stepped off the roof, landing six stories below, and Drake followed. Walking to the back door, she forced it open and entered a hallway. A short distance down the corridor was a large, black metal door. She immediately sensed the warlock on the other side of the door, and he was now coming back their way.

"Stand behind me. The warlock knows we are here."

The door slid open, and the warlock stepped through, hurling a small, blue fireball at the vampires and quickly stepping back through the opening. Katherine only had time to hold her arms in front of her face as the fireball struck her. The energy propelled her backward into Drake, and both were thrown out into the street.

"Are you all right?" Katherine asked as she rolled Drake over onto his back and saw the stunned look on his face. The weak energy wave was still a lot for a young vampire to dissipate.

"I'm all right," Drake mumbled. "It felt like the time I grab that bare wire in the cargo bay."

"Come on, stay behind me," Katherine said. "If you have to, try to dodge the fireball. You have the speed." They moved down the hall slowly, cautiously, and came to the door.

"They are in the room on the other side of this door," Katherine whispered to Drake. "Stay behind me. The warlock is preparing another fireball. Be prepared. He will throw it, and then you go after the human."

"The human won't get far," Drake promised.

Katherine forced the door aside, and they entered a small storage bay that held many boxes full of ampules of the endorphin drug. The warlock was across the room and threw another energy ball, smaller than the first. The creature was losing strength rapidly. The vampires dodged, and the energy tore through the wall that held the door and exploded with a loud *boom* that shook the walls. The man fled through a far door, and Drake went after him.

"Careful," Katherine yelled.

The warlock turned and tried to form another energy ball, but Katherine was on him, and slammed him to the floor. She picked the dazed witch up, threw him across the room, and again was quickly on him, holding him to the floor.

"Where have you come from?" Katherine demanded.

"My spirit comes from Hell, vampire. You should know that. Lucifer will send many more of my kind to kill the warrior angels of Earth and bring misery to the mortals. He is very upset about his demons. Vampires will long for the days of the demons. They will beg for Lucifer to send them back after they experience his witches."

The warlock again tried to cast a spell, and Katherine's grip tightened. "You will not be able to use your evil on me. And now I will kill you for trying."

Katherine plunged her fist into the warlock's chest, pulled the wet, slippery heart from his chest, and tossed it aside. The creature fell to the floor, his evil spirit leaving his burning body, making its way into the ether.

She followed the hall to where Drake was dropping the other man's lifeless body to the floor as he wiped the blood from his mouth.

"He didn't get away," Drake bragged with a bloody smile.

"We have to contact the authorities and tell them about the drugs."

Drake turned, pointed, and replied, "I passed a communicator down the hall. Follow me."

Katherine contacted the authorities and let them know where they could find the drugs. She and Drake went back to the flier, cleaned themselves, and went to bed. Katherine lay in Drakes soft embrace, feeling the arrival of sleep, from the beginning she had felt such love for this vampire her fledgling. That eve they left for Washington and the safety of the Bryce family compound.

Chapter Seven

T ime went on, and Katherine traveled with Drake, showing him the world, he now lived in. She took him to Egypt, showed him the room full of bright gold and sparkling jewels at the top of the pyramid. Drake loved Earth's history, and she saw how the artifacts and gold in the room amazed him. They would visit Shawn and Jessamine in the bayou and go to Colorado to visit Victoria.

She was with him now at their home in Dalton, lying naked by the side of the river. It was a hot summer's night, and she heard the grind of the crickets, the flow of the river water, and the soft rustle of the river grass in the wind. The stars were starting to disappear as the pink hue of the new day crept outward from the horizon.

They had just finished their swim, and Drake was becoming sleepy. She lay on him, let him enter her and make love to her. She loved being with Drake. The way he felt, the sounds he made, his smell and the taste of his blood, his expressions, and the way he talked—how he teased her. She stayed with him always, protecting him, and would kill anyone who tried to harm him.

Anne was with her now when she slept in the light. Herit rarely came anymore; she was strictly Shawn's angel. Anne taught her the ways of the angels and told her how she must ready herself to lead. She would bring her to Heaven; mighty angels would come and teach her about her warrior caste, and how to fight Lucifer. These days they no longer talked in riddles but told her the angels would lead the warrior vampires of earth through her. They told her she must prepare herself for the tragedies that would come to her because of this task. Lucifer would send many of his witches to Earth, so he could take his vengeance on Shawn, and then he would turn on her and Victoria.

Katherine had asked Anne if some of this tragedy would be with Drake, and this had caught Anne off-guard. Anne started to talk of Drake's purpose, but found herself and told Katherine sternly that Marilyn went to Drake when he slept. Marilyn was Drake's angel now, and that was all Anne would say about Drake. Sometimes, Katherine understood quite well, why Shawn would become irritated with the angels.

Last month Renee had visited Katherine and told her about a party, a celebration the council was having to honor the Bryce family. Katherine resisted, but Renee said she expected her to be there. She could leave Drake at the Amsterdam house. Katherine did not trust the Vampire Council, but Renee said Drake would be safe at the house. No vampire would dare harm him there. Against her better judgment, they would be leaving for Amsterdam the following week.

"Why are you so deep in thought?" Drake asked as he kissed her.

"Why did I fall so deeply in love with you?" Katherine whispered, "Would Marilyn know?"

"Why do you ask me that? Marilyn doesn't know why you fall in love. We talk about many things, and some I'm to keep to myself."

She could sense he was lying; Marilyn was helping him hide something. "I know. I fell in love because of who and what you are."

"I still miss my life in space, but now I would rather be with you than be in space. I love you so much, Katherine. Your maker was right. I was lucky when you found me. I have never loved anybody like you. Marilyn teaches me how to accept this life as a vampire and to accept my fate. Don't be jealous of Marilyn."

Drake made love to her again; she felt his wet lips on her neck, his teeth entering her and the blood flowing into him—she felt the passion of Drake's lovemaking. She rolled him over, went to his neck, and allowed her mouth to fill with his blood.

Resting her head between Drake's neck and shoulder, she drifted into sleep and slowly rode his blood back to a time when Drake was ten years old. She saw his young hands turning a metal wheel on an airlock door and watched him step through, wearing greased, stained coveralls to protect him from the cold. Drake was following a cold, dark corridor deep into a space freighter.

The pulsating hum of machinery filled the corridor. Katherine knew he lived with his parents on this freighter, and he was happy. The air was damp. Condensation hung on the metal surfaces of the space freighter. Beads of water would break loose, trickle down the curved walls of the ship, and then moved along by a channel under the grating. As they went deeper into the freighter, she heard the lonely clank of his boots hitting the metal grate, the endless purr of the machines, and the water trickling under his feet. Deeper into the freighter, they went, and she watched as Drake went through one airlock and then travel to a far-off light next to another. Cold, wet metal was everywhere, and she saw his breath amid the chill of space.

She traveled with him for a mile, only stopping to read gauges to make sure they were in the correct range. Finally, they came to the bay Drake was looking for. Meralith was his prize, a strange, purple colored metal streaked with radiant reds. The spacer miners found this metal on Saturn's moon Titan. Sometimes, he would come and take a chunk of the beautiful metal to make jewelry that he sold when docked at a space station. They opened the airlock door to the large bay that held the metal ore. Drake waved his hand over a sensor, and the lights blinked on row by row.

High above, a considerable overhead crane, its mammoth hook held in midair by thick metal cables, perched on two steel I-beams that allowed it to run the length of the bay. A stream of water poured out of a pipe that ran along the curved hull of the ship, cascading to the floor, flowing and then disappearing through a floor grate. She heard a loose chain swaying and clanging against a metal column. The bay held ten large, square metal containers, and they measured thirty feet on all sides.

They went to a ladder and started climbing; she watched his hands take hold of one rung and then another. They climbed higher and higher until they came to the crane's control cabin. Drake climbed in and took his place by the controls. He touched an activator and then pushed a control stick forward, with a lurch they were off, traveling down the massive storage bay. She heard the loud whine of the crane motor and the hiss of air escaping the relief valves of the brakes. They stopped over one of the large containers; Drake took a small, black control box and hung it on his front coverall pocket, then climbed out of the cab and down to the hook. They stood on the hook. Drake touched a button on the black box, and down they went toward the container.

As they traveled, Katherine saw out over the massive storage bay, the grey, metal piping, steel walkways, and ladders going to different levels, as well as the enormous containers. She looked overhead and saw the massive doors that allowed space transporter to come in and take the boxes. She felt the cold and the dampness, the lack of color, the vastness of space outside, and the constant drone of machinery. *What a strange world Drake fell in love with,* she thought.

They descended to the top of the container and the hook came to a stop. They stepped down onto the container, and she saw his hands turning a wheel to open the top hatch of the box. Drake took a cloth sack from his pocket, reached in, and removed a large chunk of the purple metal.

Suddenly, a voice came over his communicator. "Where are you, Drake?" His mother asked him. "You aren't taking metal again, are you?" she scolded. Katherine could feel a slight nervousness come over Drake.

"Just another little piece," she heard Blake say mischievously. "I'll be back for dinner." Katherine knew Drake's mother had discovered him, and now he would buy his mother a present with some of the money.

"Be careful, sweetie," she heard his mother's loving voice say.

Katherine woke to Drake's voice. "What did you see about me this time? Vampires… always snooping."

"You were very young, walking in a dark, damp space ship, looking for metal."

"I remember those times. How happy I was in my perfect world. I would always beg my parents to let me live with them on the ship."

"It's beyond me what you saw in that life. You can remember those times?"

"I have been alive for eighty years. Thirty years as a human and fifty as a vampire. I can remember my entire life quite well, unlike you. Five hundred years is a long time to be alive, and I'm sure it strains your memory."

"It does strain the memory. You will see someday."

"Will I?"

"Yes, you will. What is it, my love? What are you hiding from me? You are in a restless mood tonight."

"Nothing, just wondering…"

Katherine woke to a warm Amsterdam eve. Her maker had arrived earlier that day with Victoria. She looked over at Drake, who was still asleep. Foreboding about this trip filled her, and while in her sleep, she felt an unease coming from Anne.

She leaned over, kissed Drake, and brushed his brown hair from his face. "I'll be back later, my love. I must go to my maker."

Drake sat up, yawned, and stretched. "Go to him and give him your love. You have so much to give. I'll go and drink tea with my other family members."

Katherine floated out of their couch and down the hall in her white silk nightgown, came to Shawn's door, opened it, and peered inside. He was in his couch with the vampire he had loved for almost a thousand years. Katherine floated to the couch, slowly descended, lay next to him, and wrapped her arms around him. Shawn rolled over, smiled, looked into her eyes, held her, kissed her, and stroked her hair.

"How have you been?" Shawn whispered. "I miss you so much

these days."

"I'm well, and I have been busy with Drake."

"Yes, young Drake. How is he adjusting?"

"He is doing fine, but Anne won't speak of him. That worries me. His angel is Marilyn. Did you know that?"

"No, I didn't know that," Shawn said. "Again, he is lucky."

"He has a good and just angel watching over him," Victoria said sleepily. "How have you been, Katherine? I see so little of you these days."

"Okay, and I am sorry, we should spend more time together. I'm sure Drake wants to."

"The spacer who came to Earth and ran into Selene," Victoria said. "How fortunate you found him."

"Victoria, have you been running into witches?" Katherine asked.

"I have killed two, and a witch killed Eric Nicholas. I was hoping for quieter times, but Lucifer has different ideas. I even had a slayer made."

"What do you think about this party, Shawn? Why is the council throwing us a party now?"

"I don't think it is unusual of them," Shawn said. "It probably has to do with improving their image."

"Renee made it quite clear we had to be here," Katherine said. "Do you think Drake will be safe at this house?"

"Yes," Shawn answered. "They wouldn't dare attack Drake here. I would be surprised. That sort of thing is not Stephen's way."

The next eve Katherine was dressing for the party, and Drake was sitting on the bed watching her. She dressed in a light green gown and matching high heel shoes. The house was alive with activity as the Bryces prepared for the party.

"You look beautiful tonight," Drake told her.

"Thank you, love."

"I'm glad I don't have to go to this party, so don't feel bad about that."

"When it comes to the council, keeping you out of sight is the best bet. Don't leave the house while I'm gone," Katherine sternly told Drake.

"I won't. Have a good time."

"I can think of better places to have a good time." Katherine laughed. "What is it, Drake? What is bothering you? What are you hiding?"

"I hide nothing from you. You can sense that."

She watched Drake come to her. "That lipstick makes your lips so inviting," Drake told her as he embraced her. "I like your hair that way."

She felt his soft lips kiss her and felt a slight fear in him. She held his eyes with hers to see their beauty, and saw a strange look, a sorrowful look; again, she searched his mind and found nothing that would bring on such a mood.

Stroking his face, Katherine assured, "I'll be home early. I won't leave you long."

"Go to your party. I will watch a movie on the viewer."

Katherine was sitting at a round table with the Bryces and Victoria, with a crisp, white linen tablecloth, carafes of red wine, and a large, silver candelabra standing lit in the middle of the table. The night was alive with music, conversation, and laughter. They were at the council mansion, in the large ballroom with three large, ornate chandeliers hanging from the high, arched ceiling. The lighting from the chandeliers was soft, and candles burned everywhere. She saw the many lights sparkling off the large, arched glass windows of the ballroom. A hundred vampires and Crimmian servants attended the festivities.

Stephen made his way toward her and wore a smile, seeming to be in a pleasant mood, which wasn't common, especially when Shawn was around him. She also noticed that only five members of the seven-member council had attended the party.

"Greetings to the Bryces, and to you, Victoria," Stephen called out warmly. "I'm happy to see all the Bryces here. We wanted to celebrate your family tonight, Renee. The great achievements and sacrifices your family have made fighting evil in this world. And the council hopes for better relations with you, Shawn."

"I hope for better relations, too, Stephen," Shawn agreed, "But it would have meant more if all the council members were here."

"Constantine and Delphinia were called away unexpectedly. I voiced my displeasure to them, and I extend my apologies to the Bryces."

"They should have been here," Renee said sharply.

Katherine could see the eliminator across the banquet hall, and he nodded toward her. This made her feel better; at least she knew where he was.

She turned, looked at Stephen, and told him, "Not all of the Bryce family is here. Drake Bryce is absent."

"Yes, you're right, my apologies," Stephen responded quickly.

"I want to dance," Shawn said. "Would you dance with me, Katherine?"

"Yes, I would love to," Katherine answered.

"Tell me," Victoria asked Stephen, "is the Vampire Council aware of the rise of Lucifer's witches? Or do you treat the witches like you did the demons?"

Stephen became annoyed and shot back. "We are aware of the increase in Lucifer's witches, Victoria Kenmare. They have not proven themselves to be that big of a threat yet. I would have thought the demons would have been enough for you."

"They were, but Michael has more for us to do," Victoria reminded him. "I would think you would know that. Knowing this is what keeps you in power. What helps you rule."

"Is that so?" Stephen gritted at her. "And you still have a way to annoy the council!"

The night went on, and Katherine started to relax. She talked with Victoria, Juliette, and Caitlyn, catching up on the latest news and gossip. Renee made her rounds, greeting and talking to many vampires; like Anne, vampires respected her. Katherine forgot about her foreboding and even danced with Ricardo, a handsome vampire that had drawn her attention.

On returning to her table, as she took her seat, a horrible feeling hit her. A terrible panic traveled through her body, and she knew instantly that Drake was in trouble. He was at the house, there were vampires there, and they were Constantine and Delphinia. Panic flooded her senses as she looked at Shawn with horror on her face, and knew he had sensed it too. She saw him fly to Stephen and take hold of him. "If Drake dies, so will you!"

"I know nothing of this, Shawn," Stephen pleaded. "I am just as surprised about this as you are."

Katherine screamed at Shawn, "I am going to the house!"

Immediately, she rose into the air, through one of the large, arched windows, shattering it and sending shards of glass flying out onto the lawn. She accelerated and knew Shawn was behind her. Katherine had not gone far when she felt Drake's life force leave this world. A terrible scream came from her; she curled herself into a ball and fell out of the sky and toward the ground. Shawn's powerful arms scooped her up before she crashed to the earth.

"Listen to me, my dear Katherine," Shawn whispered into her ear. "You have to set the grief aside for now. Think of vengeance. You have a long time to grieve, and this, I know. Turn your sadness into anger. We have to kill two powerful vampires."

She regained her strength, and rage consumed her thoughts. "They will die!" she screamed, shoving away from Shawn's arms and changing into a fierce vampire form, the idea of killing in her head.

****

Drake had finished his movie and had gone to the kitchen to make tea. While pouring the drink, he felt the two vampires' presence. They had cloaked themselves from him so he was not sure how long they had been in the house. Setting the kettle down,

76

he turned and saw two vampires standing behind him. One was male, the other was female, and he knew they were ancient, powerful vampires.

"No eliminator this time?" Drake asked. "May I know who my executioners are?"

"My name is Constantine. This is Delphinia, and we are council members here to carry out the council sentence."

"What little I can sense from you, I know that is a lie. Do what you must."

"Why so calm? Why so brave?"

"I am a Bryce."

Drake had always known he would not live long as a vampire. The angels, from the beginning, had told him that. They said he was from space, and he had little time in this world. Marilyn had come to him early in his life as a vampire and had been with him almost constantly when he slept. She helped him hide the truth from Katherine and prepared him for this night, told him she would be with him when his death came. Michael wanted him to go to Heaven, for there was a special job for him. He would be Michael's messenger to the queen—the conduit between the angels and the queen. The death of a Bryce at the hands of the vampire council would be their final miscalculation, the catalyst for their end. This was Drakes' destiny. This had always been Drake's purpose.

"You must know you will die," Drake told them calmly. "Killing me is a death sentence for you."

"There will be no death sentence for us," Constantine insisted. "I have wanted vengeance on this family since Shawn Bryce stood by and allowed the demons to kill Hector and Hegamar. He could have prevented their deaths if he wanted. I will kill you. Then he will come, and Delphinia and I will kill him."

"You are a fool." Drake laughed. "Katherine will be here first, and she is almost as powerful as Shawn. They will kill both of you, and maybe the council, too."

"Maybe, young vampire, but your time in this world is over."

Drake watched Constantine walk toward him; he leaned his

head back and gritted his teeth. "I'm ready. Marilyn, be with me."
He felt Constantine's hand plunged into his chest, and his heart
leave him. It had served him well these eighty years, and now
darkness took him, lifted him away from this reality, and he cried
out, "Marilyn, are you there?"

I am here, Drake. I have you!

The angel gathered his life force and pushed the darkness away,
bringing him toward an immensely bright light.

****

Katherine flew with blinding speed toward the Amsterdam
house. She wiped the blood tears from her eyes and prepared
herself for the vengeance she would enact upon the two council
members. They had killed Drake, and now with Shawn beside her,
she would kill them.

Katherine flew ahead to have the first strike. The house came
into view; it was set back in a thicket of elm trees at the end of a
long, narrow road. She flew at the front door and exploded through
it and into a large foyer. Immediately, she saw Constantine flying
at her, and they met with such force, it spun them crashing through
a wall and into a large sitting room.

Holding on to Constantine, she repeatedly hit him in the face
with her right fist, screamed at him, and cursed at him, "Why
would you kill my Drake!"

The ancient vampire's powerful hands took hold of her neck
and threw her through the outside wall. Righting herself in midair,
she flew back through the opening and drove Constantine through
another wall and into the dining room. The house shook and
swayed from the assault on its structure.

Katherine shaped her hand to a point and drove it into the
vampire's side. Constantine screamed and again threw her off.

Constantine continued his assault, held her by the throat, and pushed his hand into her middle, pulling at her organs. Then he drove his hand into her chest in an attempt to take her heart. Kicking with all her strength, she propelled Constantine off her and into the far wall.

Again, she was on him and raked her long nails over his face. She cursed him, telling him what a filthy creature he was, and she stabbed at him with shards of window glass. She hit his face with all her strength, but this ancient vampire was stronger than Katherine, and again threw her off. They collided again and rolled on the floor, slipping on the blood, cursing, hitting, kicking, and clawing at each other. The vampire's hand penetrated her side, and she, in return, penetrated his stomach. Katherine ended up sitting against the wall as Constantine pierced her side again with his hand. She grabbed his arm, held it away from her, and felt her consciousness starting to fade. The vampire brought his other hand around to capture her heart, to deliver the deathblow, but Katherine caught that hand and held on. She held his hand with all her strength, felt her bloody grasp slipping, and saw the hand slowly approaching her chest.

Then she heard Delphinia's death scream and knew Shawn had killed the ancient vampire. Now, if she could just hold Constantine off a little longer. Constantine screamed his rage at her as he pushed even harder toward her chest. Slowly, his hand was slipping through hers, and then, with one powerful strike of a blade, his head rose up and left his body. Renee stood over them, holding Deceida, Victoria behind her, and ready to strike. She watched Constantine fall away, and then she rolled to the floor, felt the bloody, raw wood against her cheek. She yelled, "Shawn, get Drake's dirt so I can take him home," and then she felt her herself slipping away.

Chapter Eight

Katherine woke in a flier; she heard the hum of its engine and the low, sorrowful murmurs from the others. She knew Constantine had severely hurt her. Then the terrible pain came—Drake was dead. How would she live without him? The pain tore at her soul and penetrated her being, the very same she had once felt for Shawn long ago. Anger built in her, and she aimed it at the angels; they had lied to her and kept this horror from her.

She cried out in a panic, "Shawn, did you get Drake's dirt?"

"Yes, I have it. I'm taking you to Washington to bury you. Try to rest now, my love."

She heard Victoria say, "Rest, Katherine. I am so sorry!"

"Is Renee here?" She cried out.

"I'm here, Katherine," Renee said softly.

"Why did the council do this now?" Katherine yelled at Renee. "I don't understand! This will only further damage their reputation. Please, Renee! You can't be a member of the council anymore!"

"Stephen didn't know about the attack, but some did. It was Constantine, seeking revenge against our family. The council is in disarray, and I have resigned. I don't believe the council will survive this. Word is spreading quickly, and one member has already gone into hiding. The council is finished. You should rest. The family is here for you."

"Who is the council member that has fled?" Katherine asked

hoarsely.

"It's Farhad," Renee whispered back.

Blood tears came to Katherine's eyes, grief washed over her, and each wave was more intense than the last. Rolling over, she buried her face in the cushion, moaned, and cried. She would not forget about Farhad. Katherine would have her revenge; she'd have her revenge on all of them. Finally, allowing herself to sleep, she drifted back to the light, where she could hide from her grief and pain.

Katherine woke to warm water, washing over her. The vampires were cleaning and getting her ready for burial. Her family had buried her here before—when she was young. Katherine felt the vampires putting her in the cool, healing earth, and she welcomed the comfort of the fresh dirt. Mother Earth came to Katherine, and she felt The Mother's penetrating energy to help her with the terrible sorrow. Then she left her body and traveled to the light.

Floating in the light, Katherine allowed her senses to feel the energy, allowing the light to take her grief away, and her memories, to soothe her—all she experienced now was peace and tranquility. Marilyn was the first to come to her. Katherine felt Marilyn wrap her life force, around her, and Katherine felt Marilyn's sorrow.

I am with Drake. I am helping him. He sleeps now; he is in stasis, healing from his time on Earth. He shouldn't sleep long, he is an old soul and did not spend many years in the physical world. You don't have time to grieve, Katherine. You will be with him again, not in the physical world, but you will be with him someday. Don't grieve too long. Sleep! I will watch over Drake.

She floated, but for how long, she did not know. There was no concept of time here. Eventually, Anne came to her.

I am sorry that I hid this from you, Anne told her. *There were reasons I couldn't tell you. Events had to play out.*

Why didn't you tell me I could have prevented it? It is always what angels want. I would have done anything for your angels with Drake by my side. I don't understand.

That's why. You would have prevented it, and the angels have a purpose for Drake. They need Drake. I am taking you to Heaven. The angels will prepare you so you can enter the City of Light. Michael has requested your presence, and he will explain all to you.

Anne gathered her spirit, and she felt the change in vibrations as she traveled to Heaven. She found herself floating in intense white light, felt angels around her; they told her to rest and concentrate on the tranquility, the harmony of the light. They explained that the light would continue to intensify until she was ready to enter the City of Light.

As she floated in the light, it grew stronger, and when she became used to one kind of intensity, it would increase again. Angels were with her, soothing her, reassuring her, as she became capable of withstanding the energies of Heaven.

Suddenly, a world started to come into focus, and she was standing on a golden brick path. In the distance, she could see the City of light. The way traveled to the city through a green field scattered with colorful flowers and green-leaved trees, and then rose up and went around a majestic mountain with a waterfall cascading down to the valley below. The sky was a bright blue with a tinge of pink streaking through it. Billowy white clouds floated lazily across the heavenly sky.

She could hear birds chirping, felt and listened to a slight wind, and saw spirits floating in the sky, some with human forms, traveling—to where she did not know. The intense brightness of these ghosts was gone. The colors of this world flowed and shimmered. It was a reality not quite solid and spongy, with a feeling of absolute tranquility that permeated her being. Then she saw Anne walking toward her, and she heard her thoughts.

Welcome to the City of Light, the city of warrior angels.

The immense brightness is gone. Katherine projected.

The angels conditioned you to the light, and now you see the spirits and this world the way you want to view it. Come with me, Katherine, and we will enter the city.

Katherine walked with Anne toward the City of Light. They

followed the brick path through the field and up the side of the mountain. She thought she felt the wet mist as they went by the waterfall. Spirits floated everywhere; some wore the clothes of their time on Earth. Some had no features at all, and they barely resembled the human form. Anne told Katherine that the oldest of the angels forget their mortal look.

They followed the golden brick road into the city. Many of the spirits were busy, with a purpose—a job to do. There were many open shops and no fronts to them. She saw spirits weaving cloth and tailors making clothes. Artists were painting or decorating figurines and vases with bright, vivid colors or creating the sharp ring of metal as they forged their sculptures. She saw spirits working with leather, making, all types of musical instruments. She watched a man assembling a lamp. When he finished, he set it aside, and it disappeared. Katherine came to angels sitting on stools, holding a class with spirits gathered around them writing in books. Then Katherine heard Anne loudly in her soul.

Follow me, I want to show you something.

They rose into the sky over the golden city and traveled down the mountain valley. Below was a bright, lush, green valley that rose up to join the jagged rocks of majestic mountain peaks. They came to a place where many spirits trained with swords that looked like Deceida. She could see birds flying, small animals scampering into their holes or chewing on the grass, trees with large, green, yellow, or orange leaves. Large white and pink clouds floated in the sky. She felt this world's energy everywhere, vibrant, and then she realized she was more aware here. More awake than she had ever been.

Katherine flew with Anne, and soon they came to a large arched building made of blocks that looked to be of red sandstone, which radiated orange light. They entered a large, arched opening with no door, and the windows had no glass. The hall was enormous, with a high, curved ceiling. Katherine could see out the arched windows and saw a beautiful valley unfolding toward the horizon. Everywhere books lined the high walls of this vast building.

This is the hall of souls, and the books bear record to their existence. Come, there is something else I want to show you.

Katherine continued to float through the massive hall and soon came to an area that held many floating orbs of light. The building held rows upon rows of these orbs, as far as she could see—their number, she could not count. They flew higher, went over the brightly lit orbs, and continued a reasonable distance until Anne suddenly stopped and pointed to one, and then Katherine heard:

There is Drake, and he is in stasis. His life force is gathering his energy for Heaven.

Katherine floated down to the orb and saw the energy of Drake's life force swirling inside. Flashes of different colored lights and then, briefly, Katherine caught Drake's face. Reaching out, Katherine touched the light and felt her love—it was him. Anne came alongside her and Katherine projected, *Thank you for showing me this.*

You see? He is fine, and Marilyn checks on him regularly. She will take good care of him. You must let your grief go. You will be with him again, but here you won't experience physical love. It is a different love here. Events on Earth will develop too quickly for you to have time to grieve. This is why Michael wanted me to show you this. Come, it is time. We must go and meet him.

They floated out a large window and went up into the blue sky. A bright white mist surrounded Katherine as she floated upward, small orbs of light swirled by her, and then, like a fog on a sunny, summer morning, it lifted. Katherine was floating in front of a large palace with steeples that reached high into the blue sky. The palace shimmered in the white light it radiated. They floated through the door and down a wide hallway with a marble floor and a high, arched ceiling and chandeliers that burned so bright she could barely look at them. Through a large, white door she went, and then into a vast hall. Spirits gathered in small groups and looked as if they were talking to each other, but their mouths did not move.

They are waiting for an audience with Michael, Anne projected. *This is as far as I can go. Michael wants to see you alone.* Anne pointed toward a large, white, arched door on the far side of the hall. Katherine hesitated, and then she felt from Anne a mental shove, telling her that she must go through the door alone. Michael was testing her to see if she dared to enter. She turned and thought: *Don't leave.*

Anne replied, *I won't.*

Her spirit floated down to the floor, and she walked to the large, white, arched door, reached out, and opened the door like any other, and walked through. The angel, on the other side, looked to be a man but was three times the size of a man. Michael appeared semi-transparent, and his skin gave off a bronze hue and was draped with a white tunic to mid-thigh. The tunic gathered around his waist with a gold cord and held a bright sword that looked like Deceida. What surprised Katherine the most was the large, black wings. The span easily would have been thirty feet on her world. She approached the angel and saw his eyes burning a brilliant blue. She heard the Archangel Michael's voice resonate through her being:

Katherine, you have traveled far to be with me. Welcome! I see your surprise; Archangels have wings. Black, if they are warrior angels. I sense mortals were taught little about angels in your time.

No, not in my time. We were too busy surviving. Katherine projected.

I suppose you were. I'm afraid, dear Katherine, that Lucifer is angry about the destruction of his demons on Earth, and Eos is only inflaming the situation. Lucifer's darkness is again rising in your world, and he will send many dark witches, beware of The Tempter. Vampires must take the fight to Lucifer and his evil, and they will need leadership, far better than the Vampire Council. Eos is preparing for a great battle with Lucifer, and she will use guardians as her soldiers. This is the beginning, the great battle begins, and it will be fought on Earth in the physical plane.

Katherine pondered at the news and wondered. *Why must evil be fought on earth?*

Again, Michael sensed Katherine's thoughts. *Eons   ago, angels fought a great battle in Heaven, between the light and darkness. The angel Lucifer led the dark angels, and finally, the light drove Lucifer and his angels from Heaven.*

Now evil is fought in the physical worlds, the worlds that hold intelligent spirits. You see, dear Katherine, angels, do not want to battle in Heaven. In your world, your physical spirits are treasures for evil spirits that must be possessed. That is why angels need guardians. Hard, righteous warriors that can stand up to evil in the physical plane. In your world, this has gone astray. That is why we need a different way to lead guardians. You will be Queen of the Vampires, and I will rule through you. Many decisions you will make on your own, but some will come through me, and Drake will be my messenger.

Why me? Katherine thought.

You must bring the ancients of your kind under control. They live in luxury, they would not face Lucifer's demons, and now they do the same with the witches. I can no longer tolerate this. You are Herit. I made her first, and she was always the strongest. They will see my resolve when one as young as you bring them under her control. I chose Drake, an ancient soul that has lived many lives in the physical worlds, destined to be the messenger to the queens. That was his purpose since his birth in the cold darkness of physical space. You will rule the guardians, and I will give you high power. While queen, you will be the most powerful of all guardians. All my queens will be.

Eos even now prepares for the great battle at the Gates of Hell. She plans to send a hard, painful message to Lucifer through Shawn. She will have The Tempter killed so she can never enter the physical plane again. You must go back and prepare guardians for this assault. Lucifer sends his darkest witch for the guardian Shawn, and that is what will set these events in motion.

Katherine, you must prepare your kind for this battle. Gather an army of guardians and be ready. Be ready to pass through Hell's Hole. Only guardians can go through Hell's Hole. You are now the queen. As we speak, the angels tell the guardians they have a new leader, and their queen will expect more from them.

The Vampire Council is no more, and your reign will only be a moment in time. Already I see the next queen. Always fight evil and rule wisely, Queen Katherine.

I will do my best to do what the angels want of me, Katherine projected. *I will fight evil wherever evil shows itself, but I will never let anything happen to Shawn.*

That is what I am counting on, Katherine.

Again, Katherine pondered. *Why just queens?*

That is what The Mother will allow on Earth. The curse of Cain. I will now give you great power. Kneel and prepare yourself.

She watched Michael take the sword from his waist and tap it once on each of her shoulders, and then he handed the bright sword to her. As she took the sword in her hand, a power traveled through her.

Rise, Katherine, the power of the angels is yours, it flows through your blood, use it wisely, or bear their wrath. I give this sword, Alexa, protector of humanity, to the Queen to use against evil and all that would end her reign. Keep it close as you travel back to your world.

I will do all that you ask of me, but know this…I will be sending all of Drakes killers to you, Katherine, projected.

I have made the guardians of your world killers, so I know you you will. Go back to your world, talk to the subjects, and tell them they must do better and wait for Drake to awaken.

Katherine left the large room as Michael climbed the stairs to his throne. Anne gathered her, and they left the palace, flying down the mountain valley, over the golden city, and back to where Katherine first met Anne.

This is as far as I go, Katherine. I will come to you in the light, guide you, but soon Drake will come to you. He will be your messenger—Messenger to the Queen. Give my love to Shawn.

Katherine thought of going back to her world, her energy quickly changed, and again she went through the planes of existence. The fresh, rejuvenating earth surrounded her. Then, the tremendous thirst for blood drove her up and out of her grave. She felt the powerful arms of her maker grab her and hold her. She could hear his soothing voice.

"I have you, my love. You will need blood!"

Tasting his powerful blood as it flowed down her throat, she again felt this world and all of its hopes and agonies flooding back to her. Katherine woke to her new life as queen, and to her coronation.

Chapter Nine

K atherine had arrived home to Dalton two days ago from Amsterdam. Her duties as queen would tire her sometimes; the never-ending pettiness would weigh on her. It had been ten years since she lost Drake, and she still felt sorrow for him; it was selfish of her, but she missed the kiss of his lips. His voice, his laugh, how he looked and smelled—she missed holding his gaze so she could look into his beautiful eyes longer. How it felt making love to him, the physical parts of their life together that she would never experience with him again... She hadn't heard from him, and she didn't expect to this early.

Katherine was harder now since she lost Drake, and since she had become queen. Now, she sat in a lounger and sipped at her tea. Looking out at the night sky, a bright full moon, and stars that went on forever. She heard the rustle of the wind blowing through the treetops and the sounds of this world's insects declaring their existence. She had looked on this moon for more than five hundred years and barely could remember her beginnings. No longer could she see the faces of her brother and sister or hear their voices. She barely could even remember that she once had a brother and sister.

The angels had spread the word and told the vampires that the age of the queen had arrived. She had traveled many miles these ten years, holding gatherings, speaking to the vampires, telling them about Lucifer's witches. No longer would feeding on evil be enough, she told them. Their queen would expect more from them, and they must now fight the darkness that Lucifer would send to this world. She had met the ancients, the leaders of the covenants, and they did not seem impressed with her. They felt she was too young.

Shawn had been with her almost constantly since Drake's death, and only now had he left to travel on to Victoria's home. Angels had already set the bureaucracy that would define her rule. Crimmians had rebuilt the Vampire Council mansion and made it her palace. Vampires had named it The Citadel. The massive estate included a gathering hall complete with a large pool and fountains. In the pool, pure white marble stairs rose from the center, and a throne made of polished, light blue marble sat on a marble dais at the top of the stairs. Her banner behind her bore a gold lion's head against a sapphire blue background. Her reign would be the first of many. Katherine would hold council six times a year, make decrees and settle disputes. Michael never interfered with this part of her rule, only when it came to dealing with Lucifer and his witches. At the time of her coronation, Katherine sat on the blue throne while the ancients would pass by, grimace, and swear their allegiances.

Katherine had vampires that ran the affairs of her rule, and guards that followed her everywhere. At first, she told them not to, but through council, she had agreed, and now told them to keep their distance.

Vampires built a new camp in Dalton, where her guards were to stay when she was there. Her power as a vampire was great; she was the most powerful vampire in this world. While at her coronation, an ancient vampire had spoken to her about Farhad, trying to gain favor with her. She now knew where to look for Farhad and had decided now was the time to send him to Michael.

Katherine stared out over the river and spied a lone man fishing in the dark. He was a vampire, and by the red lion embroidered on his dark blue shirt collar, and slayer on his back, she knew he was the captain of her guard. His name was Thomas, and he came from the Germanic Covenant of Brandt. He was an older vampire, a big man with a muscular body, over a thousand years old, and he liked to fish. A handsome man with short blond hair and a close-cropped blond beard. She watched him catch a fish, reel it in, and then throw it back into the water. Every so often, he would glance up at her home on the tower. The flash of his emerald green eyes showed his covenant and strength. She felt him sensing her home, looking for anything out of place, and then saw him go back to his fishing. Thomas had been the one who spoke to her about keeping guards nearby, and she had immediately felt the sexual tension between them. Penetrating his vampire defenses, she saw the lust for her in him. Maybe, tonight she would take advantage of those feelings.

Cloaking herself, she lifted off the balcony, floated in stealth, and came around and down behind him. Standing behind him, she watched his muscular arms cast the fishing line into the water. The vampire was unaware of her presence. Slowly, she lifted her cloak, and the vampire finally sensed her. He grabbed his sword and spun to face her.

She laughed and said, "Thomas, I don't think you will need that."

"Sorry, Ma' am, I'm not used to vampires getting this close without me knowing."

"Do the fish bite this late at night?" Katherine asked as she looked into his eyes, touched his mind, and took in his smell. *A handsome man and a good man,* she thought.

"The trout feed at night, and I catch quite a lot them." Then he shrugged. "Unfortunately, I can't eat them, but I do have a memory of eating fish once. No memory of how they tasted, though."

"Let me try?" Katherine asked and watched this big man hand her the fishing pole. She fished for a while and then yelled, "I have one, Thomas!"

"Keep the line taut, and reel the fish in slowly, Ma' am."

Katherine brought the fish in and held it up for Thomas to take off the line. Then she tossed the pole aside and turned to Thomas, slowly floating toward him. "I know you want me, and I am lonely tonight. It has been a while since I have had a man. There are few takers for a queen." Coming close to him, she stroked his face with her fingers, leaned in, and smelled his neck.

"That's probably not a good idea. I am part of your guard, and my job is to protect you."

"I am the queen, and I will decide what is good or bad. Make love to me, Thomas. You want to!"

Katherine embraced the vampire with her powerful arms, kissed him passionately, and drew him to the ground with her. She pulled at his pants and shirt, felt the muscles of his arms and chest, rolled on top of him, guided him into her, and made love to him for as long as he would last. She lost herself in her lovemaking, and after, lay naked in his arms and talked about Drake—how she met him, and their short time together. How lonely she felt without him…The sun peaked above the horizon and projected its soft light down the river, showing the early morning mist drifting off the water.

"Can you feel that, Thomas, the dark energy?"

"No, Ma' am, not here."

Darkness is again descending on this world, and Lucifer's witches are gathering south of here."

"Come to me next eve at twilight. Only you. Bring your slayer and pack. We will travel south together."

"Yes, my queen."

Katherine caressed his vampire body, lay on top of him, and made love to him again. She felt the warm sun spread over her naked body, warm its coldness that Drake's death had brought her. She liked being with Thomas and the pleasure he gave her.

Katherine and Thomas traveled south to Charlottesville and was staying in a hotel midway up one of the high towers of the city. Thomas was taking a shower. He was a distraction for her, and these days she felt the best when she had one with her. There was no love for her now, only distractions. She would think of Drake often until the pain came, and then she did her best to put him out of her mind. Standing on her balcony, she watched the lights of the aircars travel around the high towers like bees around a hive. The many-colored lights of the city would flicker and wink at her. Charlottesville was a large modern city that enjoyed great prosperity. Any technology this world had to offer, it was here, in Charlottesville, located in the Carolina District.

She sensed the dark energy, and now knew it was that of two witches gathering. The witches were a hundred miles to the west, located in a vast forest north of the mountain town of Warm Springs. *Why are they there,* she wondered? Projecting her powerful sense, she felt another faint evil there.

"Ma' am, the bathroom is free."

Katherine turned and took in Thomas's large, naked body, the slight dampness on his tanned skin that made his muscles glisten, his big, pretty cock, and gave him a quizzical look. "Thomas, don't call me, Ma'am. When nobody is around, call me Katherine. We do make love to each other. Come stand with me. Hold me. Is not the city beautiful?"

"Yes, my Queen."

"Thomas!"

"Sorry."

As she stayed with Thomas, she became more curious about him and now asked him, "Thomas, how did you become a guard in my service? What made you leave your home?"

Thomas became serious. "I am from the Han family. I have not liked the Vampire Council since they had my maker killed. I have spent my long existence in learning the art of fighting. How to use weapons of all kinds to fight hand-to-hand, and military tactics. I have studied the art of warfare, as well as most of the major battles humans have fought. My angels told me to come to Amsterdam to serve you and be a guard for you."

"Well, Thomas Han, sense westward and tell me what is there."

"I sense witches, and I believe they are starting to realize we're near. So, we should be making our move as soon as possible. I am a capable warrior. You will find that out."

"We'll see. Let's hope I don't get you killed. The day is coming. Take me to bed, and we will leave next eve."

They made their way westward until they came to the Shenandoah Valley. They had cloaked themselves, but they could sense that the witches knew they were somewhere near. Large corporations that grew the vegetables for the humans used the valley. These farmlands stretched for hundreds of miles north and produced massive amounts of food. Selling vegetables to the spacers was good business.

"They are in the forest on the far side of this valley. Can you sense the witches, Thomas?"

"Yes, and they sense us. They aren't sure of where we are, though," Thomas said quickly. "I presume we are here to attack the witches. I would recommend crossing the valley under stealth and quickly. They will finally sense where we are, and then they will attack."

"The witches will certainly attack us, but there is more. Can't you sense it, Thomas? It's a different evil, and it's not coming from the witches. I felt this evil once before. I was with my maker, and it came from a cave. Have you ever heard of Hell's Hole, Thomas?"

"No, Ma' am, I never have."

"Be brave, Thomas, and you just might on this trip."

Katherine watched this powerful vampire reach back to feel his sword—to reassure himself. On her back, she wore the slayer that Michael had given her. She saw Thomas glancing at it.

"Michael gave me this sword. Angels made it in the light of Heaven. The sword's name is Alexa, defender of humankind." She pulled the blade from its sheath. The silver sword still glowed slightly. She held it out for him. "Would you like to hold it? You must hold it with a firm grip, and don't waver, vampire, or its power will burn you."

"It would be an honor, my queen." Thomas took the sword and held it firmly—even took a stroke. "I can feel Heaven's energy in the sword! How amazing!"

Katherine took the sword back and said, "Let's pay a visit to these witches."

They carefully made their way across the valley, keeping to the high grass, and trying to use the wooded areas. They cloaked and guarded themselves against a possible assault on their minds.

The vampires had just crossed a small stream when they fell into the witches' trap, a vitriolic mist, cast by the witches to encompass a small area of ground. They had walked into it, and immediately, a surreal feeling entered their heads. Their world shivered and then disappeared. They had fallen into a pit with the fires of Hell all around; wretched faces came into focus and then left them. Horrible sounds arose, grating and grinding, whispers from the evil spirits trying to turn them on each other, trying to trick them into coming to the pool and throw themselves in.

Katherine felt the panic the spell projected into her, and she willed herself back with the power Michael had given her. A thick, putrid evil is what she smelled, and she saw maggots all over her body, and black snakes slithering everywhere on the ground, flicking their red tongues at her. She brought her hands to her head to hold her ears, guarding them against the agonizing, grinding sounds, and forcing herself to think clearly, to use the high power of the angels to hold off the disorientating effects of the spell. Looking back, she saw Thomas walking in circles, bewildered, muttering chants from the angels to hold back this hopeless evil. His ears and eyes were bleeding, and she quickly went to him, grabbed hold of him, and he gave a piercing scream and fell to the ground.

"Let me help you, Thomas. We must find our way out of this." She pulled him to his feet and moved forward until eventually, she felt the spell weaken, and they found their way out. Holding him, she wiped the blood from his face. The big vampire shook from what he had seen and felt.

"Steady yourself. The spell is going away. Feel it leave you." She entered his head, calmed him, and, slowly, Thomas quieted himself.

"I felt so helpless. Never could I imagine this kind of darkness. This is what your family fought all these centuries? I don't know if I'm strong enough for this, my queen."

"You will do better next time, but you must be strong. We must ready ourselves. You said you were a warrior!"

Thomas got to his feet, shook his head, and took hold of his sword, declaring, "I am ready, my Queen."

"Follow me. We need to reach the trees. Can you sense the other evil now?"

"Yes, I can sense something different. The witches guard an evil inside that hill."

Katherine stood and stared at a spot midway up the forested slope, searching with her powerful senses, and it became clear to her what was there. "Lucifer has moved Hell's Hole, and the witches guard it," Katherine whispered in disbelief.

They quickly made their way across the valley, avoiding other diabolical traps, came to the edge of the forest, and levitated their bodies just above the ground, slithering around the trees and brush. They wove their way up the hill like vipers, and then Katherine abruptly stopped.

"The witches are going to attack," Thomas whispered excitedly, taking his slayer from his back.

"You're right. The beasts aren't going to let us go too much further." Then came the whooshing roar of the dark energy traveling through the trees, splintering and shredding the tree branches. The evil power landed all around them. The vampires dodged some, and some blew them from their feet. Katherine drew Alexa and yelled, "Follow me, Thomas!" She ran up the hill, Thomas following. The witches had left their lair and now flew down the mountain to meet them.

The evil creatures came through the trees and attacked. Both were bald and wore leather vests, leather britches, and moccasins on their feet. Their skin was pancake-white and showed their putrid black blood carrying veins. Ghostly faces these hideous creatures had, black eyes, and black mouths that contrasted against their white. They carried large daggers with black pearl hilts, and demonic symbols etched into the silver blades. A screaming witch flew at Katherine, and she felt the sting of the knife on her arm. Katherine screamed, twisted, and hit the witch in the face with the hilt of her slayer, knocking the beast back until a tree stopped her flight.

The witch got to her feet and yelled, "Beelzebub, send me fire!" The witch hurled a dark blue fireball at Katherine. She deflected the energy with Alexa, and it hit a tree, sending a loud *boom* echoing through the valley. Thomas attacked the other witch. The spell hurt him earlier, but now, with a slayer, he was the master. Katherine had never seen a sword handled so well, and he soon split the witch down the middle.

Katherine flew at the second witch and drove her slayer through its stomach, flinging the beast to the ground. The witch rolled to her feet and threw dark energy at Katherine. Holding Alexa in front of her, Katherine absorbed the heat and quickly attacked and took the witch's head with one clean slice.

"Are you all right, Thomas?" she yelled.

"I am! We certainly are amid Lucifer's sick evil tonight."

"Yes, we are!"

Walking toward her, Thomas said, "Let me tend to your wound, my Queen."

Thomas tore her leathers, placing some of his blood on her wound. Gently, he rubbed the blood into her wound. "That should help."

"We will go forward. The evil isn't far now. I'm afraid it might get worse, Thomas."

The vampires again made their way up the forested hill. They came to a small stream of spring water, winding its way down to the valley. Katherine splashed the water on her face and took sips to moisten her mouth. Thomas dunked his entire head into the water.

"Come on. It's not far now," Katherine said.

They traveled the remainder of the distance and came to a steep incline. Then the side of the hill shimmered, and a ten-foot-wide round opening appeared. Polished bricks of coal covered a large area surrounding the opening. The inside walls and floor of the cave were also made from this refined coal bricks. The blackness of this opening was remarkable, and it absorbed any light that came near. They walked to the entrance, and Katherine used her vampire eyes to see into the cave. Fifty feet in, she saw the large, red pool of evil.

"See it, Thomas? It looks like another Hell's Hole."

"I see it!"

"The putrid stench. The smell of death," Katherine whispered. "Can you feel it reaching out for you, pulling you toward the pool?"

"I can! For the love of the angels, it is horrible."

"This is what we fight. I have a task for you, warrior. You must go out and gather vampires. Gather warrior vampires that have courage and know-how to fight. Select them in my name. Make a powerful fighting force for me and wait for my command. Do you understand?"

"Yes, my queen, as you say, I will do."

"You are a strong and loyal warrior, vampire. I will call on you again. Now, I want you to leave me. What is in this cave, you do not want to see."

"Let me stay and help you!"

"The Mother will protect my mind and hide my thoughts. I must go into the cave alone. Leave. Go to Amsterdam and raise a force of magnificent warrior-vampires. Wait for my command. When I leave here, I must travel on my own. I have a debt to collect from a traitorous vampire."

Thomas walked back down the hill, and then he took flight. She looked back into the cave, and the scent of evil had disappeared as if a strong wind had blown it away. There was only stillness—no breeze could be felt. A strange scent of juniper, and then a cold thickness, came to the air, and then The Mother came into her head.

I will hide your thoughts from the dark angel Lucifer. He is in this cave and waits for you. Be strong, Katherine, it is time for you to meet the devil. Remember what you learn here. I will be with you. The Mother settled deep within her, and she started her walk into the cave.

Katherine walked the fifty feet to the large chamber that held the large pool of red liquid. Black, polished bricks of coal lined every surface of this chamber. A wave of nausea went through her, along with a sickening smell of juniper. In the far right corner, she saw a giant, black snake coiled with red eyes and a long, flickering, thin red tongue. A tail, higher than the rest of its body, moved back and forth in a hypnotic way. Suddenly, the head rose up three feet, and the red eyes burned into her. A sickness washed over her, and she heard a raspy voice in her head.

Greetings, Queen of the Vampires. Come closer, I will not harm you this time, but the next time we meet, I will take your soul. Just like, I will have your maker's soul. Do you think the angels gave you enough power to save him? No, they did not. They will never give you that power.

Then she heard a low, deep, mocking laugh echo in her head, vibrating her bones. She spoke in a loud voice, not wanting to give the devil any access to her mind. "I will never let you have Shawn!"

You have no choice. You are a weak vampire. I can sense Eos, and she is hiding your thoughts from me. How are you, Eos? I want you to know. I am sending The Temptress to bring Shawn to me. Malin is coming for Shawn, and when she is done with him, she will come for you, Queen. Do you think I would leave you out of all the fun? I know you connive with Eos, and I know Michael helps you. Leave this place! Eos hides your thoughts, but I do see something. Again, Katherine heard a deep and penetrating laugh come from the devil.

The head of the black snake slowly lowered back to the floor, its piercing red eyes fixed on her. The snake slithered over the coal brick floor, into the red pool of liquid, and disappeared. Katherine turned and walked quickly out of the cave. She felt The Mother leave her, and heard in her mind:

Be brave, Katherine, for Malin is coming.

Chapter Ten

S tephen was an old and formidable vampire and had once been an ally to the Bryce family, but now he hid from them. Katherine had been tracking him for more than a month. Stephen cloaked himself from her, but still, with help from the angels, she had a slight sense of him, even through his shroud. Now, she sat at a bar in a disco in the lower section of a tower in Munich. The disco was on the entertainment level of this tower, three levels up from the street. Colorful art and design would appear over her head and then dissipate. No sound came from them, as it would serve no purpose amid the loud music. Disco music of this age was fast-paced and pounding. The humans would throw their bodies and heads in all different directions. Sometimes, she thought, they would break their necks.

Katherine had sensed Stephen before in this disco, but each time she came, he was gone. Now, she would lie in wait for him, and shrouded herself so no vampire of this world could detect her. Twice before, she had been here, but Stephen had not shown. Shawn had told her that Stephen swore he had nothing to do with Drake's murder, but she wanted to hear this from Stephen himself. After all, he was hiding himself from her, and what reason would he have to hide if he was innocent?

She felt lonely since leaving Thomas. Her thoughts had gone back to Drake, and her anger had returned, probably because she was on a mission to kill the council member Farhad. Tonight, she drank whiskey and could feel her rage toward Stephen building.

She wanted to kill Stephen but knew Anne and Herit would be upset with her. Angels expected her to do the right thing.

Katherine suddenly felt a probing at her mind and, looking down the bar, she saw a tall, fair complexioned, blond-haired man. *Strange,* she thought, *he tried to enter my mind.* Easily, know-how fended him off, the human quickly turning away and two green symbols appearing in front of his face, telling the bartender what drink he wanted. There were times when she asked for a drink in a disco, and the bartender would give her a quizzical look. Vampires didn't need or have nanochips implanted behind their ears.

"Bartender, another whiskey!" she shouted, watching the humans give her a glance. Again, she peered down the bar at the human and sensed he knew she was a vampire. Katherine was shielding herself from vampires and never expected a human to try to enter her head. Slowly, she took hold of his mind. The man was susceptible to psychic forces, and she made him turn to look at her and sent him a message:

Careful, human...

Katherine released him; he turned in a panic and left the disco in a hurry. There was something different about this man. He was aware of psychic energy, and he seemed to know what she was. There was another vampire he was mindful of, and that vampire was Stephen. She quickly followed him out onto the street.

A warm summer rain fell from the sky, and she heard a far-off rumble of thunder. Off in the distance streaks of lightning followed the undersides of the clouds brightening the air and then fading away. The different colored lights from the flying cars and towers reflected off the wet surfaces of the city. The rain had washed the air and left it fresh and clean. Munich was a beautiful city—its shining towers stretched for miles with large, forested areas in between.

Katherine watched the man turn a corner and quickly walked after him. The man came to a corner and crossed a walkway, looked over his shoulder at her, quickened his pace, and then turned right onto another sidewalk. Katherine followed behind him and started to close the distance between them when, suddenly, he went into a building. The building had an old awning that stretched out over the walkway, and under the canopy was a hologram of a man who looked like the early Christian Jesus.

The rain had stopped, and the hologram stood with its illuminating light reflecting off the puddles around him, inviting the few people who passed by inside. Katherine entered the building and saw the man go through a stained-glass door at the end of the hallway. The inside was dim, and light filtered through the glass and projected a kaleidoscope of colors onto the walls and floor. On the door was a crucifix with words that read, "Enter and the Lord will save you." Katherine opened the door, looked inside, and saw an animated man pacing back and forth, preaching to a small crowd of people.

"Only one baby out of every three survive birth!" the preacher shouted passionately at the crowd. "Our scientists can't tell us why," the preacher yelled as he raised his arms to the ceiling. "We must return to the old religions when people worshipped the true God. These were the times when all babies survived their births. We must realize this, and pray to the one God again."

The man stood in the back, glanced back, and gave her a nervous smile. Katherine walked over, stood behind the man, and entered his mind. He tried to hide his thoughts from her, but she could feel his soul. A decent man, she saw, but he was lonely, with few friends, and kept to himself. Tonight, this human's mission was to meet her. The man believed he was a vampire once, and he defiantly knew of another vampire.

Katherine spoke softly to the man. "Sir, come outside. I wish to speak to you. You do not have to fear me."

Katherine walked outside, and the man followed. A far-off wail of a siren broke the silence as she walked, leading the man down a walkway before stopping and leaning against the wet surface of a building. She put her hands in her pants pockets to be as unthreatening as possible. The man stopped five feet from Katherine.

"Sir, you have a story to tell me," Katherine said with a friendly smile. She could see he was nervous and that he was fighting his instinct to get away from her—to stay back from her.

"I have never been this close to a vampire. How amazing this is! I have sensed vampires on occasion, but I have never made myself known to them. You are the first vampire I have talked with. I live in this tower, ten levels up from this one. I sensed you, vampire, but you were different. Great power came from you."

"What do you want to tell me, human?"

"I have always had psychic abilities-- since my birth. That is why I like going to the new age religion gatherings. As a young child, I could tell what people were thinking. I knew there was more than this physical plane of existence. Five years ago, I started to remember a past life. A long time ago, I was a vampire. I remembered drinking blood. I remembered the power I had."

"Are you sure of this, human?" Katherine asked.

"Yes, I am sure of this. I have had these abilities all my life."

The mortal became more excited, and she wondered how this man could be human now, but he believed he was telling her the truth.   "Vampire, turn me. Let me become a vampire so I can live like that again. Have that power again."

"I am sorry, human, I cannot make you a vampire. I don't love you, and I never will. Besides, I have no time for a changeling, Paul. That is your name?"

"Yes, it is. You must make me a vampire!" the man pleaded. "I now know what it is like to be a vampire. I cannot live as a human with this knowledge."

"Vampires rarely change humans. It is a long process, a personal process for a vampire. Few people have the stamina to be a vampire. You should know this if you remember being one. Tell me, Paul, have you sensed other vampires at the disco?"

"There is another, and he, too, was a powerful vampire, but he was unapproachable. That I could easily sense. He comes every Friday night."

"Every Friday Night?"

"Yes!" Paul then became agitated, turned to leave, and muttered over his shoulder, "I will find another vampire to change me."

"Good luck, friend," Katherine replied as she watched him leave.

Katherine walked back to her tower deep in thought, letting the rain wet her hair. *How strange this world can be,* and then she rose fifty levels to her hotel.

The following Friday evening, she took a place at the bar and had already had a couple of drinks when she sensed him. Stephen was coming her way, and she turned toward the door and waited. Through the entrance, Stephen strolled, turned, and quickly recognized her. Their eyes locked, he frowned, and immediately turned and left.

Stephen was walking to the edge of the terrace, where he certainly would make his escape. Katherine hurried after him, but she could only go so fast; it was a pleasant evening, and the walkways were crowded with festive humans. Stephen made his way to a secluded part of the edge and took to the air with Katherine close behind.

She flew after him and slowly gained on the ancient vampire. The fresh air rushed by her, soon turned cold, and snow pelted her face as they flew into the mountains. Occasionally, he would look over his shoulder at her. Tremendous anger built in her, at him, as she pushed on through the terrible weather. This vampire protected those who plotted and killed Drake, but Shawn would not allow her to harm him. With a burst of speed and anger, she caught Stephen over Berchtesgaden and brought him down. She dove from above and collided with his back, driving him into the mountains. They hit a high peak and fell a hundred feet, entwined in a deadly embrace, landing and rolling down the snow-covered mountain together. Stephen threw her off and screamed at her as they stood in the snow to their knees, the wind howling.

"Why can't you leave me alone? I had nothing to do with your precious Drake's death! I no longer have any responsibilities for vampires. Michael has taken that from me."

"You will address me as your queen. You were in charge of that murderous pack of vampires. I should kill all of you!"

"Look at you!" Stephen screamed. "Full of hate and revenge! You are no longer the Katherine I knew! I feel pity for you now."

Katherine launched herself at Stephen, took hold of him, and flung him into the rock face above. Stephen rolled down the side, and Katherine was on him. She struck him in his face until blood poured from his mouth and nose, staining his shirt and the snow.

"Why don't you fight me?" Katherine screamed. "What is wrong with you? Fight me, you bastard! You will fight back!"

Katherine raised her right-hand, ready to capture his heart. Her hand froze above her head and started shaking. She could not take this vampire's life; she was the queen, crowned by the Archangel Michael, and this would shame her family.

"I will not fight. Take my heart if you must. Is this what the angels have made into a queen? A vampire full of hate?"

She rolled off him, buried her face in the snow, and sobbed uncontrollably, staining the snow red with her tears. The wind howled, and the storm blew, and eventually, she raised her head to look at Stephen. Her hair hung wet and stringy against her blood-covered face. Stephen was standing, watching her with a look of pity.

"You will return to Amsterdam," Katherine commanded as she looked away and wiped the blood tears from her eyes. "Find Renee! Tell her you will be one of my advisors. Don't make me have to come looking for you again."

"Yes, my queen. I thank you for my life."

She sensed confusion in Stephen as he turned and took two steps in preparation for his flight to Amsterdam.

Katherine spoke again: "Stephen, where is Farhad?"

The vampire froze and looked back at her.

Katherine sensed, through his turmoil, his pondering—sensed him choosing his side.

He then said as he floated into the air, "He has fled to Istanbul."

Returning to Amsterdam, Katherine had her advisors find the

name of a vampire she could meet in Istanbul. Last eve, her maker came to her, and now she lay in her couch with him. There was a need for her to be with him now, as she had loved him for Six hundred years, and these days he was the only one who made her feel safe, made her feel whole. Her maker now spent time in Amsterdam with her; he was her chief advisor and proxy when she was out of touch. Katherine knew that someday her vampire army would be fighting for his life, but she did not like thinking of it— maybe she could prevent it. Lying on top of him, she brought her hand down to make him hard, but he had become serious, and would have none of it.

"You are leaving to kill Farhad, aren't you?" Shawn asked sternly.

"Yes, I am. Make love to me. I am lonely these days. Being queen has done nothing for my love life."

"This must be the last," Shawn scolded. "I will give you this one, but you must end your need for revenge. I have spoken with Stephen. You are to leave the other council members alone. Do you understand?"

Katherine could see the stern look on his face, his seriousness. She was a queen, but he was her maker and would do as he said.

"Farhad will be the last, I promise, Shawn. Don't be mad at me. Make love to me. Your queen needs you." She moved on top of him and made long, passionate love to him.

One-week later Katherine flew to Istanbul, and now stood on a roof across from a teahouse where she would meet her vampire contact. The vampire was female, and her name was Kalila. Istanbul was not a city of towers—the tallest building was ten stories, and most were a couple stories with flat or domed roofs. The city now spread from the Aegean to the Black Sea. There were only five cities in this part of the world, once known as the Middle East. Humans only lived in the cities, as the surrounding land was too harsh. The land had never sufficiently cooled since the Apocalypse. A hot breeze blew against her face, and she heard the far-off cry of the moazzen, calling the faithful to evening prayer.

Istanbul was one of the last spots on Earth that still practiced ancient religions.

Katherine sensed everything in this place, making sure nothing would come as a surprise to her. She watched the people hustling by and the anti-gravity cars slowly making their way down the crowded streets, sometimes rising higher into the air to move by. The local law only allowed cars to fly so high because of religious beliefs. Many people lived in this place, and usually, the streets were crowded with humans.

Katherine turned her senses to the vampire Kalila and cloaked herself so the younger vampire would be unaware of her presence. The vampire was not old, maybe three centuries, and had a pleasant mind. Kalila did not have another agenda, only to meet and give information to her queen, but the young vampire was nervous about meeting her. Katherine floated down to the deserted alley and walked across the street and into the teahouse. She heard the music of this culture in the background, saw waiters bringing tea to the many tables scattered throughout. A decorative carpet covered the floor, and people drew smoke from a hookah, unusual in this age. A light grey smoke drifted through the room, reflecting the dim light and giving the air a unique, rich odor. Katherine had heard of smoking but had rarely seen it. Across the room sat the vampire contact, alone. Katherine held her stealth so the vampire would be unaware.

Kalila was a small woman with jet-black, silky hair that fell to her bare shoulders. Her skin was a creamy light brown, and she had luscious ruby lips and sparkling brown eyes. She had a friendly personality, with a smile to match, which, Katherine sensed, she wore quite often. Katherine also learned that she was a master at using a slayer. Her motivation was to become more involved with the new way vampires were ruled, and being adventurous, she wanted to meet the new queen.

Katherine lifted her veil, and the vampire became aware of her presence, looked toward her, smiled, and bowed her head slightly. Katherine smiled back at her and went to sit at her table.

"Greetings, Queen Katherine," Kalila said nervously.

"Welcome to Istanbul, and it's an honor to meet you."

"Thank you, Kalila, I am grateful for your help."

Kalila picked up the teapot in front of her and asked, "Would you like some tea?"

"Yes, thank you. You are a beautiful vampire. What family do you come from?"

"My family is Sadik, and I'm from the blood covenant Zavan. I have been a vampire for three hundred and seventy-three years."

"You are lovely," Katherine said as she reached out and stroked her cheek. "What made you agree to this meeting?"

"My maker would tell me of the Bryce family, how they and Victoria Kenmare fought the demons on their own. The sacrifices your family made for all of us. Then, one day, we heard of the terrible battle between the demons and your family. We heard the angels sing of the death of the Bryces. My maker told me that was why angels gave great power to the Bryces, far more of it than they gave to other vampires. So when I heard of the information you needed, I gathered my courage and made contact, so I could meet you, my queen."

"That is kind of you, Kalila Sadik."

"I have always wanted to meet Victoria Kenmare. Tell me, is she as great a warrior as they say?"

"She is, Kalila, but she is not easy to meet. Do you live with vampires?"

"I live with a few vampires, but I have an apartment all my own."

"May I stay with you while I'm in Istanbul?" Katherine whispered seductively, leaning in to kiss her cheek and allowing her scent to fill her.

"It would be an honor, my queen."

Katherine had known almost immediately that this vampire liked women, and she now knew where Farhad was.

"Tell me, Kalila, about Farhad, and be truthful with me. I will know if you aren't," Katherine warned as she sipped her tea and easily pierced the vampire's psychic defenses.

"Farhad is of my covenant, so this is hard for me, but he turned his back on us a long ago. A cold man he is and his angels have abandoned him. Farhad contacted my family and told them he was in Istanbul. He stays behind a brothel in the Sitesi District of the city. It seems he has an appetite for mortal women."

"I see. Where does your appetite lead you? What quenches your thirst, pretty vampire?"

"You would quench my thirst, my queen," Kalila said in a nervous voice. "I hope I'm not inappropriate, but I was told you like women. I was hoping you would find me desirable."

"Take me to your apartment, Kalila. It seems tonight I have an appetite for you."

Katherine followed Kalila to a large, tan, stucco one-story home. An eight-foot stucco wall enclosed it. They walked through a courtyard with an elaborate system of pools, fountains, and waterfalls, surrounded by a lush tropical garden. Everywhere flowers of all colors were on display.

"How beautiful this is," Katherine said.

"My maker had it built. I love to spend time here and read the old books from the library. My maker collects all types of ancient books, and he taught me to read English a long time ago."

"Is your maker here?"

"No, he is traveling now. If he were here, he probably wouldn't have let me contact you. He dislikes Farhad, but he is a cautious vampire."

"Your family has nothing to fear from me. Let's go to your couch so I can show you how harmless I am."

"This way. My apartment is in the rear of this building."

Katherine followed the lovely vampire down a walkway and through the Sadik families' beautiful tropical garden. Kalila's apartment was big, with elaborate furnishings and figurines on luxurious cherry wood tables, and tile Mosaics on the walls. Colorful rugs were placed everywhere on the white marble floors.

Katherine made love to the vampire all that day. After the sun went down, they still lay naked in each other's arms. She could feel the softness of Kalila's skin, the moistness of her lips, as she caressed her and kissed her.

"I sense sadness in you, my queen," Kalila whispered as she lay next to her. "I taste it in your blood."

"My sweet Kalila," Katherine said as she brushed her hand down Kalila's back and over her soft buttocks. "I lost my fledgling a couple of years ago, and I miss him terribly. I miss his touch, his voice."

"This is why you hunt Farhad"

"Yes, he conspired with other council members to kill my love, to bring pain to my family and me. He is the last of them, and Alexa and I will have his head."

"Revenge will only give you some relief. But I'm sure you know that. Would you like me to go with you? To show you where he is."

"No, Kalila. What I will do to the vampire, I don't want you there to see. You are to travel to Amsterdam and tell my advisors to give you a place at my house. We will meet again."

Katherine spent two days with Kalila and now found herself across the street from the brothel. Shrouding herself, she could sense Farhad in the building with a mortal woman. She hoped to come as close to him as possible, but he was a three-thousand-year-old vampire, the oldest on the Vampire Council, and one of the most formidable.

Katherine waited until she sensed no humans, lifted into the air and flew to the interior courtyard of the brothel. Farhad finally had detected her, and now stood twenty feet from her, with a slayer in hand, by a fountain that flowed into a pool with bright, orange goldfish, a white statue of an ancient Persian warrior placed in its middle. Her hatred for this vampire was powerful—it took her over completely. She had to remind herself to put her emotions aside and concentrate on killing Farhad. The vampire had closed his mind to her, proof of his power.

"You have finally found me, Katherine. Who sold me out?"

"That is none of your business, and you will call me queen."

"I will call you, Katherine. You are no queen to me. You are just the changeling of that arrogant Shawn Bryce, who let my love, Hegamar, die.

"To the angels, Farhad, that's where I am going to send you! They will decide your fate," Katherine hissed as she reached for Alexa.

"Your whole family is arrogant. Just like Herit. The council sentenced your Drake to death, and I helped carry the sentence out. How does it feel, Bryce bitch! I hope you brought all your power tonight because you will need it."

As soon as Farhad had finished speaking, he picked up a large rock the size of a basketball, threw it at Katherine, and propelled himself into the night sky. She hardened herself just before the rock hit. The force lifted her up, flung her through the outside wall of the building, and into the interior, where she finally came to a stop. She lay stunned, slowly coming to her senses, and rose from the debris along with several naked humans, making their escape from the chaos. Brushing the dust off, she found Alexa and then shot through the roof in pursuit of Farhad.

Matching Farhad's speed, she flew after him, and both vampires traveled with a swiftness no human could detect. Katherine focused her vision down to only what was in front of her, and in the distance, she saw Farhad. Lowering her head, she willed her vampire energy to give her more speed, and became a missile, not really seeing what was in front of her, but sensing everything around her and slowly guiding herself to her target.

A half-hour into the chase, she finally caught Farhad, saw him look back at her, sneer at her, and pull his slayer from its sheath. Katherine flew in and delivered a slice across his thigh with Alexa. A curse from the ancient vampire and he quickly descended to an oasis in the Syrian Desert. Katherine followed, landing next to the blue waters of the Euphrates River, and saw Farhad standing amongst the palm trees, contempt on his face, feet spread, and slayer in hand, ready for a fight.

"How dare you attack me? Who do you think you are? I'm Farhad, and you don't have the power to kill me. You will pay for cutting me, Bryce."

Farhad quickly flew at her, and she deflected his slayer. The sounds of striking steel and soon a desperate fight filled the dark night. The vampires stood toe to toe and fought with their slayers, neither giving an advantage to the other. Finally, Katherine found an opening and sliced the vampire's stomach. Farhad feigned and rolled to the ground, then rose to give her a slice across her thigh. Again, they fought back and forth, their blades ringing, and sparks flying into the dark.

Katherine drew on her strength, given to her by the Archangel Michael, and slowly beat Farhad down. The sounds of their hatred for each other shattered the quiet of the desert. Then, Farhad's blade broke into pieces. Cursing, he stooped, and flung sand into Katherine's face, then took to the air to make his escape, Katherine following. Above him, she flew, and dove at him, catching him at his back, driving him down into the desert.

They crashed into the hard, packed sand, and Farhad held on, rolled his body, flinging her into the air. Farhad flew at her, and again their bodies met. Katherine parried, then feigned and pivoted, slicing Farhad deeply across his side. Springing forward, she stabbed at the vampire, only to have her blade struck away by his bloody hand. She grabbed hold of him and drove him to the ground, punching him repeatedly in the face, and plunged her hand into his side.

The vampire was starting to fade; Katherine's power was overwhelming him, and she picked him up, flung him a good distance. Again, they flew at each other, collided, and the force pivoted them to the ground. They rolled through the sand, beating on each other, tearing at each other's flesh. Finally, Katherine ended up on top of a beaten Farhad, holding him to the ground by his throat. She, too, was beaten and bloodied, blood from her face dripping on Farhad, and most of her clothes torn from her.

Farhad spat blood at her and hissed, "Unspeakable evil is coming your way, Bryce bitch. All Bryces will pay for their arrogant ways."

Katherine reached and took Alexa from the sand and said, "As Queen of the Vampires, I sentence you to death for the murder of my beloved Drake." She brought her slayer across his throat, severing his head and ending his three thousand-year life.

Chapter Eleven

A cool, brisk wind blew in Katherine's face as she leaned out into the night. She stood high on a perch at the top of a tower in Amsterdam, watching and sensing the city. It had been twenty-five years since Drake's death, and vampires had crowned her Queen. Often, she came here to clear her mind. The last two weeks, she had spent sitting on the blue throne, settling disputes, and listening to vampires drone on about their problems. The constant weight of never-ending responsibility wore on her. Looking out over the city, she would project her senses, feeling everything, sensing this sea of normalcy for that flash of evil, humans doing unspeakable things to each other.

She watched the Euro Metropolis slip silently, crossing the sky, one of the first to appear in this world. A new phenomenon was showing itself, floating cities, a half-mile high, drifting across the skies. The many-colored lights of the Metropolis and the flying vehicles swarming around would shine and light the night.

It had been fifteen years since she killed Farhad. The angels never spoke a word about the killing, only Anne, and she said it was beneath Katherine and the Bryce name. The emptiness was still with her, a hollow that Drake used to fill. Killing that despicable vampire had not helped fill this void. She longed for the time she would hear from him again and wondered what he would be like as an angel.

Two eves later, she traveled home to Dalton with Shawn,

needing a break from her responsibilities and her reign for now. It had been a long year for her. She had occupied herself with many tasks, the building of her army being the most important. She woke at her home in Dalton and lay in her maker's arms. She buried her face into his neck to smell him, to take in his thoughts and hide from the world.

He told her, with his mind, *Good morning.*

"Do you remember the first time you saw me?" She asked sleepily. "Strange, much of that time, I can't remember, but I do remember the first time I saw you."

"Yes, I do. You were working at a food stand. I thought you were the most beautiful girl I ever saw."

"I thought Victoria was the most beautiful girl you ever saw."

"She was, but you replaced her," Shawn teased.

"I bet! All I remember now of that life was meeting you and becoming a vampire. It feels like I have always been a vampire. I know nothing of what it was like being a mortal."

"Five hundred years is a long time, Katherine. We have discussed this before," Shawn told her gently. "Sometimes, time can be a burden for us. In the physical world, vampires can become lost in time. The immensity of time we deal with is why the angels gave us the ability to have more than one lover. Why you need so much love. Our lives are not fleeting, like humans. You have to accept you cannot remember your past, and a day will come when you won't remember this age. You are tired. Your spirit is low. We will stay in Dalton for a time to let you rest. Being a queen can wait."

"How is my dear Victoria?" Katherine asked, wishing she could spend more time with her, wishing she had been intimate with Victoria at least once. "I heard you spend a lot of time with her these days."

"She is well and has a slayer again. Made of titanium alloy. Folded many times and capable of keeping a razor-sharp blade. We have been practicing together. She is more serious about using a slayer, something Erdin told her. And she tells me she wants to take another changeling."

Katherine felt Shawn embrace her; she felt him enter her and move passionately on her. She also felt his blood teeth pierce her neck, felt him drink, and when he was done, she went to his neck and then whispered passionately into his ear, "I miss Drake! I wish he was here with us."

"I know you do," Shawn whispered back.

She held Shawn tightly. "Let's stay in Dalton forever. Swim in the river, and hunt your deer. You will protect me again, and I'll be your changeling."

Shawn whispered back into her ear. "You are a queen now. The angels have made it so. The angels have work for you to do, and they will not let you out of it. Trust me. That I know. You must eventually go back to Amsterdam and lead our kind. I will be with you as long as I can. I grow tired of killing Lucifer's witches. They never stop coming, and Lucifer will have me someday. You must understand this and prepare yourself for that day." Shawn rose from the couch. "Come on, let's wash up. Tonight, we hunt deer for their blood. Tell your guards we won't need them, and what is going on with the head guard? What's his name? Thomas?"

"Nothing!"

"You've slept with him," Shawn said in an exasperated voice. "Katherine, you're the queen."

"Yes, I have slept with him, and that is what this queen does. She sleeps with her subjects sometimes. I need the distraction it provides."

Later that night, Katherine found herself running through the woods, following her maker, watching him, his form, and his hair blowing back. Shawn wouldn't use his senses only his speed and cunning for hunting the deer. He would do it the human way, track the deer—follow their trail. "It is only fair," he would tell her. She had loved her maker for close to six hundred years and would fight to the death for him. Soon, they came to a fallen log and hid, peering over and seeing three deer in a clearing.

Tonight, she had a worry—her maker was slowing, he didn't run as fast as he used to. She always had a hard time keeping up with him, but tonight she easily stayed with him and could tell his speed was slowing, and his strength wasn't the same. Something was wrong, and she wasn't sure what it was.

Shawn spoke to her mind, so he didn't frighten the deer. *See, there they are. I knew they would be here.*

Yes, Shawn, you were right. She always pretended he was a great hunter. Deer's blood was not her favorite; others in her family did not mind. Anne used to tell her about the value of deer blood, but still, it tasted slightly bitter to her, and human blood was much sweeter. She would drink deer blood if she had to, or when Shawn wanted to hunt deer. *Can't we just ride them, and kill humans next eve in York?*

No, we are hunting. We will kill the deer and drink their blood. We don't always have to take human blood.

She followed Shawn out into the field and picked the big, brown buck with thick antlers, and ran after it, crashing through the trees and brush, avoiding the branches, staying close to her prey. The deer found a pine needle covered path, perfectly spaced between the trees, and they both accelerated. The buck jumped an old, stonewall, and dashed out into another small clearing. Katherine took this opportunity to launch herself at the deer and bring him down. She rolled the deer by its antlers through the field grass, and then tore at its neck with her blood teeth.

She drank the blood and then stood, wiped her face, and saw Shawn coming to her, deer's blood on his face. It was a hot, humid night; the only sound now was that of the insects. The moon peeked through the slow-moving clouds, and suddenly, Katherine sensed an evil…some other creature, not a witch.

"Can you sense it?" Shawn asked her. "I think it's trying to spy on us."

"Yes! What do you think it is?"

"I think it's a Seerabub. Follow me."

Lucifer sent Seerabubs to the physical world to spy on older guardians that could block the devil from their minds. They were not powerful creatures, but their senses were great, and they made perfect spies for Lucifer. Katherine followed Shawn through the woods. They ran at a reasonable speed, taking the shortest paths toward the Seerabub. The creature had certainly sensed them and was now trying to make its escape.

Shawn increased his speed, and Katherine quickly matched him. Soon, she came within view of the evil creature. The creature was short, close to three feet tall, and had a round, fat belly with grey, sickly, wrinkled skin that folded over itself, short arms and legs, and patches, of course, black hair scattered all over his body. He had a long, crooked nose, sores on his body, and large, thick lips that almost hid his rotted yellow teeth.

The Seerabub was running as fast as his short legs and fat body would allow, but they had caught him, and now his fate was sealed. The creature waddled when he ran and looked comical, climbing over fallen logs. Katherine took to the air, landed in front of him, and struck the Seerabub in the face with her fist, knocking him to the ground.

Shawn came from behind, "You will not escape us, spawn of Lucifer."

The ugly creature got to his feet and shoved a finger in his big nose, pulled a sickening yellow slime from it, and promptly stuck it in his mouth and chewed.

"What foul demon are you?" Katherine said as she wrinkled her nose and brow.

"I am no demon. If I was, you would not be standing here in front of me." The Seerabub spit another foul load to the ground and then scratched under one of his arms. "The vampire Shawn Bryce," the filthy creature spat at Shawn. "Malin is coming, mighty vampire. You remember Malin, don't you? She remembers you. Even now, she gathers her power and prepares a place for you in her dark castle. You will see her in the flesh this time, mighty demon slayer."

"She will never have him, foul beast," Katherine yelled at him. She took Alexa from its sheath. "Say it again, and I will cut that filthy tongue from you."

Katherine took the hilt of her slayer and struck the Seerabub in the face knocking him to the ground again. A deep, bitter coldness came from the creature, grew outward, and surrounded the vampires, ice crystals, and a melancholy formed all around them. Then dark energy went over the beast, so black it created a black hole that no light could escape. As the Seerabub was lost into this black hole, a dark creature grew from it and stood in front of them—a dark warrior of Lucifer. His face was that of a rough man; his skin, scarred and greyish black. His eyes burned red, surrounded by a grey, iron helmet. Dull, iron armor protected his shoulders, elbows, knees, and shins. A large, muscular man that stood eight feet high, he wore grey leather britches that went to his knees. Heartless evil and killing were all he knew. His body was human, but massive, a sturdy looking creature. The beast had wrapped his middle with belts that held an ax and a steel ball on a chain.

Stoic, the monster stood in front of them, holding an enormous broadsword. The iron blade, nicked from use and streaked with old blood. The dark warrior stood, staring at them, and then stretched his powerful body and said, in a deep, booming voice, "Thank you, Lucifer, for giving me this chance to kill vampires. I will kill them in your name." The monster pulled from his wrap a small, steel ball attached to a chain and a stick. He swung the ball over his head while moving toward the vampires.

Katherine felt the ground shake from his weight. Shawn flew at the creature, hitting him square in the chest with his feet, propelling him into the trees.

"Do not play with him!" Katherine shouted. "He's too dangerous."

The monster clumsily got to his feet and stomped back out of the trees and into the clearing, a menacing look on his face. The creature let out a loud, hoarse battle cry. Shawn again flew at the monster, slayer in hand, and delivered a deep cut across the side of the monster's neck. She saw him slow as he swung around the beast. *Why is he moving so slow,* she thought? The dark warrior swung the ball and caught her maker in the head, sending him crashing into the ground, sliding and rolling to a stop, unconscious.

Katherine screamed, drew Alexa, and flew at the monster. She avoided the sword and ball, driving the slayer into the creature's neck, rotating the blade and severing the monster's head from its body. The beast collapsed, turned black as coal, and dark blue flames consumed the body.

Katherine flew to Shawn and rolled him over. His skull was broken, and she frantically tore open her wrist and dripped blood on the wound.

"Can you hear me, my love?"

Shawn's eyes opened, and he mumbled, "Yes, but I have a terrible headache. You are going to have to bury me."

Then she saw him close his eyes and lose consciousness. Gathering Shawn, she flew toward her home and sent a mental message for Thomas to meet her at the house. Next, she sensed Victoria approaching at a fast speed.

Katherine landed by the river and met Thomas. "Go back in the woods and dig a grave," she hurriedly told him. She carried Shawn's limp body into the river, holding him, washing the blood from his face, and tore his clothes from him and washed his body. Victoria arrived and waded into the river.

"What has happened, Katherine?"

"Lucifer's monsters. They won't leave Shawn alone."

"We must get him to ground," a worried Victoria told her.

"I have a grave dug. Follow me."

Katherine took Shawn back into the woods, where they met Thomas.

"This is Thomas, the captain of my guard," Katherine said.

"It is an honor to meet Victoria Kenmare," Thomas quickly replied somewhat nervously. "Warrior angels sing of your battles with the demons."

"That I have heard," Victoria said. "Come, Thomas, help us bury the real Demon Slayer."

Shawn stayed buried for a month. Katherine spent that time with Victoria. They would swim in the river, walk its banks, and talk of the gathering storm.

"Do you remember when we walked this river long ago, looking for Shawn?" Katherine asked, "When we thought he was gone. When we lost Anne and Marilyn to this world."

"Yes, I do, and now you are Queen of the Vampires. With all the responsibility that comes with it. I can still remember when you were a changeling. How do you bear it?"

"I have no choice now, but Michael has hinted that I don't have to spend all my existence being queen. I look forward to those days. I want you to know, Victoria, that a time will come when you will have to stand with me and fight for Shawn. That I know, and that is all I can tell you. You should continue to practice with your slayer."

"Erdin and my angels have told me I must fight evil again. Be careful, Katherine, because they also told me to prepare to rule."

Katherine walked with Victoria in silence. "Did you know that Marilyn watches over Drake in Heaven?"

"Yes, I did. How did Shawn get caught so easily off-guard?" Victoria questioned. "It is surprising that a dark warrior did that to him."

"It was surprising," Katherine replied. "He's slower now for some reason. He has lost strength. And Shawn's future scares me!"

"Together, we must watch out for him," Victoria said. "Lucifer is going to take his vengeance on Shawn. You remember how unbearable it was last time we thought we had lost him. I can still remember that time, the sadness I felt. You and I will be next. Lucifer will come for all of us. That we can be certain of."

Katherine spent that month with Victoria and another with both her and Shawn after Shawn had awakened. Eventually, Shawn and Victoria left, and she went back to being queen.

Chapter Twelve

A cloudy night sky made the waters of the Ijmeer dark. Katherine sat on a bench, looking out over what was now Amsterdam Inlet. A cool breeze blew off the water, pushing her hair back and caressing her neck. She watched the cargo transports float across the water with the soft hum of their anti-gravity engines and the blinking of their locator lights, as they rose to travel inland to their final destinations. Artificially intelligent robots walked the catwalks on the outside of these massive machines, making their repairs. Humans, because of their low population, had finally permitted artificial intelligence into their world.

Katherine had been queen for forty-five years and had accomplished much, built her vampire army as Eos had ordered, and consolidated her power with the ancients. She had ruled wisely, and vampires knew her to be a just queen. Drake had not come to her, but she had come to a shaky truce with her emotions about his death. Now, she waited impatiently for his return. She worried about Shawn. Maybe she had always worried too much about her love.

Katherine found herself in the lower sections of Amsterdam, tracking an elusive evil that would quickly rise to an intense level and then vanish. The last time she had felt darkness of this size, it had come from the Esmanaa demon Charun. The evil had brought her here, and she had brought Alexa. Once before, the darkness brought her to an area of the city and then dissipate, leaving her the fool. It was playing with her, yet she knew it would soon show itself. This time the evil did not subside. Katherine looked down the walkway, with its neat, manicured lawns on each side, through the clump of elm trees, and knew the evil was around the bend…something terrible and wicked was coming.

This evil was Malin, finally showing herself. Now, the fight for Shawn would begin. She was The Tempter, The Succubus, a witch of tremendous power. Malin had taken more souls than any of Lucifer's evil creatures. Katherine drew from all her skills to cloak her mind from this evil, from its influence, but some still sifted through like mill dust from the cracks of the floorboards above.

She shrouded herself from Shawn because she did not want him to come to her rescue. The witch came slowly, walking—taking her time—looking around at the world as she walked, seeing and taking everything in. It was a commanding walk---she maintained a presence as if nothing could hurt her. Closer, she came, with her fog of evil, and it descended on Katherine. She could sense Malin's voice on the periphery of her defenses:

A truce, for now, vampire.

Malin was a tall creature with a woman's perfectly proportioned body, reddish-black lips, creamy white skin, eyes black as night, dark eyebrows, and long, wavy black hair that fell over her shoulders and to the small of her back. She was beautiful and wore black leather pants and black leather boots that ended above her calves. A dark green blouse, she wore that showed the top of her creamy white breast, with a grey hooded cloak, long and flowing, and at her side was a short sword the blade black as night. Katherine drew Alexa from her back and laid it next to her.

Finally, the witch strolled up to the bench and said, "May I sit, Queen of the Vampires?"

"If you must."

They looked at each for a long time, trying to penetrate each other's defenses—neither was able.

"It looks like we're going to have to talk, Queen." Malin then gave a loud, mocking laugh. "Queen, and only six hundred years old. That is a nap for me, guardian."

"Old enough to take care of you, Malin," Katherine spat back. Never had she felt such evil.

"I can sense the power in you," Malin said. "Michael must have been kind to you. And I'm sure Shawn had something to do with it." Again, Malin gave a loud laugh. "I know you are nothing but a whore vampire, and you know it, too. Did you fuck Michael for your power? You fucked the captain of your guard. All vampires are whores."

"Why are you here, Malin?" Katherine asked.

"I am here to take Shawn for my own and to kill you, mighty vampire queen. You and the Kenmare. Shawn will suffer for a thousand years for what he did to Lucifer's demons."

"You will never have Shawn," Katherine hissed back. "I will drive you from this world. You will not have that beauty for long."

Malin let out a loud, sickening laugh, and then turned and sneered at Katherine. "Stupid vampire. Look to the stars. It is already foretold he will be mine. You will never have him again. He will be mine for an eternity, and I will make sure of it."

"You lie and deceive, filthy witch!"

"No, it's the angels that have deceived. Michael did not tell you the whole truth."

Never had Katherine felt such evil coming from a living creature.

"As your strength increases, his lessens. Michael and Eos will only allow so much power in this world for vampires. You take Shawn's strength. You are a leech to him, and soon he will be weak enough for me to take to Hell."

"Shawn will always be strong enough to defeat the likes of you. I will make sure of that. Lucifer didn't tell you the whole truth, either. Many powerful angels will come for Shawn, and your time as a witch will be over."

Malin sneered at Katherine. "Did Shawn tell you that we know each other very well? I have been in his mind over the years, I have shown him my beauty, and he has felt lust for me. Did he tell you that? I am the Succubus, and I have made Shawn's cock hard."

"I believe our truce is over, Malin."

"Is it, vampire?"

Katherine reached for Alexa. Malin gave a laugh and brought her sword down on top of it. Alexa's metal rung with contempt, and then Malin pushed a dark energy wave at Katherine. The energy wrapped around her threw her up into the air and out over the freshly mowed lawn, where she skidded to a stop. Katherine quickly got to her feet. Malin took to the sky, heading west, and Katherine followed with Alexa in hand, using her speed to stay with the witch.

Katherine saw her land on a signal platform at the top of a high tower. Malin was going to make a stand and had found suitable ground for her fight. Katherine landed and watched the witch walk along the edge of the platform, facing her. A strong wind tore at their hair and clothing. The twinkling lights of the city spread out for miles in the night. Standing against the wind, Katherine kept the witch in her sight.

"Mighty Queen, are you good with your slayer? You had better be. I was going to let you live a while longer, but I see that won't be possible."

Malin drew her sword and flew at Katherine. She clenched her slayer and came to the witch. They clashed and flew by each other, both turning to advance again, striking blades, sending sparks into the air, the sharp clank of striking metal ringing through the night. Malin was skilled in how to use a sword. They fought back and forth until Katherine saw an opening and sliced the witch across the thigh.

Malin fell back and circled Katherine. "You are a powerful creature that is for sure." Malin then yelled to the night, "Father, send me more power." The witch again advanced on Katherine, striking at her, parrying, quicker now, and then turned, driving her sword into Katherine's stomach. She stumbled backward, clutching her wound. Quickly, Katherine regained her senses. No weakness could be shown to this witch.

Malin came at Katherine, struck her in the face with the hilt of her sword, cutting her, and then swung with her free fist, knocking her backward from her feet. Katherine flew up and at the witch, swinging her sword and driving the witch back. She feigned and drove Alexa into Malin's stomach. Malin screamed and fell back, holding her wound with a bloody hand.

Malin again started to walk a circle around Katherine. "How much power has that pig Michael given you, whore vampire?"

"Enough to make your time in this world short," Katherine yelled over the howling wind.

Katherine flew at Malin with blinding speed; their swords met. Katherine twirled and drove her slayer through Malin's chest, pushing her back onto the platform. She withdrew her slayer and struck Malin's face with the hilt.

"I told you, Malin, you wouldn't be beautiful for long." A massive pulse of energy blew Katherine off Malin, and she slid to the edge of the platform. Again, Malin lifted into the air and headed west.

Katherine rose to her knees, spitting blood from her mouth. She tore her shirt open and saw her stomach wound healing. "Thank you, Michael. I will take the fight to this witch in your name."

Katherine took to the air and flew out over the Atlantic, following Malin. After some time, she came within sight of the witch. Straining to fly faster and approaching from above, she slowly closed on her enemy. Malin suddenly turned and threw dark energy at her. Katherine barely avoided the dark blue ball, but the second one hit her with great force, sending immense shock waves through her, knocking her senseless. Her instincts made her roll herself into a ball as she lost control and fell from the sky.

Hitting the ocean like a bullet, she traveled a fair distance below the surface. Dazed, she allowed herself to float in the dark, cold water, felt the intense chill of the current pushing her. Allowing her body to steady itself, she went to the light and heard the angels singing. They sang to Eos that the great battle between the guardians and Malin had begun. The angels asked for the help of The Mother for the queen. Her senses slowly came back to her, and she felt the cold water rose upward and broke the surface like a phoenix, rising from the sea to fight again.

Katherine knew she could not kill this witch now and send her evil life force back to Lucifer. The Tempter could only be killed at The Gates of Hell.

But, she would not allow Shawn to be a pawn for Eos and the devil. Onward she flew, following Malin to the City of York. The city grew after the Great Dark Age, thirty miles to the west of the ruins of old New York City.

The Apocalypse had destroyed New York City, and seawater claimed the city and Long Island. Now, humans took underwater tours of the devastation that once was New York City.

The sun was now starting to rise at her back, and she flew over the coast of Old Virginia and descended into the forest to take cover. It was a rainy day, and she heard the sharp crack of the lightning echoing through the valley. Fog was gathering in the flatlands below. Cutting tree branches from the side of the hill with Alexa, she made a shelter to escape the light.

She huddled in her shelter, rain dripping on her, soaking her torn clothing, running down her face. The water washed her cuts as they healed; her hair was wet, long, and stringy, and clung to her face. Her stomach wound was healing, yet it left her weak. She heard a deep rumble of thunder in the distance, huddled, and listened to the hard rain hitting the forest leaves.

That eve she would go north, find Malin, and finish her. She thought of contacting Shawn but wanted him nowhere near Malin, so she shrouded herself. Unfortunately, Victoria was with Shawn, and Renee was too far away.

"I will kill this witch myself," she whispered. "Michael, give me the strength." Katherine huddled in her shelter, stripped her wet clothes from her body, and cleared the leaves away, exposing bare earth. She dug the dirt from the ground, making an area to lie in, and packed it on her stomach wound. Lying on the moist, bare earth, she pulled damp dirt and leaves around her. She listened to the roar of the rain-swollen creek off in the distance and felt the healing energies of The Mother penetrating her.

Katherine knew she would heal faster than Malin. She had severely hurt Malin because of her arrogance. Evil always came with vanity, but Malin would not make this mistake again. Sleep finally took hold of her, and now she floated in the light, listening to the warrior angels singing their songs of war. Waking the next eve, she cleaned herself in the creek and acquired clothing along the way to York.

Katherine rented a hotel room, took another eve to rest, and regained her strength. Now she was searching the city for the witch. Malin did not have the power to hide entirely, but she was still an extremely dangerous foe. There was a vague sense of her, and Katherine followed it to the street level of the city. Dark warriors were with her now, no doubt there to help her until she regained her strength.

Katherine prowled the ground level of the city where people with little money lived or where people who wanted a different life than work and families. A place where all types of entertainment were for sale. Where humans came to have their fun. The criminal element also operated from here. Buildings at this level were no more than ten stories high and filled in the areas between the high towers. The structures were of many different shapes, and the exterior walls were made of hardened, colored plastics and glass. Wide walkways were where the streets used to be. Trees had moved in everywhere, along with parking lots for the aircars.

The rain had stopped, and a light, white mist rose from the warm pavement. A brisk wind blew against her face, and the scattered puddles reflected the brightness of the city. Hologram advertisements played out everywhere in this city. People sat on stools at food counters and ate their different flavored noodles. She heard the hum of the aircars and watched the different colored symbols bounce in front of the human's faces and then dissipate. Times were changing again, and now she heard a new language---a world language---humans spoke along with their symbols.

Katherine traveled the walkways, projecting her powerful senses outward, trying to find Malin. Then she felt something different again, a human that knew what she was. She sensed a woman from a block back following her and knew The Mother was with her. Over the centuries, humans began developing a basic set of psychic abilities, and sometimes vampires spoke of this. The human was an old woman, had the gift of seeing, and knew Katherine was a vampire. The woman wanted relief. For Katherine to take her blood and end her tiring life. Katherine stepped into an alley, floated up into the darkness, and came down behind the woman.

"What is it, old woman? What do you want?" she asked.

The woman was with thin, grey hair, a waxiness to her skin, and a slight hunch. Katherine saw her wrinkled face and hands; dark purple veins protruded through her thin, waxy skin, and hair grew from her ears. On the rare occasion when Katherine was close to an old human, their look would surprise her. *How quickly humans' age,* she would think. *What a burden for them.* The shroud that hid Eos from the world lifted, and she felt the power of Eos. The Mother had found this old woman and led her here. A blank look came over the woman's face, and Eos spoke through her:

"Greetings, Katherine. All of Heaven is watching your fight with evil Malin. The angels watch a great battle between good and evil. They sing for your victory. I have brought you renewed strength in this woman's blood. Take her blood, give her relief of this world, and give yourself strength. Drive Malin back down Hell's Hole. The Tempter does not have the strength now to succeed with this attack, and she can't be killed here."

"Do you know where Malin is?" Katherine asked.

"She is close and is gathering dark warriors for her next attack. You have hurt her. She has lost some of her power. This is my world, and I will not let her heal quickly. I must leave now. Remember what I have said."

Katherine watched the woman as her natural expression came back to her face. She saw the woman become momentarily unsteady. She reached out and took hold of the woman.

"Are you all right, woman?" Katherine asked as she steadied the woman and guided her to a bench. "Let's sit, and you can tell me how you know of me and what you want from me."

"A voice came to me and said that it was the angel Eos, and would show me, Heaven. She wanted me to give you my blood so I can leave this world for good. I'm tired! I know you are a vampire. Please, take my blood, and help me go to Heaven!"

Katherine gathered the frail old woman in her arms. She held her gently and stroked her dry, gray hair. "Tell me, old dame, is it the body that makes you want to leave, or the spirit?"

"It's my body. It always hurts and does not work anymore. When I was young, I would dance all night. Now I am tired. I loved life and I loved Paul, but he died twenty years ago. I'm ready, vampire."

"As you wish," Katherine whispered. "Close your eyes so you can see Paul."

Katherine's mouth went to the old woman's neck. She took her blood, laid her gently on the bench, rolled up her raincoat, and placed it under the woman's head. She could feel her power return…a surprise waiting for Malin. Katherine wiped the old woman's blood from her mouth, and now she could sense Malin.

Katherine flew quickly to the nearest tower and stopped midway up on a shopping terrace. She went to a deserted area, leaned out over the railing, searched the city, and found The Tempter, three miles away at ground level. Unsheathing Alexa, she flew straight and true to begin the fight once again.

The humans knew this area as Old York, the first of the city built at the end of The Great Dark Age. The buildings were low, no more than six stories high. The humans had made them with cement and brick. Materials no longer used in this age. She walked the old street, sensed the dark energy, and saw pools of black, thick liquid splattered down the road. The evil liquid bubbled and a dark warrior formed and rose from the pool.

The monster moved toward her, large black nostrils snorting. The dark warrior was eight feet high, with an ugly look, and held a broadsword six feet in length. Katherine flew at the monster, her speed allowing her to avoid the mighty blow from his sword. She pivoted in air and severed his head from his body. The dark warrior shriveled in upon itself turned black as coal, and dark blue flames consumed it.

Another rose from a black pool and advanced toward her. Again, she moved with speed, took the monster's leg, and as he fell, she plunged her slayer into his chest. More dark warriors came at her, and she fought them, dodging or warding off their powerful blows with Alexa. She killed eight of these dark warriors, and, finally, they stopped coming.

Then she heard Malin's mocking laughter and watched her float to the ground, a short distance from her and sword in hand. A weakened Malin still bore her wounds from their last meeting. Katherine could feel the dark energy surrounding her; it was Lucifer, trying to overcome The Mother's power, trying to heal the witch as fast as his evil could.

"Did that tire you, vampire, or was it a little warm-up for you?" Malin asked with an evil laugh. "Lucifer told me that filth Eos has visited you. By the way, the old woman will never make it to Heaven. Eos and I have known each for thousands of years, and we have fought many times.

"And I'm sure she won," Katherine hissed.

"Close, but not quite."

Suddenly, Katherine felt Malin rush her senses with her despicable evil. Katherine quickly strengthened her defenses, felt the dark evil probe at the edge of her mind, trying to find a way through, trying to find an opening.

"You will not get at my mind Malin," she assured, "Michael has made sure of that, and, as you say, The Mother has helped. You are going to have to fight your way out of this."

"Will I, vampire? The angels have given you an advantage this time."

"We will finish this here," Katherine hissed.

"You will lose Shawn! That I promise! Destiny has foretold this. Remember, filthy vampire, the more the angels heal you and give you power, the weaker Shawn becomes." Malin gave a deep, evil laugh. A mocking laugh. "Lucifer, send me your strength, for I will need it tonight."

Malin drew her sword, and Katherine readied hers. They flew

at each other—clashed—sparks flying from their swords. The meeting of their bodies and swords threw both off, spinning them into a building, brick and mortar falling to the street. Katherine quickly regained her balance and flew at Malin, giving her a deep cut across the side. Malin screamed and pivoted, cutting Katherine across the thigh.

They stood, swinging their swords, both caught in a desperate fight, the sounds of battle echoing through the empty streets. Katherine evaded Malin's sword and moved in, striking the witch in the face with the hilt of her sword, then turned and gave her a slice across her neck. They fought on; Malin sliced Katherine's stomach with her sword and cut her across her face. Katherine fought back and found an opening, driving Alexa through Malin's stomach and out her back.

Katherine turned her attention to Malin's arms and delivered deep cuts. Slowly, Malin was losing her ability to swing her blade. Suddenly, her left arm lost all strength and hung at her side, putrid blood dripping from her fingers and forming small, brownish-red pools on the ground. Katherine could see the anxiety starting to show on Malin's face.

They circled each other, both bleeding from their wounds. Katherine felt the blood from the cuts to her face and neck, trickling down her back and chest. She knew Malin was trying desperately to remove her head. They circled each other, both looking for an opening. Malin moved in, striking at Katherine's neck, and Katherine blocked the blow with Alexa. Katherine feigned and parried, moving in, and, with great force, swung her sword, severing Malin's right hand. She heard the clanking of Malin's sword as it hit the pavement, her severed hand still holding the hilt.

Malin screamed, "You filthy whore! Father, protect me!"

Katherine could see that Malin was helpless, having no way to swing her sword. She circled the witch, took hold of Alexa's hilt with both hands, gripped it tighter, and prepared to take the witch's head. Suddenly, Eos was in her head:

You cannot kill her!

Powerful energy surrounded the witch. An explosion of dark energy threw Katherine back and wrapped her in black, elastic fibers that held her to the ground. Slowly it tightened on her, and she could feel the elastic threads squeezing her, burning her, trying to slice her apart. Desperately, with all her strength, she moved Alexa, and the slayer burned a bright white, melting through the fibers. A badly hurt Malin staggered and took to the air, flying south to make her escape. Katherine slowly freed her sword hand and continued to slice at the fiber, but the process was slow, and Malin widened her escape.

Suddenly, Anne's voice resounded in her head:

Use the power Michael has given you. Shapeshift into a vapor.

"How do I do that?" Katherine pleaded.

Think of what you want to become, and will it. You have the ability.

Katherine thought of it, became a white mist, drifting out of the trap, and then retook a physical form. She collapsed and lay on the ground, holding her stomach wound and hoping the energy to chase Malin would return.

Anne's voice again spoke in her head:

You must get up and go after Malin. Kill the witch in this world, and you will save Shawn. She is helpless now. Lucifer has used what energy he could to save her. Get up, Katherine. She is going to Hell's Hole!

"What of Eos!" Screamed Katherine.

Go and save Shawn!

Katherine rolled and got to her knees, gathered her thoughts and energy, and then slowly stood. Her many cuts lay open; her vampire body was concentrating on healing her stomach wound and stopping her bleeding. She rose slowly into the air, Alexa in hand. Katherine had badly hurt Malin and could easily sense where she was. Malin was headed south and not at an impressive speed.

Katherine followed and slowly gained on the witch. Malin was headed for Shenandoah and the cave that held the new Hell's Hole. The witch had weakened her, but Katherine flew after her, trying to catch Malin. Katherine used all of her energy and slowly closed on Malin, soon coming within sight of her, but it was not enough, and Malin landed on the forested hill that led to the cave. Malin, covered in blood, stumbled her way toward the entrance of Hell's Hole. Katherine landed behind her, and Malin turned and screamed, "Filthy, relentless whore! Lucifer, save me!"

Dark energy again formed and came at Katherine, and she shielded herself with Alexa, but again, it threw her back. Malin entered the cave, and Katherine quickly got to her feet in pursuit. Into the coal-lined black cave, she went, making it to the large chamber in time to see Malin fall into the pool of thick, red liquid. Her legs and body sunk into the liquid, and she hissed at Katherine.

"You think you have won, but you haven't. I am still alive. The power your angels gave you through this fight only weakens Shawn more. You and Shawn will see me again. That I promise, guardian!"

Katherine cautiously walked toward the pool, Alexa raised and glowing. She had suffered many wounds from Malin's blade, but she would kill Malin if she decided to stay and fight.

"Where are you going, Malin? Stay and face me, and we will end this now. I thought you were going to kill me, mighty witch."

"Enjoy your victory! It won't last long." Malin then pulled the red liquid over her face and retreated into Hell's Hole. The pool started to swirl and boil. Ghouls came to the surface and crawled out of the pool, hoisting their large bellies and long arms with razor-sharp nails. She had seen these creatures before, long ago, but tonight she did not have the strength to face them. Katherine turned, flew out of the cave, and made her way home to Dalton. Weak and flying slowly, she lifted the shroud that kept Shawn from knowing where she was. She then sensed him coming from Dalton, toward her; soon, he was alongside her and scooped her into his arms.

"I fought Malin and drove her from this world," Katherine said weakly. "I gave her a good beating."

"It looks like she got some good licks on you, too," Shawn said.

"Why didn't you contact me? I am disappointed that you did not. Look at yourself, all beaten up like this. I could have helped you."

"I could not have you near Malin. She wants you! Malin wants to take you away from me! It was a great victory for the angels, my love, but I do not think it was a victory for you and me. She could not be killed here, and I'm sure she will be back."

Shawn took her home and buried her. Katherine stayed in the ground for a month and then resumed her duties as Queen of the Vampires.

Chapter Thirteen

S hawn woke in a snow-covered field surrounded by a pine forest. The sun was starting its short rise from the horizon. The snow sparkled on the tops of the trees, and the scent of pine filled his sensitive nose. This world was frozen, white snow draped over everything here. It had been five years since Katherine had driven Malin down Hell's Hole. Malin was still a part of Shawn's existence, though he hid it from everyone. Malin sometimes would come into his dreams and taunt him. This time he let his guard down, and it had happened in an instant—she was able to enter his mind. Malin had led him far north, into the District of Ontario, near the shores of the Hudson Bay, where he finally fought her off. There was no poison this time for her to use to keep her grip on his mind.

He stood and brushed the snow from his body, saw the shimmer that was Malin's spirit, and then watched as she formed into a ghost, floating and resembling what she looked like when she was still of this world. She was strong again—he could tell—and so he quickly threw his defenses up to keep her out of his head.

"Why do you keep doing this to me, Malin?" he yelled.

I wanted to be with you, at least in spirit. Soon you will be mine. Lucifer is going to let me keep you. He promised me. All I have to do is kill Katherine and Victoria.

"If you show yourself again in this world, I will finish the job that Katherine started," Shawn yelled at the apparition.

Will you, vampire? Are you sure you have the strength for that?

Have you asked your Herit why you grow weaker?

"I have," Shawn raged back. "The power Michael gave me was not mine to keep. Guardian power comes from Michael, and he decides where it goes. I still have enough to take care of you."

Maybe you have it now, but soon, you won't. Then we will see. Your angels take your strength from you and give it to Katherine. Why do you want to be like them? Come to Hell's Hole and join me. I will keep my physical form so you can have me. We can live together forever.

"What makes you think I would ever come to you? I will never accept Lucifer's evil. I will kill all of Lucifer's dark angels and any mortal that harbors his evil. That is what I am Malin. That is what I have become and will always be. You're a cocky witch this morning. What is it you hide from me?"

Have you heard from that disgusting witch daughter of yours?

A chill went through Shawn, as cold as the air that surrounded him. He could not sense Jessamine, and he realized she had disappeared. "What have you done, filthy witch!"

I have done nothing. I have no physical form. Your pathetic Mother sent her to the cave and allowed a witch to trapper her their. You remember the cave. It was where the demons would have had you, if it wasn't for that whore, Katherine. Now it is up to you to save Jessamine. To use those powers, the angels gave you, pathetic vampire. You will see me soon, Demon Slayer.

Shawn stood in the snow, alone, with his fear, and heard her mocking laughter echo in his head as she left. His mind was racing—this did not make sense. But for now, he would have to take shelter and wait out the day.

The sky was a vivid blue, cloudless, the sun low, peeking above the tops of the pine trees. A deep cold had settled over Hudson Bay, and the snow crunched loudly under Shawn's feet when he moved. He lifted himself above the snow, went toward the pine forest, and huddled under the thick pine trees, covering himself with pine branches and fell into a troubled sleep. Shawn projected his thoughts to Herit.

What has happened to Jessamine? Why did The Mother allow

her to be trapped in that cave?

Drifting, he waited, and then felt Herit's presence and heard plainly:

Go to the Penn cave. A warlock holds Jessamine captive. The warlock thinks he has power over Jessamine, but he doesn't. The Mother needed her to be a distraction while she is contacting one of her witches, and you must be a part of this deception. Do not go into the cave, for the poison that had you long ago waits for you in the cave. Then you must go to New Chicago, and meet with this witch. She is a Mother's witch, and over time, The Mother has given her strength and has prepared her for your visit. Her name is Gwyn Savarin, and she runs Packard Industries, a large off-world mining business in New Chicago. I cannot tell you the purpose of this visit. Eos would not say, but be careful, Shawn, as the final preparation for Eos's plans will start there.

Shawn retrieved his slayer at Dalton and then flew to a wooded area four miles from the old Penn cave. Looking out over the valley, he saw, on the other side, slightly up the hill, the entrance to the cave. He could barely sense Jessamine. The earth hid her from his senses, but he knew she was there. The warlock was up the hill in the woods, gathering herbs for his poisons, and Shawn could sense him quite well. He cloaked himself so the creature would not be aware of his presence.

Humans had discovered titanium in this area and drilled a mine twenty miles to the east, only one of five allowed on earth. The humans could not resist the cheap, abundant titanium, and this was the reason Lucifer moved Hell's Hole. Shawn lifted and traveled slowly across the valley, twenty feet from the surface, while always sensing the warlock. Light snow covered the field grass and trees. It was a crisp, moonlit night, and soft light reflected from the ice forming at the edges of the stream that made its way through the center of this valley.

No humans lived anywhere near here. Long ago, they had gone to one of the cities of towers. Drawing his slayer, he shot up the hill with blinding speed, came upon the warlock, and dark energy met him. Once again, Shawn felt the power of The Mother come from deep inside him to protect him. He hardened himself, and the energy wave washed over him. Quickly, he regained his senses and saw the warlock pull a silver dagger and a handful of powder from a black satchel. The creature threw the dust at him, and it exploded into a horrible vapor that smelled of ammonia. The fog quickly dissipated, and Shawn started his advance.

The warlock pointed the knife at Shawn. "Attack again, vampire, and your heart will feel the pain of my blade."

The warlock wore baggy, dark blue pants with black leather boots, a black satchel at his side, and had a large, bulbous nose. His red, loose shirt opened to his stomach, and red symbols, painted with berry juice, covered his chest to protect him from the forces of good in this world. The warlock only recently came from the pool inside the cave. Another energy ball and Shawn fell to the ground as it went over him. He flew at the filthy beast, avoided his dagger, and drove his slayer through its chest. As the warlock crumpled to the ground, Shawn took his head.

Then he sensed Jessamine standing behind him. He turned and questioned, "You were not a hostage?"

She smiled, winked at him, and held her finger to her lips. "Not here, Father. Follow me." Jessamine took to the air, and Shawn followed. They flew south, and Jessamine landed in a park next to the James River, in the city of Richmond. Humans had destroyed Richmond many times over in its long history, but now it was a quaint little city with many shops and no high towers.

Jessamine gave Shawn a solid hug, kissed him on the cheek, and then he felt the force of The Mother surround them. She stepped back and said, "For secrecy, how are you, Father? It's good to see you."

"I'm fine, Jessamine. What is this all about?"

"The Mother needed to hide what she was doing from Lucifer, and this was the best way. Eos has prepared a witch for you. You must go to her, and she will tell you what Eos expects of you. Be careful, for Lucifer cannot know about this witch. Not just yet, anyway. Soon, Father, the battle will begin, and this witch will help save you in the end."

"Herit has told me about this witch. Time is growing short, Jessamine. Malin will keep coming, and The Mother has made sure of it."

Shawn left Jessamine, made his way north, and arrived a day later in New Chicago. He walked the wide walkway of a high tower on a tier lined with large buildings used for commerce as well as small shops that sold gifts made especially for the wealthy. This tier was high above the city, and the wealthy came here to work, run their business empires, and then leave for their country homes. Only the rich lived in the countryside at this age. It had been a chilly day, but now twilight was advancing across the horizon. The lights of the aircars were just starting to brighten the sky.

The witch he came to meet turned out to be extremely rich and was from a powerful business family. It was the end of the human's workday, and workers were making their way home. Traveling on small, personal, hovering transports that they stood on, they held a rail and steered using their nanochips. They went to air transports that would take them off this terrace and to their homes on other terraces.

Shawn made his way to the lobby of The Packard Building, located on the north edge of the terrace, and now he watched the humans leave for the evening. Sitting on a light green lobby sofa, he waited for Eos's witch. His wait wasn't long; she came around a corner, out into the lobby, walking with a powerful stride. She was the head of this business—that was obvious. An entourage followed, handing her a communicator through which she gave orders through speech and symbols appearing in the air, and then disappearing as she went by.

High power Shawn sensed in her. Suddenly, Gwyn turned her head and looked directly at him—she had detected him, too. The witch knew what he was, and then he felt excitement from her, and a smile came to her face. Shawn nodded at her, and she kept going out the door, out onto the walkway.

Gwyn wore a long, form-fitting grey skirt with a short, grey business jacket, a small amount of cleavage showing. Her hair was auburn, long, and flowed down her back. She was a striking woman that looked to be in her mid-thirties and walked with a steady stride. The witch was powerful and had the mark of The Mother on her neck. Few Mother witches were considered worthy of wearing this symbol.

Shawn followed her outside, and she turned briefly and smiled at him again. Standing and watching with his hands in his pockets, he smiled back and watched her leave in an aircar. Slowly, he strolled to a secluded area, taking in the sights of the neighboring towers, then rose into the sky and followed the witch out into the country. Soon he came to an estate and landed in woods on the outskirts of a large, perfectly manicured lawn. He would take his time before approaching the house, projecting his senses outward and taking in everything. Sensing and listening, he could feel no evil, only good.

The witch lived in a large, rambling two-story house. Everywhere on her home were lights, casting their beams on her dew-covered lawn. A dim candle burned in most windows. *How strange,* Shawn thought. He sensed two servants in the front of the house, guards at the sides, and the witch in the back.

Slowly, he lifted into the air and approached a back terrace where he felt the witch Gwyn. He was careful to avoid the two human guards patrolling the grounds of her estate. The patio was the only part of the house that was dark. Floating across the brick terrace, he strongly sensed the witch inside, and now he stood looking through a large sliding glass door. A cool wind blew, and he heard the rustle of the leaves. The glass door slid open, and he probed the room with his senses and entered. A curtain blew in, and he heard the tinkle of wind chimes. The rustle of papers left on a table. The room was dim, and he felt Gwyn strongly.

He walked slowly into the room, approached a sitting area, turned the corner, and saw Gwyn sitting at a table and mirror, brushing her hair. Her skin glowed in the soft light, her lips were pink and wet. She turned, looked at him, and smiled.

"Greetings, vampire. I have been waiting and preparing for a long time for you to come. And tonight, you have slowly made your way to me. I know how careful vampires are, how they love stealth, and why they live in the shadows."

"Greetings to you, witch."

"So, you are the vampire Shawn Bryce, Demon Slayer. The angels sing of your battles. It is an honor to meet you."

"I wouldn't go that far. I was tricked into most of it."

"The angels trick us all, Shawn," Gwyn revealed as she stood and walked toward him. She wore a long, light green silk robe that barely hid her female form. Her eyes sparkled an emerald green, and they drew him in. She stood in front of him and brushed her fingers over his cheek. "Neither warm nor cold--guardian. Yes, the angels trick us all, and tonight they again want something from you, Demon Slayer."

"What do you mean, witch? What is The Mother up to?" Shawn asked as he felt energy entering his head. He quickly mustered his defenses and fell back from her, watching the expression on her face turn. He felt energy and power form in her, far more than any witch of this world could gather. Stepping back further, he held his hand in front of his eyes as the bright light formed around the witch and then left her to hover in front of her. The brightness engulfed the room—he could barely see. His defenses were quickly brushed aside, and power took over him, a loud voice resonating in his head as his eyes immediately became used to the light.

It is good to be with you again. I am sure you remember me.

"I remember you, Eos. I remember your kindness, your company. The bliss you provided for me."

Do you remember the power I put in you?

His brief time with Eos quickly flooded his memory, and that memory suddenly came back to him. "I remember now and sometimes I feel it." Shawn glanced at Gwyn, and she stood frozen, not an expression on her face.

This power has lain dormant in you all these years. Soon this power will come forward at the precise time you need it. I will not leave you defenseless, remember that. When the time comes, you will have strength. You must make Gwyn a vampire. When you do this, you will lose your vampire powers. You will again have the strength of a changeling. Then Malin will come.

"You always wanted Malin to have me, and now you are making sure of it."

Yes, I always have. The chance to make sure The Tempter never walks the physical plane again is at hand. Guardians must kill her at the gates of Hell, at her dark castle. The spell I created only allows guardians to do this, and then she will never walk the physical plane again. The witch that you give your power to will turn the tide and help save you. Make her a vampire, so she can help Katherine and Victoria kill Malin. Change this powerful witch and teach her how to be a vampire. She will be a force to equal Katherine's—Lucifer and Malin will know nothing of it. While Jessamine was at the cave, I placed a powerful spell around this witch. You can talk about coming events only with Gwyn. Lucifer and Malin will not know. I wish you success, and the angels again will sing of your deeds.

The light slowly dissipated, and then it condensed around Gwyn, went into her, and disappeared. The witch's eyes came alive. Drifting above the floor, he moved back, away from the woman. Shawn stared at her, and he sensed the witch The Mother wanted him to change. What kind of woman was she? What kind of witch? He watched her, pondering what The Mother had told him.

"You have been with The Mother?" Gwyn asked.

"Yes, I have," Shawn replied. He dropped his defenses, allowing Gwyn to come rushing in; she smiled at him and allowed him to enter her mind.

Floating toward her, he embraced her, felt her body, looked into her emerald eyes. Smelling her soft neck, Shawn slowly pierced her skin with his teeth, allowing only a small amount of blood into his mouth. Her head went back, and he tasted her to learn of her. Visions of when she was a young girl, before The Mother came to her, flooded his mind. Shawn floated back from her and left her, staring at him in bewilderment.

"I thought you were going to make me a vampire," Gwyn whispered.

"Not just yet," he said. "Are you a powerful witch?"

"I am."

Shawn watched Gwyn lose form and turn into a drifting vapor—a white, misty blanket flowing across the floor. She reformed across the room and stood, smiling at him.

"And, you still need my strength?"

"I will. I see into your soul. You have opened yourself to me. Now I know why the angels take these risks with you."

Shawn watched her lift above the floor and drift toward him. He took Gwyn in his arms, Shawn pulled her close and brushed her hair back from her face. He kissed her, taking his time, feeling her lips, and again he pierced her neck with his blood teeth and drank.

"If I change you, you will be mine for a hundred years, and I will do with you what I want," he whispered in her ear.

"I understand, vampire. I will be yours, and you may do with me what you wish. Shawn, I don't think the hundred years will be all at one time, though."

"Do you drink?" He asked as he healed her puncture wounds.

"Yes, I'm a businesswoman, and we all drink."

"Good, that's the first requirement. Put something on and follow me."

Shawn walked to the terrace and lifted into the night sky, stretched outward, pointed his hand toward New Chicago, and flew at a reasonable speed back to the city. Following the outskirts of the city, he flew north and looked back to see if the witch was following him. Gwyn was flying just behind him and having no problems keeping up.

Shawn came to a secluded area on the northern fringes of the city, next to Lake Michigan, his destination—a small vampire bar located in the shadows down a small, deserted street. Gwyn landed next to him, and he sensed that she was not afraid of this place.

"This is a good place for a drink and some talk. I know the owner, a fine vampire. His name is Jermaine, and he is the changeling of the vampire Rebecca McCall. She is the head of the other family in the Herit Covenant."

"Will they allow me inside?"

"If you're with me, they will. And Jermaine is here tonight. Sometimes they let me play the piano, but probably not tonight, there is a band playing. Come on."

They walked across the street, Shawn knocked, and the door keeps let them in.

They went to the bar. "How you doing, Jermaine?"

"Shawn! Good to see you. I have a good table for you. You won't be too close to the band. Just the other night, Rebecca was asking about you."

"Was she, I hope she is well. Tonight Jermaine, I would like a bottle of your best red wine," Shawn said as they walked to the table. "This is a friend of mine, Gwyn Savarin."

"A witch? But that's not unusual for you," Jermaine said with a smile. "Glad to meet you, Gwyn."

"Good to meet you," Gwyn replied politely.

They sat at the table, and Shawn poured a large amount of wine in each glass and began the process of learning about the witch Gwyn.

"How old are you, Gwyn?"

"I am almost a hundred years old. My mother was a witch— not a powerful witch, but she taught me the aging spell. When I was twenty-one, The Mother came to me with a special mission. I have prepared my whole life for this quest. I have considerable knowledge of vampires."

"And what is that?"

"They are powerful creatures made by angels to be killers, to fight the devil's spawn. In heaven, they are known as guardians."

"I see. We do like to have fun along the way. Where does your family come from?"

"We come from Montreal. My family is an old and prominent family of that area. We're a large family. A close family."

"If you become a vampire, you cannot have any contact with them. You understand that? Is your family aware you are a witch?"

"My mother knows, and my sister, they both are witches. Eos will allow me to contact my mother and sister only. And when my task is over…"

"You cannot be part of your family business anymore. You understand that, too?"

"I have already resigned, and my sister and cousins will take over the business."

"Will you obey me, Gwyn, even though you will be much stronger than me?"

"Yes, I will obey The Mother and then you. You haven't yet decided to change me, have you? You must do what the angels want. I have spent many years preparing for this."

"We will see. I like to have my fun with the angels," Shawn told her with a wink and a grin.

"I know you are familiar with witches, and your daughter is one, but you have never changed her, either."

"My daughter was also a trick from Eos, and sometimes I think she is a part of her, one and the same, but I love her dearly. And she would not want to be a vampire. She is not a killer. Are you a killer, Gwyn?"

"I hope so!" Gwyn whispered.

Shawn reached out and stroked her cheek. "You are warm."

"Do you like warm women? I see that in you. A taste for warm flesh and blood."

"Do you?" Shawn said.

"Yes, I think I do. You can have me before you change me. I will allow it."

"We'll see. Drink up, beautiful Gwyn. Tonight, we will get to know each other. We will dance and drink, but nothing else will happen."

Shawn took Gwyn to the dance floor, felt her body through her thin silk dress. He could smell her sweet blood and allowed his teeth to slowly penetrate her neck, and again, he took a mouthful of her blood. It was like nectar to him, and it clouded his head like a drug. The Mother thought of everything.

He felt Gwyn's lips touch his ear. He heard her whisper, "If you don't change me, I will have to make you. I'm sorry. The Mother expects it of me."

"I know," Shawn whispered. "The Mother always gets what she wants."

"What was it like to fight demons?" Gwyn asked. "I have heard many stories of your battles. You killed two all by yourself. Their names were Horsa and Charun. Where they as powerful as they say?"

"They were fierce and quick, but their psychic abilities were weak. Michael took that from them. Their evil penetrated every cell in my body, and it took my strength and made me doubt myself. Terrible smell and hallucinations came with them. They were a powerful presence in this world for thousands of years. Now they are gone, and Lucifer is going to make me pay for that."

"I often wondered if I would have had the courage to face them, and the story of Pandora, saving you with her magic, is one of my favorites."

"It probably does make for good stories, but you better have that type of courage. You are going to need it."

Shawn danced and drank with Gwyn for the rest of the evening and then spent three days at her home. He did not change her or make love to her while he was at her home. All he wanted was to know her. Then he took her to his home in the bayou.

It was early evening, and Shawn had just started his night. He made his way to the dining room with his tea and sat with Jessamine and Gwyn while they ate their evening meal. The table candlelight danced off the walls and mingled with the soft lights of the chandelier overhead. He watched them eat, straining to recall what it was like, but he could not remember. It had been a long time since he could remember the taste of food.

"My father likes to watch me eat," Jessamine giggled to Gwyn. "He can't remember what it was like."

"Have you ever tried to eat, Shawn?" Gwyn asked.

"Once, a while back. I was drunk and tried to eat a piece of steak. Unfortunately, it gave me terrible pain in my blood sac, and it came back up coated with blood."

"Yuck!" The Mother's sake!" Jessamine screeched. "See what you have to look forward to, Gwyn?"

"I am aware of what I am getting into. I have studied vampires for many years. I have always admired Shawn's kind."

"I'm going to New Orleans tonight to meet a friend, so the house is yours," Jessamine said.

"Then tonight, Gwyn," Shawn said, "We will go out into the swamp and find those red berries for you."

They walked the trail that traveled west from the estate. The berries that Gwyn was looking for were on this trail. The night was hot, and the air held the moisture like a sponge. There was a full moon and plenty of stars in the clear night sky. The sounds of the insects were loud, but none landed on them, and Shawn could see small beads of perspiration form over Gwyn's soft upper lip. She wore a short sundress that exposed her beautiful legs and bare shoulders, and she walked barefoot. Gwyn was an attractive woman with dazzling green eyes and long, silky auburn hair that fell to the small of her back. Shawn now found himself wanting her.

Quickly, Gwyn turned to catch him looking at her with desire. He felt her warmth, smelled her blood, and desire for her rose in him. Now Gwyn was waiting him out, to have what she and The Mother wanted. The change was only a matter of time.

"I know the mosquitos don't like my blood, but they also have no taste for yours," Shawn said with a slight chuckle.

"A little spell for our friends, but I guess I will have to do another for this heat. Is it much farther?"

"Not too much farther. Around this bend is where I believe I saw them. Here we are!"

"Those are the berries," an excited Gwyn revealed. "They are rare in this world. I haven't had any of these for a couple of years."

"What are they used for?" Shawn asked.

"They are a dry berry, not much juice, only pulp. I dry them more and grind them into dust. A witch, using the right words and a small amount of the dust blown into the face of a human, can make them answer you truthfully. Also, using different words, you can make a human desire you. Unfortunately, the berries don't work on vampires."

"If I change you, will you still have your witch powers?"

"I will cast spells and manipulate energy. Those are the powers I keep from being a witch. I will be a vampire, with all vampire powers, lose my mortal body, drink blood, and I have spent years thinking of it, what it would be like. Do you like being a vampire?"

"I do. It grows on you. You will not spend a hundred years with me, will you?"

"No, Shawn, I will only spend a few years with you." Gwyn reached out and touched his cheek. "There is no time for us to spend many years together. I know that is a strange concept for vampires. If you survive, then I will spend the time with you."

"I remember Pandora had a special skill that came with her powers. She could see into the future. Tell me, witch, do you have a special power?"

"I do have a special power. I can call angels. Would you like me to call one for you? I believe there is an angel that would come if I create a path to this world."

"Yes, call me an angel. I would like to see this."

Gwyn raised her arms to the sky, faced north, south, east, and west, and spoke to the heavens. "Listen, and hear me. Mother, help this angel of heaven come to this world for her long-ago lover." Gwyn then began a chant that she repeated many times. "Spirit of Heaven, feel my beacon. Follow the path I show you. Do this now. Come to him."

The calling of angels took a large amount of Gwyn's energy. Shawn saw the sweat trickle down her face, her hair dampen, small droplets of sweat forming above her soft upper lip as she went on with the chant. Eventually, he saw many points of light starting to form and swirl, coming together, forming one big orb. Tears came to his eyes. It was Marilyn. Shawn hunched over, sobbing as his strength left him, blood running from his eyes and down his cheeks.

Shawn cried out, "It is you! I have waited so long to talk to you again! Are you happy where you are? Someday, I pray we will be together again."

Don't cry, my dear Shawn. I am happy as an angel. We will be together again, not as we were on earth, but we will be together. The angels have a task for you, and then, if fate wants, we will be together. Anne and I went to Michael, pleaded with him to find another way, but he would have none of it. He said The Mother needs you, and that it has already been written in the hall of records. You must follow The Mother, so you have the best chance to survive. You must give your power to this witch and prepare yourself for the evil that is coming for you, my love. But know this. Once your power is gone, Malin will come for you.

"I will give The Mother what she wants, and I give myself to Michael so they can do what they want with me. Maybe they will let me be with you again…someday," Shawn cried and wiped his eyes with the back of his hand. Shawn saw Marilyn's light start to fade.

I must leave now. The witch cannot hold me here any longer. Tell Katherine that Drake will be coming to her soon. Goodbye, my love.

Shawn saw her light fade and disappear. Desperate, he called to her but heard nothing. Gwyn fell to the ground on her knees, body trembling and clothes soaked in sweat. He went to her and picked her up, took her to his couch. He dried her, stripped her of the wet clothes, and waited for her to regain her senses. "Thank you for bringing Marilyn to me. I will give you what you want. I have become tired of all this."

Shawn stood, looking down on her naked body. Slowly, he removed his clothes, lay with her, and made love to her mortal body, not as he would a vampire, but gently because of her human body. He kissed her gently and took small amounts of her blood. When their lovemaking ended, he looked into her green eyes. "Are you ready to say goodbye to your human body?"

"Yes, vampire, I am. When you are weak, I will do everything I can to protect you."

"You will do what The Mother tells you. That I know. Ready

yourself. I have no choice." Shawn penetrated her neck, took her sweet blood, and gave her his blood and strength. He left her unconscious, went to the front yard, and rose into the hot night air, flying a short distance and falling to the ground. Still, he could see like a vampire and hear like one, but he was as he was in the beginning, when Anne first changed him. Gwyn would only stay with Shawn for three years, and through that time, she learned the ways of the vampire and grew in strength. Gwyn was a vampire and witch, needed little blood, and could walk in the daylight. Light of day did not hurt her.

Chapter Fourteen

K atherine was at The Citadel, sitting on the blue throne, staring across the large gathering hall, deep in thought. The picture of her matriarch, Anne, hanging on the far wall, came into focus. She had just finished holding council, listening to the various vampires' grievances or partitions for a favor or financing.

Shawn had consumed Katherine's thoughts lately. He had told her three years ago that Drake would soon come to her, which gave her great excitement. Now Anne and the angels were hiding something from her, and this always unsettled her. Also, three years ago, Shawn had taken the changeling Gwyn, and Katherine had pondered the purpose. Shawn had said little to her of Gwyn's origins. She asked Shawn about Gwyn, but he said he found her in New Chicago, loved her, and that was all he would say about her. Gwyn projected tremendous power, and Katherine could sense witch about her, but she was undoubtedly a vampire. Also, she could not wholly penetrate Gwyn's mental defenses. Most likely, Gwyn was part of The Mother's plan.

Katherine had recently gone to visit Shawn in the bayou, and that was when she learned Gwyn was gone. Jessamine was with Shawn now. Katherine had only seen Gwyn twice before she had disappeared. Shawn had become a weak vampire, something had happened to him; The Mother was rushing Shawn to his fate.

This past week she had sensed Malin again—could sense her there in Amsterdam. She had come back, was playing cat-and-mouse with Katherine, and now Malin was to the north where the airships came to dock. She knew the recent turn of events, and Shawn's weakness was the reasons Malin had returned.

Katherine stood, sighed, and reached for Alexa, whispering to the slayer, "I'm afraid it is time again." She strapped the slayer to her back, floated down the stairs and across the gathering hall, and left The Citadel. Foreboding was her companion as she slowly flew to the docks, floated above the warehouses, and searched the night for Malin. Suddenly, Katherine sensed Malin, knew she was close, and this time, she was not moving. Up and over the warehouses, Katherine floated, seeing the tall towers of the city to the south and hearing the revelry of drunken teenagers hiding somewhere amongst the buildings. The beam from a powerful searchlight traveled past her as she moved slowly above the warehouses. There Malin was, in an alley below. As Katherine came close, Malin walked back down the lane. Katherine moved over the alley and saw Malin a distance away. She floated down to the ground as she drew Alexa.

"I see you have returned, Malin," Katherine said.

"Yes, I have, vampire."

"You don't have your sword with you."

"I will not fight you tonight. I'm sure we will fight again, but not tonight."

"What do you want, Malin?"

"You know what I want. He is weak enough now."

"I told you once. You will never have Shawn."

"I will have him, and I have a lesson for you to show you how easy it will be…Missing anything, vampire? When was the last time you saw the captain of your guard? You know, the vampire you like to fuck."

"What have you done to Thomas?"

"I spent a night with him. He was easy to seduce. I am the Succubus, after all. He desired me and wanted me. And now that Shawn is weak, he will desire me and want me, too. You can find Thomas at the Shenandoah Cave."

"Despicable creature!" Katherine screamed as she hurled herself at Malin. A blue fireball met her and quickly turned into the black, elastic fiber from before, pinning her to the ground. Again, the thread squeezed her and burned her. Malin took to the air as Katherine quickly dissolved into a mist to free herself. Katherine gave chase, going south, but she could not catch Malin.

She now kneeled behind a tree with her head against the trunk, straining her senses toward the cave, feeling the roughness of the bark, the dampness of the dirt and moss on her knees. She heard the cry of the crows overhead. Slightly, she sensed Thomas and Malin through the earth, rock, and coal. Thomas was alive.

Maybe Lucifer was in the cave, but she had to enter and rescue Thomas. A terrible evil came from the cave. *Is the evil masking Lucifer's own?* She did not know. The wind blew through the leaves, and she felt it on her face. She licked her lips and knew she had to take the chance and enter the cave. But Malin was clever, and it could be a trap.

She slowly rose above the ground with Alexa glowing brightly in hand and floated toward the opening of the cave. Weaving her way through the trees, seeing and hearing, sensing everything, and still, she could not feel Lucifer. She came to the black opening made of coal, hesitated, and then slowly entered the cave, floating past the damp, dark walls made of coal brick, hearing the trickle of water seeping through the cracks. Into the large, black chamber, she floated, the one with the red pool in the middle. Burning torches were in the walls, and scattered flames shot from the floor. Malin was standing next to the pool, holding Thomas's arms behind him with only one of her hands. Malin's free fingers grew long, and the nails grew to become sharp, red talons.

"Thomas and I had such a good time last night. Didn't we, pathetic vampire?"

"I am sorry, my queen, I have let you down," Thomas sobbed as he lifted his head to look at her. Blood tears wet his cheeks.

"It's all right, Thomas, you didn't let me down. It's this evil witch. She has gotten hold of your mind."

Katherine changed to her vampire state, grew herself, put on the most menacing face she could. Alexa glowed and hummed as she gripped it tightly. "Let him go," she warned, "You won't make the pool this time."

Malin's long fingers and talons flicked, and in an instant, held Thomas's heart in them. His face turned grey, his veins became prominent, and Malin let him drop into a pile of dirt. Katherine stood stunned, unable to move, and then Malin threw the muscle at her. Thomas's heart bounced off her chest and landed on the black floor of the chamber. The heart burst into dust. All Katherine heard was Malin's mocking laughter.

Dark energy came from the pool, spun around the chamber, ricocheting off the walls, screeching a terrible sound. Then it veered, hitting Katherine in the chest and throwing her back out the cave entrance. Unconscious, she lay in the autumn leaves, and for how long, she did not know, but it could not have been long, for Malin would have killed her.

Katherine went back into the cave, and Malin was not there. She went to the edge of the pool, looked in, and saw faces coming to the surface—terribly distorted faces, screaming in agony. They swirled and then plunged back down Hell's Hole to their terrible fate. Falling back, she whispered, "Souls of the damned." Despair and hopelessness overcame her at the horror she had seen. Katherine quickly backed away from the pool, took her shirt off, and gathered Thomas's dirt to take home, to scatter in the river where he'd loved to fish.

Katherine sat in front of a fire in her personal chambers at The Citadel. Deep in thought, she stared into the fire, listened to its sharp crackling, watched its flames lick at the brick of the fireplace, and drank her wine. It had been a week since losing Thomas, and her guards wanted revenge, but she could not risk it. She would soon need them. Thomas was a strong, decent vampire, and she'd cared for him. He gave her pleasure, took her mind off her troubles, and made her laugh.

Katherine would need a new captain for her guard, someone that was close to her, someone she could trust in these dangerous times. Peter Kenmare fit that part; he had become a powerful vampire thanks to his maker, and he was skilled with a slayer and had studied warfare. This would not please Victoria, seeing how the last captain of her guard died, but she wanted Peter and knew there was a danger for any vampire around her or Shawn. Malin was on Earth again and was here for Shawn.

Katherine's head went up, and she turned away from the fire. Gwyn had finally come to visit her. *What is she doing here?* Her guards had stopped her at the front entrance. Soon, a guard was standing at the door to her chamber—a young, nervous vampire with limited psychic abilities, else he would have sent her a mental message. Katherine stood, sighed, floated to the door, and opened it.

"My apologies, but there is a vampire here to see you," the guard said. "She says it's important."

"Bring her to my chambers, and you need to work on your vampire skills, Ricardo. You are going to need them."

"Yes, my queen."

Soon Katherine sensed Gwyn at her door, and she went to answer. "Come in, what a surprise."

"Thank you for seeing me, my queen. It is an honor. I have something for you that will surely interest you. A gift for my first arrival."

"Come, sit down. I'm surprised to see you. I have some questions for you." Katherine took Gwyn to her sitting area, and they both slipped onto the light green sofa. Soft, low lights burned in the room. Her favorite painting of Shawn, done by Anne, was on her wall and had caught Gwyn's attention. Again, she could not penetrate Gwyn's defenses. Katherine knew she was a vampire, but there was more to her than that.

"Your maker and mine, a beautiful painting of Shawn," Gwyn said. "Who is the artist?"

"It was painted by Anne when Shawn was a hundred years old, just before he left her. More importantly, who are you, Gwyn?"

"Why, I am a vampire. Shawn's changeling, like you."

"Then why aren't you with him? I am your queen, and you must answer me truthfully."

"I am also a Mother's witch and a friend who you will need

soon. I also came to summon an angel, a gift from The Mother. I believe there is an angel you would like to see."

"What angel can you summon?" Katherine said in a quivering voice. Gwyn was opening herself, and Katherine sensed Drake.

Katherine watched Gwyn go to the center of the room, face four directions, and speak a command. Then she started a chant. She heard Gwyn repeat the song, saw her intense concentration, the sweat trickling down her face as she went rigid. Small lights formed and swirled and then came together to create an image of light in her sitting room. Katherine sensed him—it was Drake.

"Drake," she whispered.

I am here, my love. I do not want you to be sad over me. I always knew we would not be together long. The angels and Marilyn always made me aware of this. They told me that living as a vampire was not my destiny.

I knew nothing of this," Katherine said. "The angels did not tell me. Your death was a terrible loss for me."

We will never know each other in the physical world again. Now I will always be Heaven's messenger. I loved you very much, though I tried not to. You saved me and believed in me. Please, Katherine, do not be sad over me. I never wanted to be a vampire, and I didn't want to live in your world if I couldn't go back to space. I have moved on.

And I must, too! Katherine said with her heartbreaking. Now, I must find a way to save Shawn.

That is why I'm here. I have a message from Michael. Prepare yourself. Malin will take Shawn. He says you have known this, but you just wouldn't admit it to yourself. He also commands you to build another vampire army to hold in reserve. Slowly, she felt his spirit fade. *Goodbye for now. Gwyn can't keep me here any longer. I will come and bring Michael's commands. That is how we will be together now.*

"Goodbye, love." Katherine felt him leave, and her heart sank. The spirit was Drake's life force, but in many ways, he was different, and she knew it would never be the same with him. Rushing to a collapsing Gwyn, she helped her to the sofa, held her, and directed her mouth to her neck to give her blood. Gwyn's blood teeth pierced Katherine's neck, and she drank her blood.

"Thank you, Katherine," Gwyn whispered as she reached and stroked her face. Then Katherine felt the soft kiss of her lips, the caress of her tongue, and the taste of the blood on Gwyn's lips.

Gwyn whispered, "We are from the same maker, you and I. You are a powerful vampire, and very attractive, very wanting."

"And you, a mysterious Mother's witch," Katherine replied in a sad, far-off voice.

Gwyn stayed for a few days; they talked and learned about each other. Gwyn taught Katherine about The Mother and her witches, their way of life, and the hatred between The Mother and Malin. Eons ago, when Eos was a warrior vampire on another world, Malin had killed hundreds of her kind and killed Eos' lover. The attacks on them were relentless and finally drove the warrior vampires from the planet. In Lucifer's name, Malin created a dark planet that attacked other worlds and killed hundreds of millions of living souls.

Gwyn told Katherine she was jealous of her because she'd spent a hundred years with Shawn. She admitted to Katherine that she had fallen deeply in love with Shawn in the three years she spent with him. When Gwyn left, she told Katherine that if needed, she lived near The Mother's shrine, and for Katherine, she would be easy to find.

Chapter Fifteen

P erched on a high tower, Katherine and Victoria looked out over the city of Orleans. The humans had built Orleans on the north side of Pontchartrain Bay. New Orleans had sunk into the Gulf hundreds of years ago, soon after the Great War. Katherine felt the moisture in the air; felt the hot, humid breeze blow against their faces, lift their hair back. The heat lightning brightened the night sky out over the bay. Katherine had followed Malin to this city and brought Victoria with her. Drake had come in her sleep with a message from Michael. Malin was in her world, ready to take Shawn and she should prepare herself. He did not tell her where Malin was, but she sensed it from him. Turning her head to the west, she sensed Shawn and Jessamine only a hundred miles away. Malin was here, gathering her energy, preparing for her attack.

Two years ago, Katherine had summoned Peter to the blue throne and enlisted him into her service. She made him captain of her guard, the first vampire in her army and told him to form a new vampire army in her name. Victoria and Juliette had accompanied him to The Citadel, and Victoria was not happy at all about the selection of Peter. Still, she and Katherine were good friends, and, in a way, they loved each other.

Katherine sent a message to her family, told them she would need them, and expected them to serve; she also told Victoria she was going to Orleans, and that she believed Malin was there. Victoria had sensed the desperation in her and asked if she could go with her. Katherine prayed to The Mother to spare Shawn but heard nothing from her now.

"Can you sense her, Katherine?" Victoria asked. "I can't sense the witch. Not yet."

"Barely. Malin is here, though. It's been a long time since I saw you with a slayer."

"It has been almost two hundred years since I lost my slayer," Victoria replied. Twenty years ago, I had a new one made. I have been practicing since, and Shawn has helped me."

"I would have made Peter captain of my guard sooner if I had known it would bring the warrior out of you again. I will need all of my family soon, including you."

"It starts again. Another great battle with evil," Victoria said sadly. "The angels already sing of it. You know Shawn is very weak. Jessamine will not leave his side now."

"I know, The Mother thinks she is going to get what she wants. To have guardians kill Malin at the gates of Hell. I am Queen of the Vampires, and Michael has given me power. I will find a way to kill Malin in this world, and then she can never come to this world again. She will never have Shawn!"

"Do you remember, long ago, I told you that we cannot challenge The Mother?"

"I remember," Katherine said. "I'm not going to openly defy her, but I will fight for him. I will not let Malin have Shawn. You love him the same as I. You will fight for him."

"I will, that I promise you, but Shawn hasn't been the same since the time of the demons. Shawn has accepted his fate. Maybe we should, too, and plan for his rescue."

"Never will I accept this!" Katherine pleaded to Victoria. "There. I feel her again."

"Yes, there's the witch," Victoria said. "She is powerful, Katherine."

Katherine and Victoria flew past the outskirts of Orleans, to a small town twenty miles to the west, where they sensed the witch. Shawn probably could not sense Malin, but certainly, Jessamine must know how close she was. Katherine tried to sense Jessamine, touch her mind, but Jessamine had closed herself off. Jessamine was preparing for Malin and certainly knew the witch was near. It didn't matter; Katherine and Victoria would take care of Malin. This time they would capture her if they could.

Katherine and Victoria landed on the outskirts of a small town on the edge of the Great Iberian Bayou. It was a rough town; oysters were its trade, and the competition was stiff. They traveled a walkway into town, past a bonfire with drunken men drinking and partying.

"Can you sense her, Victoria?"

"I can, and the witch knows we are here."

"She does!" Katherine drew Alexa and rose into the air. "Follow me." They floated up into the darkness where no human eyes could see them. They went to the other side of town, to a long, narrow building with air cars parked along one side. Reds, pinks, and blues softly shone from its modern plastic walls. These were the only lights, no holograms to draw attention. They quietly landed on the roof.

"The witch is inside this building," Victoria said as she drew her slayer. "Katherine, are you sure about this? Malin is a powerful witch, and will certainly give us a terrible fight."

"I'm sure," Katherine said with fire in her eyes…a madness in her to end this now. "We will save Shawn! We have to kill this witch tonight! Michael, please allow her death!"

Katherine floated to the edge of the roof, and Victoria followed. She heard the whine of an arriving air car as they descended next to a side entrance. She quickly forced the door open, and they entered and walked down a long hall. The air was heavy with perfume, and lining the hallway were pedestals with holograms of women available for sex. The holograms struck different poses, showing themselves for their customers.

They moved into a large room with humans lying in loungers smoking their endorphin pipes, oblivious to their surroundings. A thick, orange smoke lazily drifted through the room. They made their way across this large room and went through a door and into another hall. Across the hall, was another large room with scantily clad women sipping wine and talking to men that worked the docks, preparing them for their nights' adventures. Seeing the guardians with their slayers, the humans quickly head for the doors. Cautiously, Katherine and Victoria walked down the hall, slayers at the ready, and came to large double doors that slid open; a dark warrior stooped and came through. Victoria immediately attacked and took the head of the evil creature. Katherine sensed the witch and the terrible evil in the room. Malin was waiting for them. Entering the room her skin quivered, and she felt as though thousands of ants were crawling on her.

A light grey mist hung in the room; the dark translucent walls shimmered. The witch floated two feet above the floor, her eyes black as coal. Black hair floated off her shoulders, a sword hung at her side, and she held a long, brown staff in her hand—the instrument had two long, yellow, sharp tips, one on each end. An evil, mocking smile spread across her face. Great darkness filled the room, an immense power surrounded Malin, and there was another spirit somewhere in hiding. Maggots crawled on the floor, and a bitter coldness swept over Katherine, accompanied by the smell of death.

"Greetings, Katherine. I told you I would be back. The time has come for me to take Shawn."

"You will take him nowhere!"

"I will take him. Bring him terrible pain at first, and make him fear me. I will turn him into a pathetic coward and then soothe him with my flesh. He will learn to serve me, and he will be mine forever." Malin told her and then gave a loud, evil laugh. "You will never have him again."

"I am going to kill you tonight!" Katherine gritted out, her eyes burning with a terrible hatred for Malin.

"Sorry, whore vampire that is not possible here!"

She changed to her most prominent and most potent form as a vampire. "You will have nothing, that I swear, and when I kill you in this world, you will never come back." Alexa glowed and rang as she raised it high. Victoria also changed to her vampire state, sword drawn and ready for the fight.

161

"I see you have brought Victoria Kenmare with you. It will do you no good, vampire. Father, remember your promise. I will kill both tonight."

"You will kill nobody, witch!" Katherine screamed as she launched herself at Malin. She swung her slayer only to have Malin parry it away with the rod. Malin twirled and hit Katherine with the rod, knocking her back. Victoria attacked and swung her blade at the witch. Malin countered, and the sounds of their blades striking rang through the room. Katherine attacked again, and the witch countered again, knocking her back, and then spun and sliced Katherine across the side with her sword. Katherine fell back, holding her wound with a bloody hand.

"Careful, Katherine!" Victoria warned. "The devil is near, and she is drawing power from him!"

"What's the matter, Katherine? Not as easy as you thought?" Malin snarled at her. "The power of Lucifer is here tonight, pathetic vampire! You are desperate and easy to fool. Where is The Mother? Where are your angels?"

Victoria attacked again as Katherine circled, their swords striking and sending sparks into the mist. Malin sidestepped, turned, and swung her rod around, hitting Victoria in the head, driving her to the floor. Katherine could see her trying to stand, blood coming from her mouth, nose, and eyes. Malin floated to the center of the room, one hand holding the rod; the other, her sword. "Come for me, Katherine, and end it now. You know you want to."

Katherine charged at the witch. Malin disappeared and reappeared at her side, deflecting Katherine's sword and driving hers through Katherine's stomach. They were face to face, and Malin smiled a cruel, wicked smile. Malin kicked Katherine back, pulled her sword from Katherine's stomach, brought the staff around, and drove the yellow tip into her chest and broke it off. Katherine felt herself losing her balance, falling back into a darkness that pulled at her, and then she felt her angel, Anne, surrounding her with energy, pulling her back into the light. She was drifting in the light, Anne telling her it would be all right—

that The Mother had always meant this to be.

****

Victoria raised her head, shook it, and wiped the blood from her eyes. Only the demons had ever hit her that hard. She saw the spear tip go into Katherine and watched as she fell and lost her fight to save Shawn. Victoria rose from the floor, circled, and picked up Alexa, held the glowing slayer in her hand, and stood her ground, facing the witch. Malin turned, stared off, and then humbled herself in a bow. "Thank you, Father. I will not need your help for this one."

"Is the other tip for me, witch?" Victoria hissed.

"No, this tip is for Shawn. It is a special tip. I won't need it for you. I will kill you before I leave, and then I'll kill Katherine. I promised my father."

Victoria raised Alexa and moved with blinding speed, cutting Malin across the shoulder. Malin fell backward, cursing at her. They circled, swords clashing; Malin spun, struck Victoria across the side, parried, and drove her sword into Victoria's stomach. Victoria fell back, holding her stomach, and quickly attacked again, surprising Malin as she feigned to one side and drove Alexa into Malin's stomach.

Malin fell back and screamed, "Where did this come from?"

"I am an old vampire, with pure blood of the angels from Erdin Kenmare, my maker. I also drank Bricius's blood, the blood of Herit. Should have thought it through, Malin, before you sent the devil away."

Malin attacked and swung at her with her slayer. Victoria parried and then twirled and caught Malin across the side. Malin disappeared and reappeared behind Victoria, striking her across the neck with the rod and quickly lunged, driving her sword into

Victoria's back. Victoria flew across the room, turned, and came back, pushing her slayer into Malin's chest. Victoria swung her fist around hitting Malin in the face, with a powerful blow knocking the witch back and off the slayer.

Malin fell back and cursed at Victoria. "I will not bloody myself anymore with you. I have business tonight, and you will not stop me. You can live, for now, vampire, and tell Katherine we will meet again."

Malin turned and disappeared through the dark wall behind her. Victoria fell to the floor, covered in blood, and knelt, trying to regain her senses. She had beaten the witch off, was hurt, and in no condition to go after her. Only Jessamine stood between Malin and Shawn. Shaking her head, she tasted blood tears, and then all the fears of losing Shawn flooded through her again. She knew she had to keep her wits and get Katherine to safety. The queen must live. That was the only way Shawn could be saved.

Victoria crawled to Katherine, turned her over, and pushed her fingers into her chest. A long time ago, she had seen this with Shawn. Digging into Katherine's chest, she found the spear tip, pulling the bloody mass from her chest, the tip burning her fingers. She threw the yellow, oozing tip to the floor, cursing, and it burst into blue flames.

Shaking Katherine, she yelled, "Can you hear me?" Gathering Katherine in her arms, she stumbled through the double doors and out into the night air. Victoria fell to the ground holding Katherine, and both lay there until a crowd of humans formed around them. Weak and covered in blood, Victoria got to her knees, flashed her vampire eyes at the humans, and hissed, "Get back! I warn you!"

She heard a man say, "Get the energizer we will capture some vampires tonight." Victoria turned, bared her fangs, and spat. "Careful humans, I will kill all of you before you move an inch."

With all her strength, she collected Katherine and the two slayers, and rose into the sky, leaving behind the wide-eyed humans and making her way slowly back to Washington.

****

Katherine was floating in the light; her angels had come to her, soothing her, telling her it was all right and that she would find a way to save Shawn. Her spirit screamed, *Anne, where are you!*

I'm here, Katherine! I'm with you!

Why did Michael do this? We could have killed Malin on Earth with a little help from him. He allowed Lucifer to give the witch strength to trick us.

Michael had no choice. Eos is a powerful angel and equals Michael. She wants Malin killed at the Gates of Hell by guardians. A thousand years ago, when Eos saw Shawn's future, she used a great deal of her strength to make a spell that made it possible to keep Malin from the physical worlds. But guardians have to kill her at her castle by the Gates of Hell. That is why she sent Pandora and a part of herself, Jessamine, to protect Shawn.

Eos knew that if Shawn survived the demons, Lucifer would seek vengeance on him. She knew he would send Malin, and felt this was her chance to kill Malin, but Lucifer's evil has made the end uncertain. Michael was in her favor and owed her this. He had to allow it!

Malin was too strong this time. I must go and protect Shawn.

You need to rest, to stay in the light, to remain in the ground, heal, and regain your strength. I pray you kill Malin! Do not let Shawn suffer long.

Katherine floated in the light and soon became aware of her beloved Drake.

Katherine... The sound of Drake's voice calmed her.

Drake, Malin took Shawn!

I know. I told you this would happen.

Katherine allowed her energy to reach out to Drake, and he allowed her to enter his being. She could feel his love and feel him soothing her. *The Archangel Michael sends you a message. He sends the way to Malin's black castle. Go to the first Hell's Hole, as it is empty now. Climb down the shaft. It is a long way down, you will come to a vast, underground cavern, follow the flow of the river of fire, and that will bring you to the black castle where Malin holds Shawn. There, you will find the Gates of Hell and the lake of fire. Michael wants you to know that he expects all guardians to fight for Shawn and your world. The angels sing of the battles to come. Your destiny has arrived. It will be you who leads the vampire army to the Gates of Hell.*

Chapter Sixteen

T he sounds of a piano melody wafted through the walls of The Last Chance Bar on the outskirts of New Hope. Shawn sat at the piano finishing his tune, sensing the crowd of humans, their moods, the sexual tension between the women and men (which always made his heart chuckle). Sal, the owner, had finally given him permission to keep a piano at the bar. Unfortunately for him, over the years, Jessamine had tired of bars and was now home asleep. He turned the keyboard off and watched the main attraction, a country band, set up for the night's festivities. Long ago, the indigenous population and the remnants of the invading Chinese army built New Hope on the edge of The Great Iberian Bayou.

He had flown the ten miles from his house to the bar, and it had tired him. Since he lost his strength, his favorite power, his flying ability, was limited. The sunlight was a new concern of his; now, he had to leave the Last Chance much earlier.

New Hope had been a small town for centuries, the type of place he liked, but now the town was starting to grow. Humans had discovered lithium gas a few thousand meters below the swamp water and the black mud of the bayou. Europa was in its second century of terraforming and paid very well for lithium gas. They used the gas to melt selected ice areas on their moon.

Gwyn had left two years ago. He tried not to fall in love with her, but her strength and kindness drew him to her. He loved her dearly, yet, while he slept, she left anyway, and left him a simple note on his desk. It read: *Goodbye, Shawn. I wish I could stay the hundred years with you but I can't. Until we meet on that horrible day... I love you, Gwyn.*

Katherine had recently visited him, and he was worried about her. She was sure she would defeat Malin and save him. All the signs pointed to a far different outcome. Shawn told her she should not forget about spending more of her time paying attention to the vampires Michael had chosen her to rule. He did not tell her that Herit had been preparing him for Malin. Anne rarely came to him now; only Herit did. She had always been his guiding angel, and now Anne was Katherine's.

The band started to play as he walked toward the table where three mortal women sat and wrinkled his sensitive nose slightly because of their perfume. They had invited him over for the company. The feeling came on suddenly, in mid-sentence, as he was greeting the women—something was wrong with Katherine. Shawn excused himself and went outside. He immediately felt Malin and knew she was close. The witch easily probed his mind, finding out how weak he was. Then a whisper spoke to him in his head:

I am coming for you.

Shawn wished he had better defenses, but those had left him, too. Now, he felt Jessamine in his head, telling him to start home, and that she would meet him on the way.

Shawn decided to run the back road through the bayou; it was hard, packed dirt with a brackish water canal running along its side. Flying would attract Malin quicker, he figured, and he could not fly very far anyway.

He had just entered the swamp when Malin caught him. Twenty feet in front of him, she appeared, hovering, two feet above the ground, dark blue energy surrounding her and lighting up the night. Her piercing black eyes stared at him as she cocked her head slightly to one side, her prize in front of her. Malin held a long staff in one hand, and a sword in the other, and a cruel smile decorated her evil face. Shawn could sense Jessamine coming, but she was hiding herself from Malin, traveling in a wide arc to confuse the witch.

Shawn pulled a locator sign from the ground that marked the trail he was on. He tore the flag from the metal post and held the metal bar with both hands. Immediately, he attacked Malin, head-on, surprising her, and then moved to the side and struck Malin's sword as she swung it in an arc to parry his blow. Dodging the second strike, he twirled and struck Malin on the back, knocking her forward. With a flash, he moved right and brought the pole down on her shoulder, bringing a yelp from the evil creature. He floated back and away from her, looking for other openings in her defenses. If he'd had his strength, he could've defeated her, and she now knew it, too.

"Always the warrior, Demon Slayer, but what you really are now is a pathetic, weak vampire." Malin spat the words at him as she turned to look into the swamp. "I can sense that witch daughter of yours. I know she is near. Is she what those whore angels have sent to save you? I'm afraid, Shawn, she won't be enough."

"If we are so weak, why have you brought Lucifer with you this time? Even I can sense his dark energy. You wear it like a cloak."

Again, Shawn attacked, and Malin dodged his blow, swinging her staff around and catching him, throwing him through the air, his flight halted by a large cypress tree. Shawn rose from the ground, and Malin flew at him. He went low to the ground, swung his metal pole, and took her feet out from under her, sending her flipping to the ground. The witch disappeared and now was next to him, striking him with her staff and driving him back to the ground. She then brought her black boot down, crushing his chest as blood spurted from his mouth.

"I told you, you are too weak to matter." She twirled her staff and drove the yellow tip into his chest. "That should hold you while I take care of that witch daughter of yours."

His strength left him, and he tried to move, rolled to his side, trying to stand, but his legs failed him. A hot, prickling heat flushed through his body. It took all his strength to use his arms to push his chest and head off the ground. The blood coming from his mouth felt warm. A white beam of plasma hit Malin in the back, throwing her down the road, but she quickly recovered, picked-up her staff and sword, and turned to face Jessamine.

Jessamine floated just above the ground with her rod in hand. Her pixie face showed contempt for Malin.

"We finally meet Malin. You will never keep him. The angels will not allow it. It doesn't matter what happens here or what you do to the vampires of Earth. Eventually, they all will come for him. He is that important to them."

"What happens here is you leave this world," Malin said as she sheathed her sword, lowered her staff, and fired, only to be met by the flame of Jessamine's rod.

Shawn saw the two plasma beams meet in the middle and heard the loud *boom* of the colliding energies, the sizzle of the energy beams as they tore and sliced into each other. The overpowering smell of ozone filled the air, and a blue world filled his sight. He saw the sparks and fire shooting away from the collision, the white of Jessamine's beam, and the blue of Malin's. Both sidestepping, trying to find an opening with their rays. Jessamine whipped her beam in an attempt to arc the energy over the top of Malin's.

"Beezlebub, stay with me!" he heard Malin yell.

They both stopped firing and were now circling each other. Neither took their eyes off the other.

"No sword?" Malin yelled. "You're not much of a warrior. Only a pathetic Mother's witch."

"I don't need a sword, and I'm not a warrior, but I can give a pitiful creature like you a fight."

"You should have brought one. You are going to need it." Malin lowered her staff and fired her blue beam, and Jessamine shot back.

Shawn felt the burning in his chest from the tip of the staff. Trying to reach the tip, he clawed at his chest, only to have his fingers seared. He gagged and again clawed at his chest. *Strange*...his breathing became faster. He rolled to his other side and looked at Jessamine; he could tell she was tiring. Malin had more endurance, and she was stronger than Jessamine. Lucifer was here, but The Mother wasn't. Eos was sacrificing Jessamine, why he didn't know.

The *booms* from their plasma beams echoed through the bayou. The intense light lit up the swamp and the night sky. They circled each other, firing their beams, each looking for an opening— witches performing a macabre dance of death. Jessamine dropped to one knee but rose again quickly.

Shawn saw she was exhausted, had little energy left, and then he heard the sickening laugh of Malin. Shawn sensed that Malin knew Jessamine was at the end of her endurance; her last obstacle was near defeat.

Malin, with a burst of energy, closed in on his daughter. Jessamine dodged, brought her energy beam around, and knocked Malin back. Malin charged again, half-crouching, dodging, and firing back, catching Jessamine in the chest and throwing her against a cypress tree, dazing her, her rod falling from her hand. Slumping over, Jessamine fell to her knees, eyed her rod, and then she tried to reach out for it. Malin was on her, kicking her in the chest and driving her back against the tree.

"I told you that you were going to need a sword," Malin hissed as she drew her own sword and drove it through Jessamine's chest. Blood quickly claimed Jessamine's blouse and spilled onto the leaves and dirt. It came from her mouth, flowed over her soft, red lips and down her white chin and neck, wetting her long, silky white hair.

Shawn screamed, "I will kill you for this! I will follow you to Hell and kill you in front of Lucifer, you filthy hag."

Malin took hold of Jessamine's throat, lifted her, and held her by her hair against the cypress tree. She turned to look at Shawn. The smile on her face turned to an evil, hateful look—an expression of cruelty he could not fathom.

"Will you kill me? Will you! I don't think that is possible now. I will take you to my castle, and I will make you bleed for a thousand days. I will strip your courage from you and make you hate the very humans you protect."

Jessamine gurgled as blood came from her mouth. "You will

never keep him, evil Malin."

"I will keep him, and you can watch what I do to him from Heaven with all the other helpless angels."

"Mother, where are you?" Jessamine cried out.

"The whore Eos is not here." Malin raised her sword, brought it across Jessamine's neck, and, with no effort, sliced her head from her body. Jessamine's blood spurted onto Malin's face and chest. Her body crumpled to the ground like a lifeless rag doll. Malin turned and laughed a sick, evil laugh at Shawn. She held Jessamine's bloody head up as if it were a trophy. "Would you like to take this with you?"

Shawn screamed his sorrow to the heavens. Tears stained his cheeks. Malin dropped the head onto the lifeless body, now lying in a pool of blood and strolled toward Shawn. She wiped at the blood on her face, wore a sadistic smile, her eyes dark and foreboding and covered in Jessamine's blood.

Shawn could feel a rise in energy as the skies darkened. He could hear the crack of lightning and the *boom* of the thunder as the fresh raindrops pelted his face. The heavens had become angry, and he felt Lucifer's dark energy steal away.

"Well, Demon Slayer, it looks like I finally woke the angels up," Malin spat at him.

Malin reached down and picked Shawn up by his throat, holding him by the jaw in front of her. Jessamine's blood was spattered on Malin's face, and her breath smelled of juniper berries. She kissed him, and he tasted dank, evil wetness.

"It is time for us to leave, for you to come with me, my love. You will be my prince, but first, you must learn how to obey me. You, Demon Slayer, will learn to fear me."

"I will never obey you, and I will kill you someday," Shawn hissed. "Kill me now, or I will kill you for what you have done here tonight."

Malin brought her blade to Shawn's face, gave it a flick, a little slice. "You are too weak to hurt me. You may have the skills, but you are too weak now. Can't you feel the warmth spread through you? Feel your face. It is not healing. Feel the warmth of your blood. It's time to go, and time for the Demon Slayer to pay for what he has done."

She twisted his head so he would look at her and gave his face a hard slap. A wave of evil went through him, a feeling of a lost soul, and it made him sick. Malin brought her staff to his chest to heal his wound and retrieve the tip from him. The Succubus threw his paralyzed body on her back and took to the air, heading toward Shawn and Jessamine's home.

A bright white light came from the stormy night sky and descended to Jessamine's bloody body. Electricity filled the wet air, and there came the sound of angels singing their sorrowful songs. Jessamine's body glowed bright white. The Mother's light absorbed this light and rose back into the night sky, into the storm clouds, through the lightning, and toward the stars and Heaven. Jessamine had always been a part of The Mother.

Shawn felt the rush of the air on his face as he lay on Malin's back, smelled a bittersweet odor that came from her. Soon they landed, and Malin threw him to the ground. He pulled himself up with his arms and found he was on the front lawn of his home. Slowly, his legs started to work as he rose to his hands and knees, only to have Malin give him a hit from her staff, sending him retching back to the ground.

"Pitiful Shawn, do you know why we are here?"

"I couldn't care less, filthy whore!" Shawn gagged as he looked at her with hate in his eyes.

"I am going to burn yours and Jessamine's house down. The home you shared with her. You will never live here again. That life is over for you. Feel the warmth spread through you." Malin pulled him up by the back of his shirt and helped him balance on his legs. She lowered her staff and fired dark energy through his windows, and soon his home was ablaze, fire shooting from the windows, breaking through and consuming the roof, staining the white columns black.

The witch walked toward him as he stood barely able to keep his balance and reached for him.

"What's the hurry, Malin?" Shawn asked. "Let's stay and

watch the fire."

Malin came to his face and hissed; he felt her acidic breath against his skin. "Do you think a vampire is coming to help you? Maybe Renee? It won't be Katherine or Victoria. No vampire can help you now." Malin took hold of him, put him on her back, and flew north toward Hell's Hole.

The lights passed below him, he tried to bring them closer with his eyes, but he couldn't, and his body was feeling strange, warm. Something was wrong. He was breathing to fast. He tried to raise his fist to strike a blow at Malin, but he couldn't.

"You are too weak to hurt me. Would you like some blood?"

Now he knew something was wrong. The thought of drinking blood had no effect on him, and panic started to make his heart race. It was a sensation he had forgotten about a long time ago.

"What have you done to me, you filthy witch?"

"The Tip I drove into you was not like the last. It was a special tip, and you will never have the strength of a vampire again. I have saved you, my love, from that life. I have made you human again, and now you will need me to survive. Weak mortals would never last by themselves, not where you are going. You will always need me."

Waves of fear traveled through him as he began to feel his new body—his human body. His fear consumed him, and his breathing became rapid, his body tingled; his face and neck became hot. How would he possibly survive being this frail, this weak? He gasped at the air and could barely catch his breath. How would he survive as a human again? He lay on Malin's back, flew through the air, and the cold wind tore at him. He started to shake and shiver violently from the cold, feelings that were strange to him. They arrived in front of the Shenandoah cave opening. Malin grabbed his arm and pulled him along into the entrance of the cave. She pulled him and led him through the darkness, sometimes pushed him so that he fell to his hands and knees. Warmblood spread over his hands from the cuts, and he could not see in the blackness, and that frightened him. Malin grabbed him, pulled him to his feet, and gave him a hard slap to the side of his head. They entered a large room made of polished blocks of coal, a red liquid pool in the middle, and fire shooting from the floor.

"Where are you taking me? I'm not going in the pool!" Shawn cried as he tried to free himself from the witch. Her grip was unbreakable.

"Yes, we are, mighty Demon Slayer," Malin said with an evil laugh. "Are you afraid? Soon you will see the Gates of Hell."

"I will drown in that pool, you stupid witch. You have made me mortal." Shawn screamed at Malin, only to receive a backhand to the face that cut his lip. Malin grabbed him by the arm and dragged him toward the pool. "You will not speak to me like that, or I will cause you terrible pain."

"Don't take me there! Don't do this," Shawn pleaded as a terrible panic went through him.

"Herit, where are you?" he screamed. "You said you would fight for me!"

Malin let out a loud and mocking laugh. "Herit, where are you! She is not here, stupid human. They have abandoned you. You are no longer a vampire. They will not help you now. You can't feel them anymore, can you?"

The witch wrapped herself, her evil, around him, and The Tempter pulled him into the pool. The hot, thick liquid consumed him, yet he could breathe. His eyes saw only small red bubbles flowing by. Then, just as quickly, he felt himself falling and landing with a hard *thud* on black stones.

The fall knocked the breath from him, and he struggled with his human lungs. All he smelled was burnt rock, earth, sulfur, and the air burned his nose and lungs. The hot stones seared his hands and knees, yet he started to regain his senses, and slowly rose to his feet. A dark warrior took hold of him, jerked him, placed a black, iron collar around his neck, and handed the metal chain to Malin with a bow. A light grey mist floated everywhere; black, jagged rocks jutted from the ground, but most of the earth was hot, black stone shaped like pieces of coal. He saw the occasional burnt human skull or bones mixed in with the rocks. Orange flames would shoot from the ground, high into the darkness, and then subside. A river of orange molten rock flowed to the horizon, lost in the glow of the flames, and all Shawn could see above him was blackness.

A hot wind blew against his face, moved along by the heat of the fires. The sound of miserable wailing traveled on the heated air. The condemned spirits drifted from Hell's Hole, shifted back into their human form, and then followed the river of fire. The convicted were whipped, and the dark warriors drove them along like cattle. Looks of horror were on their faces. They were naked, their bodies burned and their mouths sewn shut. The moans and the crack of the whips filled the hot air. Some would panic and break away from the others, only to have a dark warrior strike them down with a whip of fire. What he saw through the haze was a sad procession of condemned humans.

"Where are they going?" Shawn asked Malin.

"To the Gates of Hell, where they will enter. The dark angels wait for them. They have led Lucifer's life of evil, and now his world awaits," Malin told him as she brought her staff down on him, knocking him to the hot stone. Her evil laughter tore at his ears. "Their reward awaits them. Get up, human, and follow me," Malin hissed as she jerked the chain. Shawn pulled the chain back, and Malin only laughed at him. You are week and will not last long here."

Shawn followed behind Malin. Suddenly, she wavered and transformed herself. Now, she wore a long, grey cloak that dragged slightly on the stones, and two thick, black horns—curved like a ram's—grew from her head. Slowly and methodically, she walked, her staff in one hand and the chain in the other, dragging and pulling Shawn along. Dark energy came from her that pushed the mist away. The dark warriors stood all along the way, bowed when they saw her coming, and then beat their fists against their chests, making a thunderous sound and yelling their insults at her captive.

Shawn realized this long walk was to make him a spectacle, an example, to show the dark warriors and all dark angels what would happen to any that crossed Lucifer. He could not see as he did before, but he saw hundreds of camps with black stone huts and thousands of dark warriors as far as his human eyes could see. They occupied these camps. Smoke came from pits where they cooked their meat, and they drank some type of liquid that made them drunk.

Malin gave him a wicked smile and then told him, "If vampires try to rescue you, they will have a surprise waiting for them."

Shawn did not feel well; a sickness and a strange emptiness came over him, and his feet felt the burn of the stones through his shoes. Water came from his white, clammy skin, and he felt dizzy, lightheaded. He tried to sense, but there was nothing there. What he felt was emptiness and a terrible thirst, his mouth dry, lips cracked, his tongue like sandpaper. How did he once stand to be human? He couldn't remember as it had all happened a thousand years ago, but this, here and now, was terrible.

He followed behind Malin for hours, occasionally stumbling and falling only to receive a blow from Malin's staff along with a generous helping of ridicule. Eventually, the ground started to rise, and the incline got steeper. Off in the distance was a behemoth black stone that had heaved up from the floor of the cavern, and on top was Malin's black castle.

Next to the castle, traveling at an angle and back into the darkness was the end of the cavern, where the Gates of Hell sat, fifty feet high and fifty feet wide. Black, iron doors with strange symbols and faces cast on their surfaces, they had large, iron hinges that held them in place. These gates had not opened in ages.

At the base of these doors, a sea of blackened, burnt human bones and skulls stretched into the lake of fire, which, in turn, was fed by the river of fire. The procession of humans went to the doors where the heat was unbearable, their skin burned away, and their bare-bones crumbling to the hot rock. With a horrible scream, the black gates sucked their spirits in. As Shawn came closer to the gates, he saw thousands of faces floating in the doors with looks of unspeakable agony.

The witch dragged him up a rock outcropping that formed a road that wound its way alongside the cliff and up to the castle.

Large, blackbirds circled over the black castle. One large bird landed in front of him, its feathers replaced by black fur. The bird was easily five feet long and had bright orange, beady eyes that fixed on him, a bill that was long and sharp, meant for tearing, and feet with long talons that looked to be as sharp as a razor. The bird blocked their way, stood, and screamed at him, pecking at him and trying to tear him with its beak.

"Do you not recognize Horsa, mighty Demon Slayer? You disappoint him," Malin said, pointing her staff at the bird. "He certainly recognizes you. The demon had two chances to kill you. This is what Lucifer does to demons that guardians defeat." Shawn watched her shoo the bird off the road with her staff.

The higher they went, the more Shawn could see. This place was a vast underground cavern that took a bend to the right and then forked in two directions. His human eyes still could not see the top of the cavern. A molten river followed the floor of the cavern, and it, too, forked and went off in two different directions. The river, which formed a lake before reaching the Gates of Hell, prominently featured, in its middle, a whirlpool in which molten lava swirled and took a plunge deep into the earth.

They traveled on and eventually came to the top. Shawn found himself standing in a flat area, in a field with nothing but black, polished stones. The stones ran forty feet to the walls of the castle. There was no moat. The castle walls rose a hundred feet into the air and were made of black stones. As he got closer, Shawn could see the shards of human bones and teeth mixed in with the mortar that held the rocks together.

Again, he felt sick and started to waver. Darkness was trying to take over his mind, the evil whispers taunting him. The world began to spin, but he had to remain on his feet until he reached wherever the witch was taking him. Reaching out, he braced himself against the stone wall, waiting for the spinning to stop. Malin jerked him forward; he stumbled and fell to his knees. Looking him up and down, Malin reached and pulled him up by his iron collar. "You don't look too good, frail human," Malin said. "Maybe I made a mistake when I made you human. You might not be able to handle what I want to do to you. We'll see…"

"How do you stand this?" Shawn said weakly. "The evil of all this!"

Malin grabbed his jaw, held it tightly, and stared into his eyes. "Evil is intoxicating. It is power. There is a beauty to evil, truth to it. Accept this evil, be like me, and I will have Lucifer show you mercy. Or I will cause you unspeakable pain. Remember, Demon Slayer, if you die here as a mortal, Hell is where you will go. Nothing in this world can help you. The gates will suck you in!"

Malin pushed him ahead, and he came to a large iron door where two dark warriors stood guard. Large, brawny men with a grey cloth tied around their middles, each held a spear in one hand a shield in the other, and a broadsword hung from their waists. There were no hinges, no seams or door latch, only solid metal. Malin stepped back, lowered her staff, and a seam appeared in the middle of the door. At that moment, the two doors swung open. Shawn felt the yank of the chain as Malin pulled him inside.

The foyer was a stark contrast to the world outside. The walls were made of light brown marble, and strange, white statues were placed against the walls—figures of strange creatures, none resembling humans except for one that looked like Malin.

Malin saw him looking at the statues and told him, "Those are the forms I have taken on other worlds."

Down the corridor, a bronze door opened, and a strange creature walked through. The creature's skin was green, its lips a dark red, and its hair silver, long and curly. It looked to be a man but still had the soft features of a woman. It wore only green pants and red slippers, its body muscular, and about the size of a human. Most strange were the two small horns on his head. Gold earrings hung from his ears, and a gold chain hung around his neck that lay over a dark red symbol, the devil had burned into his chest.

Malin informed him, "This is Luvon, a powerful warlock, and the mark that you are looking at tells all of his high station with Lucifer." Malin handed him the chain and said, "Take the mighty Demon Slayer to his accommodations."

Luvon yanked the chain, and Shawn fell to the floor on his

hands and knees while both his captors laughed.

"That is how you should be when you are in the presence of your master," Luvon hissed at him. "He doesn't look much like a Demon Slayer. Only a pathetic human."

Malin walked over to Shawn, took him by his hair, and forced his head up to stare in her dark eyes. "The mighty Demon Slayer has been de-fanged. Take him away."

The warlock yanked him to his feet, dragged him down the hall, through a door, and into a large room with many more doors. The walls, white stucco, rose and were lost in the darkness of the massive hall. Lights wrapped in crystal glass hovered in the air, projecting a soft, yellow light. Large, red banners floated in the air and had strange, blue symbols sewn into them. Four giant ruling thrones, brought from worlds that evil had conquered, were placed against each of the four walls. Shawn looked up and saw a night sky with thousands of flickering stars, and in some areas, a bright spot that he later learned were worlds Malin had brought her evil to.

"Someday, earth's throne will be against that wall," Luvon hissed. "Lucifer is creating a special demon for that."

The warlock dragged him across the dark green marble floor and through a door, up a procession of stairways, and down many hallways until they arrived at a room high in the castle. The walls of the room were made of a brown plaster, the floor a rough wide, wood planking. A wooden bed with a lumpy straw mattress was placed against the far wall, and a wooden table and chair were placed in the center of the room. Attached to one wall were sets of shackles. He had a large window with no glass, only black bars. *Why the bars,* he wondered, *I could easily crawl between them and escape if I were a vampire.* Looking out over the cavern, he saw the fires, the dark orange glow of this hell.

Luvon stripped him of his clothes, leaving only his pants. He took his shoes and told him his human feet could only tolerate the floors of this castle. Outside, they would burn. The warlock forced him to the wall, shackled him, and took a switch from the wooden table. The cruel creature whipped him until he cried out, and then the warlock unshackled him, and he fell to the floor.

Drifting in and out of consciousness, he strained to feel his angels, but they were not there. He felt nothing; he was alone and had lost his psychic abilities. How closed off, he was now…How could humans be so unaware of the spiritual world? This is the question that really frightened him.

Shawn opened his eyes and saw Malin standing over him. Her hair and eyes were as black as coal, but they always were like that. She'd have been a striking woman if not for the terrible evil that clung to her.

He felt her pick him up and carry him to the bed. "I have scolded Luvon for this. I wanted to be the first to beat you. He hates you, Demon Slayer. The demon Zepar is a good friend of his."

She laid him on the bed and pulled him to a sitting position again, forcing him to stare into her eyes. "I will share a secret with you. The false angel, Michael, thinks he has rid your world of demons. Lucifer has different plans, and he is preparing the great demon Brendel to come to your world. He will be born of flesh and have great demon powers. A day will come when your world will be a battleground for the armies of good and evil, and my father will win."

"Am I supposed to be surprised?" Shawn whispered.

"I have brought you something to eat and some water," Malin said as she handed him a metal cup of water. His thirst was overwhelming, and he drank the water as if it was his last. Malin gave him a bowl of brown mush, a slimy substance with a smell that quickly made him sick to his stomach.

"You must eat. You are human now," Malin told him. "That is why you feel sick and weak. How pathetic you look! And you smell. I need you to regain some strength so I can beat you." Malin drew even closer to him, and he could smell her bittersweetness, her breath against his face. She whispered in his ear, "Love me, Shawn. Accept my evil, and I will show you mercy."

"I will never love you, and I will kill you someday," he said as the pain of losing Jessamine came back to him. "That I promise you."

Malin struck him in the face so hard with her fist that he again faded into darkness. When he woke, Malin was gone, and his gooey bowl of mush sat on the floor. Picking up the pot, he stared at its disgusting contents. There was a terrible pain in his new human stomach, and he knew he needed food, so he stuck his fingers into the mush and began to eat. He gagged and retched up a slimy hunk of mash that splattered on the floor. Again, he tried and felt the slimy food as it strangely slid down into his stomach, and this time it stayed down.

Shawn stood and felt weak, unstable, yet he could walk slowly to the table. He sat in the chair, poured himself water from the metal pitcher left on the table, and drank it straight down, poured another, and drank it slowly. He saw the open window with its black bars and spied two buckets with soap, left by the thick wooden door. He walked to the one bucket, peed, then used the other bucket of water to wash and rinse the soap from him. Shawn went to the window and looked out at his prison. Felt wetness on his cheeks, and he wiped it with his fingers, placing them in his mouth. His tears were clear and salty.

A dim, yellow-orange light sifted through the smoke from the fires shooting from the molten river. Black stones covered the ground, and jagged black rocks that jutted from the ground rose into the grey mist. The hot air brought wails of misery with it as well as the smell of Sulphur and burnt earth.

A long line of humans followed the river. Their evil spirits brought here after their earthly death, and they reformed their physical bodies only to suffer the worst kind of afterlife death at the Gates of Hell. To his right, he saw the black rock wall with huge, iron doors that never opened. It existed only to suck the wailing spirits of the evil into darkness. The condemned left a field of burnt bones spread out from the gates.

He looked back at his shabby, wooden bed with its worn, burlap blanket and a lumpy straw mattress. Suddenly, he felt dizzy and weak, stumbled back to the bed, and collapsed. The straw smelled moldy and old, but he soon fell into a deep sleep and sensed nothing but darkness; there was an emptiness to his sleep now. Only when he woke did he feel the constant fear—the horror he found himself in. He would sleep, wake, eat his mush, and sleep again. Shawn found refuge in his sleep. Sometimes he saw a strange, old woman dressed in a long, brown, ragged dress, barefoot, walking stiffly. On occasion, she would stop, curse, and pull a sliver from her barefoot.

She would switch the buckets, set his bowl of mush on the table, and pour more water into his pitcher. Most times, he would pretend to be asleep. One day he was sitting at the table, eating his mush, picking the black bugs out when the old woman came through the door.

She stared at him. Her eyes were old and bloodshot, always holding a far-off stare. "You should eat the bugs for nourishment. You will need your strength. The Tempter loves to whip," she scolded him.

Shawn could see scars on her arms and marks from the whip at the top of her back.

"How long have you been here?" Shawn asked.

"I was brought here as a young girl; payment for some terrible deed done to The Tempter. I have felt her whip many times since. You must gain your strength, Demon Slayer. You will need it soon."

There was no sense of time here; Shawn slept and woke only to eat or relieve himself. He had just started to regain his strength when Luvon woke him with his hand around his throat, yanking him from the bed and holding him against the wall. Luvon yelled at him as he flung him to the floor. "Malin waits for you! Get-up, mighty Demon Slayer!" Luvon laughed at him. "Oh, I forgot, you are just a weak human now." Luvon pulled him to his feet by his arm, dragging him out the door and down the hall. "You are strong enough now to face Malin's whip."

Luvon led him to a large door with black symbols burned into its brown, hardwood. The warlock turned the black latch, opened the door, and threw him in where, again, he landed on a wooden floor. Malin stood washing blood from her hands at a large water basin. She wore tight, black pants, black boots, and a red blouse. Her face held a cruel look, and a small streak of blood marred her cheek. Shawn was not the only unfortunate soul to visit this room today.

Bloodstained the wooden floor, and chains with hooks and cuffs hung from the ceiling. Next to the far wall was a wooden stand, and hanging from it were various black, iron instruments used for tearing and piercing flesh. An eerie orange light penetrated the small windows of the room. Malin held a whip in her hand and pulled Shawn from the floor by his jaw with the other.

"It is time to start your payment to Lucifer. I cannot wait any longer. The demons want their revenge, and Lucifer demands it of me. I have shown you mercy already and let you regain your strength. All you have to do, Shawn, is swear your love for me, your loyalty, and I will stop. Lucifer will allow this." Malin turned to Luvon and yelled, "Chain him!"

Luvon dragged Shawn to the chains with his bare feet scraping the floor, cuffed his wrists, hoisted him into the air, and did the same with his ankles. Shawn hung in the air by his arms, his legs spread apart. Luvon walked toward him with a hook and chain and pierced the hook through the skin of Shawn's chest as he screamed in agony. Luvon then gave the chain to Malin, and she pulled it tight, making him sway, pulling the skin on his chest. Pulling him forward, she held him tight, and he felt the first lash hit his stomach. The pain was agonizing, and again he screamed. His skin quivered, rising in a red welt, slightly cracked open, and blood trickled down his stomach. There came another lash, then another, as he hung, screaming in agony.

He felt the pain and the burn from twelve lashes before his head bent forward, and darkness took him. Water hit him in the face, and he felt the tight grip of Malin's hand on his jaw, the jerk that raised his head. "Tell me you will be with me, and I will end this, I swear."

"I will never be with you," Shawn gasped. "This is the only way we will be together."

"Eventually, you will agree, stupid man," Malin hissed at him.

Malin continued to whip him; he passed out three more times only to be awakened by water thrown in his face and Malin demanding his loyalty, his love. The last time, he woke in his bed with the old woman standing over him, dressing his wounds.

"You must relinquish what they want from you, or you will not last long here," the old woman advised him as she pushed a hunk of aged, moldy cheese into his hand. Taking away the pan of red water, she left him alone.

He lay in pain, stuffed the cheese into his mouth, and tried to turn to find a spot where the whip had not cut him, but he could not. He felt feverish and cried out, "Herit, where are you!" Then he heard Malin's mocking voice in his head.

"Herit, where are you! I told you, there are no angels that can help you now."

Chapter Seventeen

K atherine stayed in the ground in Washington for a month and slowly became aware of the cold, moist earth surrounding her, cradling her. She heard the despair of the angels as Malin's evil grew stronger, and felt The Mother's healing energy renewing her, adding to her power. The Mother had not come to her. When Eos did come near, Katherine felt doubt from her, and finally, she heard the call to go to her shrine.

A week had passed since she came from the ground. Victoria had left to be with Peter in Amsterdam and to begin tackling the responsibilities Katherine had imposed on her. Katherine walked the path around the lake. How beautiful it was here, how peaceful; she always came back when her responsibilities became too much for her, and always felt Anne in this place. She strained to remember the first time she saw this place when Shawn had brought her here so long ago. That was the first time she had met her family, her real family, and experienced the love that came from them. Now some were gone, and the terrible confrontations with evil dragged on and on. And now through the centuries, it had become her responsibility to carry on the fight.

Katherine felt terrible loneliness, emptiness, with her maker gone. Her thoughts always went back to Shawn and the horror, the humiliation he must be experiencing, and these thoughts would bring blood tears to her eyes and a terrible cold to her body. She had sent word to her advisors to prepare for the battle that certainly was coming, to learn all they could of the conditions they would face once they descended the shaft at the old Hell's Hole. Katherine had decided and decreed that when she was with the angels, Victoria would be in charge.

Katherine had sent word by Victoria to Peter to build and prepare the army for the assault on the black castle. The limitations of time weighed heavily on her. Off into the distance, she stared, gathering her senses, and sent a powerful psychic message to Malin. *I am coming for you.* Still, she could feel nothing from her maker, nothing at all.

Renee wanted to go with her to the shrine, but Katherine told her she must go alone. Katherine also told Renee to go to Amsterdam and help Victoria prepare for the coming battle, and to make their family to fight for Shawn. A cold, damp wind blew against her face and tossed the yellow leaves of autumn into the lake. A gust of wind rippled the water as it moved across the pond. She watched a loon take flight and swoop breaking the water, taking a break from making its winter home. How bleak everything was now. Would she ever feel happiness again? Would she ever live a normal vampire life again?

Katherine saw the aircar land at the front of the house. A Crimmian driver and Renee got out, the Crimmian walking to the front door as Renee approached Katherine.

"How are you feeling this eve?" Renee asked as she came close.

"I feel sad for the pain Shawn is going through. I sometimes don't think I can stand these thoughts, imagining what is happening to him."

"You must stay strong if there is to be any hope for Shawn," Renee said as she turned her sad gaze out over the lake. Katherine could see a blood tear come to her eye.

"Shawn made a terrible enemy of Lucifer. Caitlyn and I are leaving for Amsterdam. I have also contacted Rebecca McCall. What is left of our family will stand with you and fight to the end, for Shawn."

"All the Bryces will be there. That I know," Katherine turned and spoke with a sorrowful voice. "I pray, all will leave."

"I worry for Caitlyn, as she is not a warrior, but she is a thousand years old, and makes her own decisions. I will be at your side with Deceida either way."

"Go and help Victoria lead. Be her second," Katherine softly instructed Renee. "The Mother has summoned me. I leave for Picchu tomorrow eve. I hope someday we can all be together again here, at our home, in this beautiful place."

"As you wish, Queen Katherine." Renee turned and walked back down the path toward the house.

Katherine walked a dark street in Lima, Peru. She had received a message from Stephen to meet a courier in this part of the city. She strolled, mostly by herself, the San Miguel section of the city. Lima was a large and sprawling city. Its population was low, like most places on Earth. This was a large city but now had an aura of abandonment because of so few humans and the many empty buildings. Most cities had programs to increase the birth rate, but Lima had none. An air taxi landed to unload a resident of one of the occupied buildings. The driver was an A.I.—they were becoming much more prevalent in this world, filling many services jobs because of the population problem.

It was a dark night, and Katherine could smell the seawater close by. She walked past a staring young man, nodded, smiled, and placed the thought in his head that her looks did not matter and that he should mind his business.

She still had not sensed the courier, yet she was sure this was the area given by Stephen. Even stranger, she could not detect a vampire. She stopped, strained her powerful senses, but felt nothing and realized she was the only vampire there. Suddenly, a dim light appeared in front of her, wavered, and she heard the voice of Drake in her head:

You are in terrible danger! Look forward, concentrate, and see!

Looking down the street, bringing her powerful eyes to bear, she searched in front of her. Straining her sight, she saw a small blue spike of energy coming directly for her, appearing and disappearing, slipping in and out of this plane of existence. She leaped up and to her left just in time for the spike to miss her heart. The spike sliced through her side, spun her around with no effort at all, and then disappeared back to the plane of evil from whence it came.

Katherine fell to the ground, stunned, and then slowly sat up. She felt weak, disorientated, and the wound burned terribly. Down the street, a man walked toward her, and, in his hand, he held a vampire spike with barbs. The man was Stephen, and she sensed Lucifer's evil on him. Dazed, she tried to get to her feet but still was too weak. Stephen arrived and stared down at her, put his foot on her chest, pushed her against the building, and held her there.

"Why are you doing this, Stephen?" Katherine gasped. "Why are you killing your queen?"

"My 'queen'? That is a laugh. The biggest mistake I made in my long life was to make Anne Bryce a council member. Bryces are the scum of vampire kind, and I will kill every last one of you."

"You're mad! Lucifer has done this to you! He has gotten to you!"

"Can't you feel it? It is a great day, Katherine! With you and Shawn gone, I will lead vampires again. Only they will be Lucifer's vampires."

"The angels will never allow it, and Michael will never allow it!"

"Michael will have no choice. Lucifer is always one step ahead of him. You are certainly aware of how easy it was for him to take the mighty do-gooder, Shawn. Can you imagine the torture he is going through?"

"I showed you mercy, but you are a deceiver! I always knew you were." Again, Katherine tried desperately to get to her feet, but Stephen pushed her back.

"I'm surprised a pain in the ass like you lived for six hundred years. Prepare to be with the angels." Stephen took her hair, forced her head against the wall, and drew the vampire slayer back. The terror she felt was not for losing her life; instead, it was for Shawn because she realized she could not save him now.

Looking Stephen in the eyes, she said, "You will pay for this."

A white plasma beam hit Stephen in the side, throwing him down the street, and causing the vampire slayer to fall from his hand. A shaken Stephen got to his feet, and another plasma beam hit him, throwing him farther down the street. Gwyn landed in front of her, a powerful witch-turned vampire, carrying Shawn's original strength, Gwyn, holding a small brown rod in her hand.

"We can't have a wretched vampire like you, Stephen, ruining everything."

Katherine saw Stephen rise and immediately take to the air, making his escape. She sat, stunned, staring at Gwyn, and not quite believing she had saved her.

"I was so scared, Katherine! I didn't think I was going to make it! Who would have thought Stephen would be an assassin?"

Katherine stared at Gwyn, still amazed, she had arrived in time to save her. "Thank you! How did you know?"

"The Mother just learned of the deception," Gwyn said as she helped Katherine to her feet. Gwyn placed her rod on Katherine's wound, and Katherine saw a dark blue mist leave her and enter the rod.

"Dark energy…that's why you are so weak," Gwyn whispered as if she was afraid the devil would hear her and then scooped Katherine up and rose quickly into the air. Katherine sensed Gwyn was taking her eastward, and she felt her wound healing. The wind against her face also helped her to regain her senses. Gwyn soon landed on the banks of a river, and Katherine removed her clothes and stumbled into the moving waters, allowing the healing waters to wash over her. She watched Gwyn, naked, wade into the water, and immerse herself.

They both went back to the riverbank and sat next to each other on a large rock to dry, water dripping from their wet skin and hair. Katherine felt Gwyn wrap her arms around her and pull her close, and they sat as the dawn's light spread over them. Katherine felt the warmth of the sun, the caressing of Gwyn's hands, and heard her soothing voice.

"We will find a way to save him."

"Why must I go to The Mother?" Katherine asked. She could feel the unbearable desperation again. "I should be in Amsterdam preparing the army. I fear we are not ready."

"Time is important, and The Mother will explain all. Let's sit for a time and let the sun warm us. You will need great power to rescue Shawn, and when you are in front of The Mother in Heaven, you receive power. Your visit will not be like your last."

Katherine felt Gwyn take her face with her wet hands, kissing her softly, and heard the roar of the water. She looked at Gwyn's face, the water trickling down her cheeks, and then she looked into her eyes. Gwyn had changed to a vampire—her eyes burned a bright blue, brighter than she had ever seen. Gwyn pulled Katherine's head to her neck and said, "Take my blood. Darkness is descending on this world, and you will need strength."

Her lips felt Gwyn's soft skin, and her blood teeth slid beneath it until they found the blood artery. Sweet blood filled her mouth and flowed down her widening throat. There was high power in Gwyn's blood; it traveled through her body and filled every cell. She felt The Mother her power filling her. She fell into a trance, seeing a bright light and the angelic face of a woman. It all faded, and she was sitting next to Gwyn, a drop of blood running down her chin. Now she realized the power Gwyn had.

Katherine took hold of Gwyn's face, brought her lips to hers, kissed her on the mouth, felt Gwyn's passion, and whispered in her ear.

"You are a Bryce, and I expect you to stand with the Bryces when the time comes. I don't care about any deal you made with Shawn or The Mother."

"I will, Katherine, but I can't come just yet. I still need time. Every day I become more a part of The Mother. I walk with her in her world. Take her energy. When the fight starts, I will be there and bring this power to the Gates of Hell, I swear. The Mother also wants this."

Katherine's head fell to her chest, a sadness spread over her face, and she whispered, "You and the army are not ready. What shall I do?"

"I will tell you this," Gwyn whispered, "Eos and Michael quarrel now. The future that surrounds Shawn can no longer be seen. It is dark and uncertain, and Michael blames Eos. We may have to save Shawn by ourselves." The vampires sat in silence, warming their cold bodies in the early morning sun.

They quietly dressed and traveled on into the mountains, Katherine's feelings of foreboding only intensifying as they went, and soon they found a cave in which to take shelter. They lay close for the comfort they gave each other. Katherine was restless; her mind was racing, and she needed to talk. Fear was her constant companion now.

Katherine moved closer to Gwyn and whispered in her ear, "Do you take blood, Gwyn?"

"I take vampire blood, and if I have to, I can go a while before taking blood. I don't need human blood, but it's delicious, and I do enjoy it. I am a vampire, but my purpose in this world is different than yours."

"What is your purpose?" Katherine asked.

"You are here to help humans. I am here to help vampires. And as you can see, evil has penetrated your ranks."

"Are you hungry now?" Katherine whispered as she wrapped herself around Gwyn. "You can have some of my blood."

"Do you have your strength?" Gwyn asked softly. "I would like a taste of you."

"Yes, I'm well enough. And then Katherine felt Gwyn's teeth enter her neck and the pressure to take her blood, and then the lick of her wet tongue and the passionate kiss of her bloody lips—a kiss that surprised Katherine.

"I am sorry for your pain," Gwyn whispered.

"I tried so hard to save Shawn from Malin," Katherine said as she held onto Gwyn. "I would have killed Malin, but Lucifer was there, and the angels did nothing. They even allowed Malin to kill Jessamine. The Mother did nothing." She felt Gwyn's head come to rest on her chest.

"Jessamine is in a better place. She is part of The Mother again. Like Drake, she was never meant to live long, and the angels told you Malin would take Shawn. The Mother will explain," Gwyn whispered. "Let's sleep---I am tired. Sometimes it is hard work being a Bryce vampire."

The vampires left the following eve for the shrine at Picchu. They flew to the trail and started their long climb up the mountain that held the shrine. A red tear came to Katherine's eye. The last time she walked this trail, Jessamine and Drake was with her. Katherine followed behind Gwyn as they went higher, and the air became thin. The trees had disappeared a long way back. All they could see were grey, wet rocks, green moss, and faded green brush.

"You must prepare yourself this time for The Mother," Gwyn told her.

"What do you mean?" Katherine asked as she worked her way between two large rocks.

"The Mother will take you to Heaven. I know this won't be the first time you have been. She feels that you have the experience for this, particularly after your visit with Michael."

"Certainly won't be the first time," Katherine murmured as they relentlessly moved up the trail.

They made their way up the mountain, around the boulders, and through the mist, and came to the shrine at daybreak. Katherine sensed the electricity immediately as the power of The Mother filled the wet air. Through the early morning mist, the polished granite stone shrine came into view. Water poured from the rock face behind it and down onto and into the sanctuary. The sound of the water cascading filled the air and made rainbows in the early morning light. She tasted a saltiness in the wetness that hung in the air, felt she could reach out, and touch the clouds as they sped overhead.

"Are you ready to enter?" Gwyn asked.

"I'm ready," Katherine replied as she steadied herself.

Katherine followed Gwyn inside. The only light streamed down in beams from the opening at the top of the shrine. Worry spread over her, as she feared what The Mother was going to tell her, and she bit her bottom lip in apprehension. The water cascaded over a large, six-foot-high, clear quartz crystal. She heard the familiar tinkling, felt the electrically charged air, and the tremendous energy that filled the chamber. The mist and beams of light around the large crystal made rainbows that hung in the air.

Suddenly, a light came from the crystal, grew in size and intensity, traveled toward her, and engulfed her. Her vision went white from the strength of the light, and then she was falling as if the floor had opened beneath her. Intense vibrations traveled through her as she left the physical world, and woke lying on a dirt path.

Floating to her feet, she looked up at the bright blue sky. There was no sun, only the occasional billowy white cloud. As always, she felt the intensity of this reality and knew she was in Heaven. The path was in the middle of a field filled with wildflowers, knee-high field grass, and the buzz of bees flying amongst the flowers. The flowing brightness of the colors amazed her.

She followed the path into a forest, where squirrels climbed the trees, and small creatures scurried around them. Birds flew about everywhere, and she could hear the sounds of animals clearly in her mind. She came upon a large lion sitting next to the path and listened to its voice:

Heaven is with you, vampire. And Heaven is with our covenant. The angels have chosen our covenant to rule. Do you not recognize me? I am Bricius. I have come to tell you to believe, and Shawn will be saved.

The lion rose, sauntered back into the trees, and disappeared. Katherine walked on and came to an old man walking across the path, his clothes worn and ragged. The man had old, high brown shoes, long, grey hair, in a mess, with a small bird in it. Many other small animals clung to his clothes and followed behind him. Katherine watched the old man turn, look at her, and she projected to him.

I am looking for The Mother. She waited and heard back from the old man.

Follow the path guardian. You will find The Mother.

Katherine continued to walk the trail and came to another meadow with green grass, vibrant flowers, and a brook running through it. At the edge of this brook, sitting in the grass, was a beautiful, white-haired woman with an angelic face. The woman appeared to wear a long, white linen gown, and her feet were bare. A soft white light radiated from her. An eagle twice her size stood guard next to the woman. It turned its head to look at Katherine with ancient, yellow, burning eyes, from over its sharp, white beak. Powerful energy came from the bird.

The angel was petting a fox, and other small animals had gathered around her, waiting for their turn. She even could hear the sounds of the brook, and a gentle breeze blew across her cheek. The woman looked up at Katherine and smiled. Katherine felt the tremendous power of this woman and realized she was The Mother.

She heard, but the woman's mouth did not move:

Greetings to you, Katherine, queen of the warrior vampires of Earth.

Greetings, Katherine projected.

I know you have questions for me. That is why I brought you here, and it was a condition of Michael's.

Why did you allow that horrible Malin to kill Jessamine?

That was Jessamine's purpose in your world. To live and protect Shawn and to die for him. That was why I sent a part of my energy, and Pandora, eight hundred years ago, to the bayou for Shawn.

Where is Jessamine? Can I see her?

Jessamine was always a part of me, and you can know her now, through me.

Why didn't you let me kill Malin in my world so I could save Shawn? I could have killed her, but Lucifer's power was there. Why didn't you help? No rules would have been broken under those conditions.

Many of your years ago, so many I cannot count or remember, in another world, Malin and I were as you are on your earth. We were that world's vampires. I loved a vampire dearly, and because of jealously, Malin killed him. Malin was much older than my lover and me. I vowed to kill Malin, and we have fought on many worlds through the ages. I gave up being a warrior angel because of the loss of my lover, and eventually, this is what I became. I have kept my hate for Malin through the ages. It has been my one weakness, and I might have lost Shawn because of it.

Fear gripped Katherine as she projected, *what do you mean? What has happened?*

Lucifer has made Shawn mortal, and now I cannot see his future. He might suspect the trap I set for Malin. He might know that Shawn is my Trojan Horse.

Shawn is mortal? No, no...how could you let this happen! I could have killed Malin on Earth! I could have saved him from this!

Hear me, Katherine! You must attempt a rescue with the vampire army. Enter the Penn Shaft, go to Malin's black castle, and rescue Shawn. You must do this soon.

The army isn't ready. They need more time. I only now started to expand the army.

You have to attack if we are to save Shawn. Michael and I have come to an agreement, and he gave his consent. He wants Shawn saved, and Malin's death is secondary now. You must go as quickly as you can to the black castle.

I will take the army, ready or not, and do as you command. I will reach the black castle, and I pray he is still alive. That seems doubtful. If he is mortal, Malin surely would have killed him by now. For me, Mother, your endeavors are not worth the price I will pay.

Many souls will be saved if Malin cannot access all of the physical worlds. Not just your world. When Herit started watching Shawn, I saw the future and cast out a powerful spell to the Lesser Gods, and they accepted the spell, except for one condition, guardians had to kill Malin at the Gates of Hell. Finally, Shawn came, the Demon Slayer, and I saw my chance. That is why guardians must kill Malin at the Gates of Hell. That must be one of your priorities.

Malin will die that I promise you!

As soon as she thought the words, Katherine saw Gwyn walking down the path, and then the world in front of her started to fade and fell apart. She woke soaked, lying in a ball on the rock floor of the shrine. Slowly, she rose off the floor, righted herself, stood looking around the chamber, and found that Gwyn was nowhere to be seen. Katherine made her way outside, and still, she could not find Gwyn. She walked back down the mountain, reached the bottom, flew north to Dalton to gather her guard, and then left for Amsterdam to prepare the army for the assault on the black castle.

Chapter Eighteen

A shoeless Shawn made his way down a spiral stone stairway. Malin did not allow slaves to have shoes in the castle. In this part of the castle, the inside walls were made of light brownstone, with few windows to see out. Again, the inside was in sharp contrast to what was outside. Shawn headed to the kitchen. Baking bread was the job given to him by the old lady, and he dared not to be late, or the large, burly man that ran the kitchen would beat him.

Malin rarely beat him since she had almost killed him. She had been in a bad mood that day, and his rejection of her had sent her into a rage. He still could hear her cursing over him, about his mortality, how it limited what she could do to him, and how it had been a mistake to turn him, mortal. It had taken a long time for him to heal, but now life was a little better as long as he could make it to the kitchen. Malin would send for him sometimes, make him come to her as she lay naked on her bed. Then Malin would make him, make love to her and make him stay until he was exhausted. This also limited his beatings.

Sometimes, while he made his way to the kitchen, Luvon would be waiting for him, to fall upon him, and chase him, striking him with a wooden rod, always trying to humiliate him until he reached the safety of the kitchen. Only then Luvon usually broke off his attack. Shawn would continuously change his route in attempts to avoid cruel Luvon. Most days he was successful in tricking him, which only sent Luvon into a rage. Rarely in his thousand-year life had he come across a creature as cruel as Luvon.

He made his way through the hallways, trying to avoid the dark warriors standing guard at closed doors, and finally to the hall that held the entrance to the kitchen. Lights hovered by the ceiling to light the way. Strange glass globes sat on pedestals and lined the hallway, flashing scenes of other worlds. Most times, he met other poor wretches, mostly humans, but sometimes creatures from other physical worlds. One such thing was the brown reptilian creature with a large head that held dark, lidless eyes. When the animal passed, he heard a gravelly sound that he finally understood to mean, "Filthy human, you smell."

Escape was impossible for him now. All the old woman gave him to wear were old, brown pants with a worn, black belt to hold them up. He was mortal now, with the scars to prove it and certainly would perish outside, if he ever made it out. Sometimes, he would think about what The Mother had told him about the power, but he would quickly banish it to the back of his mind. He certainly did not feel powerful now.

There was the door to the kitchen. He had made it without attracting Luvon's wrath. Through the door, he went into the hot kitchen, smoke, and steam wafting through the air, carrying the smell of cooking meat and sauces simmering on the stoves. He saw the other poor, wretched mortals working the brick ovens, both men and women, bare-chested, their sweaty skin glistening from the heat of the kitchen. He too would sweat, but now it was clear and salty. How strange it was to find himself weak and mortal in this terrible reality.

Shawn would try to avoid the hateful stare of the large man-beast that ran the kitchen and always tried to avoid a blow from him as he passed. The hairy man would mock him, calling him "Demon Slayer" as he shoved him violently to the stone floor, skinning his soft mortal skin.

Quickly, he went to his area of the kitchen, with its barrels of flour, bread pans, buckets of warm water, and a large, wooden worktable. The wood of the table had many chips and knife marks from other poor wretches that had spent their last days there. Above, near the ceiling, were windows that glowed orange from the outside fires, and above them, the soot-stained vents in the ceiling.

Shawn had just finished his first batch of bread and had set it aside to rise when Luvon came bursting into the kitchen. The warlock was drunk on PeLa, held a long, wooden rod in his hand, and, as usual, a harsh, cruel look on his face directed toward Shawn.

"Where is the mighty Demon Slayer?" Luvon slurred. "There he is."

Shawn saw Luvon heading for him his face contorted with vengeful rage.

"You think you are so clever, avoiding me. I will teach you to take your beatings!" Luvon screamed at him as he advanced, his rod raised high. Shawn felt the first blow on his shoulder, and he felt his collarbone crack as the shock drove him to the floor. He tried to crawl under the table but Luvon stomped on him, yanked him out by his foot, and brought his rod down repeatedly on his back. Shawn thought his back would break, so he rolled over, arms held outward, protecting his head from the blows. When he was almost ready to pass out, he saw distortion in the air, a ball of dark energy hitting Luvon and knocking him into the stone wall, senseless.

Then came the screams of Malin. "I told you not to beat him that way, you filthy warlock! I am the only one to beat him! I should send you to our father! Get out of my sight!"

Luvon rose to his feet, head hanging, and stumbled to the door.

"Lucifer wants this," Luvon mumbled. "You should do what Lucifer wants."

"I know what Lucifer wants! Get out and don't come back to this kitchen!" Malin screamed as she threw his rod after him. All the slaves cowered into every corner of the kitchen, hiding their faces from the Succubus. Shawn felt Malin gather him in her arms, carry him, and then he lost consciousness.

Shawn woke to Malin sitting over him, her long, black hair

hanging freely, brushing against his face. He saw her creamy white skin, black eyes, and black lips—with a cold smile on her face. She had healed his broken bone. Malin reached down to stroke his face, and her touch was cold. She smelled of sour berries, and when her lips covered his, she tasted like spoiled vinegar. Malin rose back up and said, "Love me, Shawn, and all this pain will go away."

"Never," he said back. He felt her hand slide into his pants, trying to make him hard. When she realized he would not respond, she slapped him across the face and chanted a spell that made him erect. She held him by his throat, pulled his ragged pants from him, straddled him, and rode him for what he thought was forever. Malin would kiss him passionately, and that made him want to scream. Lying next to him, she would caress him, telling him how beautiful their evil would be together, and how she would make him powerful again. Eventually, Malin would gather her clothes and leave. This became a common occurrence for him.

****

Katherine sat on the blue throne, staring down at the marble floor, and counting the imperfections in the mortar. She looked out over the pool of water, and every so often glanced back at Peter. Peter had sent agents to hunt for Stephen after the attempt on her life. Renee, Caitlyn, and Victoria stood at her side, and Peter was giving her a readiness report on the army.

Katherine arrived back in Amsterdam one week earlier, had met with representatives of the other four vampire covenants, and decreed each would supply two hundred vampires for her army. The heads of the covenants resisted, as they had little respect for her because of her age. The negotiations went on for a week, and finally, they relented. They did not think Lucifer's witches were much of a threat, and some would not commit to the rescue of Shawn.

Katherine continued to listen to Peter and did not like what she was hearing, which only increased the desperation she felt.

"We know little of what is inside the cavern," Peter said. "We heard the cavern will dull our powers and make flying impossible, but I'm not sure of this. So the plan is simple. Follow the fire river, storm the black castle, rescue Shawn, and kill Malin."

"How many vampire soldiers will we have?" She asked.

"We will have six hundred, my queen, but half of them have just learned how to use a slayer, and most of them are only a couple centuries old. That leaves two hundred poorly trained warriors in reserve and eight hundred more supposedly coming from the covenants. We need more time."

Katherine slammed her hand down on the armrest and raised her voice. "How could it be that vampires do not know how to use a slayer? And where are the older vampires?"

"Most thought that feeding on evil would be enough and did not listen to their angels. I don't know why older vampires don't join our ranks." Peter quickly answered, surprised by this outburst, then lowered his voice and mumbled, "Maybe older vampires feel older vampires should be leading them."

Turning her head, Katherine watched Juliette throw open the large, white double doors in typical Juliette fashion. She followed her confident stride across the floor to the moat, and as she floated across to the landing near Katherine's throne, saw her glance at Peter; the look revealed affection and love for him. Katherine had known Juliette all her vampire life and trusted her with her life. Juliette was certainly a Bryce, and along with Renee and Shawn, a living vampire of Anne's making.

"You sent for me?" Juliette asked.

"Yes, I did. I have a command for you. You will stay back. When I enter the shaft, you will take over my duties here. Be in charge until I come out of the shaft. Do you understand?"

"I understand," Juliette stammered, "But...I know nothing about leading. What about the others? What about Renee?"

"I didn't either, but I learned, and so will you. I need a Bryce. Someone I can trust. Treachery has compromised my counsel. This time Renee will fight and lead. The others will go, too."

"Oh, Rebecca McCall has sent word. She and Jermaine McCall will be with you for the rescue," Juliette told her.

"I knew she would come," Katherine whispered.

Katherine stood, faced the vampires, and spoke in a loud voice. This was as good as time as any to say what she had to say. "All of you, Michael, has sent word to me. If I am killed, Victoria will become queen. It is what Michael and The Mother wants."

"Katherine, maybe it should wait until the angels make it known to all who should be queen," Victoria quickly replied.

"Vampires will not accept another Bryce, another Herit. We have made too many enemies. They will accept a Kenmare, and you know how to handle vampires. After all, you handled Shawn for many years."

A long, uncomfortable silence followed, and then Caitlyn spoke.

"Have you heard about that killer, Stephen?" Caitlyn asked as she glanced toward Renee.

"He is in hiding, but I will find him," Katherine assured her as she tried to hide her disgust for him. "He is a betrayer, an agent of Lucifer now."

She turned and looked at Peter, hoping no one noticed the pain she felt. She had spared Stephen, and he had almost doomed Shawn to Hell.

"Are there enough slayers and chest armor?" Katherine quickly asked Peter.

"Yes, my queen, all who go will have a slayer and armor."

Katherine stood and said, "I think that is enough for this eve. I'm going to my quarters. I thank you all for your help."

As she was leaving, Renee called after her. "Have you heard from Gwyn? She is Bryce."

"No, I haven't," Katherine replied as she floated over the moat and toward the large doors to her throne room.

Katherine sat at her vanity, brushing her hair and getting ready for her couch. Brushing her hair always helped relieve her tension. These days she slept alone. She missed Thomas and wished he were here. She had not heard from Drake since the attempt on her life. Michael was quiet and gave little guidance—now she only heard from The Mother.

In a way, she had hurt Renee by the selection but knew Renee was relieved, no Bryce really wanted this job. What the Bryces wanted now was to save Shawn and go home to Washington. Her thoughts went to Shawn, they always did, and she still felt a terrible fear for him. How desperate this felt for her, she had to rescue Shawn, now, he was mortal, and Malin could quickly kill him.

Six hundred warrior vampires certainly could fight their way to the black castle—they must. She set the brush down and floated from the chair toward her couch. Down she slipped into its soft mattress, pulling the top down and the covers over her head, and fell into a restless sleep.

Floating in the light, she listened to warrior angels singing their songs of war, telling her not to despair. Soon, she felt the strong presence of Drake. His spiritual energy had grown sharp.

Drake, I' m so glad you came to me tonight. I was hoping to hear from you, my love.

I can feel your pain, Katherine---you must be strong. I have news of Shawn. Michael says there is a spy in the black castle, an old woman, and she is near Shawn. Shawn is still alive, but mortal and Malin will not kill him. She has spared him, and, at times, protects him. Michael says she lives in the physical world for now and wants him for herself.

My maker's charm has saved him again. Malin told me this, but I did not believe she would want a soul as pure as Shawn's. I told her she would never keep Shawn. I will take the army to her castle, and she will pay for what she has done.

I have saved the bad news for last. Vampires cannot levitate inside the cavern, you will be too close to the Gates of Hell.

Will we lose other powers!

The dark energies of hell will affect your other powers, but flight that takes the most energy will be lost.

Nineteen

K atherine woke early and had just left her shower. She wrapped a light blue silk robe around her wet, naked body, and walked out onto her balcony. Tonight a hunger for blood had its grip on her. Katherine had not fed in a month, and soon she would gratify that need.

The sun was slowly setting into the light pink sky that was the horizon. Katherine felt a warm summer breeze caressing her wet skin, and could tell it had been a hot day. A day that humans would call sticky because of the heat. The scream of a raven, as it took flight, brought her out of her worries, and she immediately cloaked her thoughts and watched the bird swoop past her, never taking its beady eyes off her—a spy of Lucifer's no doubt. Lucifer's spies were everywhere these days. A lump formed in her throat. Was this a bad sign?

To her left were the high towers of Amsterdam, their colored lights starting to light the deepening twilight of this evening. It had been five years since Malin took Shawn, five years of desperation. It had taken time to build an army with the heads of the covenants always standing in the way.

Two eves from tonight, she would move her vampire army, six hundred warrior vampires, to Dalton to start final preparations for the assault. Two hundred warrior vampires would be left in reserve. Katherine had bought land, and the Crimmians had enlarged the guard quarters there. Now the encampment could hold hundreds, and this would be where she would garrison her army. She wanted the vampires to be close to the shaft when they started their attack. Rebecca and Jermaine McCall arrived a few days ago, and she sent them on to Dalton.

Katherine turned her head; she looked east, and a smile came to her face. It was Gwyn Bryce—she had come after all. Gwyn came over the trees with a determined look and quickly landed on her balcony.

"Greetings, queen, I hope you are well in these distressful times."

"Look at you, Gwyn, dressed as a warrior, with armor, and a small sword at your side to keep your rod company," Katherine said with a smirk and a wink. "You might need a bigger sword. I have seen the dark warriors, and they are fearsome."

"I have come to stand with you and the Bryces. I have much worse in store for those evil creatures than my sword. We will rescue Shawn. I told The Mother how important this was for you…for me to be with my vampire family."

"She still feels we should attack?" Katherine asked.

"Yes, she wants you to take the vampire army to the cavern as soon as possible. She knows Shawn is still alive, but she's not sure how long he will remain so."

"Michael sent word through Drake that Shawn is alive and that Malin wants him for herself. We fly to Dalton in two eves. From there, when we are ready, we'll leave, enter the shaft, and move into the cavern."

Five eves later, Katherine stood with the Bryces, with Victoria, Rebecca, and her army. The night of the attack had come. Once Katherine arrived in Dalton, it had taken three eves to make the final preparations. The vampire army, six hundred strong, lined the riverbank for a half-mile with slayers on their backs, silver chest armor, shields, and forearm and shin guards. She could see the anxiety on their faces. It was a clear, warm night with a full moon to mark the occasion. The moonlight reflected off the river water; Katherine could still remember Thomas fishing in this light.

She felt anxious and desperate at the same time. They knew little about the cavern and what they would find; most likely, they would meet the dark warriors, but how many, she did not know. She turned and looked at her family, the vampires she had known all her vampire life, gave them a worried smile, and they returned a half-smile, an anxious smile.

"Are we ready?" Katherine asked.

"Yes, my queen," they said in unison.

"Tonight, we save Shawn." Her voice became emotional. "He is a part of us all. His blood is our blood, and Malin will never have him, not as long as there is a Bryce, McCall, or a Kenmare alive. Am I right about that?" She stared at them, peering into their faces and looking for their resolve.

"Yes, Katherine," they all spoke.

Katherine turned back to Peter. "Is the army ready? Do they know what is expected of them?"

"They do, my queen. Some could have used more time."

"There is no more time, Peter. Prepare to attack."

"As you command," Peter answered as he nodded to one of his commanders. The commander turned with a lightsaber in hand and waved it. Far down the line, another lightsaber waved back, and with the clang of metal, the army readied themselves.

Katherine faced down the riverbank and shouted out, "Tonight, the angels watch you! Fight well! They will sing of this battle in Heaven and they will sing of you! Tonight, you fulfill your destiny!"

She stood and let the soft breeze blow against her face, listened to the flow of the river water and the wind through the trees. She felt frozen in time with a desperation building in her to end this. The sound of Victoria's voice woke her from her trance.

"Now or never, Katherine."

"Vampires, attack!" she screamed as she lifted into the air.

The warrior vampires followed and formed an arrowhead with Katherine at the tip. They flew high and fast, directly to the Penn cave.

Soon, the field in front of the cave came into view, and the vampires landed ten to twenty at a time and quickly drew their slayers. Katherine immediately sensed the dark wolves hiding just inside the cave and knew the cave had masked the wolves from them. Peter immediately called for the formation, and hundreds of snarling dark wolves stormed forth from the mouth of the cave.

The wolves rushed across the field, gnashing their saliva-coated fangs, and their vicious growls echoed out into the dark night. Peter quickly ordered the vampires to advance. The vampires and the snarling wolves clashed at the center of the field. The yelling and ringing of metal mixed with the snarls of the wolves blared in the darkness. The vampires moved quickly. With flashes of their slayers, wolf after wolf fell, slain, to the ground, changing back to their human forms. Katherine did not have the experience with wolves that her maker had, but she felt their strength and their quickness. Lucifer was sacrificing the wolves, killing them by the hundreds, to weaken the vampires before they entered the cave.

The thought, *He knows*, screamed in her head.

She would wield Alexa repeatedly; her sword from Heaven glowed and sliced the wolves' heads cleanly from their bodies.

Katherine fought like a madwoman, cutting through the wolves, but not all of the younger vampires shared in her success. The wolves swarmed over the younger ones, took some, and she saw vampire spirits leaving for Heaven. The battle went on into the night, and, finally, the vampires killed the last dark wolf.

Victoria came, grabbed Katherine's arm, and shouted to her, "Lucifer and Malin know we were coming!"

Katherine looked at her and wiped wolf blood from her face. "We can still make it," she pleaded. "Please help me!"

All of the vampires were covered in wolf's blood. She yelled at Peter, "How many did we lose?"

"We lost thirty-two vampires, my queen," Peter yelled back.

"Peter, prepare the army! We are still going down the shaft!" she commanded.

Gwyn came up next to her. "Lucifer certainly knows what we are trying to do. Are you sure?"

"Maybe we should turn back and wait. Use the element of surprise?" Renee suggested as she tended to the deep gash on Caitlyn's side.

"We can make it to the castle. This was a setback, but we are still strong. We have to make it for Shawn. He is suffering." Katherine turned and yelled, "Now, Peter, to the shaft!"

The vampires, two abreast, went into the pitch darkness of the cave, but the darkness did not matter to them. Katherine still could remember this cave of long ago, the place where she first fought a desperate fight to save her maker. The vampires split and advanced on each side of the cave wall toward the shaft.

Deeper and deeper they went into the cave, finally arriving at the large chamber that held the old, abandon Hell's Hole. Looking down the dry shaft, Katherine felt the hot air against her face as it blew her hair back. She could not see the bottom, as already her vampire senses were limited.

Katherine went first down the shaft and yelled, "Follow me, vampires, follow me to Malin's black castle! Michael is watching you!" She started her long climb down to the cavern that led to the Gates of Hell. Quickly, she descended and urged everybody to hurry. Climbing deep into the earth, she clung to the rocks as her levitating abilities left her, and finally, she reached the bottom.

Katherine fell for a distance, crouched, and looked around, knowing immediately that her power of flight had left her. One by one, the vampires emerged and fell to the black stone surface of the cavern. Katherine saw a thin, greyish mist, flames shooting into the air, black rocks jutting from the ground, and burnt bones and skulls. Moving outward, she surveyed her surroundings, stopped, and waited for all the vampires to make the trip through the shaft. The cavern was broad and high, she could barely see the ceiling. To her right was the river of molten lava, and she could easily see which way it flowed.

Katherine felt the hot air bite at her face—wave after wave of heat blew by her. They walked toward the fire river, coming as close as possible and gathering to collect their thoughts.

"Where are the dark warriors?" Rebecca asked as she looked at her changeling. "Jermaine, stay with me. What a horrible place this is."

"I don't know," Katherine answered. "And it is horrible here!"

"We must follow the flow of the river of fire," Gwyn said. "That will lead us to the black castle. And I'm sure everybody knows by now that we can't fly."

"This isn't good, Katherine, and I cannot sense the enemy," Victoria said. "I fear our senses are limited."

"Victoria is right, our senses are dulled," Gwyn said. "We are close to the gates of Hell, and it is having an effect on us."

"We will go forward," Katherine said. "How is your wound, Caitlyn?"

"It was healing, but now it has slowed. I have been hurt worse," Caitlyn said.

"You will stay with me," Renee ordered. "This is a foul place, full of danger, and I want you close."

"The evil is suffocating here," Victoria added. "I have not felt such evil since the time of the demons."

Katherine turned and yelled to Peter, "We travel on foot! Are we ready? Have we all made it through the shaft?"

"We have!" Peter yelled. "We are almost ready."

"We will follow the flow of the river of fire!" she commanded again. "Do not despair, vampires! We still have our strength and speed!"

Katherine saw the worry on Victoria's face, saw her look at Peter, and then glance quickly toward Katherine before looking away. True to her way, Katherine knew Victoria was trying to hide her worry for Peter. The vampire army moved forward, following the fire river, slowly making their way over the black rocks and around the shooting flames. Katherine could feel the heat of the stone on her feet as she walked, and could only imagine what Shawn, as a mortal, must have experienced. This environment was harsh and, indeed, the worst place she had ever been. In this place, she was thankful to be a vampire.

They had followed the river for miles when suddenly they saw the dark warrior army coming around a bend in the cavern.

Katherine spied their dark forms through the mist, thousands marching, thirty abreast, heading straight for her company. The leaders rode large, black animals that resembled giant bulls with one large horn in the center of their heads. These creatures stood twenty feet high.

Katherine commanded Peter, "Form them into a 'V' and make an arrowhead, with the most experienced toward the tip."

"We should move away from the fire river for the fight," Victoria shouted as she drew her slayer.

"Out onto the flats!" Katherine yelled. "Quickly!"

The vampires went out onto the cavern floor, moved forward, shields up, and slayers drawn, ready for the battle. It had been a long night, and now it was daytime above. She could see the exhaustion on the vampires' faces. Closer, they came to the dark warriors, and soon they could see their ugly faces.

Katherine was at the front of the arrowhead formation, drew Alexa, pointed it above, and yelled, "This is what you made this sword for, Michael! Let us not fail!"

The vampires pierced the front ranks of the dark warriors, slashing their way through, cutting the monsters down. The dark warriors were twice as big as a man and many times stronger, yet they were clumsy fighters. She could feel the hot air blow by her face, and the *whoosh* as the dark warriors' long blades came near, could hear the loud bellowing of the beasts as their hoofs came down in an attempt to crush the guardians. She would strike a leg, and, as the creature fell, she would take its head, quickly killing the rider. The other vampires did the same, and she saw their desperate looks fighting with everything they had.

Gwyn used her rod to clear a small path through the monsters, pushing them back. Katherine fought on, and the vampires penetrated into the dark warriors' ranks, slashing and cutting their way through. Soon the monsters surrounded the army, and the vampires pushed outward and forward into Hell's forces, fighting fiercely, only to have the dark warriors push them back in on themselves. The putrid blood of the dark warriors sizzled on the hot rocks, flowed in streams, and fed the fiery river. Warrior vampires fell in high numbers, and Katherine saw their spirits rising upward and moving back toward the shaft, escaping this horrible realm, flying to Heaven, and to the safety of their angels. Sorrowful wails of the angels filled the ether as they came to the cave to bring the vampire spirits to Heaven. The warrior angels pleaded with Michael to let them enter the cave, but he would not allow it. The vampires fought on and slowly advanced forward, killing hundreds of dark warriors.

A trumpet sounded, echoed through the cavern, the dark warriors fell back around the bend, and the battle ended, for now. Katherine saw that her army was exhausted; they had been fighting all night and most of a day. Scanning the cavern, she saw a grouping of black rocks jutting up that offered some cover—a place where they could lay their weary bodies.

"Peter, we will take cover behind those rocks!" Katherine yelled as she pointed toward them.

Katherine followed her army to the rocks, huddled with them amongst the black stones, and felt the intense heat of this place. Peter approached her and squatted. Katherine was afraid to ask, yet she had to…

"Peter, how many have we lost?" She looked down, and her hand shook slightly, so she clenched it tighter around Alexa.

"We have already lost two hundred vampire souls, my queen."

"We might not make it," Victoria said in a tired voice.

Katherine turned with a look of desperation on her face. "Victoria, we have to make it."

Katherine looked out and saw the vampires tending to each other's wounds. They used their blood to heal, but even that did not seem to work well here. The closer they got, the weaker they became.

"Peter, how are their spirits?" Katherine asked.

"They are tired. The younger ones want to leave, but they will not. That would shame their angels."

"Post a watch, and we will stay here and rest," Katherine commanded.

Katherine watched Renee tending Caitlyn's wounds. She now

had two severe injuries and looked pale. Deceida lay at Renee's feet on the black stone, covered in brown, putrid blood.

"Do you need to go back, Caitlyn?" A concerned Katherine asked.

"I will stay here and fight. I will not leave while my family is here in this horrible place."

Of all the Bryces, Caitlyn had never been the warrior. She was always the teacher, the voice of reason in their family. Now, Katherine and the angels had led her family here to this monstrous place. Forward was the only way for her; they had pushed the dark warriors back, and they almost broke once. The mysterious castle lay ahead, somewhere through the mist, but where, she did not know. Waves of fear would sweep through her body as the thought of all the vampires dying here haunted her.

Suddenly, a mocking laugh echoed through the cavern. Malin was floating fifty yards out from them, thirty feet above the ground. Malin's black hair and grey wool cape floated in the air, and she held her staff in hand.

"Look at the pathetic vampires, cowering amongst the rocks. You are cowards, and you know you are. You want to run from this place, and you feel it even now. You want to go back to your easy lives. Killing a few bad people here or there. Go, this one time, and I will let you leave!"

Again, Katherine heard Malin's mocking laugh, and then she saw The Tempter lower her staff, spraying fiery embers. The embers blew over her army as they dug into the small, black stone, raising their shields and trying to protect themselves from the terrible, scalding heat.

"There is plenty of fire here, vampires!" Malin yelled. "Would you like some more?"

"That is all I'm going to take from her," Renee raged as she stood and grabbed Deceida. The slayer from Heaven burned white, its blade rang—begging to cut the witch's throat.

"No, you cannot," Katherine called out as she grabbed Renee's arm. "We need to rest. She is tempting us. She wants us to attack. We are exhausted, Renee."

"Did you follow that whore queen of yours here?" Malin screamed. "You followed her here to die. Be careful, for when you fall, Lucifer might get your souls!" Malin let out a loud, taunting laugh.

Suddenly, Katherine heard Drake's voice in her head.

Confront her! Lucifer is letting her stand on her own. He is displeased with how she has handled Shawn.

If only I could fly, my love, Katherine thought in response. "Vile, evil creature!" she screamed as she stood and jumped to the top of a large, black boulder, held Alexa confidently, "Send your army back so Lucifer can have more souls. Vampires, look at her! She is nothing without Lucifer at her side! I have beaten her before, and I will again! Do not fear her! I challenge you, Malin!"

Malin sneered at her and yelled as she turned, floating back down the cavern. "You are not as strong here, mighty queen, and your army won't reach my castle! You know that! Tell her, Gwyn! I know you are here! I know you brought Eos!"

****

Shawn woke to a commotion in the castle, went to the door, and looked out to see dark warriors hustling about, grunting to each other while locking doors. He went back and looked out his window to see dark warriors everywhere. They had fortified and taken up positions all around the castle.

The old woman came into his room and quickly told him, "There are guardians in the cavern, and they are trying to fight their way here." She turned and left as soon as she arrived.

This was his chance! What he had been waiting for! He hurried to the bed and grabbed the pair of old, black shoes he had strapped to its underside and quickly put them over his feet. Peering outside his door, he waited for the dark warriors to clear out so he could start his journey of stealth. Shawn knew of a side door, which most times, the dark warriors left unguarded. Creeping down the hall, his human eyes darting everywhere, he came to a corner and made sure it was clear before he went on. Down the stairs, he went and just when he was almost there, Luvon set upon him.

Luvon threw Shawn down the hall and then pounced on his chest and putting his hands around his throat. "Where are you going, human-pig? I have bad news. Malin is off taking care of your vampire friends, and now I'm going to kill you before she returns."

Shawn felt the warlock's sturdy grip as it tightened around his neck, and slowly, his throat collapsed. His breath came with much struggle, and he felt the life leaving him—felt the evil pull on his mortal spirit. Before the last gasp left him, he brought his hands up to push at Luvon. Somewhere, hidden deep inside, tremendous energy came from him, exploded through his hands, and threw the warlock like a rag doll down the hall and into the far wall. Shawn gasped, sucked at the air, and rolled to his knees, looking to see Luvon lying against the wall, stunned. Holding his hands out in anger, he curled his fingers as if he were choking the miserable creature. The warlock's throat collapsed, his face wrinkled, and then his head caved in and broke apart into shards of black glass that dissipated into the hot air.

Shawn looked on in disbelief and slowly got to his feet, continued around a corner, and walked into two dark warriors. He tried to make his powers work again, but he couldn't. The dark warriors grabbed him and dragged him back to his room. They gave him a slap on the side of his head, threw him back in his room, and locked the door. The stupid beasts did not take his shoes.

****

Katherine sat resting against a large rock, feeling the hot air move past her skin. Only three hours of restless sleep for her; all she heard were the moans and wails of condemned souls that traveled on the hot air, and she dared not let her own spirit leave her body. She had not heard again from Drake and did not expect to. Katherine looked over and saw Victoria watching her, sensing her strength and resolve.

"We should think about turning back," Victoria warned in a low voice. "I know how difficult this will be for you."

"We can't turn back," Katherine pleaded. "You know we have to try one more time to reach him. You love him just as much as I do! Please, Victoria!"

"One more time, Katherine. That is all these vampires can take, or you will have a bigger disaster on your hands."

The sound of the trumpets filled the cavern again. Katherine looked out and saw the dark warrior army marching around the bend. Malin hovered above them and screamed, "Kill them all!" The dark warriors let out a loud battle cry and lumbered toward the vampires, trudging, and riding their beasts.

"They are coming!" Katherine yelled. "Quickly, Peter!"

Katherine helped Peter wake the vampires, and walked among them, shouting, "They are coming! Hurry! We must form up! We do not have much time!"

The vampires again formed into an arrowhead and moved toward the dark warriors. Still, they sliced into the foul beasts' ranks, giving everything they had. Through the coat of evil blood, Alexa's blade glowed white. Katherine cut through the enemy, time, and time again. She would occasionally fall back and give encouragement to the other vampires. Renee swung Deceida, cutting the dark warriors down, Rebecca and Jermaine close to her, doing the same. The vampires slowly pushed through the dark warriors' ranks, finally reaching the bend, but they came to a stop

217

and could not make the turn. The dark warriors pressed in all around the vampires, and the cries and sounds of battle filled the cavern.

Malin floated above, screaming orders to the dark warriors, cursing at them, calling them "cowards" or "filthy beasts." Katherine wished Malin would come to her, but she stayed in the air. Then she heard a terrible scream from Renee, turned, and saw Caitlyn's head falling to the black, hot rocks, her crumbling body following. Caitlyn had not seen the dark warrior's sword that came from behind.

"Michael, no!" Katherine cried out as she moved to cover Renee, who was kneeling and wailing, gathering her dirt into a pouch. Katherine stood over Renee, fighting back the dark warriors while she cried out her grief. Deceida, lying on the black rocks, glowed white. Renee picked the sword up, stuffed the bag of dirt down her chest armor, and then waded into the dark warriors, crying, cursing, and fighting like a madwoman.

Katherine and the vampires fought on, trying to make the turn, but dark warriors from the castle came and reinforced their army. Now the dark warriors had the advantage, and the warrior vampires no longer could hold their ground. Slowly the beasts pushed them back toward the shaft.

Victoria grabbed Katherine by the arm, shaking her. "Katherine, we have to escape this place, or we will lose all of the vampires. We do not have enough of the army left to stay in this miserable place."

Katherine now realized they could not make the castle. She had failed and had led her army to disaster. Blood tears came to her cheeks as she realized their desperate situation. She looked out at the sea of dark warriors that surrounded them, the fires burning everywhere, heard the yells and the screams. Now, she knew, they must escape this hell—what was left of them.

"Peter, tell the vampires to move to the shaft. We must leave this horrible place!" Katherine screamed and cried as she brought Alexa down on the monsters. The vampires gave a desperate fight as they retreated back toward the shaft and the outside world. With their numbers depleted, they, with the many spirits of the dead guardians, made their way back to the shaft.

Katherine and the older vampires stayed and fought the lumbering dark warriors while the other vampires made their escape back up through Hell's Hole. Only a hundred and eighty-five vampires climbed back up the shaft. The sorrowful songs of the angels filled the woods as the defeated vampires made their way out of the cave and took flight back to Dalton.

****

The Mother sat in her world, by the clear brook, with her defender, the eagle, at her side. She had miscalculated. Lucifer had known her plans. Lucifer became aware when he confronted Katherine at the second Hell's Hole, and now Michael was furious at the outcome. The warrior guardians of Earth had suffered a horrible defeat, and Malin had sent many vampires to Heaven. Michael was not pleased, but still, The Mother had her Trojan Horse.

Chapter Nineteen

S hawn lay on his old straw mattress, drifting between sleep and lying awake with his thoughts. Sometimes there was a part of sleep that felt familiar, but it floated by so fast he wasn't sure. Sometimes, he thought he had felt The Mother, but he couldn't be sure; this kind of sleep was still new to him. It was a heavy sleep, not what he was used to being a vampire.

A steady hand grabbed his long unwashed hair and yanked him from his bed and onto the floor. He rolled, crouched, and realized it was Malin, with a look of contempt and disgust on her face. Malin looked slightly disheveled, unusual for her, a smudge on her left cheek. Reaching down, she pulled him up by his ragged collar.

A smile came to her face. "I have some news for you, mighty Demon Slayer. Guardians entered the cavern and fought so gallantly."

Malin must have seen the glimmer of hope that came to his eyes, a quick gleam of anticipation before he could disguise his feelings. Malin took him by the throat and held him against the wall. Her lips covered his, and then she stared into his eyes, so close he could feel her breath when she spoke. "I'm afraid, filthy human, that they didn't make it. They did not make it halfway. My warriors killed most of them, and they had to turn back."

"They will come again," Shawn gasped as Malin's grip tightened.

"Do you believe that, mighty Demon Slayer? What do you

220

think the elders of your kind will be talking about now? Maybe how the young queen got hundreds of vampires killed? How long do you think she will have their support now?"

"She only needs the support of Michael and Eos," Shawn choked back.

"Does she! The two powerful angels who are at each other's throats because of you?" Malin joked. She slapped him across his face and threw him onto the bed. Sitting next to him, she pulled him close to her and again stared into his eyes. Shawn then realized she was searching for something and felt his heart speed up and anxiety build. She would certainly know what he did to Luvon.

"He knows nothing of Luvon, Father," a surprised Malin whispered to herself. "I know it is hard to believe. How could Luvon be killed without someone knowing?"

She can't see this, he thought, and quickly tried to make his mind think of something else. Malin took his face with her one hand and turned it harshly. He gasped as he felt her dark energy squeeze at his heart, making it skip.

"Careful, Shawn. I will kill you if I have to. If my father commands me." Malin rose and started toward the door and then turned around again. "Oh, I almost forgot to tell you. A Bryce was killed. How Lucifer rejoices! You see, Shawn, this turn of events has put me back in favor with my father."

Malin's laughter filled the room as she went through the door, and Shawn buried his face into his hands as he absorbed what Malin had said. A sickening heartache overcame him as he fell back into his bed, curled up, and sobbed with one burning question on his mind. *Which Bryce?*

****

Katherine lay in her couch at the Washington home. It was early evening, the time humans ate their supper. It had been a year since the rescue attempt for Shawn. She had brought Renee home to Washington and stayed with her while placing Victoria in charge in Amsterdam. Renee rarely left her room, and gaining entry had become a chore. Juliette had left a week ago to be with Peter, and now only Renee and Katherine occupied the house in Washington.

Sighing, she thought about how the sadness hung heavy in the Washington house and in the hearts of all Bryces. Washington was safe for her, and she wanted to stay there and never leave but couldn't, and she knew it. She had to save Shawn, or this despair and sadness would never end.

Katherine was afraid for Renee. Caitlyn had been a terrible loss for her. Now, Katherine was worried to leave Renee, never sure of what she would do. Renee would curse the angels and, of course, Malin. Then she would fall into a terrible melancholy, keeping Deceida by her side, and always talked about how she was going back to the cavern, and how the sword from Heaven would "take that filthy witch's head." Renee had not blamed her yet, but that could be coming, Katherine knew.

The shock of the defeat had traveled swiftly through the vampire community. The families of the dead vampires were especially angry with Katherine, and the heads of the four covenants had met in Moscow to discuss her rule. They had decided to leave her queen for the time being and to send her the vampires she needed for her army, though the arrival of these vampires was slow. The survivors of her failed attempt to rescue Shawn went home and had not returned. Nobody wanted the responsibility of rule in these turbulent times, and the elders certainly did not want their reputations tarnished. They would leave this war to Katherine for now, although they did demand she do something about Stephen and the rogues.

The mystery of why they had lost was constantly near these days. The primary reason for her defeat, was the inability to fly once they'd gotten into the cavern, and she hoped that Michael or

Eos would help with that problem. And they simply didn't have the numbers to fight their way to the black castle on foot either. She would need a bigger army, and had sent word by Juliette to Peter to grow the military and expand the garrison at Dalton. This would not be easy that she knew, the heads of the covenants always resisted everything Katherine tried to do.

Drake had not come to her since the battle. No angels came to her now. All she heard when she was in the light were their sorrowful songs for the warrior vampires of Earth.

Katherine sat on the blue throne, and Victoria stood next to her. Two years had passed before she dared leave Renee by herself. The large, white, double doors swung open, and a vampire floated through. Glancing to her side, she saw the scowl on Victoria's face. She had granted an audience to an ancient vampire known as Prodasa. The vampire was large in stature, and muscular, with a short, black beard contrasting his brown skin. As a human, he had been an adviser to Genghis Khan and part of his Mongolian horde. He was now the head of the Parfeev Covenant, a proud and hard-headed vampire, that came from Moscow. Prodasa floated across the water and to the short flight of stairs that led to the blue throne when Katherine raised her hand to stop him. He had come close enough and she wanted to be the higher.

"Greetings to you, Queen Katherine, and to you, Victoria, old, wise, and a Demon Slayer. Your skills as a warrior are known amongst vampires in my covenant."

Katherine was aware of the slight insult thrown her way. The old ones were mad at her and felt she was too young and reckless to be queen.

"Greetings to you, and I thank you for the vampires sent for the army," Katherine said as she projected her power to the vampire—a power the vampire was undoubtedly able to sense. "What can I do for you, Prodasa?"

"I'm afraid I have to start our conversation with the delivery of strong condemnation from the families of the hundred vampires of my covenant whose souls you lost on that disastrous attempt to rescue one of your family members."

"The vampire they gave their lives for was Shawn Bryce, who, you should not forget, answered the call to fight the Esmanaa. Who killed two of the demons by himself. Neither your covenant nor the others fought the demons. The Herit Covenant fought the demons for all of you. The Bryces also feel the pain of this attack. As always, the Bryce family paid with the death of one of our own."

"The covenants feel the price is too high for the vampire Shawn," Prodasa said.

"The Archangel Michael and Eos want Shawn rescued, and Malin killed. They have their reasons. This is not a Bryce decision. I expect all vampires to answer the call when it comes to fighting Lucifer. You may send my regrets and sorrow over the loss of your vampires to your covenant. Assure them the angels sing of them in Heaven."

"The Parfeev Covenant has sent the two hundred vampires you asked for," Prodasa said. "We will not send any more."

Katherine stood and walked to the edge of the stairs and looked down at Prodasa. She pointed her finger at him and shouted at him, "You will send me what I need! You will do as a say! Michael has made me queen, and he gave me the power to rule! Do not forget that, Prodasa! I will rescue Shawn, and you will be there at the next attempt, I promise you that! You will lead your covenant vampires, and you will help me fight my way to the black castle! And you will tell the other covenants to supply the needed vampires more quickly. Now, what is your other business?"

"My apologies, Queen Katherine. The covenants are not used to losing so many vampires at once. The covenants need time before they commit more vampires. Not all vampires are warriors."

"That is obvious! The covenants will lose more before this is over," Katherine said as she lowered her voice.

"The other matter is Stephen and the rogues," Prodasa said. "I am here to speak for my covenant and the others about this matter. They are killing young vampires."

"Stephen has turned to Lucifer," Katherine said as she stepped back from the edge. "The dark angels have his soul now."

"He has...a vampire told me this...also lost most of his strength. When he accepted Lucifer's evil and failed to assassinate you, he lost his vampire strength. Now he has the strength of a rogue."

"What else do you know about Stephen?" Katherine asked.

"I know he lives in Bombay. That is all."

Katherine walked back to the edge of the stairs, looked down at Prodasa. "You may leave, and remember, I will see you at the next battle." Katherine watched the upset old vampire flash his yellow eyes of his covenant before turning to leave.

"Katherine, that is not the way to win allies," An exasperated Victoria warned.

"Michael wants me to be hard on the heads of the covenants. They must be disciplined, and they must learn to follow their queen. The Herit Covenant has fought evil for thousands of years. My covenant were the ones to fight the demons. I have only been a part of this covenant for six hundred years, and even I know the sacrifices they made to fight the dark angels. And I believe there was never a vampire from the Parfeev Covenant there."

"You are stressed and tired. I want you to come with me," Victoria suggested as she took Katherine's hands. "I want to show you something. We can travel together for a few days. It will relax you. I need your advice."

"I don't know what will come of my covenant, Victoria. Our vampires die doing the angels' work. Now, I am so afraid that Shawn might be lost, too."

"I know, Katherine. I feel the pain, too, and I can feel yours. It is what we felt a long time ago, together, the desperation for Shawn. We will rescue him. We will find some way. Come with me...maybe this will give you hope."

Katherine stood on the balcony of her hotel room in Montreal. The hotel was located a half-mile up a high tower. It was night, and she looked out over the carpet of colored lights that stretched to the horizon—a sea of modern humanity. How different the sky was now, how much more crowded than when she was mortal. It was a clear night, and she was sure the humans would think it a warm night. She welcomed the gentle summer breeze that blew against her bare skin.

Victoria was still in the shower; they had slept late. The trip from Amsterdam had tired them. Victoria would relax with her, embrace and comfort her, sometimes kiss her, but that was as much as Victoria would allow--never sex with her. Katherine had not made love since losing Thomas.

The despair hung heavy tonight; it had been almost three years since the attack, and Shawn was still with Malin. The older vampires were becoming more challenging to deal with. Michael knew this would happen, and he had warned Katherine. She wondered if the ancients would ever follow her.

Tonight, Victoria was keeping a secret from her, taking her on a secretive trip. Katherine probably could have probed Victoria's mind to find out anything she'd wanted, but they loved each other, and that would have been rude.

Victoria had brought her to another tower, a commerce tower with stores lining its walkways. They now walked the Rue Cartier and made their way through a crowd of shoppers. The night was warm, and the vampires quickly smelled the many odors of human perfumes, colognes, and sweet blood.

"I wanted to talk to you tonight, Katherine," Victoria said as they sat on their stools at a food stand. They ordered two cups of tea. "You must know there is a chance that Shawn could die. He is human now, and we might not rescue him in time. That horrible place has such a harsh environment."

"We are going to save him. Malin won't kill him! I know this! I told you!" Katherine shot back in a low voice. She didn't want the humans to hear her.

"Have you thought how you would live if there wasn't a Shawn anymore?" Victoria whispered.

"I would spend my time hunting that witch and killing her."

"A powerful angel has tried to kill Malin for thousands of years, and this time she came up with this scheme. Malin can easily go to another world, and you can't." Victoria took hold of her hand. "There is a chance we won't save Shawn. I want to show you another possibility. It is down this street."

Katherine walked with Victoria; they had only gone away when Victoria stopped and pointed across the walkway at a small, quaint French restaurant. There was a hologram of a waiter with a white shirt and black apron greeting and waving to people as they passed.

"I have been watching a human for a couple of years. His name is Braden. I remember the love and joy I felt when Peter was a changeling, and I yearn for that again, so I have decided to take a changeling again if I survive. I am only waiting for this latest conflict with evil to resolve itself. Your life had something to do with food when you were human, didn't it?"

"Yes, I worked a food stand in Tacoma. That is where I met Shawn. It's funny how I can remember that so well, and all the rest is a blur in my memory. Do you want my approval? Is that why you brought me?"

"Yes, I do, but I want you to also consider an idea. Come and let me show you."

Katherine followed Victoria across the walkway and through the door of the establishment. There were twenty dining tables and a small bar. She followed Victoria to the bar; they took a seat and ordered drinks. Victoria pointed at an open door leading into a kitchen with two blond men, twins, standing together, one a cook and the other a waiter. Pictures and symbols formed around them as they spoke passionately. What struck Katherine was that both looked like Shawn, and both were very handsome men. She watched the waiter come back into the dining room. He was a charming man, the way he interacted with the guests. She sensed a strong character and intelligence about him.

"That's Braden. He will be my next changeling. The other is Julien. I have spoken with Braden briefly a couple of times, but as usual, with humans, he's not sure of me."

"He's handsome, Victoria. He looks somewhat like Shawn."

"Doesn't he? What do you think of his brother, the cook?"

"The same, handsome."

"Everything his brother is, he is, too. They are very alike. Both are humans worthy of being guardians. If we don't save Shawn, don't grieve too long. Take a changeling. You should take a changeling soon anyway. Whatever happens, it would do you good. If not Julien, there are other humans. I saw how you were with Drake."

"You can't be serious, Victoria."

Victoria had intrigued her. Katherine looked down the bar and through the open door at this human. He had blond hair and a handsome, masculine face, and an athlete's body, a glisten of sweat on his forehead and over his perfect top lip. Allowing her senses to drift toward him, she crept into his mind, softly, so he would not know, and found he was a kind man, a smart man, ambitious and strong. The man moved with confidence as he dashed the spices onto the food, shook the sizzling, steaming pans, and set them back on the stove. Every so often, he would turn and yell through the open door at his brother; an order was ready as humped over the plate, arranging the food into a perfect dish. Katherine even liked the sound of his voice.

"You are suggesting I take a changeling," Katherine said as she stared at Victoria.

"Yes, when this is over, no matter how it ends. If you are alive."

"I'm queen, I don't know if it is possible."

"It is possible, and *because* you are a queen! Where are you going?"

"To get closer," Katherine answered as she got up, making her way to the door, and stood looking through. Allowing her senses to explore this human, the smell of his sweet blood. *For a taste,* she thought. He was worried about the next payment for this restaurant. He and his brother worked hard, but now he wanted more out of life. Julien had always worked with his brother and now wanted to travel into space, to cook on a space transport, and see other worlds.

228

Julien turned, and Katherine caught his gaze. "What can I do for you, pretty lady?"

"I just wanted to take in the smells of your aromatic kitchen."

"Well, come on in. I can use some company tonight, especially from a lovely woman such as yourself."

"Aren't you a charmer?" Katherine said in a flirting way. "Are you always this friendly?"

"Not always. I'm feeling adventurous tonight. Especially when a girl as pretty as you looks through my kitchen door."

"You flatter me. How long have you been a cook?"

"All my life. Do you like to cook?"

"I did, but I haven't cooked in a long time," she purred back. "There's no need."

"Everybody should cook," Julien said with a pleasant laugh. "It's good for the soul."

"I am sure you're right," Katherine said as she caught his eyes and slowly drew him in, mesmerized him, walked toward him. She sensed nobody else was in the kitchen, brought her nose to his neck, and took him in. She could smell his human blood. The temptation was too much. She cut his flesh deep below his ear with her nail, flicked it open with her tongue, took a little, savored it in her mouth, took some more, and then healed him. He was definitely a possibility for her. Walking back to the door, she released him. Katherine was a vampire and would take from Julien what she wanted and maybe his mortal life.

"It was a pleasure talking with you, Julien. Maybe, we will see each other again."

"How did you know my name?" A puzzled Julien asked.

"I heard your brother speak it," Katherine said over her shoulder. She then turned back and swallowed the remainder of the blood. Now she would always be able to find him.

"You are impossible," Victoria said as Katherine sat. "I should have known a Bryce would do that with a human."

"You said Braden was like Julien?" Katherine inquired.

"Yes, but Braden gets excited more easily than Julien."

The man looked their way and nodded at Victoria.

"He knows you," Katherine said as she motioned him over.

"Katherine, really!"

"How are you, Victoria? It's been some time since we talked."

"I have been doing well. How is your restaurant coming?"

"We are struggling. I'm afraid that the bank wouldn't lend us the money we needed. You certainly keep pretty company."

"This is Katherine."

"Glad to meet you," Braden said.

"Good to meet you, too. I have already met your brother," Katherine said as she now captured his eyes. She quickly led him into a trance and motioned for Victoria to come closer. "Taste him. Do it quickly."

"Katherine, you're hopeless sometimes!" Victoria whispered as she rolled her eyes to the ceiling.

Katherine watched Victoria look around. Nobody was the wiser, so she moved between Victoria and the crowd, and at that precise moment, in an instant, Victoria leaned in, nicked his neck, and tasted his blood. She stayed next to him, took him in, kissed his lips softly, and then moved away. Katherine slowly released Braden, and recognition came back to his eyes.

"Whoa! Felt a little dizzy there. Working too hard."

"You are looking a little pale," Victoria said.

"Well, I better get back to work."

"It was nice to see you again, Braden," Victoria said. "Until next time."

"Uh, sure," Braden mumbled as he walked toward the kitchen.

Katherine and Victoria finished their drinks, said their farewells, and left the bar, giggling and talking.

"You're something, Katherine."

"You got to taste him, Victoria! Didn't you?"

230

Chapter Twenty

S hawn stood at his baking table in the kitchen, kneading a large ball of dough, flinging flour, and reaching for his rolling pin. He watched the large man sitting in the far corner, his head nodding down to his chest. The man had been drinking PeLa, a thick, white, intoxicating liquid. Most days, Shawn would find him sitting in the big wooden chair in the corner, drunk. This was fine with Shawn; he was an abusive man to everybody in the kitchen. Life in the kitchen was more comfortable when the big man slept.

Shawn had been captive for almost five years. Life here was becoming more manageable, especially since the death of Luvon. Malin had been gone since the vampires tried to fight their way to the castle. She had only recently returned. Malin had come to his room, forced herself on him, and that was when she told him which Bryce had lost her life. Caitlyn had never been a warrior; she had been a teacher, a writer. Shawn wondered why Katherine had brought her to this place. *She must have been desperate,* he thought. Tears came to his eyes, and he reached up to wipe them. They were clear and no longer red.

The door swung open and in marched two tiny men. They were at most three feet high, and they marched stiff-legged wherever they went, dressed as Napoleonic soldiers, with tall, black stovepipe hats, gold braids in the front, and a feather on top. A poor wretch of a woman handed them a platter with two dinner plates filled with food. Out the door, they marched, each one holding a side of the tray.

Shawn had made his way back to his room and was eating his bowl of mush and bread. Malin did not allow him to have kitchen food yet, so he stole the bread. She never allowed him to eat with the other slaves. He had to eat in his room by himself. Sitting on his chair, he looked through the window bars and out at the dark, red world outside.

Caitlyn told him once how Renee turned her. She told him she met Renee in a lounge in Paris. At that time in her life, she was a newspaper reporter and went to a bar after work. She told him she drank a lot in those days, the same as him, and had always thought it funny that a car accident was also responsible for her turning. A car accident had paralyzed her legs, and that was when Renee came and offered her a life as a vampire. Caitlyn told him how she happily accepted Renee's proposition so she could walk again.

Many times he had made love to Caitlyn when they were young vampires when Anne had taken him to Paris to visit. The first time was when they were changelings, in the lake beside the Washington house. They had been changed at the same time and were same age. Shawn remembered how she would come to visit him in the early days when he had just left Anne to keep each other company. How they laughed and made love, talked of their years as changelings. Again, tears flooded his eyes.

The door burst open, and Malin and two ugly dark warriors came through.

"Look, the mighty Demon Slayer is crying," Malin mocked.

A fist hit the side of his head, knocking him onto the floor. All he heard was the ringing in his ears and Malin's mocking laugh. Malin pulled him up by his hair and then held him by his throat. She then handed him to the dark warriors, each taking an arm as they spread him out. Malin stood in front of him, and then he saw the knife in her hand, its long, ivory hilt polished to a smooth white and accenting the long, slightly curved silver blade. The sharpness of the blade he quickly saw.

Shawn watched her walk to the bucket by the door and stick the blade in his piss. She took out a small pouch, opened it, took salt and sprinkled it on the wet edge, and then put her lips next to his ear and whispered.

"I am sorry for what I have to do, Shawn, but Lucifer thinks you are hiding something from us. He thinks you know about Luvon. My father wanted you killed right away, but I convinced him otherwise."

Malin brought the knife across his chest, cut through his flesh, the blood flowing, his skin welting, and quivering. Shawn screamed in pain, and Malin would force her way into his thoughts while he was distracted; she searched his mind, looking for his guilt. Malin knew the human mind was the most accessible when flooded with pain. Five times, she did this, each time sprinkling salt on the blade, then raised her head and screamed, "He knows nothing, Father."

She turned and bellowed, "Let him go. Fetch the healer!" and then stormed out the door. The dark warriors released him, and he fell to the floor with one thought in his mind: *She cannot see it.* Then darkness came. Only the dark came now, never any light.

He never dreamt anymore. When he woke, the old woman was over him, finishing smearing a brown ointment on his chest. She lifted him slightly as she wrapped his chest with bandages. Her face suddenly went blank, and her eyes rolled back into her head. Shawn heard a strange voice come from her.

"I have not forsaken you, Shawn." It was Eos.

****

Katherine walked the Carter Path next to the Arabian Sea. She had arrived in Bombay two eves ago and had not located Stephen, but she had sensed a powerful evil there. It was a hot night, and the smell of mortals and their blood filled her sensitive nose. The streets were crowded, and the prattle loud. Bombay was a noisy city. Holograms appeared above her head, grew large and bright, displaying their message, and then disappeared into the night.

She had called a meeting with Amrit, head of the Divjot Covenant. The vampire lounge where the meeting would be held was in a secluded area of the city, and she was going with the intent of receiving an explanation as to why he was so slow in delivering his allotted warrior vampires—why he had allowed this evil here, and why he had not brought it to her attention. As she walked past a group of men, red, sexual symbols exploded around their heads, and she hurried along. She wanted no trouble tonight from stupid, young mortals.

Then came a snide voice: "Come on, pretty...cannot sign us back?"

"I have no implant, and I want no trouble tonight. Mind yourselves!" They started after her. She turned, flashed her vampire eyes at them, and they fell back, startled.

Now Drake often came in her sleep, reassuring her that Michael and Eos were finding a way to save Shawn. Drake would distract her and quiet her fear over Shawn. Shawn had been a prisoner of Malin's for five years now, and Katherine told Drake that whatever they did, she would still build an army and rescue Shawn, no matter how many times she had to enter Hell's Hole. Drake told her that Michael was concerned about the number of guardian deaths her assaults would produce. To Michael, unlike Eos, the end of Malin was not worth the loss of that many warrior vampires. She always fought with the heads of the covenants for more vampires to fill her ranks.

Her vampire army now numbered one thousand five hundred, and she garrisoned them in Dalton, with an additional five hundred outside of Amsterdam. They consistently trained, so she would have better warriors next time.

Katherine continued her walk, and soon, the loud, colorfully dressed crowd started to thin. She turned onto Ganesh Path, walked a reasonable distance, and found herself in a secluded area under a high tower. Looking out, she saw the flashing lights marking the towers for the aircars. There were few lights in this area and, strangely, no humans. She wondered if humans avoided this area on purpose. Off in the distance, she saw some lights that came from the vampire lounge.

As she approached the silver, metal door, a hologram appeared that looked like a vampire from long ago books. *Quite scary*, she thought.

The hologram spoke. "State your business."

"The queen is here to see Amrit."

The door immediately slid open, and she entered. Soft, dim lights lit the lounge, and she saw many vampires sitting at tables, sipping their drinks. They all turned to see their young queen; some stood up slightly to get a better look. She flashed her blue eyes at them to show who she was, what covenant she came from. Most vampires here had only heard of her and had come specifically to see her. They were all from the Divjot Covenant. Some smiled, some nodded, and some just stared, stone-faced. She quickly sensed the stone faces had lost vampires under her rule. In the far corner sat Amrit with four other vampires.

As she came close, she sent a telepathic message, demanding they open themselves to her. They were uneasy and didn't know what to expect or why she wanted to see them. She sensed that they called her "the warrior queen". She immediately projected Michael's power to them, and they became more solemn. All opened themselves to her except Amrit. As she came to the table, she saw their covenant's sword from Heaven next to Amrit. She penetrated his defenses, but he was an ancient vampire, and his guards were strong.

"How dare you bring that sword here?" Katherine said in a loud voice. "That is an instrument of Michaels, and *I* am an instrument of Michaels. Raise that sword against me, and it will burn you to cinders."

The music stopped, and the lounge went silent. All the vampires stared at her. Finally, she was able to sense Amrit meant her no harm only cautious.

"The sword is not for you, my queen," Amrit said. "A

wickedness has come to our city."

"That is why I have come," Katherine scolded as her voice became louder. "Why haven't you done anything about this vile? Do you know what evil this is?"

"No, we don't. We were waiting for the high and mighty queen to come."

"Careful, Amrit," Katherine warned as she turned to meet the gaze of the other vampires in the lounge.

"You are not fighting for the Bryces, you are fighting for the Archangel. Lucifer is assaulting this world with evil." Katherine raised her voice again. "This world has descended into evil once again. Your city wreaks of it. My rule comes from Michael. It comes from The Mother. You will follow me, and you will do as I say. It is time for you to become warriors once again. Maybe you will die like a warrior if the angels smile on you. You need to talk to your angels more." Katherine turned and stared at Amrit. "You will go to Amsterdam and bring the warrior vampires I have asked for. You will also bring an additional one hundred. And you will be a part of my army. Your covenant will start doing their share."

"Our covenant has done their share," Amrit argued as he glared at her. "We lost over a hundred vampires following you down Hell's Hole."

"No, you don't do your share; that is why evil has come to your city. You will lose more than a hundred vampires before this is over. I will investigate what this foul sense is that flourishes under your idle leadership. Bring the vampires to Amsterdam. Do not question or ridicule me again, Amrit."

Katherine left the lounge and walked back the way she came. It was late, the air hot with no breeze. The crowd had thinned, and few people walked the path now. She knew a vampire followed her from the lounge, could sense him sharply, and knew this one had courage a young vampire, only two centuries old. She slowed her pace on purpose and looked into a few store windows. She spotted a beautiful piece of jewelry with different colors etched into its gold. *How pretty*, she thought. She would have to buy herself a pair of those earrings.

The vampire walked toward her, and she flooded his head with her energy, overwhelming him, searching for his intent. The Mother had been with him, so she quickly retreated. He was nervous as he came to her, with eyes that flashed the purple of his Divjot Dovenant...the "dark-eyed covenant". He was handsome, a well-built man with brown skin, black hair, and eyebrows. *What perfect lips*, she thought, and easily deflected his attempts at looking into her mind.

"Careful vampire, you cannot see into my mind if I don't want you to. Why have you followed me?" Katherine demanded.

"My pardon, my beautiful queen. It seems while at the lounge, an angel put me in a trance and told me to follow you. I woke, but the angel has left me, leaving me the fool in front of you."

"That angel is The Mother," Katherine said in a kinder tone. "She will return. You will stay with me until she does. Come along, you can keep me company."

"What is your name?" Katherine asked.

"My name is Rahul, my queen. I must say I am surprised to be here, walking with you. I was only hoping for a look."

"Where are you from, Rahul?"

"I'm from Jarhar City, north of here. I came to the lounge to see you in person. I heard you would be there. My maker is a lover of Amrit. She was one of the vampires sitting with him."

"I see. When did you feel The Mother?"

"I watched you walk in, and that's all I remember except for the angel and finding myself following you."

"You will feel her again, but for now, stay with me."

"Yes, my queen."

Katherine glanced over at Rahul. He was a handsome man, and she quickly decided he would do.

"Come with me to my hotel room. We will wait for The Mother's return there," Katherine said as she continued searching his mind. He was one hundred eighty-three years old and a gentle soul, which made her wonder why his maker changed him. The nature of a vampire should be that of a warrior. Still searching his mind, she learned that his maker had chosen him for other gifts, ones she was going to explore.

"May I ask you a question, my queen?"

"Go ahead, Rahul."

"Your maker was a great warrior and a Demon Slayer. I have spent considerable time learning about him. What was he like?"

"You would not know he was a warrior. He spent his time helping the mortals. He was always more comfortable in a bar playing his piano. But the angels wouldn't leave him alone. They always had a mission for him, and now I'm afraid he is lost, and it is me they won't leave alone."

"I am sorry for your troubles, my queen. You must know the ancients do not care to follow such a young queen."

"I am aware of that. The ancients will follow Michael's queen, or they will answer to him directly. Come. I do have a special task for you, gentle vampire."

Katherine brought Rahul to her room and took him to her bed, felt his smooth skin, his powerful arms and shoulders. She enjoyed his lovemaking, the taste of him as he kissed her.

When they had finished, she lay in his arms, stroked and kissed his muscular chest, laid her head on it, and then felt him go rigid. She quickly sat up and saw his eyes go white; they rolled back into his head, and he entered a trance.

The Mother returned and spoke through Rahul. "Greetings, Katherine. I bring you word of Shawn. He is still alive, and Malin will not kill him, only Lucifer wants him dead. Malin protects him, but Lucifer will have his life soon. We must hurry our preparations."

Katherine felt the return of her fear and desperation. A constant companion these days. "We lose too much of our power when we enter the cavern. You must help us with this, or we will never reach the black castle."

"Prepare your army and wait for Gwyn. She brings a powerful weapon for the vampires, five white pebbles. The pebbles will give the five holders flying abilities. Use the pebbles sparingly, for they will only work until Lucifer discovers what you are doing. You will save one pebble for Shawn. When you reach him, give him the stone. Remember, Shawn must have a pebble if you are to save him. Wait for Gwyn, and then you must attack again." Rahul quivered, and sweat came to his brow. "I am afraid there is more bad news for the vampires of Earth. Lucifer sends a demon to your world far more powerful than the last. He was born from a human woman, and he is of human flesh. His rise will be swift, and he will bring such heartache to your world. A great war between good and evil. The demon's name is Brendel, and he must be stopped." Rahul went rigid in the bed, and then slowly relaxed and returned to this reality.

Chapter Twenty-One

S hawn sat in a large room filled with wooden tables and chairs used by humans and creatures from other worlds for their one meal of the day. The smell of moldy, cooked grain, and rancid meat drifted through the hot air. Most ate what looked like brown slop in a bowl. Malin had finally allowed him to eat with the others, and now he would steal food from the kitchen to make his meals more palatable. He looked down at his slice of brown bread and a hunk of brownish-green meat. He couldn't remember the last time he'd eaten meat, but he did know it had to have looked and tasted better than this. The beef had a sour taste to it and would undoubtedly make him spend time squatting over his bucket. Another human affliction he had forgotten about long ago.

Almost six years had passed in this miserable place. When he wasn't working in the kitchen, he spent his time in his bed trying to sleep the time away or dealing with Malin. A game he would play often was tossing rocks toward his room's walls to see how close he could come without hitting them. He knew he needed more exercise, but wandering the castle was too dangerous. Dreams of Anne, Marilyn, Caitlyn, and Jessamine would come; he tried to talk to them in his sleep, to tell them he missed them, but they never answered. Then a melancholy would come over him for days.

Shawn knew a small part of Eos was hidden somewhere near, knowing what was happening, maybe in the old woman. If so, it was a dangerous game Eos was playing with the devil. He sat with two girls from the kitchen. Their cinnamon skin and rows of small, bony knobs on their foreheads showed they were from some other world. They were big girls that led a hard life in this horrible place, yet they had been good friends to him. They had shown him the ropes and had helped him get along. They would try to protect him from the big man, and usually took the brunt of more abuse because of it, but the big man seemed leery of the two.

The door burst open, and four dark warriors rushed into the room. One yelled, "Everybody go to your rooms quickly!" Then another took a black, leather whip from his side, cracked it, and growled. Get out of here, now. Move, you filthy creatures."

The dark warrior with the whip pointed at him. Two others came and quickly grabbed him by his arms. They dragged him out the door and down the hall. Where they were taking him, he didn't know, but he was going down the stairs, not up to his room. Shawn tried to ask them where he was going, but they would just slap him in the side of his head with their big hands. Down the stairs and deeper into the castle, the dark warriors dragged him.

Finally, they went down a dark corridor underneath the castle, where Malin suddenly appeared. She took hold of his jaw and pushed his head against the hot stonewall. The hallway filled with the smell of rotten fruit and sour vinegar. Her eyes, whereas black as night and hate, twisted her black lips.

"Vampires have come for you again. I know you killed Luvon. How you did it, I don't know. I hid it from my father, and he is mad at me. I will chain you down here until the vampires are driven from the cavern. Many vampires have died for you, and many more will die today. You will never love me or do as I say, will you?"

"I will never love you!" Shawn hissed back. "You killed Jessamine and Caitlyn."

"I think this time, when we drive the vampires from the cavern, I will send your soul to my father. Take him and chain him. Now!" Malin screamed.

They dragged him to a large metal door. There were bars over a small opening, and its tarnished metal was pitted, dented, and streaked with dark stains of blood. He heard the clanging of the keys, the turn of the lock, and the screech of the opening door that echoed through the dungeon. Dragging him in, they chained and shackled his wrists, hoisted him up, and left his feet barely touching the stone floor. The dark warriors left, shutting and locking the thick metal door.

There was no sound, and all his human eyes could see was darkness. His thoughts went to Katherine, and the vampires that must have been trying to save him. What had gone wrong the first time? Shawn knew nothing of the outside world, and he prayed to The Mother that they would reach him in time. He was not sure how much longer he could last in a place like this. Malin was tiring of him, and now he cried out to Michael in fear, "Why have you left me here? Why have you abandoned me? Please, Michael, don't let Lucifer have my soul!" He screamed at Herit, too. "You promised me you would fight for me!" Panic washed through him, and he desperately jerked at his chains, only to cut his wrists. Shawn could not break them. He was a weak human now. His head fell forward and he sobbed in the darkness.

****

Katherine had said her goodbyes to Rahul while he lay in bed---she loved the sight of Rahul naked. The next eve she strapped Alexa to her back and left to follow the sense of evil. This wickedness was something different; it had tremendous power, and she knew it must be the demon The Mother had warned her about. She followed the evil to a warehouse on the outskirts of Bombay. When she arrived, the evil grew more potent, as if it was welcoming her, leading her.

The warehouse was off by itself and had a sizeable surrounding parking lot. The building was empty now, in need of a new tenant, a tall, black metal fence sat ten feet from the building and ran around it, ending at a gate, framed by two red brick columns. On top of one of these columns was a witch, squatting, leaning forward on her hands and arms, and watching Katherine. The witch revealed immediately that she was a protector, a powerful sentinel in charge of what was inside.

Her head was bald and as smooth as glass. She had the face of a woman, but her body was muscular like a man's. She cocked her head back and forth in an unnatural manner. Her eyes were a brilliant red, with black slits in the middle. Her skin was a bronze color, and all she wore was a black leather vest, black leather pants, and red leather moccasins. The vest was closed and barely hid her well-developed chest. Katherine could see no weapons on her.

The witch continued to stare at her and slowly rose to a standing position. Katherine drew Alexa and assumed a fighting stance. A smile slowly spread over the witch's face as she stood, looking down, and then the witch spoke. "I have been expecting you, vampire. I am Samil. Lucifer has called me from another world for this important task."

"What task is that?" Katherine asked.

"I am the protector of Brendel, a dark angel. I have a welcoming party for you, warrior queen." Katherine watched the witch turn her head and look toward the entrance door. Nine rogue vampires with slayers came out, led by Stephen.

"Take your time, vampire. I will wait for you inside." Samil rose into the air and flew to the warehouse roof, stood at the edge, looking down at Katherine, pointed the finger at her with an evil smile, turned, and walked out of sight.

Katherine turned to face the vampires as they came through the gate. The bright light of the full moon lit their eerie forms and cast their hazy shadows on the ground. She looked into Stephen's mind; he had no defense against her, and he knew it. Lucifer had sentenced him to death. He held his slayer like the rest but she knew he would not fight her. Katherine saw the sorrowful look on his face as he now realized he would die and be nothing but another soul in Hell. Lucifer had brought him here for this fitting end, one designed for a traitor, a once-powerful vampire... this was his grim reward for his betrayal.

Katherine raised her sword as the rogues spread out and yelled, "Come for me, vampires!" Looking at Stephen, she said, "I will show you mercy. You will be the first to die." With blinding speed, she flew at Stephen and struck him across his stomach with Alexa. Watched him fall and, before his knees touched the ground, she took off his head, and what met the earth was his dirt.

Katherine flew back and sized up the rest. Two of the rogues had spikes meant for her heart, and she flew into them first. Whirling, she struck one across the shoulder, following up by removing the other's head. Then she spun and took the head of the first. The rogues formed around her. She felt a blade strike her across her back. She pivoted, drove her sword through the vampire's stomach, turned, took another vampire's head, and spun once more, decapitating the wounded rogue. Katherine moved much more quickly than the rogues; in and out of the fray, she darted, two more foes falling to the ground in piles of dirt. The remaining rogues fell back and made their escape.

Katherine regained her composure and drifted a foot above the ground toward the entrance door, her slayer from Heaven humming and glowing. A terrible evil, the very same she had felt so long ago with the demon Charun, drenched this place. It was a sorrowful and penetrating evil that suffocated the soul. She waved her hand in front of the little green light. The door slid open, and she entered a large corridor with doors on each side.

Katherine floated to the end of the hallway, and another door slid open. She entered what looked to be a large room, and a light mist hung in the air. The walls and ceiling of this room seemed to waver, flow unnaturally, and she knew they were not solid. Maggots crawled everywhere on the floor... the sign of the demonic presence. Staring into the mist, she raised Alexa and saw a human form lying on the floor. Slowly, she floated toward the body, sensing everything, feeling everything. The stranger was a mortal woman, and she was dead. Katherine hovered above the woman, seeing that her belly was extended, her flesh torn as if an animal had attacked her. Bite marks covered her, but they were human bite marks. She had been a pretty woman, but now her hazel eyes stared lifelessly into the mist. She was torn between her legs, afterbirth having spilled from the wound, and she lay in a red pool of blood on the dark floor. Alexa felt the extreme evil, and its metal rang. Katherine shuddered and whispered, "Quiet, Alexa."

Looking further into the mist, she saw the walls shudder, moving further away, tilting and briefly, she felt disorientated. Suddenly, a small, thick red mattress form from the mist, lying on the floor with a baby on top, and she floated cautiously to the bed. The baby looked at her with a penetrating stare and an evil smile. Horrible nausea came over her as the evil of this baby tried to pull her into its terrible darkness. *What horror is this,* she thought.

Blood tears formed in her eyes, and then she felt another presence, turned her head, and saw a shadow move. Samil came out of the mist. Still, the witch had no weapons. Katherine wiped the blood tears from her eyes, stood, and raised Alexa.

The witch laughed and said, "So sensitive, Katherine. Does Brendel make you feel sad? When he grows, he will do more than that to the guardians of this world. Brendel will bring a hundred years of war to this world."

Katherine looked at the baby. It lay naked on the mattress, and she knew it would only take a second—one blow from her—to cut this baby in two. She looked back at the witch, and the witch smiled at her, cocking her head to the side and waiting for Katherine's blow.

"Who are you?" Katherine shouted at her as she changed into her fiercest vampire form. Her eyes burned blue, and her fangs grew long. She crouched and raised Alexa, grew in size, and gathered Michael's power.

"I told you, I am Samil. Go ahead, strike at Brendel, mighty queen. I have heard about you from Malin. You almost had her, but you let her escape. Our father is not happy with you."

"That's right, I almost did, but I *will* have you, witch."

"Do you think you will save your maker?" The witch gave a

loud laugh. "Lucifer will certainly kill the Demon Slayer. You will never reach him in time. You lost him the moment he entered the black castle. Shawn is a diversion, as you can see, and Lucifer has made a new demon. The devil likes killing vampires. Leading them to the slaughter. Maybe Shawn will lead an old and powerful angel to the same fate. What do you think, queen?" Again, the witch let out a loud laugh.

"I think you must be destroyed along with that baby."

Katherine turned, and in an instant, with a blinding arc, she brought Alexa down toward the baby. She was met by a powerful energy that came from the baby itself. The dark energy wrapped itself around Katherine, lifting her, throwing her through the flowing walls and up into the dark night. Lucifer had slapped her away and was now pulling her into his darkness. Suddenly, the light came to her; she felt her angels pulling at her, pulling her away from this dark energy. Then she fell and heard the cries of her angels.

Katherine woke in tall field grass. Alexa was in her hand. She lifted her head and heard the bees buzzing around her, smelled the wildflowers, and felt the warm sun on her skin. A dog stood over her, and she felt its wet tongue on her cheek. Sitting up, she shooed the dog away.

The sun was high in the cloudless blue sky. She must have been unconscious for at least half a day. The dog came back and nuzzled her. "Stop it, dog. Go away," She ordered. Katherine stood, noticing that her skin was hot, but she could withstand a lot of sunlight. A boy's voice called for the dog from somewhere in the distance. She pushed at the dog. "Goodbye, dog. Go to your master."

Looking around, she saw a field filled with meadow grass and knew she was somewhere in the countryside. Squinting, she cupped her hands over her eyes as she looked at the bright blue sky and thought better of a trip home. Dropping to her knees, she dug into the ground, feeling the warm, moist dirt. She bore a shallow grave, fell into it, and then covered herself with the earth, sleeping until nightfall.

Chapter Twenty-Two

S hawn swayed in his chains. The time now stood still for him as he hung in the dungeon. He was human, and could not sense his surroundings as before. Light rays broke through the small openings in the door. His toes and the balls of his feet barely touched the floor, and he would have to lift them every so often because of cramping, as well as the heat of the stone. At first, sweat had poured out of him, but now it had stopped. Straining his human sense of hearing, he could detect the fighting. This time the vampires had come much closer. Even as a mere human, he could sense the tremendous upheaval going on around him. Dehydrated and becoming delirious, he thought he saw the hall light up with white light, and then it came through the door.

They are coming, Shawn. I did not forget you. Ready yourself. The sound and arrival of Herit echoed in his mind.

****

Katherine lay in a big, soft bed in a plush hotel in Montreal. She had been staying in one of their most exceptional suites for the past three months and had just woken from her day sleep and ordered tea. Now she stretched herself and was dreamily thinking of Julien, his handsome face and blonde hair, the taste of his delicious blood. It had been half a year since her encounter with Samil and Brendel. She had returned to Amsterdam to hurry the preparations for the next attack but still had to fight for vampires to join her army. She had discussed this latest turn of events with her advisors and questioned Amrit on how long this evil was in his city unobserved. He became indignant with her, and she ordered him to stay in Amsterdam—told him not to leave. Now, she realized, she must bring the head of the covenants into her rule, and made a decree that all leaders of the covenants would now sit at her advisor table.

Renee's deep sadness had now turned into fits of terrible anger. She had returned to Amsterdam and brought Deceida with her, standing at Katherine's side again and working closely with Peter and the army. These days Katherine knew Renee lived for the chance to return to the cavern and seek her revenge. Renee would tell her that Deceida also wanted to return, to take the head of Malin, and sometimes glowed in the night with a soft ring to its blade.

Three months ago, Katherine left Victoria in charge as the final preparations were being made for the attack and told her she was going to Montreal. Victoria winked, smiled at her, and told her to say "hello" to Braden for her.

On her return to Montreal, she discovered that Julien and his brother had lost their restaurant. Using the scent of his blood, she found him in the city, and now she watched and probed his thoughts almost constantly to learn if he had the stamina to be a vampire. Most nights she would shadow him, and only recently had she started speaking with him in a lounge in the city. When the time came, she had decided he would be her changeling.

The next eve Katherine walked behind stools in a disco located in the entertainment district of a high tower. Different colored lights flashed and moved to the beat of the music with Holograms overhead advertised various drinks available to order. Viewers floated in the air, depicting sporting events playing out in other parts of the city. As she slowly walked, men's heads would turn, trying to capture her gaze, trying to make her notice their smiles, their wit, and the crude, sexual symbols forming around their heads. They did not matter because she stalked another.

Taking a seat, she looked down the long bar and caught sight of her interest. She watched him as he laughed and talked with a friend. Julien could not see her in the crowd until she wanted him to see her. To his sight, she was not there. Her eyes flashed the blue of her covenant—of a vampire prowling. Julien had attracted the interest of a powerful vampire. The vampire that would someday end his mortal life.

Katherine watched the symbols form around the heads of the humans with their different emotions, their hands waving, and the chatter of their voices. Some men would stare at her, and she quickly made them look away. Ordering a glass of wine by speaking, she received her usual odd look but told the man's mind it did not matter and to go about his business.

Katherine took her drink and slipped off her stool. She wore a tight-fitting dress with a slit up the side, a little cleavage showing, and walked toward her new love. She released Julien's mind so he could see her, and probed his thoughts as she moved closer and placed in his mind there was no suspicion when it came to her. Only one of the few ideas she put in his mind. He must judge her for himself---her maker had taught her this. Slowly, she approached him, dressed in her seductive attire, and the men's eyes followed her as she walked toward her new love.

As she approached, their eyes met, and a grin spread over Julien's face. "Hi, Katherine! I didn't think I would see you again so soon. Did you have to stay longer for business?"

"Yes, but I am leaving tomorrow. I remembered you said you would be at this place. I will be gone for a while, and I wanted to see you before I left."

"You did?" Julien said with excitement to his voice. "I'm glad you came. Paul, let the lady have a seat."

Katherine sat and noticed Julien holding his jacket. "Are you leaving?"

"I'm going to meet a friend. He's showing me a little place

where I'll set up my new restaurant. It will be small, something I can afford and manage."

"You decided to open a restaurant here? Not to go into space?"

"I tried, but they won't take me. I had a bad ear infection when I was a child. The doctors cleared it up quickly, but now occasionally I get spells of vertigo. Unfortunately, space makes vertigo worse."

"That's too bad. I know how you wanted to go," Katherine said, relieved. She wouldn't have to act so quickly with Julien now. She would have more time. "Yes, I would like to see your new place. Is Braden going to be your partner?"

"Not this time. He got a job in a fancy restaurant in midtown. Oh, and I have seen your friend with him."

"Victoria is fond of Braden," Katherine answered.

Katherine was drawing him into her. He thought of her often that she could tell, and he was falling in love with her. Julien wanted her, and his lust for her built as she leaned close to him. In his thoughts, she saw what he wanted from her, what he would do to her given a chance. This made her hide what she was from him. It made her want him and wonder what it would be like to make love to him. She had not felt this kind of excitement in a long time. Thank the angels she had found him. If she survived these horrible days she found herself in, she would certainly come for him. His fate was sealed with her.

"Come on, and let me show you my new space. Then I hope you will come home with me. We can spend some time together. I want to know you better."

"I will go with you to see your new place, but I have to leave soon." She knew he was a man and would soon start making his advances toward her. "Next time I come, we will be together—I promise you."

Katherine followed Julien through the crowd and out the door, onto the wide walkway. There was a light rain and a rumble of thunder in the distance. They found public transport for the trip to the tower that held his new restaurant. This time they were only a few levels up, and she strolled with Julian enjoying his company, held his hand. A desire built in her for him, but she wasn't ready—the time was not right. Walking close to him, she took in his masculine scent, smelled his sweet blood, and longed for a taste. He was a competitor, all man, but he was kind to the weaker, the less fortunate and cared about humanity. A smooth, comfortable way he had about him. She quickly sensed he was debating whether to kiss her or not, and she slipped the suggestion not too into his mind. This made her feel guilty; she didn't like doing this, but if he kissed her, he could find her out so this time she stole his confidence.

"Why no girlfriend, Julian?" she asked.

"I am too ambitious right now. I had a girlfriend, and I loved her, but she said I was never around. She complained I didn't show her enough attention. I came home one day, and she had left, so I decided to wait for a relationship until I came back from space. But now everything is different, and I have met you."

Julian turned and looked at her, gazed into her eyes. She had taken his heart. He was a person who liked falling in love. Now he loved her, and she had a newfound desire for him.

"I have to leave for a short time, but I will be back, and your life will change. I want you to know that."

"How serious you are, Katherine." Julian continued to talk, and then she stopped him. They had walked into a less populated area of the tower. She had been preoccupied, and suddenly she sensed a powerful evil. *Oh, Michael!* She thought.

It was Malin—she had cloaked herself, and Katherine did not have Alexa with her. Julian must have seen the look of fear that came over her face.

"What is the matter, Katherine? You look like you've seen a ghost."

Grabbing him by the hand, she pulled him between two buildings. "I am sorry, Julian, for getting you into this. Your life is going to change sooner than I hoped."

"What are you talking about? Why are you pulling at me? I do have an apartment close by."

Katherine lifted her veil of secrecy, and Julian began to see her for what she was. Her eyes were not quite human, a sense, an instinct of something different. She looked around the corner of the building and saw Malin walking toward them. It was quiet, and a few humans were ways down the street, too far to matter. All she felt was the gathering of dark energy, the damp breeze on her face, and the panic for Julian's safety. Maybe she could take him to where more humans where. No, there wasn't enough time, and she only would expose him more to Malin's evil. Katherine took on her vampire form and prepared to fight.

"What is going on here? What's with the eyes? You look like those pictures of guardians. This can't be real… you're a vampire."

"I am, my love, and I'm sorry that I have got you into this. I should have waited and been more careful. My future is uncertain, and I wanted to see you before I left."

"The woman, Victoria…the one that goes around my brother. Is she a vampire, too?"

"Yes, she is. Stay here, Julian, and do not come out. I will lead this danger away from you. Wait in the darkness, and when you feel it's safe, get away from here. Go to a crowded area. Do not go home for a few days. Stay with a friend, and do not come looking for me."

"Why are you here? What do you want?"

Katherine reached out to touch Julien's cheek, and he backed away. "Because I want you, my love. I need your love."

"But you're a vampire. I could never be with a vampire. I loved you. I thought."

"I love you, Julien, and I want you. It is my nature. The angels gave me my power, and someday, hopefully, I will give it to you. You loved me before you knew what I was, and you will love me again, you will see. I have to go, but if I can, I will come back to you."

"That won't be necessary. I am not sure about all this. Just stay away from me."

She looked out to the street, sensed the evil rising, the closeness of Malin, and went to the corner of the building where Malin was standing. Malin had no weapon. She stood wearing her sadistic smile and a cloak as black as night.

"I came for a visit. I wanted you to know that Shawn and I are getting along quite well. He enjoys our lovemaking."

Katherine walked out and stood facing the witch. "You lie, Malin!"

"I have kept him alive, as I said. Soon, Lucifer will have me kill him. You will never save him, and time is running out for you."

Malin laughed, and Katherine launched herself at her. Malin shot straight up to make her escape, and Katherine followed, chasing her to the south. Slowly, she caught up with Malin, and then, suddenly, the witch descended and landed in a farming field. Malin was playing with her. Landing twenty feet from her, Katherine quickly readied herself for a fight. She yelled at the witch. "Why are you deceiving me? Why have you come here tonight?"

Malin just laughed her sick laugh. "Before you attack, I'm surprised you allowed another one of your loves to die so easily."

"You despicable creature!"

"What is his name, Julien?" Malin mocked. "He is handsome, and he does look a little like Shawn. I'm surprised the whore queen hasn't fucked him yet. You will never have love again, Queen of the Vampires. The dark angels and I will see to that."

Malin lifted her shroud, and Katherine saw the witch Samil with Julien. Her blood turned to ice as she screamed, "You evil witch!" Katherine turned, shot into the air, and flew at a tremendous speed back to Montreal. She begged Michael to give her more speed, and she accelerated. Landing, she saw Samil standing over Julien, finishing a chant. Katherine flew into the witch, knocking her backward and away from Julien, who lay unconscious.

"That wasn't very nice of you, vampire," Samil spat at her. "This is the second time you have been rude to me. It will be the last. I will leave him for you. You won't be able to do much with him."

Samil rolled her hand outward, and a blue ball of dark energy burst from it, hitting Katherine in the chest, knocking her back, stunned, onto the pavement. She rolled and got to her knees as Samil lifted into the air to make her escape.

Immediately, Katherine went to Julien and found the witch had pushed his thoughts deep inside him. She probed and searched, but there was nothing in his mind. The witch had prepared him, meaning to instill her evil into his head, but Katherine had arrived just in time to stop her. An evil spell had taken him, and now he lay in a deep trance.

Sitting next to him, she placed his head gently in her lap. Blood tears came to her. She heard a gasp and looked through her blood tears at a couple staring at them. With a look of contempt, Katherine's vampire face hurried them along.

She spoke to Julien in a soft voice, stroking his face, pushing his wet, blond hair out of his eyes. "I'm so sorry I allowed this to happen to you, my love. I should have been more careful. I should have waited before I came around you. Look what has happened to you. What I brought to you. The angels have made me queen, yet I can't have love." Katherine lifted her head, blood tears on her cheeks, and spoke. "Michael, you made vampires. You know they must have love. Why can't I have love?"

The light from a new day made its way down the walkway of the tower, crept into the alley, and softly lit Julian's lifeless face. A blood tear fell on his cheek. Katherine stood, holding Julien, and slowly lifted herself into the air. She took Julien to Dalton, and the next eve, to Amsterdam. She brought him to the basement of The Citadel and laid him on a marble slab with a red velvet cushion.

Chapter Twenty-Three

K atherine stood next to the marble slab that held Julien's motionless body. Two silver coins with etched symbols lay on his eyes to protect him from the dark angels. Two burgundy candles burned at his head, one on each side, and a blue pillow with the Herit covenant crest was placed under his head. Katherine had laid a thick, burgundy blanket over him. He was human, and she wanted to make sure he wasn't cold. Often, as she stood over him, she would beg the angels to wake him. Her only comfort was the peaceful look on his face.

Six months had passed since she came back to The Citadel with Julien. Katherine had brought a vampire schooled in human medicine to look after him, and he had told Katherine the spell kept his human condition from deteriorating. Katherine had asked Drake if the dark angels could still torment him, and Drake promised that Julien felt nothing, only oblivion. She had brought the heads of the covenants into her fold and now considered their ancient advice. She told them they would be with her on the next assault of the cavern.

Now two thousand trained warrior vampires stood ready to go with her to Hell's Hole. During the time she had been back, she had held many strategic meetings with Peter. The task of getting two thousand vampires down Hell's Hole worried her. It would take considerable time, and they would be vulnerable during their descent. Peter told her there was nothing they could do about the size of the shaft. The first vampires down would have to protect the rest as they climbed down the shaft. She was pondering this problem further when she sensed Victoria.

"I thought I would find you here. No change?" Victoria asked as she came through the door.

"No, he is the same," Katherine sighed.

"I look at him and see Braden. Do you think he is all right?"

"He should be. I don't think Malin or Samil know of him..." Katherine said, "But I didn't think they knew of a lot of things."

"We must attack soon. We are ready, Katherine. The longer we wait, the more likely it is that Lucifer discovers our plans. We will succeed this time."

"It will be soon," Katherine replied. "We have no choice. Lucifer is going to take Shawn's soul. It is only a matter of time. Drake has told me this, and Malin taunted me with it."

"Have you heard from Gwyn?"

"No, not yet, but The Mother told me she will come soon. She will come when it is time for the attack." Katherine looked at Victoria and tried to give her a smile. "Will you change Braden when this is over?"

"Yes, if I'm alive. I will go and make him my changeling."

"I would wait before I let him see Julien," Katherine said as she turned to look at him. "He should be a vampire for a while before he sees this."

"I will wait, but eventually, he will have to be told," Victoria said. "I'm sorry you are so unhappy, Katherine. You try to have love, but it eludes you."

"When I rescue my maker and my reign is over, I will have love again. My reign will be a hundred years. Michael has promised me. I think that is enough." Katherine turned and met Victoria's gaze, looking into her eyes, forcing her way in, and feeling her. "Prepare yourself, Victoria. Take your changeling and protect that love. Michael will pick you. The ancients will accept you. Drake has told me this."

"Erdin has already hinted of this," Victoria whispered, not quite believing what she said. "Soon, a Kenmare will rule," he told me. "I must change Braden before I am crowned, while I have the chance. You must give me the time to prepare."

"You will have some decades, but first we must save Shawn," Katherine said. "I am not sure anymore if that is possible, or what will be left of him when we find him."

"We will save Shawn, and he will be with us again. He will survive that hell. Shawn will find away!" Victoria told her as she took hold of Katherine's shoulders and gave her a little shake. "You will see."

It was late afternoon, and Katherine had woken early. She was walking the grounds of The Citadel. It was autumn, and she watched the yellow and orange leaves float to the ground. There was an explosion of color around The Citadel. *Some death can be beautiful,* she thought. The sun was setting, and the sky was turning a beautiful pink streaked with white.

Katherine was always sad these days, felt the loss of Jessamine and Caitlyn terribly, and worried about Renee. Now she was restless and felt the anticipation of the coming battle strongly. Renee was different now; hate had its grip on her. Her only thought was of killing Malin. She knew this would be her last chance to save Shawn. The Mother would allow the vampires to enter the cavern as many times as it took, but Michael was different. There was a limit to what he would pay for Shawn. Now, her best chance was Herit.

As she continued her walk, she felt Drake come into her thoughts, whispering in her mind:

There will be only one more attack, Katherine. Lucifer will undoubtedly know when you start the attack, and this time he will order Malin to kill Shawn when you enter the cavern. But all is not lost. Michael will allow angels to enter the cavern, and Herit will protect Shawn until you reach him. The time has come for you to bring your army to Hell's Hole and wait for the warrior angels to start the attack.

As Drake faded in her head, she told him that this time she would not leave the cavern without Shawn. Katherine continued her walk; she felt the cold wind blow at her back, looked up, and smiled. Gwyn was coming.

She watched Gwyn float to the ground. On her back was a pack, and attached was a small, round silver shield and a slayer. In her hand was a staff, a branch cut from a birch tree with the bark removed. It had turned to a reddish-brown and was the same height as Gwyn.

"Always arriving at the last minute, Gwyn," Katherine teased. She was glad to see her. Gwyn always made her feel better when she was near.

Gwyn embraced her, kissed her, and the smile left her face. "You aren't well. I'm so sorry. I'm here now, and I have brought a weapon. A weapon to rival Lucifer's."

"What does The Mother say, Gwyn?"

"She says you must attack. Time is running out."

"I see…Walk with me, Gwyn."

Darkness had descended on The Citadel. The wind had stopped, and a quiet stillness had settled over the grounds, chimes in the bell tower started to play their nightly tunes. Frost was forming on the freshly cut grass, and the silver top of the moon peaked above the dark horizon.

"I will leave Juliet to watch over my affairs. Like Caitlyn, she really is not a warrior. I will not leave the cavern without Shawn this time. I wanted you to know that. If Renee falls, and you make it out of the cavern, you must watch over Juliet. You and Juliet will be the only Bryces left."

"I will. This time I have come to stay."

Katherine and Gwyn made their way back to The Citadel, and later, Katherine sat watching Gwyn finish putting her clothes away. Gwyn was such a neat and meticulous creature. Everything had a proper place in Gwyn's world.

Gwyn finished, turned, and looked at her. "The angels know the outcome is uncertain, but I feel we will save Shawn this time."

"Who knows if any of us will leave the cavern," Katherine said. "Not even Michael can say."

"I have brought weapons," Gwyn said.

"What kind of weapons?" Katherine asked. "Did you bring the

pebbles?"

"I have brought the pebbles, and I have brought a staff," Gwyn said as she pointed to the corner. "The Mother has placed the strength of the eagle in this staff. She has given us great power. The dark warriors this time will feel the sting of the light."

"We will need it," Katherine assured.

Katherine watched Gwyn take a blue satchel and pour five white, marble-sized pebbles into her hand. "These will give us limited flying ability in the cavern. Keep your stone safe in your pocket. It takes tremendous power to fly in the cavern, and we have to use the stones sparingly."

"Can we fly when we want to?" Katherine asked.

"Yes, but there is more. Whoever reaches Shawn must give him their pebble. After the battle with the Esmanaa Demons when he lay healing in the ground, The Mother hid an immense power in him, and it has lain dormant these past centuries. The pebble will awaken this power. If I fall, you must also make sure he gets this staff. He will be a warlock, and this will be his staff."

"I will. I pray to Michael that we succeed."

Gwyn came and embraced her, and then stepped back and said, "I feel such despair in you. It has consumed you. We will save Shawn, you will see. The angels made you the transitional queen to force the ancients to accept this type of rule. The Mother says to use your power on the ancient vampires to force them into action."

"I am so tired of this," Katherine said. "Maybe the ancients are right. I am too young to be queen."

"You have forty-two more years to be queen," Gwyn said. "The Mother and Michael have agreed you must be queen for forty more years. You must accept this and end your reign with dignity."

"What choice do I have? The angels always get what they want from me."

Katherine sat at a large, round mahogany table. She had just come from welcoming Rebecca back. Only Rebecca had returned, though, and Katherine had questioned her why. Katherine informed her that the McCall's were of the Herit Covenant. Rebecca told her she led the McCall family, and that this time she would fight for her family, but she could not ask them to go to that hell. Katherine and Rebecca had separated with an uneasy peace.

Victoria sat to her right, and Renee to her left. Gwyn, Juliet, Rebecca, and Peter stood watch at the closed oak door to the large meeting hall. There were no lights, and its floors and walls were made of dark, polished marble. There were no windows—only darkness when her counsel was in session, and the doors closed. Vampires were the only creatures that could see in the hall.

Earlier, she had listened to Peter present his battle plan for the attack, which sounded much like the last time. The ancients, like her, were worried about climbing down Hell's Hole unprotected. All were sure that Lucifer would know of the attack. She had informed them that angels would protect them when they made their entrance into the cavern but told none of them about the pebbles.

"How do you know this?" asked Wodan of the Brandt Covenant.

"The Archangel Michael speaks to me through my murdered, changeling Drake. I'm sure you all remember him."

They finished the final details of the attack, and then Katherine sat and listened to the ancients drone on about why they should not have to supply any more warrior vampires. Again, she had to listened to them complain about the losses they would suffer, the reckless dangers she had brought to the vampires in her attempts to save Shawn. The latter accusation was all she could stand. She brought her hand down hard on the table, cracking the marble, and then sprung to her feet. Victoria took her hand, trying to calm her.

She screamed at the heads of the covenants. All the vampires stared at her in shock. "Again, I have to tell you?" she yelled. "It is not the Bryces ordering you to Hell's Hole! Michael and Eos have set these events in motion! You will follow me to Malin's black castle, or you will answer to Michael and Eos!"

She stood staring at the ancients, seeing the contempt on Amrit's and Prodosa's faces. "You will not have me as queen for too much longer, but two eves from tonight, we will gather at the Penn Cave and start the attack." She turned and looked at Peter. "Prepare the army and have them at the Penn Cave."

Katherine looked back at the ancients, glared at them. "Be at the Penn Cave with your swords, given to you by Heaven, or you will answer to Michael." She turned and left the hall.

Chapter Twenty-Four

A ll day, the specters of light from Heaven had gathered at the opening of the Penn Cave. Darkness came, and the spirits swirled above the cave, warrior angels with their swords of light, preparing to be the first to enter the cave.

Katherine stood with Victoria, Renee, Rebecca, and Gwyn across the field from the entrance of the cave. It had snowed, and a white powder blanketed the field grass and trees. A cold wind blew down the valley and threw the snow from the tree branches, spraying the cold, wet mist against her face. She lifted her face to enjoy the refreshing coolness, soon she would again bear the terrible, suffocating heat. A large full moon hung in the night sky, and the snow sparkled in its soft light. As the night went on, the specters increased in number. She watched the spirits flying above the opening of the cave, saw the flashes of what the lifeforce looked like when they were warrior vampires.

Through the night, warrior vampires arrived in groups of tens and twenty's, slayers in hand, carrying silver shields, breast armor, and guards. Now, close to midnight, they were reaching their full strength of two thousand, and Peter was forming them four abreast to enter the cave. The warrior vampires came from Dalton, only a short distance from the north. This time, Peter had assured her, the vampires would be better trained and well-rested when they entered the cavern.

Katherine turned and looked at Victoria. "Always at the big battles, Victoria. Michael has chosen well."

"This battle…I would not miss it. It looks like the angels will be true to their word tonight," Victoria said as she nodded toward the opening of the Penn Cave.

"Remember what I said about the staff and pebbles," Katherine called out to all.

"We remember, Katherine," Renee answered. "The time has come to kill Malin."

"There are other tasks to accomplish tonight, too, Renee."

Katherine lifted off the ground and floated to the vampires grouping for the attack. She moved in front of the heads of the covenants, nodded to them, and said, "Tonight, you will fight for your queen, not the Bryces."

She floated on and spoke to the others. "Vampires, the angels have ordered us here. As you can see, this time, they will start the attack. Prepare yourselves, the task will be hard, and the evil in that cavern will be a burden to bear. It will cause you to despair, to doubt yourself. You must put that aside, for the angels will sing your names, and Heaven's glory will be yours." Katherine floated back and heard the slayers beating against the vampires' shields—listened to their battle cries. Shouting, they declared they would fight for their queen.

A spirit broke off from the others and came to her. It was Drake, and she heard him speaking:

Ready yourselves. The attack will begin.

A bright light came down from the sky and swept across the valley, casting a glow over the snow as it went—the angel was Herit. The angel entered the field, a loud blast from a trumpet came from above, shook the snow from the trees, and the spirits followed the mighty angel into the cave. Katherine took her place with Victoria, Gwyn, Rebecca, and Renee at the head of the formation. Peter was behind them in front of the warrior vampires.

Suddenly, a bright light erupted from the tunnel, poured out into the field, and engulfed the vampires. The world sparkled and shimmered in front of her eyes. Katherine could barely see through the light, and then as quick as it came, it left. She looked back and screamed, "Now, Peter! For the love of Heaven, now!

Start the attack!"

For the second time, the vampires entered the cave and followed the darkness until they came to the shaft that led to the cavern below. The angels had blown the shaft open with the light, and made a much larger opening. Now many more vampires could climb down at the same time.

Katherine went to the opening, felt the heat from the shaft, hit her face, and smelled the terrible odor of Sulphur. Looking at Victoria, she said, "The time has come. Let's save Shawn." Victoria nodded in agreement and started her climb down the shaft.

Katherine followed Victoria down the shaft; Gwyn was next to her, and Renee was above, with Rebecca. She played out scenarios in her mind and thought of the terrible task that was at hand, as she made her descent. All she could hear was the clanking of armor, and she felt the dirt and rock falling from above as she made her way down the shaft. Thirty minutes later, she reached the bottom and was met by the hot, black stones, the heat, and the burnt human bones. The river of fire lay off to the right of them. Her thoughts went to Shawn. What would he be like now as a human, having spent so long in this terrible place? This time, dark warriors had come right to the entrance of the shaft, and the spirits swirled around them, striking them down with their swords of light, pushing them back, securing the arrival of the vampire warriors. Dark warriors screamed and cursed as they swung their broadswords at the ghosts, only to watch their blades pass through the specters. The warrior angels had driven the dark warriors back and away from the entrance of the shaft, and this gave the vampires time to make their way down and move into formation.

Katherine saw Gwyn lower her staff and fire a white plasma beam. Dark warriors shimmered in its powerful, light, and disintegrated. Firing the staff again, Gwyn cut a path through the dark warriors, pushing them away from the entrance. Katherine looked up and saw Herit's light travel down the cavern, around the bend, out of sight, and then she saw Malin in the distance, floating above the dark warriors, her staff in hand, screaming orders to them. Gwyn and Malin fired at each other, white and blue plasma beams colliding, booming through the cavern.

Katherine screamed at Peter, "Form them into an arrowhead and then move forward! Victoria, Rebecca, and Renee in the lead!"

Katherine eyed Malin, drew Alexa, and flew directly toward her enemy. Katherine swung her sword, and Malin deflected it with her staff, but still, she parried and delivered a slice to Malin's arm. Malin pivoted in the air and struck Katherine across her back with the staff, driving her down into a sea of dark warriors. Standing, she swung Alexa like a madwoman, taking their arms, their legs, and spilling their insides onto the hot, black stone. She sliced through the monsters, removing their heads and covering herself in their thick, brown blood. She fought, with abandon, to save Shawn, to end her despair and misery.

Soon the main vampire forces caught up with her, and she took her place at the lead. The spirits had left and gone back up the shaft, but this time the vampires were moving forward at a faster pace, and hope started to build inside of Katherine. The warrior vampires were cutting through the dark warriors, their putrid blood covering the hot stones and flowing into the river of fire, burning, creating a terrible stench, and filling the air with acrid smoke.

****

In Heaven, the Archangel Michael sat on his throne, resting his head in his hand, watching the desperate battle unfold. He had allowed Eos to get himself in a terrible situation. His choir of angels was not happy about Shawn's predicament. Eos was an ancient and powerful angel that he was forced to come to terms with. Michael would need her help and power to defeat the demon, Brendel.

****

Repeatedly, Katherine would bring a dark warrior down and take his head. Victoria to her right and Renee and Rebecca to her left, Gwyn fired her staff and cleared a path through the monsters.

Katherine looked out and saw Gormal, leader of the Zavan Covenant, moving into the dark warriors, swinging his glowing sword from Heaven and taking a terrible toll on the Dark Warriors' ranks. All of the covenant leaders fought with the full fury of their ancient power, sending hundreds of dark warriors to Hell. Warrior vampires also fell, and their spirits flew back toward the shaft, finding their way to Heaven. The upheaval shook the rock walls of the cavern. Dust and dirt now joined the mist and drifted through the hot air.

More and more, they pushed the monsters back, slicing through them, stepping over their grotesque bodies. The vampires faced a sea of monsters, fighting a desperate fight. All that Katherine heard was the sound of battle, the clashing of metal, the grunts, groans from the dark warriors, the yells and screams from the warrior vampires. Katherine could see the bend in the cavern now, and she screamed to Victoria and Renee, "We are going to make it this time!"

Then she saw Malin return, swooping down into the vampires and killing many. Katherine immediately flew to her, and the sounds of their swords clashing echoed through the cavern. They both flew backward from the force of their collision, and both hovered looking for an opening.

Malin laughed at her and said, "Shawn will be dead, and his soul in Hell before you get to him."

"I don't think so, witch!" Katherine screamed. "I am pretty sure

Herit will have something to say about that!"

"Vampire whore!" Malin screamed as she came to Katherine. Again, they clashed their swords, looking for an opening. Suddenly, Malin feigned right, then went left and plunged her sword into Katherine's side. "How does that feel, vampire!"

Katherine parried Malin's second strike and brought Alexa around, slicing across Malin's stomach. Malin kicked Katherine back into the dark warriors. She felt their filthy hands grabbing at her, tearing at her, lifting her, and trying to pull her apart. She swung Alexa, killing the ones that held her. Katherine fell and rolled to her feet, and, looking up, she saw Renee attacking Malin, Deceida glowing in her hands. Renee and Malin were circling, clashing, and withdrawing, looking for an advantage—each slicing flesh with their swords. Katherine lifted into the air and flew toward Malin, only to meet a wave of dark energy that knocked her to the ground, dazed. The vampire formation again caught up with her, circling her protecting her. Quickly, she got to her feet and looked up to see a severely wounded Renee. Malin was behind her, holding Renee's head by her hair. Malin had pierced her spine, and she was helpless.

Malin brought her sword to Renee's neck and heard her scream, "Father, tonight I will end the Herit Covenant! No, Herit will leave here!" Malin, covered in blood, brought her sword across Renee's neck, taking her head. Katherine saw Renee's body and Deceida fall to the ground, followed by her head.

Katherine yelled, "Take Alexa!" as she threw Victoria her slayer. Flying into the dark warriors, she beat them back, plunging her fists into them as she fought her way to Renee. When she arrived, all she saw was a pile of fine dirt. Deceida lay on the hot, black stone, covered in brown blood. Wiping the blood tears from her eyes with the back of her filthy, blood-stained hand, Katherine reached down, picked up Deceida, and Heaven's slayer glowed with a bright light, and she held it high for all to see. The sounds of fighting and dying filled the cavern with many vampire spirits leaving their ranks and flying back toward the shaft. Katherine again wiped her bloody face and screamed to the warrior vampires, "Follow your queen! We will prevail!"

A wounded Malin had again vanished. Katherine charged into the dark warriors with Deceida, taking a terrible vengeance on the monsters. Many fell before her. The warrior vampires fought their way to the bend, turned, and moved slowly toward the black castle and the Gates of Hell.

Just when the anticipation of victory started to move through the ranks of the warrior vampires, a loud, coarse blast from a trumpet sounded, and the dark warriors fell back, allowing for an opening. Huge, black-haired bulls with long, sharp horns pored through their evil ranks. Dark warriors rode atop of the beast, holding long pikes with razor-sharp tips. The sounds of battle, trumpeting, and the thunder of the beasts' hooves striking the black rock echoed through the cavern. Briefly, the vampires lost formation, and the monsters pushed them back, but with great determination, they reformed and moved forward again.

Malin was standing on a beast, riding toward Katherine, holding the reins in one hand and a black, iron shield with the other hand. Malin was screaming at her dark warriors to fight harder, to stop the vampires' assault, or they would suffer for eternity the wrath of Lucifer.

Gwyn floated up, lowered her staff, and fired at Malin, the fiend's shield absorb the beam. Still, the energy forced her off the beast, tumbling her back down the cavern.

The vampires fought on. Gwyn would lower her staff and fire, disintegrating any dark warrior in its path. The warrior vampires would push forward slowly, driving the horde of dark warriors back. Katherine fought with recklessness, killing many dark warriors. Five hours into the battle, she finally saw the black castle sitting on its rock plateau, to the left the fire river that ended at the massive Gates of Hell.

Suddenly, a black mist sifted through the iron gates, reforming and then changing to take the shape of long tendrils that intertwined and spread out from their point of origin. They came from all over the gates, grasping fingers oscillating in the hot air currents in the cavern. The dark warriors stiffened their resolve as these tendrils whipped out at them, prodding them to fight harder. Katherine sensed the fear in the monsters toward these tendrils. Her vampire warriors fought on, pushing the dark warriors toward the Gates of Hell. Finally, they had come close enough for Katherine, Victoria, and Gwyn to make their assault on the black castle.

Katherine now saw Malin standing on a high turret of the castle, pacing back and forth, screaming her disgust at the dark warriors.

Katherine screamed to Peter, "You and Rebecca will have to hold this ground!" She then yelled to Victoria and Gwyn over the roar of the battle, "Follow me into the castle!" She then whispered, "Be with us, Michael."

"Make it as quick as you can, my queen! The army is starting to tire!" Peter called back.

The warrior vampires mustered another offensive push. The rear of the dark warriors' horde met with the black fingers. They wrapped themselves around the dark warriors, bringing them kicking and screaming toward the Gates of Hell, the black doors absorbed them. The dark warriors pushed back in terror, caught between Lucifer's wrath and the warrior vampires'. Flaming balls of fire came from the high turrets of the black castle and landed amongst the vampires, exploding and sending flames high into the cavern.

"Quickly, my queen! Go now!" Peter yelled as he pulled his slayer from a dark warrior. "We will hold these miserable creatures."

"Victoria, Gwyn!" Katherine screamed and pointed. "Follow me! We will fly to the top of the turret and end that bitch's life!"

They flew to the high turret to find Malin gone. Where she'd stood, a wooden trap door lay open on the floor of the tower. Balls of fire from the other towers rained down around them, and they quickly dove for the trap door, climbing down a ladder to a wooden catwalk below. They followed the curved, stonewall to a door that led to stairs descending into the castle.

Anticipation and hope now replaced her sense of fear,

desperation, and sorrow. Katherine was close to Shawn. She could feel him and knew he was alive, yet a tear came to her eye as she remembered that he was mortal. She turned, saw the look on Victoria's face, and knew she had felt the same. Katherine drew Deceida and started down the stairs to rescue her maker. What she would find, she could not be sure.

She followed behind Gwyn. Dark warriors came up the stairs, and Gwyn would lower her staff and disintegrate them. Down the stairs they went, killing any dark warrior that lay in wait; soon, they came to the main section of the castle, followed the corridors to more stairs, and continued their descent. They had gone down three floors when Katherine sensed Malin down a hallway. Frozen in place, she stared at a large wooden door at the end of the hall.

"Malin is somewhere on the other side of that door," Katherine said, pointing, "Victoria, take Gwyn and follow the sense of Shawn. Save him. I will go for Malin."

"Are you sure?" Victoria questioned.

"Katherine, let us go with you," Gwyn pleaded.

"No, it has to be me. Go and save Shawn. I beg you!" Katherine pleaded, then pointed. "Follow those stairs."

Katherine moved slowly down the corridor, Deceida glowing and vibrating like a string on a violin. Her senses were at their highest, yet still, they were cloudy, dampened by the influence of this despicable place. Coming to the door, she forced it open and entered a room where she could feel strongly that Shawn had been recent. This had been his prison; she saw a horrible straw bed, his bowl of mush, and his piss pot. Her concentration waned because of all this, the horror she felt, and then the rage. Malin appeared sifting through the bars in the open window. The witch flew into Katherine, knocking her into the far wall. Katherine quickly got to her feet and took a fighting stance.

"You will pay for what you have done to Shawn," Katherine shouted as she raised Deceida.

"Your covenant's sword, I see…" Malin spat. "Did you get it off of dead Renee? It will do you no good here."

"Deceida and I will have something to say about that,"

Katherine yelled back.

"Do you approve of Shawn's room? Filthy whore of a vampire. I could have kept him in the dungeon."

They clashed in the center of the room, quickly obliterating the wooden table and chair. Only the screams of hate, the sound of metal striking metal, and the chaos outside could be heard. Sparks flew from their swords; metal ringing filled the room as both fought a desperate fight. Katherine twirled and caught Malin across the arm, but her foe had anticipated this and plunged her sword into Katherine's stomach. Katherine screamed and fell back. After having already fought for eight hours, she was exhausted, and her senses had become dulled.

"I can read you, vampire. In this place, I can see your thoughts. You've had a hard trip," Malin laughed. "Here, I have the upper hand. I thought you would have known that."

Katherine launched herself at Malin, forcing her against the wall. Malin gasped, and then dark energy formed, blowing Katherine away, across the room and against the far stonewall where she fell to the floor. Again, Katherine quickly got to her feet, flew toward Malin, and their swords rang out.

They fought, striking at each other, both delivering cuts to arms, legs, and body. Both tried to find an opening, their blood spilling to the wooden planks of the floor. Malin parried and thrust her sword at Katherine, missing her mark. Katherine faked a blow and then brought Deceida across Malin's sword hand, causing her to drop the weapon. Katherine quickly stomped on it and connected her fist with Malin's jaw. Malin grabbed Katherine's sword arm and wrapped her other arm around her neck, forcing her to the floor.

They rolled in the blood, gouged at each other, pummeling each other with their fists, cursing at each other, fighting a vicious fight to the death. Deceida fell from her hand as she needed both hands to stop Malin from tearing her head off.

Malin ended up on top, wrapping her hands around Katherine's throat. The witch pushed her hand out and growled, "Beelzebub, give me the knife." A dagger appeared in her hand, silver-bladed, an evil symbol carved into the black pearl hilt. Katherine, at the last minute, was able to deflect the blade before it could enter her heart squarely, but it still sliced the edge. She screamed and pushed the witch from her, rolling to her knees, blood pouring from her mouth. Malin was quickly upon her, drawing the dagger across her throat, slowly slicing into her neck, trying to remove her head from her body. Katherine was helpless, her power leaving her. Darkness approached.

Malin snarled, "Father, I have killed two of Herit's! The leader of the covenant and, now, the Herit Queen. Now, you must believe I am the greatest of all your witches!"

Malin hesitated for a moment, her face pressed against the side of Katherine's. Katherine could feel and smell her sour breath.

Malin whispered, "Prepare to die. You have failed."

Katherine then saw a bright light engulf them, and a plasma beam hit Malin, wrapped itself around her, and threw her against the far stonewall like a rag doll.

Shawn was standing by the door with a staff, energy flowing from him, and he appeared to be magnificent, brand new, and big—his head almost touched the ceiling. He was holding a staff, and then the room faded, and darkness came to her. Katherine heard the wail of the condemned, felt darkness surrounding her, pulling at her, and then Anne was with her, wrapping her spirit around Katherine's, bringing her away from the chaos and toward Heaven.

Chapter Twenty-Five

S hawn's dungeon cell filled with intense, white light. It seeped through the cracks, through the door window, and drove the evil from his cell. Herit was all around him; he closed his eyes, bathed in her light, and felt her rejuvenating energy.

Shawn, try to wake yourself. Help is almost here.

Then the light blew the metal doors out into the hallway, his chains came apart, and he fell to the floor. Many dark warriors went into the fire, sent by Lucifer to kill Shawn. Their swords raised, they too, fell dead and dissipated in the intense energy. For the first time in a long time, he felt relief. Then Herit's voice came again.

I am with you. Help has finally arrived.

The light subsided, and he was staring at two fierce creatures, one with eyes that burned blue; the other, emerald green. They held slayers and were covered in dark warrior blood. He blinked his eyes and at first drew away from these vampires. Then he came to his senses and looked again.

"Victoria, Gwyn," he said.

"Yes, it's us, Shawn, we have come to take you out of here. You know us!"

"Yes, for Heaven's sake, I do recognize you."

"Look what that witch has done to you..." Victoria said as she helped him to his feet.

"I know you," Shawn said. "But there is definitely a difference about you, though. We must go and find Katherine. We should hurry."

Gwyn came to him and grabbed his arm. He tried to free himself, but she was far stronger than he was. "It's all right. We are here to help you to awaken a power in you. Listen to me, Shawn. I have a white pebble to give you. Centuries ago, when you lay in your grave for those many years, Eos created a tremendous power, placed half in you and the other in her protector, the eagle. When I give you the stone, it will awaken this power in you. The staff I give you now has the other half of this power. You will be The Mother's most powerful witch. A warlock of tremendous power. You must ready yourself to receive this power. This energy will be a shock to your soul."

Gwyn let him go, and he simply took the stone and staff and went out the door.

"Shawn, wait," Gwyn said as she and Victoria looked at each other and then went after him.

"We have to go. Katherine needs us," he said urgently. "Don't you understand?"

Shawn started down the hall with one, though, to go to Katherine. But a power surged through him. It began in his head, traveled through his body, and he thought this energy would tear him apart. Shifting into Hell, he saw the horrible dark angels, felt the evil, and saw Lucifer with another demon, laughing at him. Then he knew the truth. This was all a sick game, a drug for the devil, a perversion for him. It was the tragedy of destroying all lives, good or evil. All were his to torment throughout the many worlds. The devil would always bring chaos and darkness. Malin meant nothing to him because the devil could make evil disciples for an eternity. Shawn saw Earth as a ruined battleground between good and evil, stripped of humanity. Then he was back in the hall, and fell against the stonewall, bathed in sweat, thrashing and screaming in terror. Gwyn came to him, held him to stop his convulsions.

Shawn screamed, his eyes wide with terror. "This will happen over and over through eternity. Lucifer's evil will never end, and he will bring demons and destruction again to our world."

"Is he all right, Gwyn? For the love of Michael," Victoria gasped. "What is happening to him? What is he saying? What did you do?"

"Help me with him. The Mother has given him great power, and he has seen something…something he was not meant to see. Most are in Heaven when they receive this kind of power."

Slowly he awakened to electricity moving through his body, energy pulsating in him. Then all subsided, and he stood with a new, healed body, perfect in every way, covered with the rags he had worn since coming to this horrible place. The stench had left him. Physically, he felt much better, stronger, but still, he was terribly afraid of this place. Before, his power was contained within a vampire's body. Now his strength was in a mortal's body, not built for such stress and wear.

"Are you all right, my love?" Victoria asked.

"Yes, I think I'm all right. We must go to my room. Katherine is there, and she needs our help!"

Shawn led Victoria and Gwyn as they made their way out of the dungeon, through the long corridors, and up the hot, stone stairs of the castle to his room. He heard the terrible battle beyond the castle walls. Dark warriors moved quickly to their stations, preparing to repel the vampires if needed. Some would stop and engage them, but Victoria and Gwyn would swiftly cut them down with their swords. Shawn carried the staff and felt the smooth wood of his new weapon, the latent energy within, and the vibrations in his hand. The power he held in his hands was beyond his imagination.

They came to the last corridor, and Shawn could hear the terrible fighting, the screams, and cursing coming from his room. Suddenly, the hall became cold, with a deep chill that reached out and wrapped around them, penetrated their beings. The air shimmered, and dark energy formed around the entrance to his room. He saw faces of horrible creatures in this energy—grim visages of dark angels. Immediately, a wave of dark energy moved down the hallway and washed over them, throwing them to the other end of the corridor. Shawn got to his feet with the staff and

276

looked to Gwyn.

"Think what you want the staff to do, and it will do it," Gwyn said.

Lowering the staff, he fired a white plasma beam, and the dark energy around the door collapsed in on itself and disappeared. He ran to the door and into the room to see Malin holding a severely wounded Katherine, starting a slice across her neck. Immediately, he fired the staff and hit Malin, lifting her and throwing her into the far wall. Shawn handed the staff to Gwyn, went and picked up Deceida, and moved to a stunned Malin. Stretching out her hand, Malin rolled, reached for her sword, and Shawn kicked it away. Deceida started to glow, and its metal rang in anticipation. Shawn reached down, picked the witch up by her hair, and held her to the wall.

"Spare me, Shawn. I spared you. I did not kill you. I should have, but I didn't," a defeated Malin whispered. "I see now. This power was always in him. Father!" Malin cried out. "Save me! I know I allowed this vampire to cloud my judgment!"

"You will get no sympathy from me, Malin," Shawn spat. "I told you what I would do to you for killing my daughter and Caitlyn."

Victoria placed her hand on his sword hand. "You cannot kill her. You are not a vampire. I will do it." Shawn gave the witch to her and watched Victoria hold her against the wall, staring into her black eyes. "It is a Kenmare that takes your life." Shawn handed Deceida to Victoria, she drew the blade across The Tempter's throat, and her body fell to the floor. Shawn saw Victoria dropped Malin's head onto her body, her black eyes staring lifelessly into oblivion. A pool of blood grew, spread over the wooden floor, and the slippery warmth surrounded Shawn's bare feet. She'd spent eons in the service of the devil, only to die, yet still, he left her there lying in an ugly, disgraceful death and did not consume her body.

Suddenly, trumpets sounded throughout the cavern. Shawn jumped onto the ledge of his prison window, looked out through the bars, and saw the titanic iron gates starting to move. Rock, dirt, and ash fell from around the gates and from the ceiling of the cavern. A thunderous rumble filled the void. The Gates of Hell were opening! Jumping back to the floor, he went to Katherine, scooped her into his arms, took Deceida, and said, "It is time to leave here, and quickly."

Victoria bent the bars back; Shawn followed her and Gwyn through the window and thanked the angels that he could fly again. He landed among the vampire warriors' formation, and they quickly surrounded Katherine. Victoria and Gwyn fell next to him, and Victoria yelled to Peter, "I have command now! Start an orderly retreat back to the shaft. We are leaving this place!"

The Gates of Hell opened only slightly, and black specters flew from the opening, followed by an agonized wail of lost souls. More and more came swirling and flying en masse, all moving in time with each other like a flock of swallows would. They flew into the warrior vampire formation, killing many, and then swarmed the vampire spirits as they flew back toward the cave opening.

Another blast from a trumpet and white specters came down the cavern, led by the bright light of Herit. Black and white phantoms swirled around each other, locked in battle. The distraction allowed the vampires to make their escape. The vampires fought the dark warriors back, and the cursing and moaning, the desperate cry of battle, continued as they slowly made their way back to the shaft.

Shawn held the vampire queen in his arms and stayed in the middle of the formation to protect her. Gwyn had taken the staff and fired it repeatedly, killing the dark warriors in large numbers as they made their exit back down the cavern. Victoria had taken her position in the back of the formation with her changeling Peter to protect the vampires as they made their escape.

Finally, they reached the shaft, and Gwyn planted the staff, pointing up to the opening and freedom from this terrible place. An intensely bright light came from the staff and projected up through the shaft. Gwyn yelled to the vampires, "Come into the light, quickly!"

The warrior vampires went into the light, and the beam lifted them to the top and freedom. In droves, the vampires fled into the light and up to the surface until the very last was accounted for. The weary vampires stumbled out of the cave and out onto the field, all covered in dark warrior blood. Some held the wounded. They collapsed to the ground, exhausted, crying at the horror they had just been through. Some cried for the loss of their friends and some for the loss of their lovers. Six hundred warrior vampires did not come back up the shaft, Renee, the leader of the Herit Covenant, among them.

Shawn carried Katherine out of the cave, brought her out onto the field, and laid her on the frosted field grass. Last out of the cave were the warrior angels. They flew above and around the vampires singing songs of battle, singing the warrior vampires' greatness, and then they lifted into the night sky and disappeared. Herit's bright light came from the cave, traveled to Shawn, and hovered above him.

Katherine will live. Malin is dead, and you are free. The Mother claims a great victory because of Katherine and our covenant. Anne has taken her spirit, and you must bury her body. The angels will sing songs of her deeds.

An enormous explosion of light and the hill shook as the cave and shaft collapsed in on itself. The spirit of Herit moved off and up into the star-filled sky. The heads of the covenants came to Shawn before they left. They had fought hard, and without them, the vampires' losses would have been much higher. Shawn saw looks of exhaustion and sorrow on their faces.

Gormal of the Zavan Covenant spoke first. "We were horrified to see the death of the leader of your covenant. We grieve with you. Renee was a great warrior vampire, and we will miss her. The warrior vampires of Earth have suffered for the death of Malin and your rescue. I hope it was worth it. My maker and Herit were lovers, and it grieves me to see the Herit Covenant near destruction."

"I thank you for your concern," Shawn said.

"Will the Herit Queen live?"

"She will live," Shawn said.

Amrit of the Divjot Covenant stepped forward. "You are mortal, Shawn. You are not a vampire anymore. Who will lead your covenant?"

"Rebecca McCall will lead what's left of it," Prodosa of the Parfeev Covenant said wearily.

"You will not decide who leads our covenant," Rebecca argued.

"Herit's own should decide who leads the covenant," Gwyn agreed.

"And you are a witch, vampire, and a changeling. Why are you speaking?" Wodan of the Brandt covenant demanded.

"She is right. The vampires of the Herit Covenant will decide who leads them," Shawn said. "And now I have to get Katherine buried."

Shawn knelt down and took Katherine's head, brushed her blood-soaked hair from her face. He saw the cuts and slices to her body and saw them on her face and neck as well. Twice a sword had pierced her, a dagger had sliced her heart, and he saw the cut to her neck that was meant to end her life.

"Look what they did to you, my love," Shawn whispered. "I will take you home, bury you, and protect you from now on."

The warrior vampires slowly gathered themselves and, in small groups, flew back to Dalton, went to the Susquehanna, and washed the dark warrior blood from their bodies. After the vampires rested, they left Dalton and made their way back to their homes.

Shawn gathered Katherine, strapped Deceida to his back, and took to the air bringing Katherine home. Gwyn followed with his staff, and Victoria went with Peter to Amsterdam. Before the battle, Katherine had decreed that Victoria would rule if she were not capable.

Shawn stood over a fresh grave in the basement of the Washington home. He and Gwyn had just finished burying Katherine. Standing in thought, he remembered when Anne had buried him and Victoria here. Humor came to him, a thought, and he didn't know why...now he was mortal, and a vampire stood next to him. That vampire had given blood to Katherine. He wondered why vampires made humans uncomfortable. Glancing at Gwyn, he pondered, was it the way they blinked, or their piercing eyes? The way light did not behave quite right around them? Gwyn had told him of the sacrifices Katherine had made to save him. She told him Katherine had made many enemies because of her persistence. Now, he knew, it would be hard for Katherine to continue being queen, because of the older vampires and her enemies. Shawn was tired, a melancholy tried to creep into him. But tonight, he would sleep with a cleansed body in a decent bed.

Gwyn came up next to him and put her arm around him. "Are you all right, love? I feel your sadness."

"I'm okay. Did you know, Gwyn, that for humans, vampires take a little getting used to?"

He felt her moist lips against his ear, the tingle of their touch, and she whispered. "Really? I guess I will have to be gentle with you. Let's go to bed. You are tired. Do you think I could have a taste of that blood of yours?"

"I suppose I can spare a little, and you have some years with me, by the way. I don't expect you to disappear again."

Gwyn laughed. "I'm not going anywhere. A mortal with a vampire changeling! The ancients will love that! How long do you think Michael will allow you to be a mortal?"

Shawn shrugged his shoulders. "I'm tired. I going to bed where it is safe, and there are no witches except for you." Shawn made his way to his room and looked at the bed, and then the couch. "Bed or couch?" he asked Gwyn.

"Couch, my love," Gwyn whispered.

"I thought so."

Chapter Twenty-Six

K atherine sat on a porch of an old-time beach house. Before the battle, she had visited a store, seen a hologram of this old-fashioned kind of dwelling on a beautiful beach, and that is where she wanted to stay while in Heaven. Anne had brought her here, and she had only recently awoken from a deep, spiritual sleep—a sleep that helped quell the sadness and fears lingering after the events she had witnessed and participated in. How long she had slept, she wasn't sure, as there was no way to measure time there. When Katherine woke, Anne was with her, and Anne's spirit hovered over her. Katherine smiled and wondered if Anne saw the smile.

How are you, Katherine?

That depends.

Victoria and Gwyn made it to Shawn and rescued him. Shawn arrived just in time, saved you, and Victoria killed Malin.

Then I am glad for Shawn and sad over the losses our family must bear again. Was it right to lose Jessamine, Caitlyn, and Renee for Shawn? A thousand other vampires...I am not sure. It leaves me with so much guilt.

Evil must always be confronted, Katherine. If not, it will spread through humankind, just like a plague. Without goodness, mortal man could not survive or exist. Humans would destroy themselves.

It was a perfect, sunny day, and the waves rolled onto a beautiful, white sandy beach. The seagulls skimmed the water and then flew up into a blue, spiritual sky. A few billowy, white clouds hung against the blue, and she could hear the surf, the roar of the waves and the call of the seagulls. In the back of the house, she had thought up a beautiful, green meadow with colorful flowers, birds, and a path to take walks.

Drake was with her. He had been with her constantly since she had woken. He still had his human looks but now was becoming transparent, more of a spirit. Drake told her that she had won a great victory for Heaven. Katherine tried to get the picture of Renee's death out of her mind, but she could not. She asked Drake if he would take her to Renee and Caitlyn, but he told her he couldn't, as they were in a spiritual stasis. Drake's spiritual body walked toward her; the strangeness of it still startled her sometimes.

How are you today, Katherine?

Fine, Drake. I feel better knowing that Shawn is safe. I still feel terrible about Jessamine, Caitlyn, and Renee. I have destroyed the Herit Covenant, and I must learn to live with that. I even still feel bad about your death.

It has been sixty years, Katherine. Have you given any thought to going back? It has been a year on Earth.

Soon, but not just yet. I'm not ready. I want to enjoy my beautiful surroundings a little while longer.

Katherine continued her walk with Drake along the surf. Kicking at the water, she searched for the perfect seashell to put in her green cloth sack. She hadn't felt this carefree in a long time.

Drake had been behind her but now seemed to have disappeared, and then she saw the light in front of her, descending toward her. *A spirit,* she thought. It came to the beach and formed into a person but was still white, and very transparent. Katherine could make out the features, but Anne was now very much a spirit.

How are you, Katherine? How is your rest going? Enjoyable, I hope.

Quite well, I have enjoyed being here. No responsibilities. What has Michael to say about the turn of events?

He is pleased that Shawn survived, but he has gone on to other matters. The demon child you saw now occupies his time. Lucifer and the witch Samil have hidden it well, and nobody knows where he is.

There was a terrible evil attached to that baby. Is Michael still in agreement? In letting me step down as queen?

In a way, you have another forty years to be queen. Victoria will be crowned queen when your reign is over. When the time comes, and she is crowned, you are to give her Deceida, and take back Alexa. The sword will transform her into a Herit, and she will lead the covenant. She has never been of a covenant, but now, Eos wants her to be a Herit.

I will give her the sword. Victoria, as a Herit leading our covenant...what next?

It is time for you to go back, Katherine. Face your responsibilities. I have news for you, though. It seems that over the year, because of the death of Malin, a human has slowly awakened. Julien is awake and nervously awaits your return. Shawn and Gwyn took him to the house in Washington.

He is awake?

Yes, Katherine, and now you must go back. Remember, the angels sing of your deeds. Eos and Michael, thank you for your sacrifice.

Heaven started to fade, the beauty disappearing, falling apart slowly in front of her. She felt the vibration begin in her spirit, and she moved into darkness and gradually became aware of the moist dirt encasing her skin. The Mother had her, cradled her, soothing her physical body, healing it; she felt Mother Earth's energy flowing through her, and then the intense need for blood. She pushed up, out of her grave, and into Gwyn's arms. Instincts took over, and they compelled her to find blood.

"Help me, Shawn! She's hard to hold!" Katherine heard Gwyn shout.

"I certainly won't be able to hold her," Shawn replied. "Katherine, stop fighting, we have blood for you. You don't have to go anywhere."

It was Shawn. She sensed him strongly, and he was next to her. She also sensed his mortal body.

"Shawn, is that you?" she cried out. "Thank the angels you are alive."

"Gwyn, give her some of your blood. I'll get the collars."

Katherine felt Gwyn's blood fill her mouth and flow down her opened throat. She felt Shawn wrapping the metal blood collars around her arms, and initiating the infusion of blood into her. Her mental self-started to wake, yet she felt tired and wanted to sleep.

"Shawn, wash my eyes so I can see you."

Shawn took her in his arms and brought her to the marble table. Warm water washed over her, over her face, and then she saw him. He looked mortal, but he was definitely her Shawn. She reached up and stroked his face. "You are human. I can feel your heat. I will have to talk to Michael about that."

She felt his warm lips kiss her, brush against her ear, and then she heard him whisper. "Thank you for saving me. Sleep, my love. I am here."

"Is Julien here?"

"Yes, my love. We have taken good care of him."

Sleep came to her quickly, and she drifted in the light, heard the angels sing of the warrior queen, and the battles that were fought by the guardians of Earth. How the guardians had made Lucifer cower behind his gates.

It had been a week since she left her grave. She had woken three times now and was feeling like herself again. It was late afternoon, a cloudy day with a spring chill. Standing on her balcony, she watched the brisk April wind blow across the lake, forming little waves that rolled onto the shore, washing the winter debris from the water.

Two humans walked together by the lake—Shawn and Julien, talking, getting on as if they were old friends. Shawn always had a way with humans, but now he was human, too. She also sensed the immense power in Shawn from The Mother. Eavesdropping on their conversation, Katherine listened to Shawn and Julien talking.

"It seems, my dear friend, it is time for me to tell you a few things," Shawn said. "There is no need for you to be anxious. All is well, and no harm will come to you here."

"If this has to do with Katherine's kind, there is no need. She has no right to keep me here. And you should let me go."

"I cannot let you go. A queen has decided your fate, and the angels give her the right. You will pay a debt for all humanity. It's a great honor for you, and that I cannot change."

Fear and uncertainty, that was what she sensed from Julien when talking of vampires. Then Shawn would reassure him that everything was all right.

"Braden is a vampire," Shawn said, looking at Julien for his reaction. "Victoria changed him soon after the battle that hurt Katherine. He has been a vampire for almost a year."

"Is he all right?" Julien asked. "And I'm sure he didn't ask to be a vampire."

"Yes, he is well and is feeding. It seems he is starting to like being a vampire. You will see him soon."

"What does that mean?"

"That brings me to the other thing I have to tell you. Katherine is healed, and she is here. She is going to come to you."

"I am not going to be made a vampire," Julien said as he stopped, stood firm, and looked at the trail heading into the woods and off the grounds.

"I see you are thinking of escape again. You should know by now that is not possible. Have courage, Julien… a great life awaits you."

Katherine sensed his fear from the news. Julien was confused about the turn of events in his life, and he worried about the horrible woman that had put him in that horrific sleep. Tonight she would hunt for blood, fill her blood sac, prepare herself, and tomorrow, she would go to him.

It was late afternoon the following day, and Katherine had just risen from her couch. Last eve she had fed and regained her strength. Now Shawn was at her door, and she hurried to let him in.

"As beautiful as always," Shawn told her with a wink. "Not bad for a creepy vampire."

Embracing him, she drew him to her, and they kissed passionately. She nuzzled his neck with her cheek, felt his slight resistance to her, and knew he was tolerating her. Toward the end, Katherine thought Shawn would be lost, yet she had saved him. Victoria had killed Malin, and her misery and despair had left her. Excitement filled Katherine tonight; she would go to her love, Julien.

Katherine whispered in Shawn's ear. "Let me have a taste. I want to taste your human blood."

"All right, a taste, but do it quickly. I have something to show you."

Changing to her vampire form, Katherine embraced him, gently inserted her blood teeth into his neck, and allowed his sweet human blood to fill her mouth.

"Shawn, you taste delicious."

"That's all you can have," Shawn said.

"For now," Katherine teased.

"Come to the balcony. I want to talk," Shawn told her.

Katherine looked out over the lake and on the far side, she saw Julien fishing. She smiled. Thomas had loved to fish…

"Does he like to fish?" Katherine asked.

"I guess he likes it. He has done a lot of fishing since being here. It also gets him away from us. I think Gwyn makes him nervous."

"Is Gwyn going to stay with you?"

"Yes, she is going to finish her hundred years with me. If I live that long. I am mortal."

Katherine turned, faced Shawn, and said, with no lack of exasperation, "And how long do you think Victoria and I will let you stay mortal?"

"I will be mortal as long as I want. No vampire in the world can change that."

"You will be mortal until you start to age, and then we'll see!"

"Are you going to change Julien?"

"Yes, I am going to take him as a changeling."

"You should do it sooner rather than later. The anticipation is not doing him any good. Gwyn has gone after him several times to bring him back. Change him and then take him to his brother. Gwyn and I will be leaving soon. I had my home rebuilt in the bayou, and I will live there with Gwyn."

"Back to your swamp?"

"Yes. And you have responsibilities in Amsterdam. I will leave the bayou and travel. I promise."

Katherine turned and looked across the lake; Julien was packing his gear and starting back toward the house. It was dusk, a gentle, moist spring breeze traveled across the water. The lone croak of a bullfrog echoed over the small lake. Earlier she had dressed and prettied herself.

Katherine rose into the air. "Wish me luck."

"Good luck," Shawn told her as he turned to go in.

Katherine floated to the ground and started on the path that traveled its way around the lake, came to a wooden bench, and sat by the lakeshore, waiting for him. Julien walked out of the wooded area with a confident stride and spied her sitting, dropped his gear, and froze. His mind searched for a way to avoid this meeting. Fear is what she sensed from him, but he was not going to show it, he was going to deal with her. She gave him a loving look and spoke softly.

"How are you, my love? I missed you. You don't have to be afraid of me. I would never hurt you."

"Why did you let that woman do what she did to me?"

"I had no choice. Those women tricked me, but things are different. We can be together now."

"I know you are a vampire, and I know you want to make me one. But I have decided I don't want to be a vampire, and I will be leaving to go home. Please tell Braden to come to see me."

"I am a vampire, my dearest love, that is true, and what you want doesn't matter when it comes to this. I'm going to tell you what my maker told me long ago. I am not going to let you go. I want you. I love you, and the angels allow me to have you."

Katherine got up and walked toward Julien. "I know you are

afraid. It will be all right. Afterward, I will take you to see your brother. I hear he has adjusted quite well. You loved me once, and you will again."

"You can stop right there, Katherine. I do not want to be a vampire," Julien commanded as he took a defensive stance. His eyes darted about, and his mind worked, trying to find some escape.

Katherine stopped, smiled at him, and calmed him. "I will not let anything happen to you. I will be with you through the change. You will be with me for a hundred years, and I will make you strong, and teach you how to be a vampire. We are warrior angels, Heaven's killers, here on Earth. I will take your blood, and you will have mine. You cannot escape me. This is your fate."

Katherine changed and felt the quickening, the scent of jasmine filling the air. In an instant, Katherine was on Julien, and his struggle against her embrace was in vain. "Quiet yourself, my love. A great life awaits you." Her mouth went to his neck, to have what she craved—his blood and his love. She took him to her apartment in the house and laid him in the couch, brushed his hair from his face, and kissed his lips softly.

"Now, I will have love," she whispered.

Chapter Twenty-Seven

F orty years had passed since the battle at Hell's Gate. Katherine sat on the blue throne and held her last court. Shawn, Rebecca, and Gwyn stood to her right and Victoria, with Braden, were in seclusion, preparing for her coronation. Victoria would be crowned the following eve, at midnight. Michael had finally given his permission for Katherine to step down.

Vampires droned on and on about their problems or their disputes with each other while she listened. She watched the hovering platforms, the workers hanging the banner signifying her reign at the far end of the hall. The flag was the Bryces', bearing a striking blue background with a yellow lion's head woven in its middle. The symbol for the Herit Covenant was at the top, and at the bottom was the symbol marking her reign. Vampires would know her as the Hundred-Year Queen; the warrior queen that fought great battles and led the guardians to the Gates of Hell and shook them with the fury of the angels.

Last eve, Victoria had given Alexa back to Katherine and told her that Erdin had brought her to Heaven to see Michael. Michael said that Deceida would be Victoria's and that she would become the leader of the Herit Covenant. Victoria would be one of Herit's, and the Kenmare family would be a part of the Herit Covenant after that. Victoria laughed and said, "I couldn't believe what Michael was telling me, but I have drunk so much of Shawn's blood over the years, I'm probably already a Herit."

They talked most of the night, and Katherine spoke of how she had almost called off the last attack, how she nearly lost her nerve. How despair had clouded her decisions. Katherine told Victoria she must prepare for the coming of The Demon and Samil. Prepare herself for the dark times to follow. This would be her challenge.

Finally, Victoria told her that Drake would not be coming to her anymore. His destiny had always been reserved to the Heavens—he was still to be a conduit to the queen, and he would be Victoria's messenger to Michael now. Katherine then told Victoria, as a blood tear ran down her cheek, that she was ready to say goodbye to Drake.

Katherine had seen her last vampire and given her final decree. Now she watched four ancient vampires come into the hall and float across the pool of water. The leaders of the other four covenants had arrived. They went to the foot of the stairs, and Katherine, as usual, raised her hand.

"You may stop there."

"We bring greetings to the Herit Queen, slayer of Malin," Amrit said as the others nodded their agreement.

"I can assure you, gentlemen, I was unconscious when Malin lost her life. Victoria, with Deceida, killed Malin. You must be pleased that an ancient will now be queen."

"We haven't come to disrespect you, my queen, we came to honor you," Gormal insisted. Again, the others nodded in agreement.

"We all are curious, my queen," Prodasa said. "When will the Herit Covenant select a leader?"

"I believe we all will find out the answer to that question tomorrow."

A smile came to her, Julien had poked his head through the door, and was making faces at her. A thought entered her head, coming from him, now they were very much a part of each other.

I'm bored with packing, and Braden is busy with Victoria.

They had grown to love each other deeply, and she could not imagine this world without him. Julien had adjusted well to vampire life, learned his lessons well, and was growing stronger as the years passed.

Katherine rose from her throne, made her excuses to the visiting vampires; she would much rather be with her love. She drifted down the stairs and across the pool with a smile on her face. Queen Katherine went to her changeling. "All right, we will go into the city, to the disco you like. Go get dressed. But tomorrow, after the ceremony, we have to finish packing."

"Can we hunt for blood?" Julien asked. "I'm hungry."

"Yes, my love. After the disco."

The next eve she sat on her throne again. Julien, Rebecca, and Juliet stood to her left, and Shawn, dressed in a long, grey robe, his staff in hand, stood to her right with Gwyn. Deceida lay on a gold table in front of her. The hall had filled with vampires from all over the world, and she sensed the angels hovering above.

The sound of trumpets announced the arrival of the new queen. The large double doors opened, and Victoria's procession entered the hall. They followed the banner of her reign—green, with gold stars sprinkled about its cloth. Victoria wore a long, emerald green gown that streamed behind her as she walked. Her long, blond hair flowed down and over her beautiful, bare shoulders. A simple crown of daisies encircled her beautiful head. Peter, with his marred battle armor and slayer, followed behind her, and then came Braden, in a dashing, modern suit. Katherine looked to her left and saw the loving smile on Shawn's face. Victoria's procession made its way to the stairs, then Victoria, Peter, and Braden made the climb to the throne.

Katherine stood and faced the crowd. "I have been your queen for a century. Our world has never known the onslaught of evil that came during my reign. It was not the Bryces or the Herit Covenant alone that beat them back. It was the warrior vampires of this world. Without your strength and courage, we would never have prevailed. I thank you all, and you will always have my gratitude. Now, I give you your next queen, Victoria Kenmare."

The hall filled with the applause of the vampires. Smiles spread over the faces of the leaders of the covenants. They were getting what they wanted—an ancient, a hero warrior to be queen and not a Herit. Katherine smiled and nodded to them as they had yet to receive their surprise.

"Are you ready, Victoria?"

"I am, my queen."

Katherine took the simple gold crown from her head, held it high, and then placed it on Victoria's head.

"I give you Queen Victoria. Long may she reign."

The hall erupted with loud applause and cheers. The trumpets sounded. Katherine looked at Shawn and smiled, a blood tear rolling down her cheek.

Reaching for Deceida, she looked at the leaders of the covenants, took the slayer, held it high, the sword glowing white light, the ringing of its metal filling the hall.

"Deceida, demon slayer and now witch slayer!" Katherine shouted. "Sword from Heaven! Given to Herit! The sword of the Herit Covenant, the eternal companion of the leader of the Herit Covenant!"

Katherine turned, holding the sword out with both hands, giving it to Victoria. "I pass this sword to you, my queen."

Victoria turned and held the sword high. Deceida brightened, and the light grew in intensity, then enclosed Victoria in its light and faded. Victoria's eyes glowed white and then turned to the blue of a sapphire.

Katherine faced the leaders of the covenants and shouted, "The Herit Covenant has been chosen because of their sacrifices, by the Archangel Michael, and Eos, to be the leaders of vampires. I give you the next Herit Queen and the leader of the Herit Covenant. Queen Victoria!"

Katherine heard the surprised murmurs travel through the hall as the vampires realized their next queen would be a vampire of Herit, and all that followed would be Herit as well. Again, the hall broke out into a loud round of applause. Katherine looked at the leaders of the covenant, gave them a big smile, and winked.

Katherine and had just left her couch and a sleeping Julien and now stood on the balcony of her home in Washington. The soft, early summer breeze blew through her short, silk nightgown, caressing her skin. It had been two years since Katherine had left The Citadel, and she had not been back since. The sun slowly traveled below the tree line. Twilight spread over her beautiful mountain lake, a new night unfolding. Only Julien and she lived there now, and they led a quiet life, staying close to home, only traveling to Seattle to feed and to seek entertainment. Shawn and Gwyn lived in the bayou, and Juliet lived with Peter in the house on the outskirts of Amsterdam. Now Katherine understood why Shawn lived in a swamp. After her reign, she wanted privacy and seclusion. Her home by the river in Dalton was still there. The vampire army rebuilt Dalton and now lived in the town with the Crimmians, interfacing with the outside world.

Katherine often thought of her vampire family, of the vampires that had lived in this house. Anne, Marilyn, Renee, Caitlyn, and Drake. She had known them all and had loved them all. They were in Heaven, and now the Herit Covenant had three families: the Bryces, McCall's and Kenmare's.

Katherine felt Julien's naked body come up behind her, press against her. Quickly felt his hardness against her buttocks. Julien embraced her, slid his hands down her stomach and between her legs, and she gave a slight gasp as he kissed her neck.

"Do I have to pack a bedroll?" Julien whispered into her ear.

She laughed. "Yes, we will be spending a lot of time on the road."

"The road? I don't think there are roads anymore. Only walking paths."

"You're right, it used to be the road."

Katherine was going to travel again, was going to start to live again, and a trip was just what she needed. Katherine would take Julien, travel like she and Shawn used to. On the road, they'd go to the bayou to visit Shawn and Gwyn, and then they'd move on to Amsterdam to visit Juliet, Victoria, Peter, and Braden. After that, maybe she would show him the pyramids, who knew…Katherine turned, kissed Julien, again felt him against her belly, took his hand, and led him back to the couch.

****

Shawn walked to the end of his porch and leaned out against the railing, sensing and listening to the night. He had loved Jessamine and missed her terribly. Now he felt intense hatred for Malin, but she was in a place he would not go. Katherine had survived the horrors of the ordeal to save him and now spent much of her time traveling with her changeling Julien. Katherine would come and visit him and Gwyn often.

Shawn knew the great love Katherine had for Julien and knew that was Katherine's way, always falling in love so deeply. The transition from her reign to Victoria's went smoothly, and now Katherine rarely spoke of The Citadel. It was mid-summer, and the heat in the bayou would have been stifling for his mortal body, but he'd devised a spell to surrounded his house and body. It kept the insects out and regulated a perfect seventy degrees for his human body. Out in the bayou, he saw a brown pelican raise one leg, preparing to take its evening nap. The night glittered, the stars filling the sky, and the fireflies lit the swamp. A big, silver moon hung low in the sky, peeking out from a passing cloud, only to have the next cloud hide it again.

He was sipping his bourbon, sitting in his rocker, when he sensed the evil. Forty-five years had passed since his rescue, and this was the first time he had sensed Lucifer's evil. This was an evil witch calling to him with a singsong melody, playing with him.

Shawn sat his sweaty glass of bourbon down on the railing and turned to watch Gwyn come out the front door, carrying his staff. Gwyn had taught him the magic of The Mother, and with the eagle's staff he was a formidable foe.

"You've sensed it, too?"

"Yes, I have. We must be cautious. It's a powerful witch, and she is toying with us," Gwyn said.

"Give me the staff," Shawn said with a sigh, "and I will go see what this is."

"Let me go with you."

"No, stay here. If I need help, then come. This witch is not here to fight. She is calling to me. Lucifer likes to have his fun at first."

"I must go with you, Shawn. It is starting again."

"No, you are the changeling. Do as I say."

Shawn took the staff and walked out into the bayou, following the sense of the witch. Cautiously, he moved down a path that led to a large pool of black bayou water and held his staff in front of him, keeping it at the ready. Thirty feet out, the witch stepped out of the brush and into the moonlight and stood, staring at him. The moon cast its light across the black water and on the hag.

Her head was bald, and her eyes burned a dark red. A muscular woman with perfect facial features, she had smooth, bronze skin. She was dressed in leather, an open vest that showed her well-developed breasts and moccasins on her feet. Black gloves with embedded rhinestones covered her arms to her elbows.

"What is it you want, bald witch?" Shawn yelled to her.

The witch cocked her head from side to side and yelled back, "Aren't you a funny warlock. I heard that about you, and now it is time for us to meet Shawn Bryce. My name is Samil. I'm sure the whore Katherine told you about me."

"She has!"

"Malin is with our father now, and she is not happy with you, Demon Slayer. You got her in a lot of trouble with Beezlebub. She is no longer favored."

"She is where you will be if you come any closer."

"Now, now, there is no need for fighting. Not tonight. We are getting to know each other."

"Something tells me that in time, we will know each other quite well," Shawn yelled.

"You are still mortal but a powerful warlock. I can tell. And you carry the eagle's staff."

"Tell me, Samil, where is Brendel?"

"I will not tell you that. You will have to find out for yourself. Beware, though. Guardian will hear from Brendel soon enough, and he will make them weep. We will meet again, Shawn Bryce. It is time for me to leave. That pathetic queen is coming. Say 'hello' to the whore for me. She can follow me, but she will not find Brendel. Not until he is ready." Shawn watched her take a few steps before lifting herself into the hot, night sky.

Shawn sensed the vampire coming to him and knew the vampire had a purpose. She was an old vampire, two thousand years old, one he had loved all his long life, and she was queen. The vampire landed, with Deceida on her back, came to him, and kissed him passionately.

Shawn smiled a loving smile and said, "I thought you didn't like to kiss mortals."

"For you, as always, I will make an exception," Victoria laughed. "You already look older, human!"

"I have pondered the longevity spell, but I'm not ready."

"What did Samil want?" Victoria asked.

"She wanted to meet me."

"I follow her sometimes, and this time she came to you. She is a sly one and loves to tease. Someday I will find the demon, and then we will have to kill him, love."

"Is this what Michael has commanded, my queen? I will always help you, Victoria, but do you think Michael could find somebody else to kill the demon?"

Victoria reached out and stroked his cheek tenderly. "I'm sorry. Like me, the angels haven't finished with you, my dearest love. How warm you feel…"

"Humans usually are."

"The angels will never leave us alone." Victory sighed. "Not you or me. I tried to live a life of peace, but that is not why we are here, or what the angels expect from us."

"You have something else on your mind, Victoria. I can sense it in you. I see it in your eyes."

Victoria's eyes flashed the blue of the Herit Covenant. "I have my love."

Shawn looked down the sandy path and saw Gwyn a distance away, standing, watching, and a nervous smile on her face. She waved, and he could sense her excitement. Now he knew why Victoria was here. Smiling at Victoria, he reached out and touched her soft cheek.

"Have Michael and Eos come to an agreement about me?"

"They have, my love. The time has come. Your solitude is over. They have needs again, and they have decided on you."

"What will it be? Vampire or warlock?"

"Both my love. You will be like Gwyn."

Shawn watched the pearl-white blood teeth form in the vampire's moist, beautiful mouth. Her eyes burned the blue of a sapphire, and the scent of jasmine filled the air. A warm breeze tossed her silky blond hair so he could see her beautiful neck once again. The blink of her eyes. He had always seen such beauty in this vampire, and tonight she was indeed the most beautiful.

"You will be the one? I thought it would be Katherine or Gwyn."

"No, my love. The angels have given me this great honor. They promised me if I became queen, you would be of my making."

Victoria strolled toward him, a look of love on her face, and she wrapped herself around him, held him, and kissed him passionately. Shawn felt her moist lips against his, the brush of her tongue, and then her teeth against his neck. For the second time in his long life, he felt the embrace of a vampire and the bite that would make him one. Deceida glowed the white light of Heaven.

Richard R Hall

The End

www.ingramcontent.com/pod-product-compliance
Lightning Source LLC
Chambersburg PA
CBHW071447170626
46811CB00007B/2496